# The Collected Supernatural Fiction of Bram Stoker

## Volume 5

Contains the novel 'The Snake's Pass'
two novelettes 'The Watter's Mou' and
'The Chain of Destiny"
and five short stories to chill the blood

Bram Stoker

LEONAUR

*The Collected
Supernatural and Weird
Fiction of Bram Stoker
Volume 5
Contains the novel 'The Snake's Pass'
two novelettes 'The Watter's Mou' and
'The Chain of Destiny"
and five short stories to chill the blood*
by Bram Stoker

FIRST EDITION

Leonaur is an imprint
of Oakpast Ltd

ISBN: 978-1-84677-836-0 (hardcover)
ISBN: 978-1-84677-835-3 (softcover)

http://www.leonaur.com

# Contents

# The Snake's Pass

## Chapter 1

### A Sudden Storm

Between two great mountains of gray and green, as the rock cropped out between the tufts of emerald verdure, the valley, almost as narrow as a gorge, ran due west towards the sea. There was just room for the roadway, half cut in the rock, beside the narrow strip of dark lake of seemingly unfathomable depth that lay far below, between perpendicular walls of frowning rock. As the valley opened. the land dipped steeply, and the lake became a foam-fringed torrent, widening out into pools and miniature lakes as it reached the lower ground. In the wide terrace-like steps of the shelving mountain there were occasional glimpses of civilization emerging from the almost primal desolation which immediately surrounded us—clumps of trees, cottages, and the irregular outlines of stone-walled fields, with black stacks of turf for winter firing piled here and there.

Far beyond was the sea—the great Atlantic—with a wildly irregular coast-line studded with a myriad of clustering rock)' islands. A sea of deep dark blue, with the distant horizon tinged with a line of faint white light, and here and there, where its margin was visible through the breaks in the rocky coast, fringed with a line of foam as the waxes broke on the rocks or swept in great rollers over the level expanse of sands.

The sky was a revelation to me, and seemed almost to obliterate memories of beautiful skies, although I had just come from the south, and had felt the intoxication of the Italian night, where, in the deep blue sky, the nightingale's note seems to hang as though its sound and the colour were but different expressions of one common feeling.

The whole west was a gorgeous mass of violet and sulphur and gold—great masses of storm-cloud piling up and up till the very heavens seemed weighted with a burden too great to bear. Clouds of violet, whose centres were almost black, and whose outer edges were tinged with living gold; great streaks and piled up clouds of palest yellow deepening into saffron and flame-colour which seemed to catch the coming sunset and to throw its radiance back to the eastern sky.

The view was the most beautiful that I had ever seen; and accustomed as I had been only to the quiet pastoral beauty of a grass country, with occasional visits to my great aunt's well-wooded estate in the south of England, it was no wonder that it arrested my attention and absorbed my imagination. Even my brief half-a-year's travel in Europe, now just concluded, had shown me nothing of the same kind.

Earth, sea, and air all evidenced the triumph of Nature, and told of her wild majesty and beauty. The air was still—ominously still. So still was all, that through the silence, that seemed to hedge us in with a sense of oppression, came the booming of the distant sea, as the great Atlantic swell broke in surf on the rocks or stormed the hollow caverns of the shore.

Even Andy, the driver, was for the nonce awed into comparative silence. Hitherto, for nearly forty miles of a drive, he had been giving me his experiences—propounding his views—airing his opinions; in fact, he had been making me acquainted with his store of knowledge touching the whole district and its people—including their names, histories, romances, hopes and fears—all that goes to make up the life and interest of a countryside.

No barber—taking this tradesman to illustrate the popular idea of loquacity *in excelsis*—is more consistently talkative than an Irish car-driver to whom has been granted the gift of speech. There is absolutely no limit to his capability, for every change of surrounding affords a new theme and brings on the tapis a host of matters requiring to be set forth.

I was rather glad of Andy's "brilliant flash of silence" just at present, for not only did I wish to drink in and absorb the grand and novel beauty of the scene that opened out before me, but I wanted to understand as fully as I could some deep thought which it awoke within me. It may have been merely the grandeur and beauty of the scene—or perhaps it was the thunder which filled the air that July evening—but I felt exalted in a strange way, and impressed at the same time with a new sense of the reality of things. It almost seemed as if through that opening valley, with the mighty Atlantic beyond and the piling up of the storm-clouds overhead, I passed into a new and more real life.

Somehow I had of late seemed to myself to be waking up. My foreign tour had been gradually dissipating my old sleepy ideas, or perhaps overcoming the negative forces that had hitherto dominated my life; and now this glorious burst of wild natural beauty—the majesty of nature at its fullest—seemed to have completed my awakening, and I felt as though I looked for the first time with open eyes on the beauty and reality of the world.

Hitherto my life had been but an inert one, and I was younger in many ways and more deficient in knowledge of the world in all ways than other young men of my own age. I had stepped but lately from boyhood, with all boyhood's surroundings, into manhood, and as yet I was hardly at ease in my new position.

For the first time in my life I had had a holiday—a real holiday, as one can take it who can choose his own way of amusing himself.

I had been brought up in an exceedingly quiet way with an old clergyman and his wife in the west of England, and except my fellow pupils, of whom there was never at any time more than one other, I had had little companionship. Altogether I knew very few people. I was the ward of a great aunt, who was wealthy and eccentric and of a sternly uncompromising disposition. When my father and mother were lost at sea, leaving me, an only child, quite unprovided for, she undertook to pay for my schooling and to start me in a profession if I should show sufficient aptitude for any. My father had been pretty well cut off by his family on account of his marriage with what they considered his inferior, and times had been, I was always told, pretty hard for them both. I was only a very small boy when they were lost in a fog when crossing the Channel; and the blank that their loss caused me made me, I dare say, seem even a duller boy than I was.

As I did not get into much trouble, and did not exhibit any special restlessness of disposition, my great aunt took it, I suppose, for granted that I was very well off where I was; and when, through growing years, the fiction of my being a school-boy could be no longer supported, the old clergyman was called "guardian" instead of "tutor," and I passed with him the years that young men of the better class usually spend in college life. The nominal change of position made little difference to me, except that I was taught to ride and shoot, and was generally given the rudiments of an education which was to fit me for being a country gentleman. I dare say that my tutor had some secret understanding with my great aunt, but he never gave me any hint whatever of her feelings towards me.

A part of my holidays each year was spent in her place, a beautiful country-seat. Here I was always treated by the old lady with rigid severity but with the best of good manners, and by the servants with affection as well as respect. There were a host of cousins, both male and female, who came to the house; but I can honestly say that by not one of them was I ever treated with cordiality. It may have been my fault, or the misfortune of my shyness; but I never met one of them without being made to feel that I was an "outsider."

I can understand now the cause of this treatment as arising from their suspicions when I remember that the old lady, who had been so severe with me all my life, sent for me when she lay on her deathbed, and, taking my hand in hers and holding it tight, said, between her gasps:

"Arthur, I hope I have not done wrong, but I have reared you so that the world may for you have good as well as bad—happiness as well as unhappiness; that you may find many pleasures where you thought there were but few. Your youth, I know, my dear boy, has not been a happy one; but it was because I, who loved your dear father as if he had been my own son—and from whom I unhappily allowed myself to be estranged until it was too late—wanted you to have a good and happy manhood."

She did not say any more, but closed her eyes and still held my hand. I feared to take it away lest I should disturb her; but presently the clasp seemed to relax, and I found that she was dead.

I had never seen a dead person, much less any one die, and the event made a great impression on me. But youth is elastic, and the aid lady had never been much in my heart.

When the will was read, it was found that I had been left heir to all her property, and that I would be called upon to take a place among the magnates of the county. I could not fall at once into the position, and, as I was of a shy nature, resolved to spend at least a few months in travel. This I did, and when I had returned, after a six months' tour, I accepted the cordial invitation of some friends, made an my travels, to pay them a visit at their place in the county of Clare.

As my time was my own, and as I had a week or two to spare, I had determined to improve my knowledge of Irish affairs by making a detour through some of the counties in the west on my way to Clare.

By this time I was just beginning to realize that life has many pleasures. Each day a new world of interest seemed to open before me. The experiment of my great aunt might yet be crowned with success.

And now the consciousness of the change in myself had come home to me—come with the unexpected suddenness of the first streak of the dawn through the morning mists. The moment was to be to me a notable one; and as I wished to remember it to the full, I tried to take in all the scene where such a revelation first dawned upon me. I had fixed in my mind, as the central point for my memory to rest on, a promontory right under the direct line of the sun, when I was interrupted by a remark made, not to me but seemingly to the universe in general:

"Musha![1] but it's comin' quick."

"What is coming?" I asked.

"The shtorm! Don't ye see the way thim clouds is dhriftin? Faix, but it's fine times the ducks'll be afther havin' before many minutes is past!"

I did not heed his words much, for my thoughts were intent on the scene. We were rapidly descending the valley, and, as we got lower, the promontory seemed to take bolder shape, and was beginning to stand out as a round-topped hill of somewhat noble proportions.

"Tell me, Andy," I said, "what do they call the hill beyond?"

"The hill beyant there, is it? Well, now, they call the place Shleenanaher."

"Then that is Shleenanaher Mountain?"

"Begor, it's not. The mountain is called Knockcalltecrore. It's Irish."

"And what does it mean?"

"Faix, I believe it's a short name for the Hill iv the Lost Goolden Crown."

"And what is Shleenanaher, Andy?"

"Throth, it's a bit iv a gap in the rocks beyant that they call Shleenanaher."

"And what does that mean? It is Irish, I suppose?"

"Thrue for ye! Irish it is, an' it manes The Shnake's Pass."

"Indeed! And can you tell me why it is so called?"

"Begor, there's a power iv raysons guv for callin' it that. Wait till we get Jerry Scanlan or Bat Moynahan, beyant in Carnaclif! Sure they knows every laygend and shtory in the bar'ny, anil tell them all, av ye like. Whew! Musha, here it comes!"

1. Indeed (from the Irish *utilise*).

Surely enough, it did come. The storm seemed to sweep through the valley in a single instant; the stillness changed to a roar, the air became dark with the clouds of drifting rain. It was like the bursting of a water-spout in volume, and came so quickly that I was drenched to the skin before I could throw my mackintosh round me. The mare seemed frightened at first; but Andy held her in with a steady hand and with comforting words, and after the first rush of the tempest she went on as calmly and steadily as hitherto, only shrinking a little at the lightning and the thunder.

The grandeur of that storm was something to remember. The lightning came in brilliant sheets that seemed to cleave the sky, and threw weird lights among the hills, now strange with black, sweeping shadows. The thunder broke with startling violence right over our heads, and flapped and buffeted from hill-side to hillside, rolling and reverberating away into the distance, its farther voices being lost in the crash of each succeeding peal.

On we went, through the driving storm, faster and faster; but the storm abated not a jot. Andy was too much occupied with his work to speak; and as for me, it took all my time to keep on the rocking and swaying car, and to hold my hat and mackintosh so as to shield myself as well as I could from the pelting storm. Andy seemed to be above all considerations of personal comfort. He turned up his coat collar, that was all, and soon he was as shiny as my own waterproof rug. Indeed, altogether, he seemed quite as well off as I was, or even better, for we were both as wet as we could be, and while I was painfully endeavouring to keep off the rain, he was free from all responsibility and anxiety of endeavour whatever.

At length, as we entered on a long, straight stretch of level road, he turned to me and said:

"Yer 'an'r it's no kind iv use dhrivin' like this all the way to Carnaclif. This shtorm'll go on for hours. I know thim well up on these mountains, wid' a nor'-aist wind blowin'. Wouldn't it be betther for us to get shelther for a bit?"

"Of course it would," said I. "Try it at once. Where can you go?"

"There's a place nigh at hand, yer 'an'r, the Widdy Kelligan's shebeen,[2] at the cross-roads of Glennashaughlin: it's quite contagious. Gee-up, ye ould corn-crake! hurry up to Widdy Kelligan's."

It seemed almost as if the mare understood him and shared his wishes, for she started with increased speed down a lane-way that opened out a little on our left. In a few minutes we reached the crossroads, and also the shebeen of Widow Kelligan, a low whitewashed thatched house, in a deep hollow between high banks in the south-western corner of the cross. Andy jumped down and hurried to the door.

"Here's a sthrange gintleman, Widdy. Take care iv him," he called out, as I entered.

Before I had succeeded in closing the door behind me, he was unharnessing the mare, preparatory to placing her in the lean-to stable, built behind the house against the high bank.

Already the storm seemed to have sent quite an assemblage to Mrs. Kelligan's hospitable shelter. A great fire of turf roared up the chimney, and round it stood, and sat, and lay a steaming mass of nearly a dozen people, men and women. The room was a large one, and the inglenook so roomy that nearly all those present found a place in it. The roof was black, rafters and thatch alike; quite a number of cocks and hens found shelter in the rafters at the end of the room. Over the fire was a large pot suspended on a wire, and there was a savoury and inexpressibly appetizing smell of marked volume throughout the room of roasted herrings and whiskey punch.

As I came in all rose up, and I found myself placed in a warm seat close to the fire, while various salutations of welcome buzzed all around me. The warmth was most grateful, and I was trying to convey my thanks for the shelter and the welcome, and feeling very awkward over it, w hen, with a "God save all here!" Andy entered the room through the back door.

---

2. An unlicensed drinking establishment (from the Irish *séibín*), also spelled "shebeen" at other points in the novel.

He was evidently a popular favourite, for there was a perfect rain of hearty expressions to him. He, too, was placed close to the fire, and a steaming jorum of punch placed in his hands—a similar one to that which had been already placed in my own. Andy lost no time in sampling that punch. Neither did I; and I can honestly say that if he enjoyed his more than I did mine, he must have had a very happy few minutes. He lost no time in making himself and all the rest comfortable.

"Hurroo!" said he. "Musha! but we're just in time. Mother, is the herrin's done? Up with the creel, and turn out the pitaties; they're done, or me senses desaves me. Yer 'an'r, we're in the hoight iv good luck! Herrin's it is, and it might have been only pitaties an' point."

"What is that?" I asked.

"Oh, that is whin there is only wan herrin' among a crowd—too little to give aich a taste, and so they put it in the middle and point the pitaties at it to give them a flaviour."

All lent a hand with the preparation of supper. A great potato basket, which would hold some two hundred-weight, was turned bottom up, the pot was taken off the fire, and the contents turned out on it in a great steaming mass of potatoes. A handful of coarse salt was taken from a box and put on one side of the basket, and another on the other side. The herrings were cut in pieces, and a piece given to each—the dinner was served.

There were no plates—no knives, forks or, spoons—no ceremony—no precedence—nor was there any heart-burning, jealousy, or greed. A happier meal I never took a part in, nor did I ever enjoy food more. Such as it was, it was perfect. The potatoes were fine and cooked to perfection; we took them in our fingers, peeled them how we could, dipped them in the salt, and ate till we were satisfied.

During the meal several more strangers dropped in, and all reported the storm as showing no signs of abating. Indeed, little such assurance was wanting, for the fierce lash of the rain, and the howling of the storm as it beat on the face of the house, told the tale well enough for the meanest comprehension.

15

When dinner was over and the basket removed, we drew around the fire again, pipes were lit, a great steaming jug of punch made its appearance, and conversation became general. Of course, as a stranger, I came in for a good share of attention.

Andy helped to make things interesting for me, and his statement, made by my request, that I hoped to be allowed to provide the punch for the evening, even increased his popularity, while it established mine. After calling attention to several matters which evoked local stories and jokes and anecdotes, he remarked:

"His 'an'r was axin' me just afore the shtorm kem on as to why the Shleenanaher was called so. I tould him that none could tell him like Jerry Scanlan or Bat Moynahan, an' here is the both of them, sure enough. Now, boys, won't ye oblige the sthrange gintleman, an' tell him what yez know iv the shtories anent the hill?"

"Wid all the plisure in life," said Jerry Scanlan, a tall man of middle age, with a long thin clean-shaven face, a humorous eye, and a shirt collar whose points in front came up almost to his eyes, while the back part disappeared into the depths of his frieze coat collar behind.

"Begor, yer 'an'r, I'll tell ye all I iver heerd. Sure there's a lay-gend, and there's a shtory—musha! but there's a wheen o' both lay-gends and shtories—but there's wan laygend beyant all—here Mother Kelligan, fill up me glass, fur sorra one o' me is a good dhrj shpaker. Tell me, now, sor, do they allow punch to the Mimbers iv Parlymint whin they're shpakin?" I shook my head.

"Musha! thin, but it's meself they'll niver git as a number till they alther that law! Thank ye, Mrs. Kelligan, this is just my shtyle But now for the laygend that they tell of Shleenanaher."

## CHAPTER 2

### THE LOST CROWN OF GOLD

"Well, in the ould ancient times, before St. Pathrick banished the shnakes from out iv Ireland, the hill beyant was a mighty important place intirely. For more betoken, none other lived in it than the King iv the Shnakes himself. In thim times there was

16

up at the top iv the hill a wee bit iv a lake wid threes and sedges and the like growin' round it; and 'twas there that the King iv the Shnakes made his nist—or whativer it is that shnakes calls their home. Glory be to God! but none us of knows anythin' of them at all, at all, since Saint Pathrick tuk them in hand."

Here an old man in the chimney corner struck in:"Thrue for ye, acushla;[1] sure the bit lake is there still, though, more belike it's dhry now, it is, and the threes is all gone."

"Well," went on Jerry, not ill-pleased with this corroboration oi his story, "the King iv the Shnakes was mighty important, intirely. He was more nor tin times as big as any shnake as any man's eyes had iver saw; an' he had a goolden crown on to the top of his head, wid a big jool in it that tuk the colour iv the light, whether that same was from the sun or the moon; an' all the shnakes had to take it in turns to bring food, and lave it for him in the cool iv the evenin', whin he would come out and ate it up and go back to his own place.

"An' they do say that whiniver two shnakes had a quarr'll they had to come to the King, an' he decided betune them; an' he tould aich iv them where he was to live, and what he was to do. An' wanst in ivery year there had to be brought to him a live baby; and they do say that he would wait until the moon was at the full, an' thin would be heerd one wild wail that made every sowl widin miles shuddher, an' thin there would be black silence, and clouds would come over the moon, and for three days it would never be seen agin."

"Oh, glory be to God!" murmured one of the women, "but it was a terrible thing!" and she rocked herself to and fro, moaning, all the motherhood in her awake.

"But did none of the min do nothin?" said a powerful-look-ing young fellow in the orange and green jersey of the Gaelic Athletic Club, with his eyes flashing; and he clinched his teeth.

"Musha! how could they? Sure, no man ever seen the King iv the Shnakes!"

"Thin how did they know about him?" he queried, doubt-

---

1. Darling (from the Irish phrase *a chuisle mo chroí*, literally "a pulse of my heart.")

fully.

"Sure, wasn't one of their childher tuk away iv'ry year? But, anyhow, it's all over now! an' so it was that none iv the min iver wint. They do say that one woman what lost her child, run up to the top of the hill; but what she seen, none could tell, for whin they found her she was a ravin' lunatic, wid white hair an' eyes like a corpse—an' the mornin' afther they found her dead in her bed wid a black mark round her neck as if she had been choked, an' the mark was in the shape iv a shnake. Well, there was much sorra and much fear, and whin St. Pathrick tuk the shnakes in hand the bonfires was lit all over the counthry. Never was such a flittin' seen as whin the shnakes came from all parts wrigglin' and crawlin' an' shkwirmin'."

Here the narrator dramatically threw himself into an attitude, and with the skill of a true improvisatore, suggested in every pose and with every limb and in every motion the serpentine movements.

"They all came away to the west, and seemed to come to this wan mountain. From the north and the south and the east they came be millions an' thousands an' hundhreds—for whin St. Pathrick ordhered them out he only tould them to go, but he didn't name the place—an' there was he up on top of Brandon Mountain, wid his vistments on to him an' his crozier in his hand, and the shnakes movin' below him, all goin' up north, an' sez he to himself:

"'I must see about this.' An' he got down from aff iv the mountain, and he folly'd the shnakes, and he see them move along to the hill beyant that they call Knockcalltecrore. An' be this time they wor all come from all oxer Ireland, and they wor all round the mountain—exceptin' on the say-side—an' they all had their heads pointed up the hill, and their tails pointed to the Saint, so that they didn't see him, an' they all gave wan great hiss, an' then another, an' another, like wan, two, three! An' at the third hiss the King iv the Shnakes rose up out of the wee fen at the top of the hill, wid his goold crown gleamin'; an' more be-token it was harvest time, an' the moon was up. an' the sun was settin', so the big jool in the crown had the light oi both the sun an' the moon, an' it shone so bright that right away in Lensther the people thought the whole counthry was afire. But whin the Saint seen him, his whole forrum seemed to swell out an' get bigger an' bigger, an' he lifted his crozier, an' he pointed west, an' sez he, in a voice like a shtorm, 'To the say, all ye shnakes! At wanst! to the say!'

"An' in the instant, wid wan movement, an' wid a hiss that made the air seem full iv watherfalls, the whole iv the shnakes that was round the hill wriggled away into the say as if the fire was at their tails. There was so many iv them that they filled up the say out beyant to Cusheen Island, and them that was behind, had to shlide over their bodies. An' the say piled up till it sent a wave mountains high rollin' away across the Atlantic till it sthruck upon the shore iv America—though more betoken it wasn't America thin, for it wasn't discovered till long afther. An' there was so many shnakes that they do say that all the white sand that dhrifts up on the coast from the Blaskets to Achill Head is made from their bones." Here Andy cut in:

"But, Jerry, you haven't tould us if the King iv the Shnakes wint too."

"Musha! but it's in a hurry ye are. How can I tell ye the whole laygend at wanst; an', moreover, when me mouth is that dhry I can hardly spake at all—an' me punch is all dhrunk—"

He turned his glass face down on the table, with an air of comic resignation. Mrs. Kelligan took the hint and refilled his glass while he went on:

"Well! whin the shnakes tuk to say-bathin' an' forgot to come in to clhry themsehes, the ould King iv thim sunk down agin into the lake, an' Saint Pathrick row Is his eyes, an' sez he to himself:

"'Musha! is it dhramin' I am, or what? or is it laughin' at me he is? Does he mane to defy me?' An' seein' that no notice was tuk iv him at all, he lifts his crozier, and calls out:

"'Hi! here! you! Come here! I want ye!'" As he spoke, Jerry went through all the pantomime of the occasion, exemplify-

19

ing by every movement the speech pf both the Saint and the Snake.

"Well, thin the King iv the Shnakes puts up his head out iv the lake, an' sez he:

"'Who calls?'

"'I do,' says St. Pathrick, an' he was so much mulvathered at the Shnake presumin' to sthay, afther he tould thim all to go that for a while he didn't think it quare that he could sphake at all. "Well, what do ye want wid me?' sez the Shnake. "'I want to know why you didn't lave Irish soil wid all th' other Shnakes,' sez the Saint.

"'Ye tould the Shnakes to go,' sez the King, 'an' I am their King, so I am; and your wurrds didn't apply to me!' an' with that he dhrops like a flash of lightnin' into the lake again.

"Well! St. Pathrick was so tuk back wid his impidence that he had to think for a minit, an' then he calls again: "'Hi! here! you!'

"What do you want now?' sez the King iv the Shnakes, again poppin' up his head.

"'I want to know why you didn't obey me ordhers?' sez the Saint. An' the King hiked at him an' laughed; and he looked mighty evil, I can tell ye, for be this time the sun was down and the moon up, an' the jool in his crown threw out a pale cold light that would make you shuddher to see. 'An',' says he, as slow an' as hard as an attorney (saving your prisence) when he has a bad case:

"'I didn't obey,' sez he, 'because I thraverse the jurisdiction.'

"'How do ye mane?' asks St. Pathrick.

"'Because,' sez he, 'this is my own houldin',' sez he, 'be perscriptive right,' sez he. I'm the whole govermint here, and I put a nexeat on meself not to lave widout me own permission,' and he ducks down agin into the pond.

"Well, the Saint began to get mighty angry, an' he raises his crozier, and he calls him agin:

"'Hi! here! you!' and the Shnake pops up.

"'Well! Saint, what do you want now? Amn't I to be quit iv

20

ye at all?'

"'Are ye goin', or are ye not?' sez the Saint.

"'I'm King here, an' I'm not goin'.'

"'Thin, says the Saint, 'I depose ye!'

"You can't, sez the Shnake, 'while I have me crown.'

"'Then I'll take it from ye,' sez St. Pathrick.

"'Catch me first!' sez the Shnake; an' wid that he pops undher the wather, what began to bubble up and boil. Well, thin, the good Saint stood bewildhered, for as he was lukin' the wather began to disappear out of the wee lake; and then the ground iv the hill began to be shaken as if the big Shnake was rushin' round and round it down deep down undher the ground.

"So the Saint stood on the edge of the empty lake an' held up his crozier, and called on the Shnake to come forth. And when he hiked down, lo! an' behold ye! there lay the King iv the Shnakes coiled round the bottom iv the lake, though how he had got there the Saint could niver tell, for he hadn't been there when he began to summons him. Then the Shnake raised his head, and, lo! and behold ye! there was no crown onto it.

"Where is your crown?' sez the Saint.

"'It's hid,' sez the Shnake, leerin' at him.

"'Where is it hid?'

"'It's hid in the mountain! Buried where you nor the likes iv you can't touch it in a thousand years!' an' he leered agin.

"'Tell me where it may be found?' sez the Saint starnly. An' thin the Shnake leers at him agin wid an eviller smile than before; an' sez he:

"'Did ye see the wather what was in the lake?'

"'I did,' sez St. Pathrick.

"'Thin, when ye find that wather ye may find me jool'd crown, too,' sez he; an' before the Saint could say a word, he wint on:

"An' till ye git me crown I'm king here still, though ye banish me. An' mayhap I'll come in some forrum what ye don't suspect, for I must watch me crown. An' now I go away—iv me own accord.' An' widout one word more, good or bad, he shlid right away into the say, dhrivin' through the rock an' makin' the clift that they call the Shleenanaher—an' that's Irish for the Shnake's Pass—until this day."

"An' now, sir, if Mrs. Kelligan hasn't dhrunk up the whole bar'l, I'd like a dhrop iv punch, for talkin' is dhry wurrk," and he buried his head in the steaming jorum, which the hostess had already prepared.

The company then began to discuss the legend. Said one of the women:

"I wondher what forrum he tuk when he kem back!" Jerry answered:

"Sure, they do say that the shiftin' bog wor the forrum he tuk. rhe mountain wid the lake on top used to be the fertilest shpot in the whole counthry; but iver since the bog began to shift this was niver the same."

Here a hard-faced man named McGlown, who had been silent, struck in with a question:

"But who knows when the bog did begin to shift?"

"Musha! sorra one of me knows; but it was whin th' ould Shnake druv the wather iv the lake into the hill!" There was a twinkle in the eyes of the story-teller, which made one doubt his own belief in his story.

"Well, for ma own part," said McGlown, "A don't believe a sengle word of it."

"An' for why not?" said one of the women. "Isn't the mountain called 'Knockcalltecrore,' or 'The Hill of the Lost Crown iv Gold,' till this day?" Said another:

"Musha! how could Misther McGlown believe anythin', an' him a Protestan'."

"A'll tell ye that A much prefer the facs," said McGlown. "Ef hestory es till be believed, A much prefer the story told till me by yon old man. Damn me! but A believe he's old enough till remember the theng itself."

He pointed as he spoke to old Moynahan, who, shrivelled up and white-haired, crouched in a corner of the inglenook, holding close to the fire his wrinkled, shaky hands.

"What is the story that Mr. Moynahan has, may I ask?" said I. "Pray oblige, me, won't you? I am anxious to hear all I can of the mountain, for it has taken my fancy strangely."

The old man took the glass of punch, which Mrs. Kelligan handed him as the necessary condition antecedent to a story, and began:

"Oh, sorra one of me knows anythin' except what I've heerd from me father. But I oft heerd him say that he was tould that it was said that in the Frinch invasion that didn't come off undher Gineral Humbert, whin the attimpt was over an' all hope was gone, the English sodgers made sure of great prize-money whin they should git hould of the threasure-chist. For it was known that there was much money goin' an' that they had brought a lot more than iver they wanted for pay and expenses in ordher to help bribe some of the other people that was houldin' off to be bought by wan side or the other—if they couldn't manage to git bought be both. But, sure enough, they wor all sould, bad cess to thim! and the divil a bit of money could they lay their hands on at all."

Here the old man took a pull at his jug of punch, with so transparent a wish to be further interrogated that a smile flashed round the company. One of the old crones remarked, in an audible *sotto voce*.[2]

"Musha! but Bat is the cute story-teller intirely. Ye have to dhrag it out iv him! Go on, Bat, go on! Tell us what become iv the money."

"Oh, what become iv the money? So ye would like to hear? Well, I'll tell ye—-just one more fill of the jug, Mrs. Kelligan, as the gintleman wishes to know all about it—well, they did say that the officer what had charge of the money got well away with some five or six others. The chist was a heavy wan—an iron chist bang full up iv goold! Oh, my! but it was fine! A big chist—that high, an' as long as the table, an' full up to the led wid goolden money an' paper money, an' divil a piece of white money in it at all! All goold, every pound note iv it."

---

2. In soft tones, so as not to be overheard.

He paused, and glanced anxiously at Mrs. Kelligan, who was engaged in the new brew.

"Not too much wather, if *ye* love me, Katty; you know me wakeness! Well, the)' do say that it tuk hard work to lift the chist into the boat; an' thin they put in a gun-carriage to carry it on, an' tuk out two horses, an' whin the shmoke was all round an' the darkness of night was on, they got on shore, an' made away down south from where the landin' was made at Killala. But, anyhow, they' say that none of them was ever heerd of agin. But they was thraced through Ardnaree an' Lough Conn, an' through Castlebar Lake an' Lough Carra, an' through Lough Mask an' Lough Corrib. But they niver kem out through Galway, for the river was watched for thim day an' night be the sodgers; and how they got along God knows, for 'twas said they suffered quare hardships.

"They tuk the chist an' the gun-carriage an' the horses in the boat, an' whin they couldn't go no farther the)' dhragged the boat over the land to the next lake, an' so on. Sure, one dhry sayson, when the wathers iv Corrib was down feet lower nor they was iver known afore, a boat was found up at the Bealanabrack end that had lay there for years; but the min nor the horses nor the treasure was never heerd of from that day to this—so they say," he added, in a mysterious way, and he renewed his attention to the punch, as if his tale was ended.

"But, man alive!" said McGlown, "that's only a part. Go on, man dear! an' fenesh the punch after."

"Oh, oh! Yes, of course, you want to know the end. Well, no wan knows the end. But they used to say that whin the min lift the boat they wint due west, till one night they sthruck the mountain beyant; an' that there they buried the chist an' killed the horses, or rode away on them. But anyhow, they wor niver seen again; an', as sure as you're alive, the money is there in the hill! For luk at the name iv it! Why did any wan iver call it 'Knockcalltore'—an' that's Irish for 'The Hill of the Lost Gold'—if the money isn't there?"

"Thrue for ye!" murmured an old woman with a cutty pipe.

"For why, indeed? There's some people what won't believe nothin' altho' it's undher their eyes!" and she puffed away in silent rebuke to the spirit of scepticism—which, by the way, had not been manifested by any person present.

There was a long pause, broken only by one of the old women, who occasionally gave a sort of half-grunt, half-sigh, as if unconsciously to fill up the hiatus in the talk. She was a "keener"[3] by profession, and was evidently well fitted to and well drilled in her work. Presently old Moynahan broke the silence:

"Well, it's a mighty quare thing, anyhow, that the hill beyant has been singled out for laygends and sthories and gossip iv all kinds consarnin' shnakes an' the like. An' I'm not so sure, naythur, that some iv thim isn't there shtill; for, mind ye! it's a mighty curious thin' that the bog beyant keeps shiftin' till this day. And I'm not so sure, naythur, that the shnakes has all left the hill yit!"

There was a chorus of "Thrue for ye!"

"Aye, an' it's a black shnake too!" said one.

"An' wid side-whishkers!" said another.

"Begorra! we want St. Pathrick to luk in here agin!" said a third.

I whispered to Andy the driver:

"Who is it they mean?"

"Whisht!" he answered, but without moving his lips; "but don't let on I tould ye! Sure an' it's Black Murdock they mane."

"Who or what is Murdock?" I queried.

"Sure an' he is the Gombeen Man."

"What is that? What is a gombeen man?"

"Whisper me now," said Andy; "ax some iv the others. They'll larn it ye more betther nor I can."

"What is a gombeen man?" I asked to the company generally.

"A gombeen man, is it? Well, I'll tell ye," said an old, shrewd-looking man at the other side of the hearth. "He's a man that finds you a few shillin's or a few pounds whin ye want it bad,

---

3. A person who wails in lamentation for the dead.

and then niver laves ye till he has tuk all ye've got—yer land an' yer shanty an' yer holdin' an' yer money an' yer craps; an' he would take the blood out of yer body if he could sell it or use it anyhow!"

"Oh, I see—a sort of usurer."

"Ushurer? aye, that's it; but a ushurer lives in the city, an' has laws to hould him in. But the Gombeen has nayther law nor the fear iv law. He's like wan that the Scriptures says 'grinds the faces iv the poor.' Begor, it's him that'd do little for God's sake if the divil was dead!"

"Then I suppose this man Murdock is a man of means—a rich man in his way?"

"Rich is it? Sure an' it's him as has plinty. He could lave this place if he chose an' settle in Galway—aye, or in Dublin itself if he liked betther, and lind money to big min—landlords an' the like— instead iv playin' wid poor min here an' swallyin' them up, wan be wan. But he can't go! He can't go!" This he said with a vengeful light in his eyes; I turned to Andy for explanation.

"Can't go! How does he mean? What does he mean?"

"Whisht! Don't ax me. Ax Dan, there. He doesn't owe him any money!"

"Which is Dan?"

"The ould man there be the settle what has just spoke—Dan Moriarty. He's a warrum man, wid money in bank an' what owns his houldin'; an' he's not afeerd to have his say about Murdock.'

"Can any of you tell me why Murdock can't leave the Hill?" I spoke out.

"Begor, I can," said Dan quickly. "He can't lave it because the Hill houlds him!"

"What on earth do you mean? How can the Hill hold him?"

"It can hould tight enough! There may be raysons that a man gives—sometimes wan thing, an' sometimes another; but the Hill houlds—an' houlds tight all the same!"

Here the door was opened suddenly, and the fire blazed up

with the rush of wind that entered. All stood up suddenly, for the newcomer was a priest. He was a sturdy man of middle age, with a cheerful countenance. Sturdy as he was, however, it took all his strength to shut the door, but he succeeded before any of the men could get near enough to help him. Then he turned and saluted all the company:

"God save all here."

All present tried to do him some service. One took his wet great-coat, another his dripping hat, and a third pressed him into the warmest seat in the chimney-corner, where, in a very few seconds, Mrs. Kelligan handed him a steaming glass of punch, saying, "Dhrink that up, yer riv'rence. 'Twill help to kape ye from catchin' cowld."

"Thank ye, kindly," he answered, as he took it. When he had half emptied the glass, he said:

"What was it I heard as I came in about the Hill holding some one?" Dan answered:

"'Twas me, yer riv'rence. I said that the Hill had hould of Black Murdock, and could hould him tight."

"Pooh! pooh! man; don't talk such nonsense. The fact is, sir," said he, turning to me, after throwing a searching glance round the company, "the people here have all sorts of stories about that unlucky Hill—why, God knows; and this man Murdock, that they call Black Murdock, is a money-lender as well as a farmer, and none of them like him, for he is a hard man and has done some cruel things among them. When they say the Hill holds him, they mean that he doesn't like to leave it because he hopes to find a treasure that is said to be buried in it.

"I'm not sure but that the blame is to be thrown on the different names given to the Hill. That most commonly given is Knockcalltecrore, which is a corruption of the Irish phrase Knock-na-callte-cróin-óir, meaning, 'The Hill of the Lost Golden Crown;' but it has been sometimes called Knockcalltore—short for the Irish words Knock-na-callte-óir, or 'The Hill of the Lost Gold'. It is said that in some old past time it was called Knocknanaher, or The Hill of the Snake;' and, indeed, there's one place on it they call Shleenahaher, meaning the 'Snake's Pass'. I dare say, now, that they have been giving you the legends and stories and all the rubbish of that kind. I suppose you know, sir, that in most places the local fancy has run riot at some period and has left a good crop of absurdities and impossibilities behind it?"

I acquiesced warmly, for I felt touched by the good priest's desire to explain matters, and to hold his own people blameless for crude ideas which he did not share. He went on:

"It is a queer thing that men must be always putting abstract ideas into concrete shape. No doubt there have been some strange matters regarding this mountain that they've been talking about— the Shifting Bog, for instance; and as the people could not account for it in any way that they can understand, they knocked up a legend about it. Indeed, to be just to them, the legend is a very old one, and is mentioned in a manuscript of the twelfth century.

"But somehow it was lost sight of till about a hundred ago, when the loss of the treasure-chest from the French invasion at Killala set all the imaginations of the people at work, from Donegal to Cork, and they fixed the Hill of the Lost Gold as the spot where the money was to be found. There is not a word of fact in the story from beginning to end, and"—here he gave a somewhat stern glance round the room—"I'm a little ashamed to hear so much chat and nonsense given to a strange gentleman like as if it was so much gospel. However, you mustn't be too hard in your thoughts on the poor people here, sir, for they're good people—none better in all Ireland—in all the world for that—but they talk too free to do themselves justice."

All those present were silent for awhile. Old Moynahan was the first to speak.

"Well, Father Pether, I don't say nothin' about St. Pathrick an' the shnakes meself, because I don't know nothin' about them; but I know that me own father tould me that he seen the Frinchmin wid his own eyes crossin' the sthrame below, an' facin' up the mountain. The moon was risin' in the west, an' the hill threw a big shadda. There was two min an' two horses, an' they had a big box on a gun-carriage. Me father seen them cross the sthrame. The load was so heavy that the wheels sunk in the clay, an' the min had to pull at them to git them up again. An' didn't he see the marks iv the wheels in the ground the very nixt day?"

"Bartholomew Moynahan, are you telling the truth?" interrupted the priest, speaking sternly.

"Throth an' I am, Father Pether; divil a word iv a lie in all I've said."

"Then how is it you've never told a word of this before?"

"But I have tould it, Father Pether. There's more nor wan here low what has heerd me tell it; but they wor tould as a saycret!"

"Thrue for ye!" came the chorus of almost every person in the room. The unanimity was somewhat comic and caused among them a shamefaced silence, which lasted quite several seconds. The pause was not wasted, for by this time Mrs. Kelligan had brewed another jug of punch, and glasses were replenished. This interested the little crowd, and they entered afresh into the subject. As for myself, however, I felt strangely uncomfortable. I could not quite account for it in any reasonable way.

I suppose there must be an instinct in men as well as in the lower orders of animal creation—I felt as though there were a strange presence near me.

I quietly looked round. Close to where I sat, on the sheltered side of the house, was a little window built in the deep recess of the wall, and, farther, almost obliterated by the shadow of the priest as he sat close to the fire, pressed against the empty lattice, where the glass had once been, I saw the face of a man—a dark, forbidding face it seemed in the slight glimpse I caught of it. The profile was towards me, for he was evidently listening intently, and he did not see me. Old Moynahan went on with his story:

"Me father hid behind a whin bush, an' lay as close as a hare in his forrum. The min seemed suspicious of bein' seen, and they looked carefully all round for the sign of any wan. Thin they started up the side of the Hill; an' a cloud came over the moon, so that for a bit me father could see nothin'. But prisintly he seen the two min up on the side of the Hill at the south, near Joyce's mearin'.[4] Thin they disappeared agin, an' prisintly he seen the horses an' the gun-carriage, an' all, up in the same place, an' the moonlight sthruck thim as they wint out iv the shadda; and min, an' horses, an' gun-carriage, an' chist, an' all wint round to the back iv the hill at the west an' disappeared. Me father waited a minute or two to make sure, an' thin he run round as hard as he could an' hid behind the projectin' rock at the enthrance iv the Shleenanaher, an' there foreninst[5] him, right up the hill-side, he seen two min carryin' the chist, an' it nigh weighed thim down.

"But the horses an' the gun-carriage was nowhere to be seen. Well, me father was stealin' out to folly thim when he loosened a sthone, an' it clattered down through the rocks at the Shnake's Pass wid a noise like a dhrum, an' the two min sot down the chist an' they turned; an' whin they seen me father, one of them runs at him, and he turned an' run. An' thin another black cloud crossed the moon; but me father knew ivery foot of the mountain-side, and he run on through the dark. He heerd the footsteps behind him for a bit, but they seemed to get fainter an' fainter; but he niver stopped runnin' till he got to his own cabin. And that was the last he iver see iv the men, or the horses, or the chist. Maybe they wint into the air or the say, or the mountin; but, anyhow, they vanished, and from that day to this no sight, or sound, or word iv them was ever known!"

There was a universal, "Oh!" of relief as he concluded, while he drained his glass.

I looked round again at the little window; but the dark face was gone.

Then there arose a perfect babel of sounds. All commented on the story, some in Irish, some in English, and some in a speech, English indeed, but so purely and locally idiomatic that I could only guess at what was intended to be conveyed. The comment

---

4. A well-marked boundary, such as a fence or ditch, between two farms.
5. Opposite.

generally took the form that two men were to be envied—one of them, the Gombeen Man, Murdock, who owned a portion of the western side of the hill; the other one, Joyce, who owned another portion of the same aspect.

In the midst of the buzz of conversation the clattering of hoofs was heard. There was a shout, and the door opened again and admitted a stalwart stranger of some fifty years of age, with a strong, determined face, with kindly eyes, well-dressed, but wringing wet and haggard, and seemingly disturbed in mind. One arm hung useless by his side.

"Here's one of them!" said Father Peter.

## CHAPTER 3

### THE GOMBEEN MAN

"God save all here," said the man as he entered.

Room was made for him at the fire. He no sooner came near it and tasted the heat than a cloud of steam arose from him.

"Man! but ye're wet," said Mrs. Kelligan. "One'd think ye'd been in the lake beyant!"

"So I have," he answered, "worse luck! I rid all the way from Galway this blessed day to be here in time, but the mare slipped coming down Curragh Hill and threw me over the bank into the lake. I wor in the wather nigh three hours before I could get out, for I was foreninst the Curragh Rock an' only got a foothold in a chink, an' had to hold on wid me one arm, for I fear the other is broke."

"Dear! dear! dear!" interrupted the woman. "Sthrip yer coat off, acushla, an' let us see if we can do anythin'."

He shook his head, as he answered:

"Not now; there's not a minute to spare. I must get up the Hill at once. I should have been there be six o'clock. But I mayn't be too late yit. The mare has broke down entirely. Can anyone here lend me a horse?"

There was no answer till Andy spoke:

"Me mare is in the shtable, but this gintleman has me an' her for the day, an' I have to lave him at Carnaclif tonight."

Here I struck in:

"Never mind me, Andy. If you can help this gentleman, do so. I'm better off here than driving through the storm. He wouldn't want to go on with a broken arm if he hadn't good reason!"

The man looked at me with grateful eagerness:

"Thank yer honor kindly. It's a rale gintleman ye are! An' I hope ye'll never be sorry for helpin' a poor fellow in sore trouble."

"What's wrong, Phelim?" asked the priest. "Is there anything troubling you that anyone here can get rid of?"

"Nothin', Father Pether, thank ye kindly. The trouble is me own intirely, an' no wan here could help me. But I must see Murdock tonight."

There was a general sigh of commiseration; all understood the situation.

"Musha!" said old Dan Moriarty, *sotto voce.* "An' is that the way of it? An' is he, too, in the clutches iv that wolf—him that we all thought was so warrum? Glory be to God! but it's a quare wurrld it is; an' it's few there is in it that is what they seems. Me poor frind, is there any way I can help ye? I have a bit iv money by me that yer welkim to the lend iv av ye want it."

The other shook his head gratefully:

"Thank ye kindly, Dan, but I have the money all right; it's only the time I'm in trouble about!"

"Only the time, me poor chap! It's be time that the divil help.' Black Murdock an' the likes iv him, the most iv all! God be good tc ye if he has got his clutch on yer back, an' has time on his side, for yell want it!"

"Well! anyhow, I must be goin' now. Thank ye kindly, neighbours all. When a man's in throuble, sure the good-will of his frinds is the greatest comfort he can have."

"All but one, remember that—all but one!" said the priest.

"Thank ye kindly. Father, I shan't forget. Thank ye Andy: an' you, too, young sir; I'm much beholden to ye. I hope someday I may have it to do a good turn for ye in return. Thank ye kindly again, and goodnight." He shook my hand warmly, and was going to the door, when old Dan said:

"An' as for that black-jawed ruffian, Murdock—" He paused, for the door suddenly opened, and a harsh voice said:

"Murtagh Murdock is here to answer for himself!" It was my man at the window.

There was a sort of paralyzed silence in the room, through which came the whisper of one of the old women:

"Musha! talk iv the divil!"

Joyce's face grew very white; one hand instinctively grasped his riding-switch, the other hung uselessly by his side. Murdock spoke:

"I kem here expectin' to meet Phelim Joyce. I thought I'd save him the throuble of comin' wid the money." Joyce said in a husky voice:

"What do ye mane? I have the money right enough here. I'm sorry I'm a bit late, but I had a bad accident—bruk me arrum, an' was nigh dhrownded in the Curragh Lake. But I was goin' up to ye at once, bad as I am, to pay ye yer money, Murdock." The Gombeen Man interrupted him:

"But it isn't to me ye'd have to come, me good man. Sure, it's the sheriff himself that was waitin' for ye, an' whin ye didn't come"—here Joyce winced; the speaker smiled—"he done his work."

"What wurrk, acushla?" asked one of the women. Murdock answered slowly:

"He sould the lease iv the farrum known as the Shleenanaher in open sale, in accordance wid the terrains of his notice, duly posted, and wid warnin' given to the houldher iv the lease."

There was a long pause. Joyce was the first to speak:

"Ye're jokin', Murdock. For God's sake, say ye're jokin'! Ye tould me yerself that I might have time to git the money. An' ye tould me that the puttin' me farrum up for sale was only a matther iv forrum to let me pay ye back in me own way. Nay, more, ye asked me not to tell any iv the neighbours, for fear some iv them might want to buy some iv me land. An' it's niver so, that whin ye got me aff to Galway to rise the money, ye went on

33

wid the sale, behind me back—wid not a soul by to spake for me or mine—an' sould up all I have! No! Murtagh Murdock, ye're a hard man, I know, but ye wouldn't do that! Ye wouldn't do that!"

Murdock made no direct reply to him, but said, seemingly to the company generally:

"I ixpected to see Phelim Joyce at the sale today, but as I had some business in which he was consarned, I kem here where I knew there'd be neighbours—an', sure, so there is."

He took out his pocket-book and wrote names: "Father Pether Ryan, Daniel Moriarty, Bartholomew Moynahan, Andhrew McGlown, Mrs. Katty Kelligan—that's enough! I want ye all to see what I done. There's nothin' undherhand about me! Phelim Joyce, I give ye formial notice that yer land was sould an' bought by me, for ye broke yer word to repay me the money lint ye before the time fixed. Here's the sheriffs assignmint, an' I tell ye before all these witnesses that I'll proceed with ejectment on title at wanst."

All in the room were as still as statues. Joyce was fearfully still and pale, but when Murdock spoke the word "ejectment" he seemed to wake in a moment to frenzied life. The blood flushed up in his face, and he seemed about to do something rash; but with a great effort he controlled himself and said:

"Mr. Murdock, ye won't be too hard. I got the money to-day—it's here—but I had an accident that delayed me. I was thrown into the Curragh Lake and nigh dhrownded an' me arrum is bruk. Don't be so close as an hour or two; ye'll never be sorry for it. I'll pay ye all, and more, and thank ye into the bargain all me life. Ye'll take back the paper, won't ye, for me childhren's sake—for Norah's sake?"

He faltered; the other answered with an evil smile:

"Phelim Joyce, I've waited years for this moment. Don't ye know me betther nor to think I would go back on meself whin I have shtarted on a road? I wouldn't take yer money, not if ivery pound note was spread into an acre and cut up in tin-pound notes. I want yer land—I have waited for it, an' I mane to have it! Now don't beg me anymore, for I won't go back; an' tho' it's many a grudge I own ye, I square them all before the neighbours be refusin' yer prayer. The land is mine, bought be open sale; an' all the judges an' coorts in Ireland can't take it from me! An' what do ye say to that now, Phelim Joyce?"

The tortured man had been clutching the ash sapling which he had used as a riding-whip, and from the nervous twitching of his fingers I knew that something was coming. And it came; for, without a word, he struck the evil face before him—struck as quick as a flash of lightning—such a blow that the blood seemed to leap out round the stick, and a vivid welt rose in an instant. With a wild, savage cry the Gombeen Man jumped at him; but there were others in the room as quick, and before another blow could be struck on either side both men were grasped by strong hands and held back.

Murdock's rage was tragic. He yelled, like a wild beast, to be let' get at his opponent. He cursed and blasphemed so outrageously that all were silent, and only the stern voice of the priest was heard:

"Be silent, Murtagh Murdock! Aren't you afraid that the God overhead will strike you dead? With such a storm as is raging as a sign of his power, you are a foolish man to tempt him."

The man stopped suddenly, and a stern, clogged sullenness took the place of his passion. The priest went on:

"As for you, Phelim Joyce, you ought to be ashamed of yourself. Ye're not one of my people, but I speak as your own clergyman would if he were here. Only this day has the Lord seen fit to spare you from a terrible death; and yet you dare to go back of his mercy with your angry passion. You had cause for anger—or temptation to it, I know—but you must learn to kiss the chastening rod, not spurn it. The Lord knows what he is doing for you as for others, and it may be that you will look back on this day in gratitude for his doing, and in shame for your own anger. Men, hold off your hands—let those two men go; they'll quarrel no more—before me at any rate, I hope."

The men drew back. Joyce held his head down, and a more

despairing figure or a sadder one I never saw. He turned slowly away, and, leaning against the wall, put his face between his hands and sobbed. Murdock scowled, and the scowl gave place to an evil smile, as looking all around he said:

"Well, now that me work is done, I must be gettin' home."

"An' get some wan to iron that mark out iv yer face," said Dan.

Murdock turned again and glared around him savagely as he hissed aut:

"There'll be iron for someone before I'm done—Mark me well! I've never gone back or wakened yit whin I promised to have me own turn. There's thim here what'll rue this day yit! If I am the Shnake on the Hill—thin beware the Shnake. An' for him what shtruck me, he'll be in bitther sorra for it yit—him an' his!" He turned his back and went to the door.

"Stop!" said the priest. "Murtagh Murdock, I have a word to say to you—a solemn word of warning. Ye have today acted the part of Ahab towards Naboth the Jezreelite; beware of his fate! You have coveted your neighbour's goods; you have used your power without mercy; you have made the law an engine of oppression. Mark me! It was said of old that what measure men meted should be meted out to them again.

"God is very just. 'Be not deceived, God is not mocked. For what things a man shall sow, those also shall he reap.' Ye have sowed the wind this day; beware lest you reap the whirlwind! Even as God visited his sin upon Ahab the Samarian, and as he has visited similar sins on others in his own way—so shall he visit yours on you. You are worse than the land-grabber—worse than the man who only covets. Saintough is a virtue compared with your act. Remember the story of Naboth's vineyard, and the dreadful end of it. Don't answer me! Go and repent if you can, and leave sorrow and misery to be comforted by others, unless you wish to undo your wrong yourself. If you don't, then remember the curse that may come upon you yet!"

Without a word Murdock opened the door and went out, and a little later we heard the clattering of his horse's feet on the rocky road to Shleenanaher.

When it was apparent to all that he was really gone, a torrent of commiseration, sympathy, and pity broke over Joyce. The Irish nature is essentially emotional, and a more genuine and stronger feeling I never saw. Not a few had tears in their eyes, and one and all were manifestly deeply touched. The least moved was, to all appearance, poor Joyce himself. He seemed to have pulled himself together, and his sterling manhood and courage and pride stood by him. He seemed, however, to yield to the kindly wishes of his friends, and when we suggested that his hurt should be looked to, he acquiesced:

"Yes, if you will. Betther not go home to poor Norah and distress her with it. Poor child! she'll have enough to bear without that."

His coat was taken off, and between us we managed to bandage the wound. The priest, who had some surgical knowledge, came to the conclusion that there was only a simple fracture. He splinted and bandaged the arm, and we all agreed that it would be better for Joyce to wait until the storm was over before starting for home. Andy said he could take him on the car, as he knew the road well, and that as it was partly on the road to Carnaclif, we should only have to make a short detour and would pass the house of the doctor, by whom the arm could be properly attended to.

So we sat around the fire again, while without the storm howled and the fierce gusts which swept the valley seemed at times as if they would break in the door, lift off the roof, or in some way annihilate the time-worn cabin which gave us shelter.

There could, of course, be only one subject of conversation now, and old Dan simply interpreted the public wish when he said:

"Tell us, Phelim—sure we're all friends here—how Black Murdock got ye in his clutches? Sine any wan of us would get you out of thim if he could."

There was a general acquiescence. Joyce yielded himself, and said:

"Let me thank ye, neighbours all, for yer kindness to me and mine this sorraful night. Well, I'll say no more about that; but I'll tell ye how it was that Murdock got me into his power. Ye know that boy of mine—Eugene?"

"Oh, and he's the fine lad, God bless him! an' the good lad, too!"—this from the women.

"Well, ye know, too, that he got on so well whin I sint him to school that Dr. Walsh recommended me to make an ingineer of him. He said he had such promise that it was a pity not to see him get the right start in life, and he gave me, himself, a letther to Sir George Henshaw, the great ingineer. I wint and seen him, and he said he would take the boy. He tould me that there was a big fee to be paid, but I was not to throuble about that; at any rate, that he himself didn't want any fee, and he would ask his partner if he would give up his share too. But the latther was hard up for money. He said he couldn't give up all fee, but that he would take half the fee, provided it was paid down in dhry money.

"Well, the regular fee to the firm was five hundhred pounds, and as Sir George had giv up half an' only half, th' other half was to be paid, if that was possible. I hadn't got more'n a few pounds by me; for what wid dhrainin' and plantin' and fencin', and the payin' the boy's schoolin' and the girl's at the Nuns' in Galway, it had put me to the pin iv me collar to find the money up to now. But I didn't like to let the boy lose his chance in life for want of an effort, an' I put me pride in me pocket an' kem an' asked Murdock for the money. He was very smooth an' nice wid me—I know why now—an' promised he would give it at wanst if I would give him security on me land. Sure, he joked an' laughed wid me, an' was that cheerful that I didn't misthrust him. He tould me it was only forrums I was signin' that'd never be used." Here Dan Moriarty interrupted him:

"What did ye sign, Phelim?"

"There wor two papers. Wan was a writin' iv some kind, that in considheration iv the money lent an' his own land—which I was to take over if the money wasn't paid at the time appointed—he was to get me lease from me; an' the other was a power of attorney to Enther Judgment for the amount if the money wasn't paid at the right time. I thought I was all safe, as I could repay him in the time named, an' if the worst kem to the worst I might borry the money from some wan else—for the lease is worth the sum tin times over— an' repay him. Well, what's the use of lookin' back, anyhow? I signed the papers—that was a year ago, an' one week. An' a week ago the time was up!" He gulped down a sob, and went on:

"Well, ye all know the year gone has been a terrible bad wan, an' as for me it was all I could do to hould on—to make up the money was impossible. Thrue, the lad cost me next to nothin', for he arned his keep be exthra work, an' the girl, Norah, kem home from school and laboured wid me, an' we saved every penny we could. But it was all no use; we couldn't get the money together anyhow. Thin we had the misfortin wid the cattle that ye all know of; an' three horses that I sould in Dublin, up an' died before the time I guaranteed them free from sickness." Here Andy stuck in:

"Thrue for ye! Sure there was some dhreadful disordher in Dublin among the horse cattle, intirely; an' even Misther Docther Perfesshinal Ferguson himself couldn't git undher it!" Joyce went on:

"An' as the time grew nigh I began to fear, but Murdock came down to see me whin I was alone, an' tould me not to throuble about the money, an' not to mind about the sheriff, for he had to give him notice. 'An',' says he, 'I wouldn't, if I was you, tell Norah anythin' about it, for it might frighten the girl; for weemin is apt to take to heart things like that that's only small things to min like us.' An' so, God forgive me, I believed him; an' I niver tould me child anything about it—even whin I got the notice from the sheriff. An' whin the notice tellin' iv the sale was posted up on me land, I tuk it down meself, so that the poor child wouldn't be frightened—God help me!" He broke down for a bit, but then went on:

"But somehow I wasn't asy in me mind, an' whin the time iv

the sale dhrew nigh I couldn't keep it to meself am' longer, an' I tould Norah. That was only yisterday, and look at me today! Norah agreed wid me that we shouldn't trust the Gombeen, an' she sent me off to the Galway Bank to borry the money. She said I was an honest man an' farmed me own land, and that the bank might lind the money on it.

"An', sure enough, whin I wint there this mornin' be appointment, wid the Coadjuthor himself to inthroduce me, though he didn't know why I wanted the money—that was Norah's idea, and the Mother Superior settled it for her—the manager, who is a nice gintleman, tould me at wanst that I might have the money on me own note iv hand. I only gave him a formal writin', an' I took away the money. Here it is in me pocket in good notes; they're wet wid the lake, but, I'm thankful to say, all safe. But it's too late, God help me!" Here he broke down for a minute, but recovered himself with an effort:

"Anyhow, the bank that thrusted me musn't be wronged. Back the money goes to Galway as soon as iver I can get it there. If I am a ruined man, I needn't be a dishonest wan! But poor Norah! God help her! it will break her poor heart."

There was a spell of silence, only broken by sympathetic moans. The first to speak was the priest:

"Phelim Joyce, I told you a while ago, in the midst of your passion, that God knows what he is doin', and works in his own way. You're an honest man, Phelim, and God knows it, and, mark me, he won't let you nor yours suffer. 'I have been young,' said the Psalmist, 'and now am old; and I have not seen the just forsaken, nor his seed seeking bread.' Think of that, Phelim!—may it comfort you and poor Norah. God bless her, but she's the good girl! You have much to be thankful for, with a daughter like her to comfort you at home and take the place of her poor mother, who was the best of women; and with such a boy as Eugene, winnin' name and credit, and perhaps fame to come, even in England itself. Thank God for his many merges, Phelim, and trust him."

There was a dead silence in the room. The stern man rose,

and coming over took the priest's hand.

"God bless ye, Father!" he said, "it's the true comforter ye are."

The scene was a most touching one; I shall never forget it. The worst of the poor man's trouble seemed now past. He had faced the darkest hour; he had told his trouble, and was now prepared to make the best of everything—for the time at least—for I could not reconcile to my mind the idea that that proud, stern man, would not take the blow to heart for many a long day, that it might even embitter his life.

Old Dan tried comfort in a practical way by thinking of what was to be done. Said he:

"Iv course, Phelim, it's a mighty throuble to give up yer own foine land an' take Murdock's bleak shpot instead, but I dare say ye will be able to work it well enough. Tell me, have ye signed away all the land, or only the lower farm? I mane, is the Cliff Fields yours or his?"

Here was a gleam of comfort evidently to the poor man. His face lightened as he replied:

"Only the lower farm, thank God! Indeed, I couldn't part wid the Cliff Fields, for they don't belong to me—they are No-rah's, that her poor mother left her—they wor settled on her, whin we married, be her father, and whin he died we got them. But, indeed, I fear they're but small use by themselves; shure, there's no wather in them at all, savin' what runs off me ould land; an' if we have to carry wather all the way down the hill from—from me new land"—this was said with a smile, which was a sturdy effort at cheerfulness—"it will be but poor work to raise anythin' there—ayther shtock or craps. No doubt but Murdock will take away the sthrame iv wather that runs there now. He'll want to get the cliff lands, too, I suppose."

I ventured to ask a question:

"How do your lands lie compared with Mr. Murdock's?"

There was a bitterness in his tone as he answered, in true Irish fashion:

"Do you mane me ould land, or me new?"

41

"The lands that were—that ought still to be yours," I answered.

He was pleased at the reply, and his face softened as he replied:

"Well, the way of it is this. We two owns the west side of the Hill between us. Murdock's land—I'm spakin' iv them as they are till he gets possession iv mine—lies at the top iv the Hill; mine lies below. My land is the best bit on the mountain, while the Gombeen's is poor soil, with only a few good patches here and there. Moreover there is another thing. There is a bog which is high up the Hill mostly on his houldin', but my land is free from bog, except one end of the big bog, an' a stretch of dry turf, the best in the counthry, an wid enough turf to last for a hundhred years, it's that deep."

Old Dan joined in:

"Thrue enough! that bog of the Gombeen's isn't much use anyhow. It's rank and rotten wid wather. Whin it made up its mind to sthay, it might have done betther!"

"The bog? Made up its mind to stay! What on earth do you mean?" I asked. I was fairly puzzled.

"Didn't ye hear talk already," said Dan, "of the Shiftin' Bog on the mountain?"

"I did."

"Well, that's it. It moved an' moved an' moved longer than anywan can remimber. Me grandfather wanst tould me that whin he was a gossoon it wasn't nigh so big as it was when he tould me. It hasn't shifted in my time, and I make bould to say that it has made up its mind to settle down where it is. Ye must only make the best of it, Phelim. I dare say ye will turn it to some account."

"I'll try what I can do, anyhow. I don't mane to fould me arms an' sit down oppawsit me property an' ate it!" was the brave answer.

For myself, the whole idea was most interesting. I had never before even heard of a shifting bog, and I determined to visit it before I left this part of the country.

By this time the storm was beginning to abate. The rain had ceased, and Andy said we might proceed on our journey. So after a while we were on our way; the wounded man and I sitting on one side of the car, and Andy on the other. The whole company came out to wish us God-speed, and with such comfort as good counsel and good wishes could give we ventured into the inky darkness of the night.

Andy was certainly a born car-driver. Not even the darkness, the comparative strangeness of the road, or the amount of whiskey-punch which he had on board could disturb his driving in the least; he went steadily on. The car rocked and swayed and bumped, for the road was a by one, and in but poor condition; but Andy and the mare went on alike unmoved. Once or twice only, in a journey of some three miles of winding by-lanes, crossed and crossed again by lanes or watercourses, did he ask me the way. I could not tell which was roadway and which waterway, for they were all watercourses at present, and the darkness was profound. Still, both Andy and Joyce seemed to have a sense lacking in myself, for now and again they spoke of things which I could not see at all. As, for instance, when Andy asked:

"Do we go up or down where the road branches beyant?" Or again: "I disremimber, but is that Micky Dolan's ould apple-three, or didn't he cut it down? an' is it Tim's fornent us on the lift?"

Presently we turned to the right, and drove up a short avenue towards a house. I knew it to be a house by the light in the windows, for shape it had none. Andy jumped down and knocked, and after a short colloquy, Joyce got down and went into the doctor's house.

I was asked to go too, but thought it better not to, as it would only have disturbed the doctor in his work; and so Andy and I possessed our souls in patience until Joyce came out again, with his arm in a proper splint. And then we resumed our journey through the inky darkness.

However, after a while, either there came more light into the sky, or my eyes became accustomed to the darkness, for I thought that now and again I beheld *men as trees walking.*[1]

Presently something dark and massive seemed outlined in the sky before us—a blackness projected on a darkness—and, said Andy, turning to me:

"That's Knockcalltecrore; we're nigh the foot iv it now, and pretty shortly we'll be at the enthrance iv the boreen,[2] where Misther Joyce'll git aff."

We plodded on for a while, and the hill before us seemed to overshadow whatever glimmer of light there was, for the darkness grew more profound than ever; then Andy turned to my companion:

"Sure, isn't that Miss Norah I see sittin' on the sthile beyant?" I looked eagerly in the direction in which he evidently pointed, but for the life of me I could see nothing.

"No, I hope not," said the father, hastily. "She's never come out in the shtorm. Yes, It is her; she sees us."

Just then there came a sweet sound down the lane:

"Is that you, father?"

"Yes, my child; but I hope you've not been out in the shtorm."

"Only a bit, father; I was anxious about you. Is it all right, father? Did you get what you wanted?" She had jumped off the stile and had drawn nearer to us, and she evidently saw me, and went on in a changed and shyer voice:

"Oh, I beg your pardon. I did not see you had a stranger with you."

This was all bewildering to me. I could hear it all—and a sweeter voice I never heard—but yet I felt like a blind man, for not a thing could I see, while each of the three others was seemingly as much at ease as in the daylight.

"This gentleman has been very kind to me, Norah. He has given me a seat on his car, and indeed he's come out of his way to lave me here."

I am sure we're all grateful to you, sir; but, father, where is

---

1. *Mark* 8:24.

2. A small road or country lane (from the Irish *bótharín*).

your horse? Why are you on a car at all? Father, I hope you haven't met with any accident—I have been so fearful for you all the day." This was spoken in a fainter voice; had my eyes been of service, I was sure I would have seen her grow pale.

"Yes, my darlin', I got a fall on the Curragh Hill, but I'm all right. Norah dear! Quick, quick! catch her, she's faintin'!—my God! I can't stir!"

I jumped off the car in the direction of the voice, but my arms sought the empty air. However, I heard Andy's voice beside me:

"All right; I have her. Hould up, Miss Norah; yer dada's all right. Don't ye see him there, sittin' on me car? All right, sir; she's a brave girrul! She hasn't fainted."

"I am all right," she murmured, faintly; "but, father, I hope you are not hurt?"

"Only a little, my darlin'—just enough for ye to nurse me a while; I dare say a few days will make me all right again. Thank ye, Andy; steady now, till I get down; I'm feelin' a wee bit stiff." Andy evidently helped him to the ground.

"Goodnight, Andy, and goodnight you too, sir, and thank you kindly for your goodness to me all this night. I hope I'll see you again." He took my hand in his uninjured one, and shook it warmly.

"Goodnight," I said, and "goodbye: I am sure I hope we shall meet again."

Another hand took mine as he relinquished it—a warm, strong one—and a sweet voice said, shyly:

"Goodnight, sir, and thank you for your kindness to father."

I faltered "Goodnight", as I raised my hat; the aggravation of the darkness at such a moment was more than I could equably bear. We heard them pass up the boreen, and I climbed on the car again.

The night seemed darker than ever as we turned our steps towards Carnaclif, and the journey was the dreariest one I have ever taken. I had only one thought which gave me any pleasure, but that was a pretty constant one through the long miles of damp, sodden road—the warm hand and the sweet voice coming out of the darkness, and all in the shadow of that mysterious mountain, which seemed to have become a part of my life. The words of the old storyteller came back to me again and again:

"The Hill can hould tight enough! A man has raysons—sometimes wan thing and sometimes another—but the Hill houlds him all the same!"

And a vague wonder drew upon me as to whether it could ever hold me, and how!

## Chapter 4

### The Secrets of the Bog

Some six weeks elapsed before my visits to Irish friends were completed, and I was about to return home. I had had everywhere a hearty welcome: the best of sport of all kinds, and an appetite beyond all praise, and one pretty well required to tackle with any show of success the excellent food and wine put before me. The West of Ireland not only produces good viands in plenty and of the highest excellence, but there is remaining a keen recollection, accompanied by tangible results, of the days when open house and its hospitable accompaniments made wine-merchants prosperous—at the expense of their customers.

In the midst of all my pleasure, however, I could not shake from my mind—nor, indeed, did I want to—the interest which Shleenanaher and its surroundings had created in me. Nor did the experience of that strange night, with the sweet voice coming through the darkness in the shadow of the Hill, become dim with the passing of the time. When I look back and try to analyse myself and my feelings, with the aid of the knowledge and experience of life received since then, I think that I must have been in love. I do not know if philosophers have ever undertaken to say whether it is possible for a human being to be in love in the abstract—whether the something which the heart has a tendency to send forth needs a concrete objective point! It may be so; the swarm of bees goes from the parent hive with only the impulse of going—its settling is a matter of chance. At any rate I may say that no philosopher, logician, metaphysician, psychologist, or other thinker, of whatsoever shade of opinion, ever held that a man could be in love with a voice.

True that the unknown has a charm—*omne ignotum pro magnifico.*[1] If my heart did not love, at least it had a tendency to worship. Here I am on solid ground; for which of us but can understand the feelings of those men of old in Athens, who devoted their altars "To the Unknown God?" I leave the philosophers to say how far apart, or how near, are love and worship: which is first in historical sequence, which is greatest or most sacred! Being human, I cannot see any grace or beauty in worship without love.

However, be the cause w hat it might, I made up my mind to return home *via* Carnaclif. To go from Clare to Dublin by way of Galway and Mayo is to challenge opinion as to one's motive. I did not challenge opinion; I distinctly avoided doing so, and I am inclined to think that there was more of Norah than of Shleenanaher in the cause of my reticence. I could bear to be "chaffed" about a superstitious feeling respecting a mountain, or I could endure the same process regarding a girl of whom I had no high ideal, no sweet illusive memory.

I would never complete the argument, even to myself—then; later on, the cause or subject of it varied!

It was not without a certain conflict of feelings that I approached Carnaclif, even though on this occasion I approached it from the south, whereas on my former visit I had come from the north. I felt that the time went miserably, slowly, and yet nothing would have induced me to admit so much. I almost regretted that I had come, even while I was harrowed with thoughts that I might not be able to arrive at all at Knockcalltecrore. At times I felt as though the whole thing had been a dream; and again as though the romantic nimbus with which imagination had surrounded and hallowed all things must pass away and show that my unknown beings and my Pacts of delicate fantasy were but stern and vulgar realities.

---

1. Everything unknown is taken for magnificent.

The people at the little hotel made me welcome with the usual effusive hospitable intention of the West. Indeed, I was somewhat nettled at how well they remembered me, as, for instance, when the buxom landlady said:

"I'm glad to be able to tell ye, sir, that yer car-man, Andy Sullivan, is here now. He kem with a commercial from Westport to Roundwood, an' is on his way back, an' hopin' for a return job. I think ye'll be able to make a bargain with him if ye wish."

I made to this kindly speech a hasty, and, I felt, an ill-conditioned reply, to the effect that I was going to stay in the neighbourhood for only a few days and would not require the car. I then went to my room and locked my door, muttering a malediction on officious people. I stayed there for some time, until I thought that probably Andy had gone on his way, and then ventured out.

I little knew Andy, however. When I came to the hall, the first person that I saw was the cheerful driver, who came forward to welcome me:

"Musha! but it's glad I am to see yer 'an'r. An' it'll be the proud man I'll be to bhring ye back to Westport wid me."

"I'm sorry, Andy," I began, "that I shall not want you, as I am going to stay in this neighbourhood for a few days."

"Sthay is it? Begor! but it's more gladerer shtill I am. Sure, the mare wants a rist, an' it'll shute her an' me all to nothin'; an' thin while ye're here I can be dhrivin' yer 'an'r out to Shleenanaher. It isn't far enough to intherfere wid her rist."

I answered in, I thought, a dignified way—I certainly intended to be dignified:

"I did not say, Sullivan, that I purposed going out to Shleenanaher or any other place in the neighbourhood."

"Shure, no, yer 'an'r, but I remimber ye said ye'd like to see the Shiftin' Bog; an' thin Misther Joyce and Miss Norah is in throuble, and ye might be a comfort to thim."

"Mr. Joyce! Miss Norah! who are they?" I felt that I was getting red and that the tone of my voice was most unnatural.

Andy's sole answer was as comical a look as I ever saw, the

central object in which was a wink which there was no mistaking. I could not face it, and had to say:

"Oh yes, I remember now. Was not that the man we took on the car to a dark mountain?"

"Yes, surr—him and his daughther!"

"His daughter! I do not remember her. Surely we only took him on the car." Again I felt angry, and with the anger an inward determination not to have Andy or anyone else prying around me when I should choose to visit even such an uncompromising phenomenon as a shifting bog. Andy, like all humorists, understood human nature, and summed up the situation conclusively in his reply—inconsequential though it was:

"Shure yer 'an'r can thrust me; it's blind or deaf an' dumb I am, an' them as knows me knows I'm not the man to go back on a young gintleman goin' to luk at a bog. Sure, doesn't all young min do that same? I've been there meself times out iv mind! There's nothin' in the wurrld foreninst it! Lukin' at bogs is the most intherestin' thin' I knows."

There was no arguing with Andy; and as he knew the place and the people, I then and there concluded an engagement with him. He was to stay in Carnaclif while I wanted him, and then drive me over to Westport.

As I was now fairly launched on the enterprise, I thought it better to lose no time, but arranged to visit the bog early the next morning.

As I was lighting my cigar after dinner that evening, Mrs. Keating, my hostess, came in to ask me a favour. She said that there was staying in the house a gentleman who went over every day to Knockcalltecrore, and as she understood that I was going there in the morning, she made bold to ask if I would mind giving a seat on my car to him, as he had turned his ankle that day and feared he would not be able to walk. Under the circumstances I could only say "Yes," as it would have been a churlish thing to refuse. Accordingly, I gave permission with seeming cheerfulness, but when I was alone my true feelings found vent in muttered grumbling: "I ought to travel in an ambulance instead of a car." "I seem never to be able to get near this Shleen-anaher without an invalid." "Once ought to be enough; but it has become the regulation thing now." "I wish to goodness Andy would hold his infernal tongue; I'd as lief have a detective after me all the time." "It's all very well to be a good Samaritan as a luxury, but as a profession it becomes monotonous." "Confound Andy! I wish I'd never seen him at all."

This last thought brought me up standing, and set me face to face with my baseless ill-humour. If I had never seen Andy, I should never have heard at all of Shleenanaher. I should not have known the legend—I should not have heard Norah's voice.

"And so," said I to myself, "this ideal fantasy—this embodiment of a woman's voice—has a concrete name already. Aye, a concrete name, and a sweet one too."

And so I took another step on my way to the bog, and lost my ill-humour at the same time. When my cigar was half through and my feelings were proportionately soothed, I strolled into the bar and asked Mrs. Keating as to my companion of the morrow. She told me that he was a young engineer named Sutherland.

"What Sutherland?" I asked, adding that I had been at school with a Dick Sutherland, who had, I believed, gone into the Irish College of Science.

"Perhaps it's the same gentleman, sir. This is Mr. Richard Sutherland, and I've heerd him say that he was at Stephen's Green."

"The same man!" said I. "This is jolly! Tell me, Mrs. Keating, what brings him here?"

"He's doin' some work on Knockcalltecrore for Mr. Murdock, some quare thing or another. They do tell me, sir, that it's a most mystayrious thing, wid poles an' lines an' magnets an' all kinds of divilments. They say that Mr. Murdock is goin' from off his head ever since he had the law of poor Phelim Joyce. My! but he's the decent man, that same Mr. Joyce, an' the Gombeen has been hard upon him."

"What was the lawsuit?" I asked.

"All about a sellin' his land on an agreement. Mr. Joyce borryed some money, an' promised if it wasn't paid back at a certain time that he would swop lands. Poor Joyce met wid an accident comin' home wid the money from Galway an' was late, an' when he got home found that the Gombeen had got the sheriff to sell up his land on to him. Mr. Joyce thried it on the coorts, but now Murdock has got a decree on to him an' the poor man'll have to give up his fat lands an' take the Gombeen's poor ones instead."

"That's bad! When has he to give up?"

"Well, I disremember meself exactly, but Mr. Sutherland will be able to tell ye all about it as ye drive over in the mornin'."

"Where is he now? I should like to see him; it may be my old school-fellow."

"Troth, it's in his bed he is; for he rises mighty arly, I can tell."

After a stroll through the town (so-called) to finish my cigar I went to bed also, for we started early. In the morning, when I came down to my breakfast, I found Mr. Sutherland finishing his. It was my old school-fellow; but from being a slight, pale boy, he had grown into a burly, hale, stalwart man, with keen eyes and a flowing brown beard. The only pallor noticeable was the whiteness of his brow, which was ample and lofty as of old.

We greeted each other cordially, and I felt as if old times had come again, for Dick and I had been great friends at school. When we were on our way I renewed my inquiries about Shleenanaher and its inhabitants. I began by asking Sutherland as to what brought him there. He answered:

"I was just about to ask you the same question. 'What brings you here?'"

I felt a difficulty in answering as freely as I could have wished, for I knew that Andy's alert ears were close to us, so I said:

"I have been paying some visits along the west coast, and I thought I would take the opportunity on my way home of investigating a very curious phenomenon of whose existence I became casually acquainted on my way here—a shifting bog."

Andy here must strike in:

"Shure, the masther is mighty fond iv bogs, intirely. I don't

51

know there's anything in the wurruld what intherests him so much." Here he winked at me in a manner that said as plainly as if spoken in so many words, "All right, yer 'an'r, I'll back ye up!" Sutherland laughed as he answered:

"Well, you're in the right place here. Art; the difficulty they have in this part of the world is to find a place that is *not* bog. However, about the Shifting Bog on Knockcalltecrore, I can, perhaps, help you as much as anyone. As you know, geology has been one of my favourite studies, and lately I have taken to investigate in my spare time the phenomena of this very subject. The bog at Shleenanaher is most interesting. As yet, however, my investigation can only be partial, but very soon I shall have the opportunity which I require."

"How is that?" I asked.

"The difficulty arises," he answered, "from a local feud between two men, one of them my employer, Murdock, and his neighbour, Joyce."

"Yes," I interrupted, "I know something of it. I was present when the sheriff's assignment was shown to Joyce, and saw the quarrel. But how does it affect you and your study?"

"This way: the bog is partly on Murdock's land and partly on Joyce's, and until I can investigate the whole extent I cannot come to a definite conclusion. The feud is so bitter at present that neither man will allow the other to set foot over his boundary, or the foot of any one to whom the other is friendly. However, tomorrow the exchange of lands is to be effected, and then I shall be able to continue my investigation. I have already gone nearly all over Murdock's present ground, and after tomorrow I shall be able to go over his new ground—up to now forbidden to me."

"How does Joyce take his defeat?"

"Badly, poor fellow, I am told; indeed, from what I see of him, I am sure of it. They tell me that up to lately he was a bright, happy fellow, but now he is a stern, hard-faced, scowling man—essentially a man with a grievance, which makes him take a jaundiced view of everything else. The only one who is not afraid to speak to him is his daughter, and they are inseparable. It certainly is cruelly hard on him. His farm is almost an ideal one for this part of the world; it has good soil, water, shelter, trees, everything that makes a farm pretty and comfortable, as well as being good for farming purposes; and he has to change it for a piece of land as irregular in shape as the other is compact; without shelter, and partly taken up with this very bog and the utter waste and chaos which, when it shifted in former times, it left behind."

"And how does the other, Murdock, act?"

"Shamefully; I feel so angry with him at times that I could strike him. There is not a thing he can say or do, or leave unsaid or undone, that is not aggravating and insulting to his neighbour. Only that he had the precaution to bind me to an agreement for a given time, I'm blessed if I would work for him, or with him at all— interesting as the work is in itself, and valuable as is the opportunity it gives me of studying that strange phenomenon, the Shifting Bog."

"What is your work with him," I asked—"mining, or draining, or what?"

He seemed embarrassed at my question. He "'hum'd and 'ha'd"— then with a smile he said quite frankly:

"The fact is that I am not at liberty to say. The worthy Gombeen Man put a special clause in our agreement that I was not, during the time of my engagement, to mention to any one the object of my work. He wanted the clause to run that I was never to mention it; but I kicked at that, and only signed in the modified form."

I thought to myself, "More mysteries at Shleenanaher!" Dick went on:

"However, I have no doubt that you will very soon gather the object for yourself. You are yourself something of a scientist, if I remember?"

"Not me," I answered, "my great aunt took care of that when she sent me to our old tutor—or, indeed, to do the old boy justice, he tried to teach me something of the kind; but I found out it wasn't my vogue—anyhow, I haven't done anything lately."

"How do you mean?"

"I haven't got over being idle yet. It's not a year since I came into my fortune. Perhaps—indeed I hope—that I may settle down to work again."

"I'm sure I hope so, too, old fellow," he answered gravely. "When a man has once tasted the pleasure of real work, especially work that taxes the mind and the imagination, the world seems only a poor place without it."

"Like the wurrld widout girruls for me, or widout bog for his 'an'r!" said Andy, grinning as he turned round on his seat.

Dick Sutherland, I was glad to see, did not suspect the joke. He took Andy's remark quite seriously, and said to me:

"My dear fellow, it is delightful to find you so interested in my own topic."

I could not allow him to think me a *savant*. In the first place, he would very soon find me out, and would then suspect my motives ever after. And, again, I had to accept Andy's statement, or let it appear that I had some other reason or motive—or what would seem even more suspicious still, none at all; so I answered:

"My dear Dick, my zeal regarding bog is new; it is at present in its incipient stage, in so far as erudition is concerned. The fact is, that although I would like to learn a lot about it, I am at the present moment profoundly ignorant on the subject."

"Like the rest of mankind," said Dick. "You will hardly believe that, although the subject is one of vital interest to thousands of persons in our own country—one in which national prosperity is mixed up to a large extent—one which touches deeply the happiness and material prosperity of a large section of Irish people, and so helps to mould their political action, there are hardly any works on the subject in existence."

"Surely you are mistaken," I answered.

"No, unfortunately, I am not. There is a Danish book, but it is geographically local; and some information can be derived from the blue-book containing the report of the International

Commission on turf-cutting, but the special authorities are scant indeed. Some day, when you want occupation, just you try to find in any library, in any city of the world, any works of a scientific character devoted to the subject. Nay; more; try to find a fair share of chapters in scientific books devoted to it. You can imagine how devoid of knowledge we are, when I tell you that even the last edition of the *Encyclopaedia Britannica* does not contain the heading 'bog.'"

"You amaze me!" was all I could say.

Then, as we bumped and jolted over the rough by-road, Dick Sutherland gave me a rapid but masterly survey of the condition of knowledge on the subject of bogs, with special application to Irish bogs, beginning with such records as those of Giraldus Cambrensis, of Dr. Boate, of Edmund Spenser, from the time of the first invasion, when the state of the land was such that, as is recorded, when a spade was driven into the ground a pool of water gathered forthwith. He told me of the extent and nature of the bog-lands, of the means taken to reclaim them, and of his hopes of some heroic measures being ultimately taken by Government to reclaim the vast Bog of Allen, which remains as a great evidence of official ineptitude.

"It will be something," he said, "to redeem the character for indifference to such matters so long established, as when Mr. King wrote two hundred years ago, 'We live in an island almost infamous for bogs, and yet I do not remember that any one has attempted much concerning them.'" We were close to Knock-calltecrore when he finished his impromptu lecture thus:

"In fine, we cure bog by both a surgical and a medical process. We drain it so that its mechanical action as a sponge may be stopped, and we put in lime to kill the vital principle of its growth. Without the other, neither process is sufficient; but together, scientific and executive man asserts his dominance."

"Hear! hear!" said Andy. "Musha, but Docther Wilde himself (rest his sowl!) couldn't have put it aisier to grip. It's a purfessionaler the young gintleman is, intirely!"

We shortly arrived at the south side of the western slope of the Hill, and, as Andy took care to inform me, at the end of the boreen leading to the two farms, and close to the head of the Snake's Pass.

Accordingly, I let Sutherland start on his way to Murdock's, while I myself strolled away to the left, where Andy had pointed out to me, rising over the slope of the intervening spur of the Hill, the top of one of the rocks which formed the Snake's Pass. After a few minutes of climbing up a steep slope, and down a steeper one, I arrived at the place itself.

From the first moment that my eyes lit on it, it seemed to me to be a very remarkable spot, and quite worthy of being taken as the scene of strange stories, for it certainly had something "uncanny" about it.

I stood in a deep valley, or rather bowl, with behind me a remarkably steep slope of greensward, while on either hand the sides of the hollow rose steeply—that on the left, clown which I had climbed, being by far the steeper and rockier of the two. In front was the Pass itself.

It was a gorge or cleft through a great wall of rock, which rose on the sea-side of the promontory formed by the Hill. This natural wall, except at the actual Pass itself, rose some fifty or sixty feet over the summit of the slope on either side of the little valley; but right and left of the Pass rose two great masses of rock, like the pillars of a giant gate-way. Between these lay the narrow gorge, with its walls of rock rising sheer some two hundred feet. It was about three hundred feet long, and widened slightly outward, being shaped something funnel-wise, and on the inner side was about a hundred feet wide.

The floor did not go so far as the flanking rocks, but, at about two-thirds of its length, there was a perpendicular descent, like a groove cut in the rock, running sheer down to the sea, some three hundred feet below, and as far under it as we could see. From the northern of the flanking rocks which formed the Pass the rocky wall ran northward, completely sheltering the lower lands from the west, and running into a towering rock that rose on the extreme north, and which stood up in jagged peaks something like The Needles off the coast of the Isle of Wight.

There was no doubt that poor Joyce's farm, thus sheltered, was an exceptionally favoured spot, and I could well understand how loath he must be to leave it.

Murdock's land, even under the enchantment of its distance, seemed very different, and was just as bleak as Sutherland had told me. Its south-western end ran down towards the Snake's Pass. I mounted the wall of rock on the north of the Pass to look down, and was surprised to find that down below me was the end of a large plateau of some acres in extent which ran up northward, and was sheltered north and west by a somewhat similar formation of rock to that which protected Joyce's land. This, then, was evidently the place called the Cliff Fields, of which mention had been made at Widow Kelligan's.

The view from where I stood was one of ravishing beauty. Westward in the deep sea, under gray clouds of endless variety, rose a myriad of clustering islets, some of them covered with grass and heather, where cattle and sheep grazed; others were mere rocks rising boldly from the depths of the sea, and surrounded by a myriad of screaming wild-fowl. As the birds dipped and swept and wheeled in endless circles, their white breasts and gray wings varying in infinite phase of motion, and as the long Atlantic swell, tempered by its rude shocks on the outer fringe of islets, broke in fleecy foam and sent living streams through the crevices of the rocks and sheets of white water over the bowlders where the sea-rack rose and fell, I thought that the earth could give nothing more lovely or more grand. Andy's voice beside me grated on me unpleasantly: "Musha! but it's the fine sight it is intirely; it only wants wan thing."

"What does it want?" I asked, rather shortly.

"Begor, a bit of bog to put your arrum around while ye're lukin' at it," and he grinned at me knowingly.

He was incorrigible. I jumped down from the rock and scrambled into the boreen. My friend Sutherland had gone on his way to Murdock's, so calling to Andy to wait till I returned, I followed him.

I hurried up the boreen and caught up with him, for his progress was slow along the rough lane-way. In reality I felt that it would be far less awkward having him with me; but I pretended that my only care was for his sprained ankle. Some emotions make hypocrites of us all!

With Dick on my arm limping along we passed up the boreen, leaving Joyce's house on our left. I looked out anxiously in case I should see Joyce—or his daughter; but there was no sign of anyone about. In a few minutes Dick, pausing for a moment, pointed out to me the Shifting Bog.

"You see," he said, "those two poles? The line between them marks the mearing of the two lands. We have worked along the bog down from there." He pointed as he spoke to some considerable distance up the Hill to the north where the bog began to be dangerous, and where it curved around the base of a grassy mound, or shoulder of the mountain.

"Is it a dangerous bog?" I queried.

"Rather! It is just as bad a bit of soft bog as ever I saw. I wouldn't like to see anyone or anything that I cared for try to cross it!"

"Why not?"

"Because at any moment they might sink through it; and then, goodbye—no human strength or skill could ever save them."

"Is it a quagmire, then, or like a quicksand?"

"Like either, or both. Nay, it is more treacherous than either. You may call it, if you are poetically inclined, a 'carpet of death!' What you see is simply a film or skin of vegetation of a very low kind, mixed with the mould of decayed vegetable fibre and grit and rubbish of all kinds, which have somehow got mixed into it, floating on a sea of ooze and slime—of something half liquid, half solid, and of an unknown depth. It will bear up a certain weight, for there is a degree of cohesion in it; but it is not all of equal cohesive power, and if one were to step on the wrong spot—" He was silent.

"What then?"

"Only a matter of specific gravity! A body suddenly immersed would, when the air of the lungs had escaped and the *rigor mortis* had set in, probably sink a considerable distance; then it would rise after nine days, when decomposition began to generate gases, and make an effort to reach the top. Not succeeding in this, it would ultimately waste away, and the bones would become incorporated with the existing vegetation somewhere about the roots, or would lie among the slime at the bottom."

"Well," said I, "for real cold-blooded horror, commend me to your men of science."

This passage brought us to the door of Murdock's house—a plain, strongly-built cottage, standing on a knoll of rock that cropped up from the plateau round it. It was surrounded with a garden hedged in by a belt of pollard ash and stunted alders.

Murdoch had evidently been peering surreptitiously through the window of his sitting-room, for, as we passed in by the gate, he came out to the porch. His salutation was not an encouraging one:

"You're somethin' late this mornin', Mr. Sutherland. I hope ye didn't throuble to delay in ordher to bring up this sthrange gintleman. Ye know how particular I am about any wan knowin' aught of me affairs."

Dick flushed up to the roots of his hair, and, much to my surprise, burst out quite in a passionate way:

"Look you here, Mr. Murdock, I'm not going to take any cheek from you, so don't you give any. Of course I don't expect a fellow of your stamp to understand a gentleman's feelings— damn it! how can you have a gentleman's understanding when you haven't even a man's? You ought to know right well what I said I would do, I shall do I despise you and your miserable secrets and your miserable trickery too much to take to myself anything in which they have a part; but when I bring with me a friend, but for whom I shouldn't have been here at all—for I couldn't have walked—I expect that neither he nor I shall be insulted. For two pins I'd not set foot on your dirty ground again!"

Here Murdock interrupted him:

"Aisy now! Ye're undher agreement to me; an' I hould ye to it."

"So you can, you miserable scoundrel, because you know I shall keep my word; but remember that I expect proper treatment; and remember, too, that if I want an assistant I am to have one.

Again Murdock interrupted, but this time much more soothingly:

"Aisy! aisy! Haven't I done every livin' thing ye wanted, and helped ye meself every time? Sure arn't I yer assistant?"

"Yes, because you wanted to get something, and couldn't do without me. And mind this: you can't do without me yet. But be so good as to remember that I choose my own assistant; and I shall not choose you unless I like. You can keep me here and pay me for staying as we agreed; but don't you think that I could fool you if I would?"

"Ye wouldn't do that, I know—an' me thrusted ye!"

"You trusted me! you miserable wretch—Yes! you trusted me by a deed, signed, sealed, and delivered. I don't owe you anything for that."

"Mr. Sutherland, sir, ye're too sharp wid me. Yer frind is very welkim. Do what you like—go where you choose—bring whom you will—only get on wid the worrk and kape it saycret."

"Aye!" sneered Dick, "you are ready to climb down because you want something done, and you know that this is the last day for work on this side of the hill. Well, let me tell you this—for you'll do anything for greed—that you and I together, doing all we can, shall not be able to cover all the ground. I haven't said a word to my friend—and I don't know how he will take any request from you after your impudence; but he is my friend, and a clever man, and if you ask him nicely, perhaps he will be good enough to stay and lend us a hand."

The man made me a low bow and asked me in suitable terms if I would kindly stop part of the day and help in the work. Needless to say I acquiesced. Murdock eyed me keenly, as though to make up his mind whether or no I recollected him—he evidently remembered me—but I affected ignorance, and he seemed satisfied. I was glad to notice that the blow of Joyce's riding-switch still remained across his face as a livid scar. He went away to get the appliances ready for work, in obedience to a direction from Sutherland.

"One has to cut that hound's corns rather roughly," said the latter, with a nice confusion of metaphors, as soon as Murdock had disappeared.

Dick then told me that his work was to make magnetic experiments to ascertain, if possible, if there was any iron hidden in the ground.

"The idea," he said, "is Murdock's own, and I have neither lot nor part in it. My work is simply to carry out his ideas, with what mechanical skill I can command, and to invent or arrange such appliances as he may want. Where his theories are hopelessly wrong, I point this out to him, but he goes on or stops just as he chooses. You can imagine that a fellow of his low character is too suspicious to ever take a hint from anyone. We have been working for three weeks past and have been all over the solid ground, and are just finishing the bog."

"How did you first come across him?" I asked.

"Very nearly a month ago he called on me in Dublin, having been sent by old Gascoigne, of the College of Science. He wanted me to search for iron on his property. I asked if it was regarding opening mines? He said, 'No, just to see if there should be any old iron lying about.' As he offered me excellent terms for my time, I thought he must have some good—or rather, I should say, some strong motive. I know now, though he has never told me, that he is trying for the money that is said to have been lost and buried here by the French after Humbert's expedition to Killala."

"How do you work?" I asked.

"The simplest thing in the world; just carry about a strong magnet—only we have to do it systematically." "And have you found anything as yet?"

61

"Only old scraps—horseshoes, nails, buckles, buttons; our most important find was the tire of a wheel. The old Gombeen thought he had it that time!" and Dick laughed. "How did you manage the bog?"

"That is the only difficult part; we have poles on opposite sides of the bog with lines between them. The magnet is fixed, suspended from a free wheel, and I let it down to the centre from each side in turn. If there were any attraction I should feel it by the thread attached to the magnet which I hold in my hand."

"It is something like fishing?"

"Exactly."

Murdoch now returned and told us that he was ready, so we all went to work. I kept with Sutherland at the far side of the bog, Murdoch remaining on the near side. We planted, or rather placed, a short stake in the solid ground, as close as we could get it to the bog, and steadied it with a guy from the top; the latter I held, while Murdoch, on the other side, fulfilled a similar function. A thin wire connected the two stakes; on this Sutherland now fixed the wheel, from which the magnet depended.

On each side we deflected the stake until the magnet almost touched the surface of the bog. After a few minutes' practice I got accustomed to the work, and acquired sufficient dexterity to be able to allow the magnet to run freely. Inch by inch we went over the surface of the bog, moving slightly to the south-west each time we shifted, following the edges of the bog. Every little while Dick had to change sides, so as to cover the whole extent of the bog, and when he came round again had to go back to where he had last stopped on the same side.

All this made the process very tedious, and the day was drawing to a close when we neared the posts set up to mark the bounds of the two lands. Several times during the day Joyce had come up from his cottage and inspected our work, standing at his own side of the post.

He looked at me closely, but did not seem to recognize me. I nodded to him once, but he did not seem to see my salutation, and I did not repeat it.

All day long I never heard the sweet voice; and as we returned to Carnaclif after a blank day—blank in every sense of the word—the air seemed chillier and the sunset less beautiful than before. The last words I heard on the mountain were from Murdock:

"Nothin' tomorrow, Mr. Sutherland! I've a flittin' to make, but I pay the day all the same; I hould ye to your conthract. An' remember, surr, we're in no hurry wid the wurrk now, so yell not need help anymore."

Andy made no remark till we were well away from the Hill, and then said, dryly:

"I'm afeerd yer 'an'r has had but a poor day; ye lnk as if ye hadn't seen a bit iv bog at all, at all. Gee up, ye ould corn-crake! the gintlemin does be hurryin' home fur their tay, an' fur more wurrk w id bogs tomorra!"

## CHAPTER 5

### ON KNOCKNACAR

When Sutherland and I had finished dinner that evening we took up the subject of bogs where we had left it in the morning. This was rather a movement of my own making, for I felt an awkwardness about touching on the special subject of the domestic relations of the inhabitants of Knockcalltecrore. After several interesting remarks, Dick said:

"There is one thing that I wish to investigate thoroughly: the correlation of bog and special geological formations."

"For instance?" said I.

"Well, specially with regard to limestone. Just at this part of the country I find it almost impossible to pursue the investigation any more than Van Troil could have pursued snake studies in Iceland."

"Is there no limestone at all in this part of the country?" I queried.

"Oh yes, in lots of places; but as yet I have not been able to find any about here. I say 'as yet' on purpose, because it seems to me that there must be some on Knockcalltecrore."

Needless to say the conversation here became to me much more interesting. Dick went on:

"The main feature of the geological formation of all this part of the country is the vast amount of slate and granite, either in isolated patches or lying side by side. And as there are instances of limestone found in quaint ways, I am not without hopes that we may yet find the same phenomenon."

"Where do you find the instances of these limestone formations?" I queried, for I felt that as he was bound to come back to, or towards Shleenanaher, I could ease my own mind by pretending to divert his from it.

"Well, as one instance, I can give you the Corrib River—the stream that drains Lough Corrib into Galway Bay; in fact, the river on which the town of Galway is built. At one place one side of the stream all is granite, and the other is all limestone; I believe the river runs over the union of the two formations. Now, if there should happen to be a similar formation, even in the least degree, at Knockcalltecrore, it will be a great thing."

"Why will it be a great thing?" I asked.

"Because there is no lime near the place at all; because, with limestone on the spot, a hundred things could be done that, as thing are at present, would not repay the effort. With limestone we could reclaim the bogs cheaply all over the neighbourhood—in fact a limekiln there would be worth a small fortune. We could build walls in the right places; I can see how a lovely little harbour could be made there at a small expense. And then, beyond all else, would be the certainty—which is at present in my mind only a hope or a dream— that we could fathom the secret of the Shifting Bog, and perhaps abolish or reclaim it."

"This is exceedingly interesting," said I, as I drew my chair closer. And I only spoke the exact truth, for at that moment I had no other thought in my mind. "Do you mind telling me more, Dick? I suppose you are not like Lamb's Scotchman that will not broach a half-formed idea!"

"Not the least in the world. It will be a real pleasure to have such a good listener. To begin at the beginning, I was much struck with that old cavity on the top of the Hill. It is one of the oddest things I have ever seen or heard of. If it were in any other place or among any other geological formation, I would think its origin must

have been volcanic. But here such a thing is quite impossible. It was evidently once a lake."

"So goes the legend. I suppose you have heard it?"

"Yes; and it rather confirms my theory. Legends have always a base in fact; and whatever cause gave rise to the myth of St. Patrick and the King of the Snakes, the fact remains that the legend is correct in at least one particular—that at some distant time there was a lake or pond on the spot."

"Are you certain?"

"A very cursory glance satisfied me of that. I could not go into the matter thoroughly, for that old wolf of mine was so manifestly impatient that I should get to his wild-goose chase for the lost treasure-chest, that the time and opportunity were wanting. However, I saw quite enough to convince me."

"Well, how do you account for the change? What is your theory regarding the existence of limestone?"

"Simply this, that a lake or reservoir on the top of a mountain means the existence of a spring or springs. Now, springs in granite or hard slate do not wear away the substance of the rock in the same way as they do when they come through limestone. And, moreover, the natures of the two rocks are quite different. There are fissures and cavities in the limestone which are wanting, or which are, at any rate, not so common or perpetually re-current in the other rock. Now, if it should be, as I surmise, that the reservoir was ever fed by a spring passing through a streak or bed of limestone, we shall probably find that in the progress of time the rock became worn, and that the spring found a way in some other direction—either some natural passage through a gap or fissure already formed, or by a channel made for itself."

"And then?"

"And then the process is easily understandable. The spring

naturally sent its waters where there was the least resistance, and they found their way out on some level lower than the top of the Hill. You perhaps noticed the peculiar formation of the Hill, specially on its west side—great sloping tables of rock suddenly ended by a wall of a different stratum—a sort of serrated edge all the way down the inclined plane; you could not miss seeing it, for it cuts the view like the teeth of a saw! Now, if the water, instead of rising to the top and then trickling down the old channel, which is still noticeable, had once found a vent on one of those shelving planes it would gradually fill up the whole cavity formed by the two planes, unless, in the meantime, it found some natural escape.

"As we know, the mountain is covered in a number of places with a growth or formation of bog, and this water, once accumulating under the bog, would not only saturate it, but would raise it—being of less specific gravity than itself—till it actually floated. Given such a state of things as this, it would only require sufficient time for the bog to become soft and less cohesive than when it was more dry and compact, and you have a dangerous bog, something like the carpet of death that we spoke of this morning."

"So far I can quite understand," said I. "But if this be so, how can the bog shift as this one undoubtedly has? It seems, so far, to be hedged with walls of rock. Surely these cannot move."

Sutherland smiled. "I see you do apprehend. Now we are at the second stage. Did you notice, as we went across the hillside, that there were distinct beds or banks of clay?"

"Certainly; do they come in?"

"Of course. If my theory is correct, the shifting is due to them."

"Explain!"

"So far as I can. But here I am only on surmise, or theory pure and simple. I may be all wrong, or I may be right—I shall know-more before I am done with Shleenanaher. My theory is that the shifting is due to the change in the beds of clay, as, for instance, by rains washing them by degrees to lower levels; this is notably the case in that high clay bank just opposite the Snake's Pass. The rocks are fixed, and so the clay becomes massed in banks between them, perhaps aided in the first instance by trees falling across the chasm or opening.

"But then the perpetually accumulating water from the spring has to find a way of escape; and as it cannot cut through the rock, it rises to the earth bed, till it either tops the bed of clay which confines it or finds a gap or fissure through which it can escape. In either case it make a perpetually deepening channel for itself, for the soft clay yields little by little to the stream passing over it, and so the surface of the outer level falls, and the water escapes, to perhaps find new reservoirs ready-made to receive it, and a similar process as before takes place."

"Then the bog extends, and the extended part takes the place of the old bog, which gradually drains."

"Just so; but such would, of course, depend on the level; there might be two or more reservoirs, each with a deep bottom of its own and united only near the surface; or if the bank or bed of clay lay in the surface of one shelving rock, the water would naturally drain to the lowest point, and the upper land would be shallow in proportion."

"But," I ventured to remark, "if this be so, one of two things must happen: either the water would wear away the clay so quickly that the accumulation would not be dangerous, or else the process would be a very gradual one, and would not be attended with such results as we are told of. There would be a change in the position of the bog, but there would not be the upheaval and complete displacement and chaos that I have heard of, for instance, with regard to this very bog of Knockcalltecrore."

"Your 'if' is a great peacemaker. If what I have supposed were all, then the result would be as you have said; but there are lots of other supposes; as yet we have only considered one method of change. Suppose, for instance, that the water found a natural means of escape—as, for instance, where this very bog sends a stream over the rocks into the Cliff Fields—it would not attack the clay bed at all, unless under some unusual pressure. Then suppose that when such pressure had come the water did not rise and top the clay bed, but that it found a small fissure part of the way down. Suppose there were several such reservoirs as I have mentioned—and from the formation of the ground I think it very likely, for in several places jutting rocks from either side come close together, and suggest a sort of gap or canon in the rock formation, easily forming it into a reservoir.

"Then, if the barrier between the two upper ones were to be weakened and a sudden weight of water were to be thrown on the lower wall, suppose such wall were to partially collapse, and bring down, say, a clay bank, which would make a temporary barrier loftier than any yet existing, but only temporary; suppose that the quick accumulation of waters behind this barrier lifted the w hole mass of water and slime and bog to its utmost height. Then, when such obstruction had been reached, the whole lower barrier, weakened by infiltration and attacked with sudden and new force, would give way at once, and the stream, kept down from above by the floating bog, would force its way along the bed-rock and lift the whole spongy mass resting on it.

"Then, with this new extent of bog suddenly saturated and weakened—demoralized as it were—and devoid of resisting power, the whole floating mass of the upper bog might descend on it, mingle with it, become incorporated with its semi-fluid substance, and form a new and dangerous quagmire incapable of sustaining solid weight, but leaving behind on the higher level only the refuse and sediment of its former existence—all the rubble and grit too heavy to float, and which would gradually settle down on the upper bed-rock."

"Really, Dick, you put it most graphically. What a terrible thing it would be to live on the line of such a change."

"Terrible, indeed! At such a moment a house in the track of the movement—unless it were built on the rock—would go down like a ship in a storm—go down solid and in a moment, without warning and without hope!"

"Then, with such a neighbour as a shifting bog, the only safe place for a house would be on a rock?"—Before my eyes, as I spoke, rose the vision of Murdock's house, resting on its knoll of rock, and I was glad, for one reason, that there, at least, would be safety for Joyce—and his daughter.

"Exactly. Now Murdock's house is as safe as a church. I must look at his new house when I go up tomorrow."

As I really did not care about Murdock's future, I asked no further questions; so we sat in silence and smoked in the gathering twilight.

There was a knock at the door. I called, "Come in." The door opened slowly, and through a narrow opening Andy's shock head presented itself.

"Come in, Andy," said Dick. "Come here and try if you can manage a glass of punch."

"Begor!" was Andy's sole expression of acquiescence. The punch was brewed and handed to him.

"Is that as good as Widow Kelligan's?" I asked him. Andy grinned:

"All punch is good, yer 'an'rs. Here's both yer good healths, an' here's The Girls' an'"—turning to me, "'the Bog.'" He winked, threw up his hand—and put down the empty glass. "Glory be to God!" was his grace after drink.

"Well, Andy! what is it?" said Dick.

"I've heerd," said he, "that yer 'an'rs isn't goin' in the mornin' to Shleenanaher, and I thought that yez couldn't do betther nor dhrive over to Knocknacar tomorra an' spind the day there."

"And why Knocknacar?" said I.

Andy twirled his cap between his hands in a sheepish way. I felt that he was acting a part, but could not see any want of reality. With a little hesitation he said:

"I've gother from what yer 'an'rs wor sayin' on the car this mornin', that yez is both intherested in bogs, an' there's the beautifulest bit iv bog in all the counthry there beyant. An', moreover, it's a lovely shpot intirely. If you gintlemen have nothin' betther to do, ye'd dhrive over there—if ye'd take me advice."

"What kind of bog is it, Andy?" said Dick. "Is there anythin' peculiar about it. Does it shift?"

Andy grinned a most unaccountable grin.

"Begor, it does, surr!" he answered, quickly. "Sure, all bogs does shift!" And he grinned again.

"Andy," said Dick, laughing, "you have some joke in your mind. What is it?"

"Oh, sorra wan, surr—ask the masther there."

As it did not need a surgical operation to get the joke intended into the head of a man—of whatever nationality—who understood Andy's allusion, and as I did not want to explain it, I replied:

"Oh, don't ask me, Andy; I'm no authority on the subject," and I looked rather angrily at him, when Dick was not looking.

Andy hastened to put matters right; he evidently did not want to lose his day's hire on the morrow:

"Yer 'an'rs, ye may take me wurrd for it. There's a bog beyant at Knocknacar which'll intherest yez intirely; I rimimber it meself a lot higher up the mountain whin I was a spalpeen,[1] an' it's been crawlin' down iver since. It's a mighty quare shpot, intirely!"

This settled the matter, and we arranged forthwith to start early on the following morning for Knocknacar, Andy, before he left, having a nightcap—out of a tumbler.

We were astir fairly early in the morning, and having finished a breakfast sufficiently substantial to tide us over till dinner-time, we started on our journey. The mare was in good condition for work, the road was level and the prospect fine, and altogether we enjoyed our drive immensely. As we looked back we could see Knockcalltecrore rising on the edge of the coast away to our right, and seemingly surrounded by a network of foam-girt islands, for a breeze was blowing freshly from the southwest.

At the foot of the mountain—or, rather, hill—there was a small, clean-looking sheebeen. Here Andy stopped and put up the mare; then he brought us up a narrow lane bounded by

---

1. From the Irish *spailpín* meaning "rascal," or, sometimes, "seasonal labourer."

thick hedges of wild brier to where we could see the bog which was the object of our visit. Dick's foot was still painful, so I had to give him an arm, as on yesterday. We crossed over two fields, from which the stones had been collected and placed in heaps. The land was evidently very rocky, for here and there—more especially in the lower part—the gray rock cropped up in places. At the top of the farthest field, Andy pointed out an isolated rock rising sharply from the grass.

"Look there, yer 'an'rs; whin I remimber first, that rock was as far aff from the bog as we are now from the boreen; an' luk at it now: why, the bog is close to it, so it is." He then turned and looked at a small heap of stones. "Murther! but there is a quare thing. Why that heap, not a year ago, was as high as the top iv that rock. Begor, it's bein' buried, it is!"

Dick looked quite excited as he turned to me and said:

"Why, Art, old fellow, here is the very thing we were talking about. This bog is an instance of the gradual changing of the locality of a bog by the filtration of its water through the clay beds resting on the bed-rock. I wonder if the people here will let me make some investigations! Andy, who owns this land?"

"Oh, I can tell yer 'an'r that well enough; it's Mishter Moriarty from Knockcalltecrore. Him, surr," turning to me, "that ye seen at Widda Kelligan's that night in the shtorm."

"Does he farm it himself?"

"No, surr—me father rints it. The ould mare was riz on this very shpot."

"Do you think your father will let me make some investigations here, if I get Mr. Moriarty's permission also?"

"Throth, an' he will, surr—wid all the plisure in life—iv coorse," he added, with native shrewdness, "if there's no harrum done to his land—or, if there's harrum done, it's ped for."

"All right, Andy," said I; "I'll be answerable for that part of it."

We went straight away with Andy to see the elder Sullivan. We found him in his cabin at the foot of the hill—a hale old man of nearly eighty, with all his senses untouched, and he was all that could be agreeable. I told him who I was, and that I could afford to reimburse him if any damage should be done. Dick explained to him that, so far from doing harm, what he would do would probably prevent the spreading of the bog, and would in such case much enhance the value of his holding, and in addition give him the use of a spring on his land. Accordingly we went back to make further investigations. Dick had out his notebook in an instant, and took accurate note of everything; he measured and probed the earth, tapped the rocks with the little geological hammer which he always carried, and finally set himself down to make an accurate map of the locality, I acting as his assistant in the measurements. Andy left us for a while, but presently appeared, hot and flushed. As he approached, Dick observed:

"Andy has been drinking the health of all his relatives. We must keep him employed here, or we may get a spill going home."

The object of his solicitude came and sat on a rock beside us, and looked on. Presently he came over, and said to Dick:

"Yer 'an'r, can I help ye in yer wurrk? Sure, if ye only want wan hand to help ye, mayhap mine id do. An' thin his 'an'r here might hop up to the top iv the mountain; there's a mighty purty view there intirely, an' he could enjoy it, though ye can't get up wid yer lame fut."

"Good idea!" said Dick. "You go up on top. Art. This is very dull work, and Andy can hold the tape for me as well as you or anyone else. You can tell me all about it when you come down."

"Do, yer 'an'r. Tell him all ye see!" said Andy, as I prepared to ascend. "If ye go up soft be the shady parts, mayhap ye'd shtrike another bit of bog be the way."

I had grown so suspicious of Andy's *double entente*,[2] that I looked at him keenly, to see if there was any fresh joke on; but his face was immovably grave, and he was seemingly intent on the steel tape which he was holding.

---

2. Double meaning.

I proceeded up the mountain. It was a very pleasant one to climb, or rather, to ascend, for it was nearly all covered with grass. Here and there, on the lower half, were clumps of stunted trees, all warped eastwards by the prevailing westerly wind— alders, mountain-ash, and thorn. Higher up these disappeared, but there was still a pleasant sprinkling of hedge-rows. As the verdure grew on the south side higher than on the north or west, I followed it and drew near the top. As I got closer, I heard someone singing. "By Jove," said I to myself, "the women of this country have sweet voices!"—indeed, this was by no means the first time I had noticed the fact. I listened, and as I drew nearer to the top of the hill I took care not to make any noise which might disturb the singer. It was an odd sensation to stand in the shadow of the hill-top, on that September day, and listen to *Ave Maria* sung by the unknown voice of an unseen singer. I made a feeble joke all to myself:

"My experience of the girls of the west is that of *vox et præteria nihil*."[3]

There was an infinity of *pathos* in the voice—some sweet, sad yearning, as though the earthly spirit was singing with an unearthly voice—and the idea came on me with a sense of conviction that some deep unhappiness underlay that appeal to the Mother of Sorrows. I listened, and somehow felt guilty. It almost seemed that I was profaning some shrine of womanhood, and I took myself to task severely in something of the following strain:

"That poor girl has come to this hill-top for solitude. She thinks she is alone with Nature and Nature's God, and pours forth her soul freely; and you, wretched, tainted man, break in on the sanctity of her solitude—of her prayer. For shame! for shame!"

Then—men are all hypocrites—I stole guiltily forward to gain a peep at the singer who thus communed with Nature and Nature's God, and the sanctity of whose solitude and prayer I was violating.

---

3. Latin for "words, and nothing else."

A tuft of heath grew just at the top; behind this I crouched, and parting its luxuriance looked through.

For my pains I only saw a back, and that back presented in the most ungainly way of which graceful woman is capable. She was seated on the ground, not even raised upon a stone. Her knees were raised to the level of her shoulders, and her outstretched arms confined her legs below the knees—she was, in fact, in much the same attitude as boys are at games of cock-fighting. And yet there was something very touching in the attitude—something of self-oblivion so complete that I felt a renewed feeling of guiltiness as an intruder. Whether her reasons be aesthetic, moral, educational, or disciplinary, no self-respecting woman ever sits in such a manner when a man is by.

The song died away, and then there was a gulp and a low suppressed moan. Her head drooped between her knees, her shoulders shook, and I could see that she was weeping. I wished to get away, but for a few moments I was afraid to stir lest she should hear me. The solitude, now that the vibration of her song had died out of the air, seemed oppressive. In those few seconds a new mood seemed to come over her. She suddenly abandoned her dejected position, and, with the grace and agility of a young fawn, leaped to her feet. I could see that she was tall and exquisitely built, on the slim side—what the French call *svelte*. With a grace and *pathos* which were beyond expression she stretched forth her arms towards the sea, as to something that she loved, and then, letting them fall by her side, remained in a kind of waking dream.

I slipped away, and when I was well out of sight ran down the hill about a hundred yards, and then commenced the re-ascent, making a fair proportion of noise as I came, now striking at the weeds with my heavy stick, now whistling, and again humming a popular air.

When I gained the top of the hill I started as though surprised at seeing anyone, much less a girl, in such a place. I think I acted the part well: again I say that at times the hypocrite in us can be depended upon. She was looking straight towards me, and certainly, so far as I could tell, took me in good faith. I doffed my hat and made some kind of stammering salutation, as one would to a stranger—the stammering not being, of course, in the routine of such occasions, but incidental to the special circumstances. She made me a graceful courtesy and a blush overspread her cheeks. I was afraid to look too hard at her, especially at first, lest I should frighten her away, but I stole a glance towards her at every moment when I could.

How lovely she was! I had heard that along the west coast of Ireland there are traces of Spanish blood and Spanish beauty, and here was a living evidence of the truth of the hearsay. Not even at sunset in the parades of Madrid or Seville, could one see more perfect beauty of the Spanish type—beauty perhaps all the more perfect for being tempered with northern calm. As I said, she was tall and beautifully proportioned. Her neck was long and slender, gracefully set in her rounded shoulders, and supporting a beautiful head, borne with the free grace of the lily on its stem.

There is nothing in woman more capable of complete beauty than the head, and crowned as this head was with a rich mass of hair as black and as glossy as the raven's wing, it was a thing to remember. She wore no bonnet, but a gray homespun shawl was thrown loosely over her shoulders; her hair was coiled in one rich mass at the top and back of her head, and fastened with an old-fashioned tortoise-shell comb. Her face was a delicate oval, showing what Rossetti calls "the pure wide curve from ear to chin." Luxuriant black eyebrows were arched over large black-blue eyes swept by curling lashes of extraordinary length, and showed off the beauty of a rounded, ample forehead—somewhat sunburnt, be it said.

The nose was straight and wide between the eyes, with delicate sensitive nostrils; the chin wide and firm, and the mouth full and not small, with lips of scarlet, forming a perfect Cupid's bow, and just sufficiently open to show two rows of small teeth, regular and white as pearls. Her dress was that of a well-to-do peasant—a sort of body or jacket of printed chintz over a dress or petticoat of homespun of the shade of crimson given by a madder dye. The dress was short, and showed trim ankles in gray homespun with pretty feet in thick, country-made, wide-toed shoes. Her hands were shapely, with long fingers, and were very sunburnt and manifestly used to work.

As she stood there, with the western breeze playing with her dress and tossing about the stray ends of her raven tresses, I thought that I had never in my life seen anything so lovely. And yet she was only a peasant girl, manifestly and unmistakably, and had no pretence of being anything else.

She was evidently as shy as I was, and for a little while we were both silent. As is usual, the woman was the first to recover her self-possession, and while I was torturing my brain in vain for proper words to commence a conversation, she remarked:

"What a lovely view there is from here! I suppose, sir, you have never been on the top of this hill before?"

"Never," said I, feeling that I was equivocating if not lying. "I had no idea that there was anything so lovely here." I meant this to have a double meaning, although I was afraid to make it apparent to her. "Do you often come up here?" I continued.

"Not very often. It is quite a long time since I was here last; but the view seems fairer and dearer to me every time I come." As she spoke the words, my memory leaped back to that eloquent gesture as she raised her arms.

I thought I might as well improve the occasion and lay the foundation for another meeting without giving offence or fright, so I said:

"This hill is quite a discovery; and as I am likely to be here in this neighbourhood for some time, I dare say I shall often find myself enjoying this lovely view."

She made no reply or comment whatever to this statement. I looked over the scene, and it was certainly a fit setting for so lovely a figure; but it was the general beauty of the scene, and not, as had hitherto been the case, one part of it only, that struck my fancy. Away on the edge of the coast-line rose Knockcalltecrore; but it somehow looked lower than before, and less important.

The comparative insignificance was, of course, due to the fact that I was regarding it from a superior altitude, but it seemed to me that it was because it did not now seem to interest me so much. That sweet voice through the darkness seemed very far away now; here was a voice as sweet, and in such habitation! The invisible charm with which Shleenanaher had latterly seemed to hold me, or the spell which it had laid upon me, seemed to pass away, and I found myself smiling that I should ever have entertained such an absurd idea.

Youth is not naturally standoff, and before many minutes the two visitors to the hill-top had laid aside reserve and were chatting freely. I had many questions to ask of local matters, for I wanted to find out what I could of my fair companion without seeming to be too inquisitive; but she seemed to fight shy of all such topics, and when we parted my ignorance of her name and surroundings remained as profound as it had been at first. She, however, wanted to know all about London. She knew it only by hearsay; for some of the questions which she asked me were amazingly simple; manifestly she had something of the true peasant belief that London is the only home of luxury, power, and learning. She was so frank, however, and made her queries with such a gentle modesty, that something within my heart seemed to grow and grow; and the conviction was borne upon me that I stood before my fate. Sir Geraint's ejaculation rose to my lips:

*Here, by God's rood, is the one maid for me!*[4]

One thing gave me much delight. The sadness seemed to have passed quite away—for the time, at all events. Her eyes, which had at first been glassy with recent tears, were now lit with keenest interest, and she seemed to have entirely forgotten the cause of her sorrow.

"Good!" thought I to myself, complacently. "At least I have helped to brighten her life, though it be but for one hour."

---

4. Alfred, Lord Tennyson, *The Marriage of Geraint*, from *The Idylls of the King*.

Even while I was thinking she rose up suddenly—we had been sitting on a bowlder—"Goodness! how the time passes!" she said; "I must run home at once."

"Let me see you home," I said, eagerly. Her great eyes opened, and she said, with a grave simplicity that took me "way down" to use American slang:

"Why?"

"Just to see that you get home safely," I stammered. She laughed merrily.

"No fear for me. I'm safer on this mountain than anywhere in the world—almost," she added, and the grave, sad look stole again over her face.

"Well, but I would like to," I urged. Again she answered, with grave, sweet seriousness:

"Oh no, sir; that would not do. What would folk say to see me walking with a gentleman like you?" The answer was conclusive. I shrugged my shoulders because I was a man, and had a man's petulance under disappointment; and then I took off my hat and bowed—not ironically, but cheerfully, so as to set her at ease; for I had the good fortune to have been bred a gentleman. My reward came when she held out her hand frankly and said:

"Goodbye, sir," gave a little graceful curtsey, and tripped away over the edge of the hill.

I stood bareheaded looking at her until she disappeared. Then I went to the edge of the little plateau and looked over the distant prospect of land and sea, with a heart so full that the tears rushed to my eyes. There are those who hold that any good emotion is an act of prayer. If this be so, then on that wild mountain-top as fervent a prayer as the heart of man is capable of went up to the Giver of all good things!

When I reached the foot of the mountain I found Dick and Andy waiting for me at the sheebeen. As I came close Dick called out:

"What a time you were, old chap. I thought you had taken root on the hill-top! What on earth kept you?"

"The view from the top is lovely beyond compare," I said, as an evasive reply.

"Is what ye see there more lovelier nor what ye see at Shleen-anaher?" said Andy, with seeming gravity.

"Far more so!" I replied instantly and with decision.

"I told yer 'an'r there was somethin' worth lukin' at," said he. "An' may I ask if yer 'an'r seen any bog on the mountain?"

I looked at him with a smile. I seemed to rather like his chaff now. "Begor I did, yer 'an'r," I answered, mimicking his accent.

We had proceeded on our way for a long distance, Andy apparently quite occupied with his driving, Dick studying his notebook, and I quite content with my thoughts, when Andy said, apropos of nothing and looking at nobody:

"I seen a young girrul comin' down the hill beyant a wee while before yer 'an'r. I hope she didn't disturb any iv yez?"

The question passed unnoticed, for Dick apparently did not hear, and I did not feel called upon to answer it.

I could not have truthfully replied with a simple negative or positive.

## Chapter 6

### Confidences

The next day Sutherland would have to resume his work with Murdock, but on his newly-acquired land. I could think of his visit to Knockcalltecrore without a twinge of jealousy; and, for my own part, I contemplated a walk in a different direction. Dick was full of his experiment regarding the bog at Knocknacar, and could talk of nothing else—a disposition of things which suited me all to nothing, for I had only to acquiesce in all he said, and let my own thoughts have free and pleasant range.

"I have everything cut and dry in my head, and I'll have it all on paper before I sleep tonight," said the enthusiast. "Unfortunately, I am tied for a while longer to the amiable Mr. Murdock; but since you're good enough, old fellow, to offer to stay to look after the cutting, I can see my way to getting along. We can't begin until the day after tomorrow, for I can't by any possibility get old Moriarty's permission before that. But then we'll start in earnest. You must get some men up there and set them to work at once.

"By tomorrow evening I'll have an exact map ready for you to work by, and all you will have to do will be to see that the men are kept up to the mark, look at the work now and then and take a note of results. I expect it will take quite a week or two to make the preliminary drainage, for we must have a decided fall for the water. We can't depend on less than twenty or thirty feet, and I should not be surprised if we want twice as much. I suppose I sha'n't see you till tomorrow night; for I'm going up to my room now, and shall work late, and I must be off early in the morning. As you're going to have a walk I suppose I may take Andy, for my foot is not right yet?"

"By all means," I replied, and we bade each other good-night.

When I went to my own room I locked the door and looked out of the open window at the fair prospect bathed in soft moonlight. For a long time I stood there. What my thoughts were I need tell no young man or young woman, for without shame I admitted to myself that I was over head and ears in love. If any young person of either sex requires any further enlightenment, well, then, all I can say is that their education in life has been shamefully neglected, or their opportunities have been scant; or, worse still, some very grave omission has been made in their equipment for the understanding of life. If anyone not young wants such enlightenment, I simply say, "Sir, or madam, either you are a fool, or your memory is gone!"

One thing I will say, that I never felt so much at one with my kind; and before going to bed I sat down and wrote a letter of instructions to my agent, directing him to make accurate personal inquiries all over the estate, and at the forthcoming rent-day make such remissions of rent that would relieve any trouble, or aid in any plan of improvements such as his kinder nature could guess at or suggest.

I need not say that for a long time I did not sleep, and although my thoughts were full of such hope and happiness that the darkness seemed ever changing into sunshine, there were, at times, such harrowing thoughts of difficulties to come—in the shape of previous attachments; of my being late in my endeavours to win her as my wife; of my never being able to find her again—that, now and again, I had to jump from my bed and pace the floor. Towards daylight I slept, and went through a series of dreams of alternating joy and pain.

At first, hope held full sway, and my sweet experience of the day became renewed and multiplied; again, I climbed the hill and saw her and heard her voice; again, the tearful look faded from her eyes; again, I held her hand in mine and bade goodbye, and a thousand happy fancies filled me with exquisite joy. Then doubts began to come. I saw her once more on the hilltop, but she was looking out for some other than myself, and a shadow of disappointment passed over her sweet face when she recognized me.

Again, I saw myself kneeling at her feet and imploring her love, while only cold, hard looks were my lot; or I found myself climbing the hill, but never able to reach the top, or on reaching it finding it empty. Then I would find myself hurrying through all sorts of difficult places—high, bleak mountains, and lonely wind-swept strands, dark paths through gloomy forests, and over sun-smitten plains, looking for her whom I had lost, and in vain trying to call her, for I could not remember her name. This last nightmare was quite a possibility, for I had never heard it.

I awoke many times from such dreams in an agony of fear; but after a time both pleasure and pain seemed to have had their share of my sleep, and I slept the dreamless sleep that Plato eulogizes in the *Apologia Socratis*.

I was awakened to a sense that my hour of rising had not yet come by a knocking at my door. I opened it, and on the landing without saw Andy standing, cap in hand.

"Holloa, Andy!" I said. "What on earth do you want?"

"Yer 'an'r 'll parden me, but I'm jist off wid Misther Sutherland; an' as I undherstand ye was goin' for a walk, I made bould t' ask yer 'an'r if ye'll give a missage to me father?"

"Certainly, Andy, with pleasure."

"Maybe ye'd tell him that I'd like the white mare tuk off the grash an' gave some hard atin' for a few days, as I'll want her brung into Wistport before long."

"All right, Andy. Is that all?"

"That's all, yer 'an'r." Then he added, with a sly look at me:

"Maybe ye'll keep yer eye out for a nice bit o' bog as ye go along."

"Get on, Andy," said I. "Shut up, you ould corn-crake!" I felt I could afford to chaff with him, as we were alone.

He grinned, and went away. But he had hardly gone a few steps when he returned and said, with an air of extreme seriousness:

"As I'm goin' to Knockcalltecrore, is there any message I kin take for ye to Miss Norah?"

"Oh, go on!" said I. "What message should I have to send, when I never saw the girl in my life?"

For reply he winked at me with a wink big enough to cover a perch of land, and, looking back over his shoulder so that I could see his grin to the last, he went along the corridor, and I went back to bed.

It did not strike me till a long time afterwards—when I was quite close to Knocknacar—how odd it was that Andy had asked me to give the message to his father. I had not told him I was even coming in the direction—I had not told anyone; indeed, I had rather tried to mislead when I spoke of taking a walk that day, by saying some commonplace about "the advisability of breaking new ground," and so forth. Andy had evidently taken it for granted; and it annoyed me somewhat that he could find me so transparent. However, I gave the message to the old man, to which he promised to attend, and had a drink of milk, which is the hospitality of the West of Ireland farmhouse. Then, in the most nonchalant way I could, I began to saunter up the hill.

I loitered awhile here and there on the way up. I diverted my steps now and then as if to make inquiry into some interesting object. I tapped rocks and turned stones over, to the discomfiture of various swollen pale-coloured worms and nests of creeping things. With the end of my stick I dug up plants, and made here and there unmeaning holes in the ground, as though I were actuated by some direct purpose known to myself and not understood of others. In fact, I acted as a hypocrite in many harmless and unmeaning ways, and rendered myself generally obnoxious to the fauna and flora of Knocknacar.

As I approached the hilltop my heart beat loudly and fast, and a genuine supineness took possession of my limbs, and a dimness came over my sight and senses. I had experienced something of the same feeling at other times in my life—as, for instance, just before my first fight when a school-boy, and when I stood up to make my maiden speech at the village debating society. Such feelings—or lack of feelings—however, do not kill; and it is the privilege and strength of advancing years to know this fact.

I proceeded up the hill. I did not whistle this time, or hum, or make any noise; matters were far too serious with me for any such levity. I reached the top, and found myself alone! A sense of blank disappointment came over me, which was only relieved when, on looking at my watch, I found that it was as yet still early in the forenoon. It was three o'clock yesterday when I had met—when I had made the ascent.

As I had evidently to while away a considerable time, I determined to make an accurate investigation of the hill of Knocknacar—much, very much, fuller than I had made as yet. As my unknown had descended the hill by the east, and would probably make the ascent—if she ascended at all—by the same side; and as it was my object not to alarm her, I determined to confine my investigations to the west side. Accordingly, I descended about half way down the slope, and then commenced my prying into the secrets of Nature under a sense of the just execration of me and my efforts on the part of the whole of the animate and inanimate occupants of the mountainside.

Hours to me had never seemed of the same inexhaustible proportions as the hours thus spent. At first I was strong with a dogged patience; but this in time gave way to an impatient eagerness that merged into a despairing irritability. More than once I felt an almost irresistible inclination to rush to the top of the hill and shout, or conceived an equally foolish idea to make a call at every house, cottage, and cabin in the neighbourhood. In this latter desire my impatience was somewhat held in check by a sense of the ludicrous; for, as I thought of the detail of the doing it, I seemed to see myself, when trying to reduce my abstract longing to a concrete effort, meeting only jeers and laughter from both men and women in my seemingly asinine effort to make inquiries regarding a person whose name even I did not know, and for what purpose I could assign no sensible reason.

I verily believe I must have counted the leaves of grass on portions of that mountain. Unfortunately, hunger or thirst did not assail me, for they would have afforded some diversion to my thoughts. I sturdily stuck to my resolution not to ascend to the top until after three o'clock, and I gave myself much *kudos* for the stern manner in which I adhered to my resolve.

My satisfaction at so bravely adhering to my resolution, in spite of so much mental torment and temptation, may be imagined when, at the expiration of the appointed time, on ascending to the hilltop, I saw my beautiful friend sitting on the edge of the plateau and heard her first remark after our mutual salutations:

"I have been here nearly two hours, and am just going home! I have been wondering and wondering what on earth you were workinsg at all over the hillside! May I ask, are you a botanist?"

"No."

"Or a geologist?"

"No."

"Or a naturalist?"

"No."

There she stopped; this simple interrogation as to the pursuits of a stranger evidently struck her as unmaidenly, for she blushed and turned away.

I did not know what to say; but youth has its own wisdom—which is sincerity—and I blurted out:

"In reality I was doing nothing; I was only trying to pass the time."

There was a query in the glance of the glorious blue-black eyes and in the lifting of the ebon lashes; and I went on, conscious as I proceeded that the ground before me was marked "Dangerous":

"The fact is, I did not want to come up here till after three, and the time seemed precious long, I can tell you."

"Indeed. But you have missed the best part of the view. Between one and two o'clock, when the sun strikes in between the islands—Cusheen there to the right, and Mishear—the view is the finest of the whole day."

"Oh, yes," I answered, "I know now what I have missed."

Perhaps my voice betrayed me. I certainly felt full of bitter regret; but there was no possibility of mistaking the smile which rose to her eyes and faded into the blush that followed the reception of the thought.

There are some things which a woman *cannot* misunderstand or fail to understand; and surely my regret and its cause were within the category.

It thrilled through me with a sweet intoxication, to realize that she was not displeased. Man is predatory even in his affections, and there is some conscious power to him which follows the conviction that the danger of him—which is his intention— is recognized.

However, I thought it best to be prudent, and to rest on success—for a while, at least. I therefore commenced to talk of London, whose wonders were but fresh to myself, and was rewarded by the blight smile that had now become incorporated with my dreams by day and by night.

And so we talked—talked in simple companionship; and the time fled by on golden wings. No word of love was spoken or even hinted at, but with joy and gratitude unspeakable I began to realize that we were *en rapport* And, more than this, I realized that the beautiful peasant girl had great gifts—a heart of gold, a sweet, pure nature, and a rare intelligence. I gathered that she had had some education, though not an extensive one, and that she had followed up at home such subjects as she had learned in school. But this was all I gathered. I was still as ignorant as ever of her name, and all else beside, as when I had first heard her sweet voice on the hilltop.

Perhaps I might have learned more had there been time; but the limit of my know ledge had been fixed. The time had fled so quickly, because so happily, that neither of us had taken account of it; and suddenly, as a long red ray struck over the hilltop from the sun, now preparing for his plunge into the western wave, she jumped to her feet with a startled cry:

"The sunset! What am I thinking of! Goodnight! goodnight! No, you must not come—it would never do! Goodnight!" And before I could say a word, she was speeding down the eastern slope of the mountain.

The revulsion from such a dream of happiness made me for the moment ungrateful; and I felt that it was with an angry sneer on my lip that I muttered, as I looked at her retreating form:

"Why are the happy hours so short, while misery and anxiety spread out endlessly?"

But as the red light of the sunset smote my face, a better and a holier feeling came to me; and there on the top of the hill I knelt and prayed, with a directness and fervour that are the spiritual gifts of youth, that every blessing might light on her— the *arrière pensée* being—her, my wife. Slowly I went down the mountain after the sun had set; and when I got to the foot I stood bareheaded for a long time, looking at the summit which had given me so much happiness.

Do not sneer or make light of such moments, ye whose lives are gray. Would to God that the gray-haired and gray-souled watchers of life, could feel such moments once again!

I walked home with rare briskness, but did not feel tired at all by it; I seemed to tread on air. As I drew near the hotel I had some vague idea of hurrying at once to my own room, and avoiding dinner altogether as something too gross and carnal for my present exalted condition; but a moment's reflection was sufficient to reject any such folly. I therefore achieved the other extreme, and made Mrs. Keating's kindly face beam by the vehemence with which I demanded food. I found that Dick had not yet returned—a fact which did not displease me, as it insured me a temporary exemption from Andy's ill-timed banter, which I did not feel in a humour to enjoy at present.

I was just sitting down to my dinner when Dick arrived. He, too, had a keen appetite; and it was not until we had finished our fish, and were well into our roast duck, that conversation began. Once he was started, Dick was full of matters to tell me. He had seen Moriarty— that was what had kept him so late—and had got his permission to investigate and experiment on the bog. He had thought out the whole method of work to be pursued, and had, during Murdock's dinner-time, made to scale a rough diagram for me to work by.

We had our cigars lit before he had exhausted himself on this subject. He had asked me a few casual questions about my walk, and, so as not to arouse any suspicions, I had answered him vaguely that I had had a lovely day, had enjoyed myself immensely, and had seen some very pretty things—all of which was literally and exactly true. I had then asked him as to how he had got on with his operations in connection with the bog. It amused me to think how small and secondary a place Shleen-anaher, and all belonging to it, now had in my thoughts. He told me that they had covered a large portion of the new section of the bog; that there was very little left to do now, in so far as the bog was concerned; and he descanted on the richness and the fine position of Murdock's new farm.

"It makes me angry," said he, "to think that that human-shaped wolf should get hold of such a lovely spot, and oust such a good fellow as the man whom he has robbed—yes, it is robbery, and nothing short of it. I feel something like a criminal myself for working for such a wretch at all."

"Never mind, old chap," said I; "you can't help it. Whatever he may have done wrong, you have had neither act nor part in it. It will all come right in time." In my present state of mind I could not imagine that there was, or could be, anything in the world that would not come all right in time.

We strolled into the street, and met Andy, who immediately hurried up to me:

"Good-evenin', yer 'anr'! An' did ye give me insthructions to me father?"

"I did, Andy; and he asked me to tell you that all shall be done exactly as you wish."

"Thank yer 'an'r." He turned away, and my heart rejoiced, for I thought I would be free from his badinage; but he turned and came back, and asked, with a senility which I felt to be hypocritical and assumed:

"Any luck, yer 'an'r, wid bogs today?" I know I got red as I answered him:

"Oh, I don't know—yes, a little—not much."

"Shure, an' I'm glad to hear it, surr; but I might have known be the Ink iv ye and be yer shtep. Faix, it's aisy known whin a man has been lucky wid bogs!" The latter sentence was spoken in a pronounced "aside."

Dick laughed, for although he was not in the secret he could see that there was some fun intended. I did not like his laugh, and said hotly:

"I don't understand you, Andy!"

"Is it undershtand me ye don't do? Well, surr, if I've said anythin' that I shouldn't, I ax yer pardon. Bogs isn't to be lightly shpoke iv at all, at all;" then, after a pause: "Poor Miss Norah!"

"What do you mean?" said I.

"Shure yer 'an'r, I was only pityin' the poor crathur. Poor thing! but this'll be a bitther blow to her intirely!" The villain was so manifestly acting a part, and he grinned at me in such a provoking way, that I got quite annoyed.

"Andy, what do you mean?—out with it!" I said, hotly.

"Mane, yer 'an'r? Shure nawthin'. All I mane is, poor Miss Norah! Musha! but it'll be the sore thrial to her. Bad cess to Knocknacar, anyhow!"

"This is infernal impertinence! Here—" I was stopped by

Dick's hand on my breast:

"Easy, easy, old chap! What is this all about? Don't get angry, old man. Andy is only joking, whatever it is. I'm not in the secret myself, and so can give no opinion; but there is a joke somewhere. Don't let it go beyond a joke."

"All right, Dick," said I, having had time to recover my temper. "The fact is that Andy has started some chaff on me about bogs— meaning girls thereby—every time he mentions the word to me; and now he seems to accuse me in some way about a girl that came to meet her father that night I left him home at Knockcalltecrore. You know Joyce, that Murdock has ousted from his farm. Now, look here, Andy! You're a very good fellow, and don't mean any harm; but I entirely object to the way you're going on. I don't mind a button about a joke. I hope I'm not such an ass as to be thin-skinned about a trifle, but it is another matter when you mention a young lady's name alongside mine. You don't think of the harm you may do. People are very talkative, and generally get a story the wrong end up. If you mention this girl—whatever her name is—"

"Poor Miss Norah!" struck in Andy, and then ostentatiously corrected himself—"I big yer 'an'r's pardon, Miss Norah, I mane."

—"this Miss Norah—along with me," I went on, "and especially in that objectionable form, people may begin to think she is wronged in some way, and you may do her an evil that you couldn't undo in all your lifetime. As for me, I never even saw the girl. I heard her speak in the dark for about half a minute, but I never set eyes on her in my life. Now, let this be the last of all this nonsense! Don't worry me anymore; but run in and tell Mrs. Keating to give you a skinful of punch, and to chalk it up to me."

Andy grinned, ducked his head, and made his exit into the house as though propelled or drawn by some unseen agency. When I remarked this to Dick he replied, "Some spirit draws him, I dare say."

Dick had not said a word beyond advising me not to lose my

temper. He did not appear to take any notice of my lecture to Andy, and puffed unconcernedly at his cigar till the driver had disappeared. He then took me by the arm, and said:

"Let us stroll a bit up the road." Arm in arm we passed out of the town and into the silence of the common. The moon was rising, and there was a soft, tender light over everything. Presently, without looking at me, Dick said:

"Art, I don't want to be inquisitive or to press for any confidences, but you and I are too old friends not to be interested in what concerns each other. What did Andy mean? Is there any girl in question?"

I was glad to have a friend to whom to open my mind, and without further thought I answered:

"There is, Dick."

Dick grasped my arm and looked keenly into my face, and then said:

"Art, answer me one question—answer me truly, old fellow, by ill you hold dear—answer me on your honour."

"I shall, Dick. What is it?"

"Is it Norah Joyce?" I had felt some vague alarm from the seriousness of his manner, but his question put me at ease again, and with a high heart, I answered:

"No, Dick, it is not." We strolled on, and after a pause, that seemed a little oppressive to me, he spoke again:

"Andy mentioned a poor 'Miss Norah'—don't get riled, old man—and you both agreed that a certain young lady was the only one alluded to. Are you sure there is no mistake? Is not your young lady called Norah?" This was a difficult question to answer, and made me feel rather awkward. Being awkward, I got a little hot:

"Andy's an infernal fool. What I said to him—you heard me—"

"Yes; I heard you."

—"was literally and exactly true. I never set eyes on Norah Joyce in my life. The girl I mean—the one you mean also—was one I saw by chance yesterday—and today—on the top of

90

Knocknacar."

"Who is she?"—there was a more joyous sound in Dick's voice.

"Eh—eh," I stammered; "the fact is, Dick, I don't know."

"What is her name?"

"I don't know."

"You don't know her name?"

"No."

"Where does she come from?"

"I don't know. I don't know anything about her except this, Dick—that I love her with all my heart and soul!" I could not help it—I could not account for it—but the tears rushed to my eyes, and I had to keep my head turned away from Dick lest he should notice me. He said nothing, and when I had surreptitiously wiped away what I thought were unmanly tears of emotion, I looked round at him. He, too, had his head turned away and, if my eyes did not deceive me, he, too, had some unmanly signs of emotion.

"Dick," said I. He turned on the instant. We looked in one another's faces, and the story was all told. We grasped hands warmly.

"We're both in the same boat, old boy," said he.

"Who is it, Dick?"

"Norah Joyce!"—I gave a low whistle.

"But," he went on, "you are well ahead of me. I have never even exchanged a word with her yet. I have only seen her a couple of times; but the whole world is nothing to me beside her. There, I've nothing to tell. *Veni, Vidi, Victus sum!*—I came, I saw, I was conquered. She has beauty enough, and if I'm not an idiot, worth enough to conquer a nation.—Now, tell me all about yours."

"There's nothing to tell, Dick; as yet I have only exchanged a few words. I shall hope to know more soon." We walked along in silence, turning our steps back to the hotel.

"I must hurry and finish up my plans tonight so as to be ready for you tomorrow. You won't look on it as a labour to go to Knocknacar, old chap," said he, slapping me on the back.

"Nor you to go to Shleenanaher," said I, as we shook hands and parted for the night.

It was quite two hours after this when I began to undress for bed. I suppose the whole truth, however foolish, must be told, but those two hours were mainly spent in trying to compose some suitable verses to my unknown. I had consumed a vast amount of paper—consumed literally, for what lover was ever yet content to trust his unsuccessful poetic efforts to the waste basket? and my grate was thickly strewn with filmy ashes. Hitherto the Muse had persistently and successfully evaded me. She did not even grant me a feather from her wing, and my "woeful ballad made to my mistress' eyebrow" was among the things that were not. There was a gentle tap at the door. I opened it, and saw Dick with his coat off. He came in.

"I thought I would look in, Art, as I saw the light under your door, and knew that you had not gone to bed. I only wanted to tell you this: You don't know what a relief it is to me to be able to speak of it to any living soul—how maddening it is to me to work for that scoundrel Murdock. You can understand now why I flared up at him so suddenly ere yesterday. I have a strong conviction on me that his service is devil's service as far as my happiness is concerned, and that I shall pay some terrible penalty for it."

"Nonsense, old fellow," said I, "Norah only wants to see you to know what a fine fellow you are. You won't mind my saying it, but you are the class of man that any woman would be proud of!"

"Ah! old chap," he answered sadly, "I'm afraid it will never get that far. There isn't, so to speak, a fair start for me. She has seen me already—worse luck!—has seen me doing work which must seem to her to aid in ruining her father. I could not mistake the scornful glance she has thrown on me each time we have met. However, *che sara sara!* It's not use fretting beforehand. Goodnight!"

# CHAPTER 7

## VANISHED

We were all astir shortly after daylight on Monday morning. Dick's foot was well enough for his walk to Knockcalltecrore, and Andy came with me to Knocknacar, as had been arranged, for I wanted his help in engaging labourers and beginning the work. We got to the sheebeen about nine o'clock, and Andy, having put up the mare, went out to get labourers. As I was morally certain that at that hour in the morning there would be no chance of seeing my unknown on the hilltop, I went at once to the bog, taking my map with me and studying the ground where we were to commence operations.

Andy joined me in about half an hour with five men—all he had been able to get in the time. They were fine strapping young fellows and seemed interested in the work, so I thought the contingent would be strong enough. By this time I had the ground marked out according to the plan, and so, without more ado, we commenced work.

We had attacked the hill some two hundred feet lower down than the bog, where the land suddenly rose steeply from a wide sloping extent of wilderness of invincible barrenness. It was over this spot that Sutherland hoped ultimately to send the waters of the bog. We began at the foot and made a trench some four feet wide at the bottom, and with sloping walls, so that when we got in so far the drain would be twenty feet deep, the external aperture would measure about twice as much.

The soil was heavy and full of moderate-sized bowlders, but was not unworkable, and among us we came to the conclusion that a week of solid work would, bar accidents and our coming across unforeseen difficulties, at any rate break the back of the job. The men worked in sections—one marking out the trench by cutting the surface to some foot and a half deep, and the others following in succession. Andy sat on a stone hard by, filled his pipe, and endeavoured in his own cheery way to relieve the monotony of the labour of the others. After about an hour he grew tired and went away—perhaps it was that he became interested in a country car, loaded with persons, that came down the road and stopped a few minutes at the sheebeen on its way to join the main road to Carnaclif.

Things went steadily on for some time. The men worked well, and I possessed my soul in such patience as I could, and studied the map and the ground most carefully. When dinner-time came the men went off each to his own home, and as soon as the place was free from them I hurried to the top of the mountain. The prospect was the same as yesterday. There was the same stretch of wild moor and rugged coast, of clustering islands and foam-girt rocks, of blue sky laden with such masses of luminous clouds as are only found in Ireland. But all was to me dreary and desolate, for the place was empty and *she* was not there. I sat down to wait with what patience I could.

It was dreary work at best; but at any rate there was hope—and its more immediate kinsman, expectation—and I waited. Somehow the view seemed to tranquillize me in some degree. It may have been that there was some unconscious working of the mind which told me, in some imperfect way, that in a region quite within my range of vision nothing could long remain hidden or unknown. Perhaps it was the stilly silence of the place. There was hardly a sound—the country people were all within doors at dinner, and even the sounds of their toil were lacking. From the west came a very faint breeze, just enough to bring the far-off, eternal roar of the surf.

There was scarcely a sign of life. The cattle far below were sheltering under trees, or in the shadows of hedges, or standing still knee-deep in the pools of the shallow streams. The only moving thing which I could see was the car which had left so long before, and was now far off, and was each moment becoming smaller and smaller as it went into the distance.

So I sat for quite an hour with my heart half sick with longing, but she never came. Then I thought I heard a step coming up the path at the far side. My heart beat strangely. I sat silent, and did not pretend to hear. She was walking more slowly than usual, and with a firmer tread. She was coming. I heard the steps on the plateau, and a voice came:

"Och! an' isn't it a purty view, yer 'an'r?" I leaped to my feet with a feeling that was positively murderous. The revulsion was too great, and I broke into a burst of semi-hysterical laughter. There stood Andy, with ragged red head and sun-scorched face, in his garb of eternal patches, bleached and discoloured by sun and rain into a veritable coat of many colours, gazing at the view with a rapt expression, and yet with one eye half closed in a fixed but unmistakable wink, as though taking the whole majesty of nature into his confidence.

When he heard my burst of laughter he turned to me quiz-zically:

"Musha! but it's the merry gentleman yer 'an'r is this day. Shure, the view here is the laughablest thing I ever see!" and he affected to laugh, but in such a soulless, unspontaneous way that it became a real burlesque. I waited for him to go on. I was naturally very vexed, but I was afraid to say anything lest I might cause him to interfere in *this* affair—the last thing on earth that I wished for.

He did go on—no one ever found Andy abashed or ill at ease:

"Begor! but yer 'an'r lepped like a deer when ye heerd me shpake. Did ye think I was goin' to shoot ye? Faix, an' I thought that ye wor about to jump from aff iv the mountain into the say, like a shtag."

"Why, what do you know about stags, Andy? There are none in this part of the country, are there?" I thought I would drag a new subject across his path. The ruse of the red herring drawn across the scent succeeded.

"Phwhat do I know iv shtags? Faix, I know this, that there does be plinty in me lard's demesne beyant at Wistport. Shure, wan iv thim got out last autumn an' nigh ruined me garden. He kem in at night an' ate up all me cabbages an' all the vigitables I'd got. I frightened him away a lot iv times, but he kem back all the same. At last I could shtand him no longer, and I wint meself an' complained to the lard. He tould me he was very sorry fur the damage he done, an',' sez he, 'Andy, I think he's a bankrup',' sez he, an' we must take his body.' 'How is that, me lard?' sez I. Sez he, 'I give him to ye, Andy. Do what ye like wid him.' An' wid that I wint home an' I med a thrap iv a clothes-line wid a loop in it, an' I put it betune two threes; and, shure enough in the night I got him."

"And what did you do with him, Andy?" said I.

"Faith, surr, I shkinned him and ate him." He said this just in the same tone in which he would speak of the most ordinary occurrence, leaving the impression on one's mind that the skinning and eating were matters done at the moment and quite off-hand.

I fondly hoped that Andy's mind was now in quite another state from his usual mental condition; but I hardly knew the man yet. He had the true humorist's persistence, and before I was ready with another intellectual herring he was off on the original track.

"I thrust I didn't dishturb yer 'an'r. I know some gintlemin likes to luk at views and say nothin'. I'm tould that a young gintleman like yer 'an'r might be up on top iv a mountain like this, an' he'd luk at the view so hard day afther day that he wouldn't even shpake to a purty girrul—if there was wan forninst him all the time!"

"Then they lied to you, Andy." I said this quite decisively.

"Faix, yer 'an'r, an' it's glad I am to hear that same, for I wouldn't like to think that a young gintleman was afraid of a girrul, however purty she might be."

"But, tell me, Andy," I said, "what idiot could have started such an idea? And even if it was told to you, how could you be such a fool as to believe it?"

"Me belave it! surr, I didn't belave a wurrd iv it—not until I met yer 'an'r." His face was quite grave, and I was not sorry to find him in a sober mood, for I wanted to have a serious chat with him. It struck me that he, having relatives at Knocknacar, might be able to give me some information about my unknown.

"Until you met me, Andy! Surely I never gave you any ground for holding such a ridiculous idea."

"Begor, yer 'an'r, but ye did. But p'r'aps I had better not say any more—yer 'an'r mightn't like it."

This both surprised and nettled me, and I was determined now to have it out, so I said, "You quite surprise me, Andy. What have I ever done? Do not be afraid; out with it," for he kept looking at me in a timorous kind of way.

"Well, then, yer 'an'r, about poor Miss Norah."

This was a surprise, but I wanted to know more.

"Well, Andy, what about her?"

"Shure, an' didn't you refuse to shpake iv her intirely an' sot on me fur only mintionin' her—an' she wan iv the purtiest girruls in the place?"

"My dear Andy," said I, "I thought I had explained to you last night all about that. I don't suppose you quite understand; but it might do a girl in her position harm to be spoken about with a—a man like me."

"Wid a man like you—an' for why? Isn't she as good a girrul as iver broke bread?"

"Oh, it's not that, Andy; people might think harm."

"Think harrum! Phwhat harrum, an' who'd think it?"

"Oh, you don't understand; a man in your position can hardly know."

"But, yer 'an'r, I don't git comprehindin'. What harrum could there be, an' who'd think it? The people here is all somethin iv me own position—workin' people—an' whin they knows a girrul is a good, dacent girrul, why should they think harrum because a nice young gintleman goes out iv his way to shpake to her? Doesn't he shpake to the quality like himself, an' no wan thinks any harrum iv ayther iv them?"

Andy's simple, honest argument made me feel ashamed of the finer sophistries belonging to the more artificial existence of those of my own station.

"Sure, yer 'an'r, there isn't a bhoy in Connaught that wouldn't like to be shpoke of wid Miss Norah. She's that good, that even the nuns in Galway, where she was at school, loves her and thrates her like wan iv themselves, for all she's a Protestan'."

"My dear Andy," said I, "don't you think you're a little hard on me? You're putting me in the dock, and trying me for a series of offences that I never even thought of committing with regard to her or anyone else. Miss Norah may be an angel in petticoats, and I'm quite prepared to take it for granted that she is so; your word on the subject is quite enough for me. But just please to remember that I never set eyes on her in my life. The only time I was ever in her presence was when you were by yourself, and it was so dark that I could not see her, to help her when she fainted. Why, in the name of common-sense, you should keep holding her up to me, I do not understand."

"But yer 'an'r said that it might do her harrum even to mintion her wid you."

"Oh, well, Andy, I give it up—it's no use trying to explain. Either you *won't* understand, or I am unable to express myself properly."

"Surr, there can be only one harrum to a girrul from a gintleman"—he laid his hand on my arm, and said this impressively; whatever else he may have ever said in jest, he was in grim earnest now—"an' that's whin he's a villain. Ye wouldn't do the black thrick, and desave a girrul that thrusted ye?"

"No, Andy, no! God forbid! I would rather go to the highest rock on some island there beyond, where the surf is loudest, and throw myself into the sea, than do such a thing. No, Andy; there are lots of men that hold such matters lightly, but I don't think I'm one of them. Whatever sins I have, or may ever have upon my soul, I hope such a one as *that* will never be there."

All the comment Andy made was, "I thought so." Then the habitual quizzical look stole over his face again, and he said:

"There does be some that does fear braches iv promise. Mind ye, a man has to be mighty careful on the subject, for some weemin is that cute there's no bein' up to them."

Andy's sudden change to this new theme was a little embarrassing, since the idea leading to it—or rather preceding it—had been one purely personal to myself; but he was off, and I thought it better that he should go on.

"Indeed!" said I.

"Yes, surr. Oh my, but they're cute. The first thing that a girrul does when a man looks twice at her, is t' ask him to write her a letther, an' thin she has him—tight."

"How so, Andy?"

"Well, ye see, surr, when you're writin' a letther to a girrul, ye can't begin widout a 'My dear' or a 'My darlin', an' thin she has the grip iv the law onto ye! An' ye do be badgered be the counsillors, an' ye do be frowned at be the judge, an' ye do be laughed at be the people, an' ye do have to pay yer money, an' there ye are!"

"I say, Andy," said I, "I think you must have been in trouble yourself in that way; you seem to have it all off pat."

"Oh, throth, not me, yer 'an'r. Glory be to God! but I niver was a defindant in me life—an' more betoken, I don't want to be—but I was wance a witness in a case iv the kind."

"And what did you witness?"

"Faix, I was called to prove that I seen the gintleman's arrum around the girrul's waist. The counsillors made a deal out iv that— just as if it warn't only manners to hould up a girrul on a car!"

"What was the case, Andy? Tell me all about it."

I did not mind his waiting, as it gave me an excuse for staying on the top of the hill. I knew I could easily get rid of him when she came—if she came—by sending him on a message.

"Well, this was a young woman what had an action agin Shquire Murphy, iv Ballynashoughlin himself—a woman as was no more nor a mere simple governess!"

It would be impossible to convey the depth of social unimportance conveyed by his tone and manner; and coming from a man of "shreds and patches," it was more than comic. Andy had his good suit of frieze and homespun; but while he was on mountain duty, he spared these and appeared almost in the guise of a scarecrow.

"Well, what happened?"

"Faix, whin she tould her shtory the shquire's councillor hiked up at the jury, an' he whispered a wurrd to the shquire and his 'an'r wrote out a shlip iv paper an' banded it to him, an' the councillor ups an' says he:'Me lard and gintlemin iv the jury, me client is prepared to have the honour iv the lady's hand if she will so, for let by-gones be by-gones.' An', sure enough, they was married on the Sunday next four weeks; an' there she is now dhrivin' him about the counthry in her pony-shay, an' all the quality comin' to tay in the garden, an' she as affable as iver to all the farmers round. Aye, an' be the hokey, the shquire himself sez that it was a good day for him whin he sot eyes on her first, an' that he don't know why he was such a damn fool as iver to thry to say 'no' to her, or to wish it."

"Quite a tale with a moral, Andy. Bravo, Mrs. Murphy."

"A morial is it? Now, may I make bould to ask yer 'an'r what morial ye take out iv it?"

"The moral, Andy, that I see is, When you see the right woman go for her for all you're worth, and thank God for giving you the chance." Andy jumped up and gave me a great slap on the back.

"Hurroo! more power to yer elbow! but it's a bhoy afther me own h'arrt y' are. I big yer pardon, surr, for the liberty; but it's mighty glad I am."

"Granted, Andy; I like a man to be hearty, and you certainly are. But why are you so glad about me?"

"Because I like yer 'an'r. Shure in all me life I niver see so much iv a young gentleman as I've done iv yer 'an'r. Surr, I'm an ould man compared wid ye—I'm the beginnin' iv wan, at any rate—an' I'd like to give ye a wurrd iv advice; git marrid while ye can! I tell ye this, surr, it's not whin the hair is beginnin' to git thin on to the top iv yer head that a nice young girrul ill love ye for yerself. It's the people that goes all their lives makin' money and lukin' after all kinds iv things that's no kind iv use to thim, that makes the mishtake.

"Suppose ye do git marrid when ye're ould and bald, an' yer legs is shaky, an' ye want to be let sit close to the fire in the warrum corner, an' ye've lashins iv money that ye don't know what to do wid! Do you think that it's thin that yer wives does be dhramin' iv ye all the time and worshippin' the ground ye thrid? Not a bit iv it! They do be wantin'—aye and thryin' too—to help God away wid ye!"

"Andy," said I, "you preach, on a practical text, a sermon that any and every young man ought to hear." I thought I saw an opening here for gaining some information, and at once jumped in.

"By Jove! you set me off wishing to marry! Tell me, is there any pretty girl in this neighbourhood that would suit a young man like me?"

"Oho! begor, there's girruls enough to shute any man."

"Aye, Andy—but pretty girls!"

"Well surr, that depinds. Now what might be yer 'an'r's idea iv a purty girrul?"

"My dear Andy, there are so many different kinds of prettiness that it is hard to say."

"Faix, an' I'll tell ye if there's a girrul to shute in the counthry, for bedad I think I've seen thim all. But you must let me know what would shute ye best?"

"How can I well tell that, Andy, when I don't know myself? Show me the girl, and I'll very soon tell you."

"Unless I was to ax yer 'an'r questions;" this was said very slyly.

"Go on, Andy; there is nothing like the Socratic method."

"Very well, thin; I'll ax two kinds iv things, an' yer 'an'r will tell me which ye'd like the best."

"All right, go on."

"Long or short?"

"Tall; not short, certainly."

"Fat or lane?"

"Fie! fie! Andy, for shame; you talk as if they were cattle or pigs."

101

"Begor, there's only wan kind iv fat an' lane that I knows of; but av ye like I'll call it thick or thin; which is it?"

"Not too fat, but certainly not skinny." Andy held up his hands in mock horror:

"Yer 'an'r shpakes as if ye was talkin' iv powlthry."

"I mean, Andy," said I, with a certain sense of shame, "she is not to be either too fat or too lean, as you put it."

"Ye mane 'shtreaky'!"

"Streaky!" said I, "what do you mean?" He answered promptly:

"Shtreaky—thick an' thin—like belly bacon." I said nothing. I felt certain it would be useless and out of place. He went on:

"Nixt, fair or dark?"

"Dark, by all means."

"Dark be it, surr. What kind iv eyes might she have?"

"Ah! eyes like darkness on the bosom of the azure deep!"

"Musha! but that's a quare kind iv eye fur a girrul to have intirely! Is she to be all dark, surr, or only the hair of her?"

"I don't mean a nigger, Andy!" I thought I would be even with him for once in a way. He laughed heartily.

"Oh, my, but that's a good wan. Be the hokey, a girrul can be dark enough fur any man widout bein' a naygur. Glory be to God, but I niver seen a faymale naygur meself, but I suppose there's such things; God's very good to all his craythurs! But, ban-in' naygurs, must she be all dark?"

"Well, not of necessity, but I certainly prefer what we call a brunette."

"A brunet. What's that now? I've heerd a wheen o' quare things in me time, but I niver heerd a woman called that before."

I tried to explain the term; he seemed to understand, but his only comment was:

"Well, God is very good," and then went on with his queries.

"How might she be dressed?" he looked very sly as he asked the question.

"Simply. The dress is not particular—that can easily be altered. For myself, just at present, I should like her in the dress they all wear here, some pretty kind of body and a red petticoat."

"Thrue for ye," said Andy. Then he went over the list, ticking off the items on his fingers as he went along:

"A long, dark girrul, like belly bakin, but not a naygur, some kind iv a net, an' wid a rid petticoat, an' a quare kind iv an eye! Is that the kind iv a girrul that yer 'an'r wants to set yer eyes on?"

"Well," said I, "item by item, as you explain them, Andy, the description is correct; but I must say that never in my life did I know a man to so knock the bottom out of romance as you have done in summing up the lady's charms."

"Her charrums, is it? Be the powers! I only tuk what yer 'an'r tould me. An' so that's the girrul that id shute yer?"

"Yes, Andy, I think she would." I waited in expectation, but he said nothing. So I jogged his memory.

"Well?" He looked at me in a most peculiar manner, and said, slowly and impressively:

"Thin I can sahtisfy yer 'an'r. There's no such girrul in all Knocknacar!" I smiled a smile of triumph:

"You're wrong for once, Andy. I saw such a girl only yesterday, here on the top of this mountain, just where we're sitting now."

Andy jumped up as if he had been sitting on an ant-hill, and had suddenly been made aware of it. He looked all round in a frightened way, but I could see that he was only acting, and said:

"Glory be to God! but maybe it's the fairies, it was, or the pixies! Shure, they do say that there's lots an' lots an' lashins iv them on this hill. Don't ye have nothin' to say to thim, surr! There's only sorra follys thim. Take an ould man's advice, an' don't come up here anymore. The shpot is dangerous to ye. If ye want to see a fine girrul go to Shleenanaher, an' have a good Ink at Miss Norah in the daylight."

"Oh, bother Miss Norah!" said I. "Get along with you, do! I think you've got Miss Norah on the brain, or perhaps you're in love with her yourself." Andy murmured, *sotto voce*, but manifestly for me to hear:

"Begor, I am, like the rist iv the bhoys, av course!"

Here I looked at my watch, and found it was three o'clock, so thought it was time to get rid of him.

"Here," said I, "run down to the men at the cutting and tell them that I'm coming down presently to measure up their work, as Mr. Sutherland will want to know how they've got on."

Andy moved off. Before going, however, he had something to say, as usual:

"Tell me, Misther Art"—this new name startled me, Andy had evidently taken me into his public family—"do ye think Misther Dick"—this was another surprise—"has an eye on Miss Norah?" There was a real shock this time.

"I see him lukin' at her wance or twice as if he'd like to ate her; but, bedad, it's no use if he has, for she wouldn't luk at him. No wondher, an' him helpin' to be takin' her father's houldin' away from him."

I could not answer Andy's question as to poor old Dick's feelings, for such was his secret and not mine; but I determined not to let there be any misapprehension regarding his having a hand in Murdock's dirty work, so I spoke hotly:

"You tell anyone that dares to say that Dick Sutherland has any act or part, good or bad, large or small, in that dirty ruffian's dishonourable conduct, that he is either a knave or a fool, at any rate he is a liar. Dick is simply a man of science engaged by Murdock, as any other man of science might be, to look after some operations in regard to his bog."

Andy's comment was made *sotto voce*, so I thought it better not to notice it.

"Musha! but the bogs iv all kinds is gettin' mixed up quarely. Here's another iv them. Misther Dick is engaged to luk afther the bogs. An' so he does, but his eyes goes wandherin' among thim. There does be bogs iv all kinds now all over these parts. It's quare times we're in, or I'm gettin' ould!"

With this Parthian shaft Andy took himself down the hill,

and presently I saw the good effects of his presence in stimulating the workmen to more ardent endeavours, for they all leaned on their spades while he told them a long story, which ended in a tumult of laughter.

I might have enjoyed the man's fun, but I was in no laughing humour. I had got anxious long ago because *she* had not visited the hilltop. I looked all round, but could see no sign of her anywhere. I waited and waited, and the time truly went on leaden wings. The afternoon sun smote the hilltop with its glare, more oppressive always than even the noontide heat.

I lingered on and lingered still, and hope died within me.

When six o'clock had come I felt that there was no more chance for me that clay; so I went sadly down the hill, and, after a glance for Dick's sake at the cutting, sought the sheebeen where Andy had the horse ready harnessed in the car. I assumed as cheerful an aspect as I could, and flattered myself that I carried off the occasion very well. It was not at all flattering, however, to my histrionic powers to hear Andy, as we were driving off, whisper in answer to a remark deploring how sad I looked, made by the old lady who kept the sheebeen:

"Whisht! Don't appear to notice him, or yell dhrive him mad. Me opinion is that he's been wandherin' on the mountain too long, an' tamperin' wid the rings on the grass—you know—an' that he has seen the fairies!" Then he said aloud and ostentatiously:

"Gee up, ye old corn-crake! Ye ought to be fresh enough; ye've niver left the flit iv the hill all the day." Then turning to me, "An' sure, surr, it's goin' to the top that takes it out iv wan—ayther a horse or a man."

I made no answer, and in silence we drove to Carnaclif, where I found Dick impatiently waiting dinner for me.

I was glad to find that he was full of queries concerning the cutting, for it saved me from the consideration of subjects more difficult to answer satisfactorily. Fortunately I was able to give a good account of the time spent, for the work done had far exceeded my expectations. I thought that Dick was in much better spirits than he had been; but it was not until the subject of the bog at Knocknacar was completely exhausted that I got any clew on the subject. I then asked Dick if he had had a good time at Shleenanaher?

"Yes!" he answered. "Thank God, the work is nearly done! We went over the whole place today, and there was only one indication of iron. This was in the bog just beside an elbow where Joyce's land—his present land—touches ours—no, I mean on Murdock's, the scoundrel!" He was quite angry with himself for using the word "ours" even accidentally.

"And has anything come of it?" I asked him.

"Nothing. Now that he knows it is there, he would not let me go near it on any account. I'm in hopes he'll quarrel with me soon in order to get rid of me, so that he may try by himself to fish it— whatever it may be—out of the bog. If he does quarrel with me! Well, I only hope he will; I have been longing for weeks past to get a chance at him. Then she'll believe, perhaps—" He stopped.

"You saw her today, Dick!"

"How did you know that?"

"Because you look so happy, old man."

"Yes, I did see her; but only for a moment. She drove up in the middle of the day, and I saw her go up to the new house. But she didn't even see me," and his face fell. Presently he asked:

"You didn't see your girl?"

"No, Dick, I did not. But how did you know?"

"I saw it in your face when you came in."

We sat and smoked in silence. The interruption came in the shape of Andy.

"I suppose, Masther Art, the same agin tomorra—unless ye'd like me to bring ye wid Masther Dick to see Shleenanaher; ye know the shpot, surr—where Miss Norah is!"

He grinned, and as we said nothing, made his exit.

# CHAPTER 8
## A VISIT TO JOYCE

With renewed hope I set out in the morning for Knocknacar.

It is one of the many privileges of youth that a few hours' sleep will change the darkest aspect of the entire universe to one of the rosiest tint. Since the previous evening, sleeping and waking, my mind had been framing reasons and excuses for the absence of ———. It was a perpetual grief to me that I did not even know her name. The journey to the mountain seemed longer than usual; but, even at the time, this seemed to me only natural under the circumstances.

Andy was today seemingly saturated or overwhelmed with a superstitious gravity. Without laying any personal basis for his remarks, but accepting as a stand-point his own remark of the previous evening concerning my having seen a fairy, he proceeded to develop his fears on the subject. I will do him the justice to say that his knowledge of folklore was immense, and that nothing but a gigantic memory for detail, cultivated to the full, or else an equally stupendous imagination working on the facts that momentarily came before his view, could have enabled him to keep up such a flow of narrative and legend.

The general result to me was, that if I had been inclined to believe such matters I would have remained under the impression that, although the whole seaboard, with adjacent mountains, from Westport to Gal way, was in a state of plethora as regards uncanny existences, Knocknacar, as a habitat for such, easily bore off the palm. Indeed, that remarkable mountain must have been a solid mass of gnomes, fairies, pixies, leprechauns, and all genii, species and varieties of the same. No Chicago grain elevator in the early days of a wheat corner could have been more solidly packed. It would seem that so many inhabitants had been allured by fairies, and consequently had mysteriously disappeared, that this method of minimisation of the census must have formed a distinct drain on the local population, which, by the way, did not seem to be excessive.

I reserved to myself the right of interrogating Andy on this subject later in the day, if, unhappily, there should be any opportunity. Now that we had drawn near the hill, my fears began to return.

While Andy stabled the mare I went to the cutting and found the men already at work. During the night there had evidently been a considerable drainage from the cutting, not from the bog, but entirely local. This was now Friday morning, and I thought that if equal progress were made in the two days, it would be quite necessary that Dick should see the working on Sunday, and advise before proceeding further.

As I knew that gossip and the requirements of his horse would keep Andy away for a while, I determined to take advantage of his absence to run up to the top of the hill, just to make sure that no one was there. It did not take long to get up, but when I arrived there was no reward, except in the shape of a very magnificent view. The weather was evidently changing, for great clouds seemed to gather from the west and south, and far away over the distant rim of the horizon the sky was as dark as night. Still, the clouds were not hurrying as before a storm, and the gloom did not seem to have come shoreward as yet; it was rather a presage of prolonged bad weather than bad itself. I did not remain long, as I wished to escape Andy's scrutiny. Indeed, as I descended the hill I began to think that Andy had become like the "Old Man of the Sea," and that my own experience seemed likely to rival that of Sinbad.

When I arrived at the cutting I found Andy already seated, enjoying his pipe. When he saw me he looked up with a grin, and said audibly:

"The Good People don't seem to be workin' so 'arly in the mornin'. Here he is safe an' sound among us."

That was a very long day. Whenever I thought I could do so, without attracting too much attention, I strolled to the top of the hill, but only to suffer a new disappointment.

At dinner-time I went up and sat all the time. I was bitterly disappointed, and also began to be seriously alarmed. I seemed to have lost my Unknown.

When the men got back to their work, and I saw Andy beginning to climb the hill in an artless, purposeless manner, I thought I would kill two birds with one stone, and, while avoiding my incubus, make some inquiries. As I could easily see from the top of the hill, there were only a few houses all told in the little hamlet; and including those most isolated, there were not twenty in all. Of these I had seen in the sheebeen and in old Sullivan's, so that a stroll of an hour or two, properly organized, would cover the whole ground; and so I set out on my task to try and get some sight or report of my unknown. I knew I could always get an opportunity of opening conversation by asking for a light for my cigar.

It was a profitless task. Two hours after I had started I returned to the top of the hill as ignorant as I had gone, and the richer only by some dozen or more drinks of milk, for I found that the acceptance of some form of hospitality was an easy opening to general conversation. The top was still empty, but I had not been there a quarter of an hour when I was joined by Andy. His first remark was evidently calculated to set me at ease:

"Begor, yer 'an'r comes to the top iv this hill nigh as often as I do meself."

I felt that my answer was inconsequential as well as ill-tempered:

"Well, why on earth, Andy, do you come so often? Surely there is no need to come, unless you like it."

"Faix, I came this time lest yer 'an'r might feel lonely. I niver see a man yit be himself on top iv a hill that he didn't want a companion iv some kind or another."

"Andy," I remarked, as I thought, rather cuttingly, "you judge life and men too much by your own experience. There are people and emotions which are quite out of your scope—far too high, or perhaps too low, for your psychic or intellectual grasp."

Andy was quite unabashed. He looked at me admiringly.

"It's a pity yer 'an'r isn't a mimber iv Parlyment. Shure, wid a flow iv language like that ye could do anythin'!"

As satire was no use, I thought I would draw him out on the subject of the fairies and pixies.

"I suppose you were looking for more fairies; the supply you had this morning was hardly enough to suit you, was it?"

"Begor, it's meself is not the only wan that does be lukin' for the fairies!" and he grinned.

"Well, I must say, Andy, you seem to have a good supply on hand. Indeed, it seems to me that if there were any more fairies to be located on this hill it would have to be enlarged, for it's pretty solid with them already, as far as I can gather."

"Augh! there's room for wan more! I'm tould there's wan missin' since ere yistherday."

It was no good trying to beat Andy at this game, so I gave it up and sat silent. After a while he asked me:

"Will I be dhrivin' yer 'an'r over to Knockcalltecrore?"

"Why do you ask me?"

"I'm thinking it's glad yer 'an'r will be to see Miss Norah."

"Upon my soul, Andy, you are too bad. A joke is a joke, but there are limits to it; and I don't let any man joke with me when I prefer not. If you want to talk of your Miss Norah, go and talk to Mr. Sutherland about her. He's there every day and can make use of your aid. Why on earth do you single me out as your father-confessor? You're unfair to the girl, after all, for if I ever do see her I'm prepared to hate her."

"Ah! yer 'an'r wouldn't be that hard! What harrum has the poor crathur done that ye'd hate her—a thing no mortial man iver done yit?"

"Oh, go on! don't bother me anymore; I think it's about time we were getting home. You go down to the sheebeen and rattle up that old corn-crake of yours; I'll come down presently and see how the work goes on."

He went off, but came back as usual; I could have thrown something at him.

"Take me advice, surr: pay a visit to Shleenanaher, an' see Miss Norah," and he hurried down the hill.

His going did me no good; no one came, and after a linger-
ing glance around, and noting the gathering of the rain clouds,
I descended the hill.

When I got up on the car I was not at all in a talkative humour, and said but little to the group surrounding me. I heard
Andy account for it to them:

"Whisht! don't notice his 'an'r's silence! It's stupid wid
shmokin' he is. He lit no less nor siventeen cigars this blessed
day. Ax the neighbours av ye doubt me. Gee up!"

The evening was spent with Dick as the last had been. I knew
that he had seen his girl; he knew that I had not seen mine,
but neither had anything to tell. Before parting he told me that
he expected to shortly finish his work at Knockcalltecrore, and
asked me if I would come over.

"Do come," he said, when I expressed a doubt; "do come, I
may want a witness;" so I promised to go.

Andy had on his best suit, and a clean wash, when he met us
smiling in the early morning. "Look at him," I said; "wouldn't
you know he was going to meet his best girl?"

"Begor," he answered, "mayhap we'll all do that same!" It was
only ten o'clock when we arrived at Knockcalltecrore, and vent
up the boreen to Murdock's new farm. The Gombeen Man was
standing at the gate with his watch in his hand. When we came
up, he said:

"I feared you would be late. It's just conthract time now.
Hadn't ye betther say goodbye to your frind an' git to work?"
He was so transparently inclined to be rude, and possibly to pick
a quarrel, that I whispered a warning to Dick. To my great satisfaction he whispered back:

"I see he wants to quarrel; nothing in the world will make me
lose temper today." Then he took out his pocketbook, searched
for and found a folded paper. Opening this he read: "'and the
said Richard Sutherland shall be at liberty to make use of such
assistant as he may choose or appoint whensoever he may wish
during the said engagement at his own expense.' You see, Mr.
Murdock, I am quite within the four walls of the agreement,

and exercise my right. I now tell you formally that Mr. Arthur Severn has kindly undertaken to assist me for today." Murdock glared at him for a minute, and then opened the gate and said:

"Come in, gintlemin." We entered.

"Now, Mr. Murdock!" said Dick, briskly, "what do you wish done today? Shall we make further examination of the bog where the iron indication is, or shall we finish the survey of the rest of the land?"

"Finish the rough survey."

The operation was much less complicated than when we had examined the bog. We simply "quartered" the land, as the constabulary say when they make search for hidden arms; and taking it bit by bit, passed the magnet over its surface. We had the usual finds of nails, horseshoes, and scrap-iron, but no result of importance. The last place we examined was the house. It was a much better built and more roomy structure than the one he had left. It was not, however, like the other, built on a rock, but in a sheltered hollow. Dick pointed out this to me, and re-marked:

"I don't know but that Joyce is better off, all told, in the ex-change. I wouldn't care myself to live in a house built in a place like this, and directly in the track of the bog."

"Not even," said I, "if Norah was living in it too?"

"Ah, that's another thing. With Norah I'd take my chance, and live in the bog itself, if I could get no other place."

When this happened our day's work was nearly done, and very soon we took our leave for the evening, Murdock saying, as I thought, rather offensively:

"Now, you, sir, be sure to be here in time on Monday morn-ing."

"All right," said Dick, nonchalantly; and we passed out. In the boreen he said to me:

"Let us stroll up this way, Art," and we walked up the hill towards Joyce's house, Murdock coming down to his gate and looking at us. When we came to Joyce's gate we stopped. There was no sign of Norah; but Joyce himself stood at his door. I was opening the gate when he came forward.

"Good-evening, Mr. Joyce," said I. "How is your arm? I hope quite well by this time. Perhaps you don't remember me. I had the pleasure of giving you a seat up here in my car, from Mrs. Kelligan's, the night of the storm."

"I remember well," he said; "and I was thankful to you, for I was in trouble that night; it's all done now." And he looked round the land with a sneer, and then he looked yearningly towards his old farm.

"Let me introduce my friend, Mr. Sutherland," said I.

"I ax yer pardon, sir, an' I don't wish to be rude; but I don't want to know him. He's no frind to me and mine!"

Dick's honest, manly face grew red with shame. I thought he was going to say something angrily, so cut in as quickly as I could:

"You are sadly mistaken, Mr. Joyce; Dick Sutherland is too good a gentleman to do wrong to you or any man. How can you think such a thing?"

"A man what consorts wid me enemy can be no frind of mine!"

"But he doesn't consort with him; he hates him. He was simply engaged to make certain investigations for him as a scientific man. Why, I don't suppose you yourself hate Murdock more than Dick does."

"Thin I ax yer pardon, sir," said Joyce. "I like to wrong no man, an' I'm glad to be set right."

Things were going admirably, and we were all beginning to feel at ease, when we saw Andy approach. I groaned in spirit; Andy was gradually taking shape to me as an evil genius. He approached, and making his best bow, said:

"Fine evenin', Misther Joyce. I hope yer arrum is betther; an' how is Miss Norah?"

"Thank ye kindly, Andy; both me arm and the girl's well."

"Is she widin?"

"No; she wint this mornin' to stay over Monday in the convent. Poor girl, she's broken-hearted, lavin' her home and gettin'

113

settled here. I med the changin' as light for her as I could; but weemin takes things to heart more nor min does, an' that's bad enough, God knows!"

"Thrue for ye," said Andy. "This gintleman here, Mashter Art, says he hasn't seen her since the night she met us below in the dark."

"I hope," said Joyce, "you'll look in and see us, if you're in these parts, sir, whin she comes back. I know she thought a dale of your kindness to me that night."

"I'll be here for some days, and I'll certainly come, if I may."

"And I hope I may come, too, Mr. Joyce," said Dick, "now that you know me."

"Ye'll be welkim, sir."

We all shook hands, coming away; but as we turned to go home, at the gate we had a surprise. There, in the boreen, stood Murdock, livid with fury. He attacked Dick with a tirade of the utmost virulence. He called him every name he could lay his tongue to—traitor, liar, thief, and, indeed, exhausted the whole terminology of abuse, and accused him of stealing his secrets and of betraying his trust. Dick bore the ordeal splendidly; he never turned a hair, but calmly went on smoking his cigar. When Murdock had somewhat exhausted himself and stopped, he said, calmly:

"My good fellow, now that your ill-manners are exhausted, perhaps you will tell me what it is all about?"

Whereupon Murdock opened again the phials of his wrath. This time he dragged us all into it—I had been brought in as a spy, to help in betraying him, and Joyce had suborned him to the act of treachery. For myself I fired up at once, and would have struck him, only Dick had laid his hand on me, and in a whisper cautioned me to desist.

"Easy, old man, easy! Don't spoil a good position. What does it matter what a man like that can say? Give him rope enough; we'll have our turn in time, don't fear!"

I held back, but unfortunately Joyce pressed forward. He had his say pretty plainly.

"What do ye mane, ye ill-tongued scoundhrel, comin' here to make a quarrel? Why don't ye shtay on the land you have robbed from me, and lave us alone? I am not like these gintlemen here, that can afford to hould their tongues and despise ye; I'm a man like yerself, though I hope I'm not the wolf that ye are—fattenin' on the blood of the poor! How dare you say I suborned any one—me that never told a lie, or done a dirty thing in me life? I tell you, Murtagh Murdock, I put my mark upon ye once—I see it now comin' up white through the red of yer passion! Don't provoke me further, or I'll put another mark on ye that ye'll carry to yer grave!"

No one said a word more. Murdock moved off and entered his own house; Dick and I said "goodnight" to Joyce again, and went down the boreen.

## Chapter 9

### My New Property

The following week was a time to me of absolute bitterness. I went each day to Knocknacar, where the cutting was proceeding at a rapid rate. I haunted the hill-top, but without the slightest result. Dick had walked over with me on Sunday, and had been rejoiced at the progress made; he said that if all went well we could about Friday next actually cut into the bog. Already there was a distinct infiltration through the cutting, and we discussed the best means to achieve the last few feet of the work so as not in any way to endanger the safety of the men working.

All this time Dick was in good spirits. His meeting with Norah's father had taken a great and harrowing weight off his mind, and to him all things were now possible in the future. He tried his best to console me for my disappointment. He was full of hope—indeed he refused to see anything but a delay, and I could see that in his secret heart he was not altogether sorry that my love affair had received a temporary check. This belief was emphasized by the tendency of certain of his remarks to the effect that marriages between persons of unequal social status were inadvisable—he, dear old fellow, seemingly in his transparent honesty unaware that he was laying himself out with all his power to violate his own principles.

But all the time I was simply heart-broken. To say that I was consumed with a burning anxiety would be to understate the matter; I was simply in a fever. I could neither eat nor sleep satisfactorily, and, sleeping or waking, my brain was in a whirl of doubts, conjectures, fears, and hopes. The most difficult part to bear was my utter inability to do anything. I could not proclaim my love or my loss on the hilltop; I did not know where to make inquiries, and I had no idea who to inquire for. I did not even like to tell Dick the full extent of my woes.

Love has a modesty of its own, whose lines are boldly drawn, and whose rules are stern.

On more than one occasion I left the hotel secretly—after having ostensibly retired for the night—and wended my way to Knocknacar. As I passed through the sleeping country I heard the dogs bark in the cottages as I went by, but little other sound I ever heard except the booming of the distant sea. On more than one of these occasions I was drenched with rain, for the weather had now become thoroughly unsettled. But I heeded it not; indeed the physical discomfort—when I felt it—was in some measure an anodyne to the torture of my restless soul.

I always managed to get back before daylight, so as to avoid any questioning. After three or four days, however, the "boots" of the hotel began evidently to notice the state of my clothes and boots, and ventured to speak to me. He cautioned me against going out too much alone at night, as there were two dangers: one from the moonlighters who now and again raided the district, and who, being composed of the scum of the countryside—"corner-boys" and loafers of all kinds—would be only too glad to find an unexpected victim to rob; and the other, lest in wandering about I should get into trouble with the police under suspicion of being one of these very ruffians.

The latter difficulty seemed to me to be even more obnoxious than the former; and to avoid any suspicion I thought it best to make my night wanderings known to all. Accordingly, I asked Mrs. Keating to have some milk and bread and butter left in my room each night, as I would probably require something after my late walk. When she expressed surprise as to my movements, I told her that I was making a study of the beauty of the country by night, and was much interested in moonlight effects. This last was an unhappy setting forth of my desires, for it went round in a whisper among the servants and others outside the hotel, until at last it reached the ears of an astute Ulster-born policeman, from whom I was much surprised to receive a visit one morning. I asked him to what the honour was due. His answer spoke for itself:

"From information received, A come to talk till ye regardin' the interest ye profess to take in moonlichtin'."

"What on earth do you mean?" I asked.

"A hear ye're a stranger in these parts; an' as ye might take away a wrong impression weth ye, A thenk it ma duty to tell ye that the people round here are nothin' more nor less than leears, an' that ye mustn't believe a single word they say."

"Really," said I, "I am quite in the dark. Do try and explain. Tell me what it is all about."

"Why, A larn that ye're always out at nicht all over the country, and that ye've openly told people here that ye're interested in moonlichtin'."

"My dear sir, some one is quite mad. I never said such a thing—indeed, I don't know anything about moonlighting."

"Then why do ye go out at nicht?"

"Simply to see the country at night—to look at the views— to enjoy the effects of moonlight."

"There ye are, ye see—ye enjoy the moonlicht effect."

"Good lord! I mean the view—the purely esthetic effect— the *chiaroscuro*—the pretty pictures!"

"Oh, aye! A see now—A ken weel! Then A needn't trouble ye further. But let ma tell ye that it's a dangerous practice to walk out be nicht. There's many a man in these parts watched and laid for. Why in Knockcalltecrore there's one man that's in danger all the time. An' as for ye—why ye'd better be careful that yer nicht

117

wanderins doesn't bring ye ento trouble," and he went away.

As last I got so miserable about my own love affair that I thought I might do a good turn to Dick; and so I determined to try to buy from Murdock his holding on Knockcalltecrore, and then to give it to my friend, as I felt that the possession of the place, with power to re-exchange with Joyce, would in no way militate against his interests with Norah.

With this object in view I went out one afternoon to Knockcalltecrore, when I knew that Dick had arranged to visit the cutting at Knocknacar. I did not tell anyone where I was going, and took good care that Andy went with Dick. I had acquired a dread of that astute gentleman's inferences.

It was well in the afternoon when I got to Knockcalltecrore. Murdock was out at the edge of the bog making some investigations on his own account with the aid of the magnets. He flew into a great rage when he saw me, and roundly accused me of coming to spy upon him. I disclaimed any such meanness, and told him that he should be ashamed of such a suspicion. It was not my cue to quarrel with him, so I restrained myself as well as I could, and quietly told him that I had come on a matter of business.

He was anxious to get me away from the bog, and took me into the house. Here I broached my subject to him, for I knew he was too astute a man for my going round the question to be of any use.

At first my offer was a confirmation of his suspicion of me as a spy; and, indeed, he did not burke this aspect of the question in expressing his opinion.

"Oh, aye!" he sneered. "Isn't it likely I'm goin' to give up me land to ye, so that ye may hand it over to Mr. Sutherland— an' him havin' saycrets from me all the time—maybe knowin' where what I want to find is hid. Didn't I know it's a thraitor he is, an' ye a shpy."

"Dick Sutherland is no traitor and I am no spy. I wouldn't hear such words from anyone else; but, unfortunately, I know already that your ideas regarding us both are so hopelessly wrong that it's no use trying to alter them. I simply came here to make you an offer to buy this piece of land. The place is a pretty one, and I, or some friend of mine, may like some day to put up a house here. Of course if you don't want to sell there's an end to the matter; but do try to keep a decent tongue in your head—if you can."

My speech had evidently some effect on him, for he said:

"I didn't mane any offinse—an' as for sellin', I'd sell anything in the wurrld av I got me price fur it!"

"Well, why not enter on this matter? You're a man of the world, and so am I. I want to buy; I have money and can afford to give a good price, as it is a fancy with me. What objection have you to sell?"

"Ye know well enough I'll not sell—not yit, at all evints. I wouldn't part wid a perch iv this land fur all ye cud offer—not till I'm done wid me sarch. I mane to get what I'm lukin' fur—if it's there!"

"I quite understand. Well, I am prepared to meet you in the matter. I am willing to purchase the land—it to be given over to me at whatever time you may choose to name. Would a year suit you to make your investigations?"

He thought for a moment; then took out an old letter, and on the back of it made some calculations. Then he said:

"I suppose ye'd pay the money down at wanst?"

"Certainly," said I, "the very day I get possession." I had intended paying the money down, and waiting for possession as a sort of inducement to him to close with me; but there was so much greed in his manner that I saw I would do better by holding off payment until I got possession. My judgment was correct, for his answer surprised me:

"A month'll do what I wanted—or, to be certain, say five weeks from today. But the money would have to be payed to the minit."

"Certainly," said I. "Suit yourself as to time, and let me know the terms, so that I can see if we agree. I suppose you will want to see your attorney, so name any day to suit you.'

"I'm me own attorney. Do ye think I'd thrust any iv them wid me affairs? Whin I have a lawsuit I'll have thim, but not before. If ye want to know me price I'll tell it to ye now."

"Go on," said I, concealing my delight as well as I could. He accordingly named a sum which, to me, accustomed only as I had hitherto been to the price of land in a good English county, seemed very small indeed.

He evidently thought he was driving a hard bargain, for he said, with a cunning look:

"I suppose ye'll want to see lawyers and the like. So you may; but only to see that ye get ye bargin hard and fast. I'll not discuss the terrums wid any one else; an' if y' accept, ye must sign me a writin' now, that ye buy me land right here, an' that yell pay the money widin a month before ye take possession on the day we fix."

"All right," said I. "That will suit me quite well. Make out your paper in duplicate, and we will both sign. Of course, you must put in a clause guaranteeing title, and allowing the deed to be made with the approval of my solicitor, not as to value, but as to form and completeness."

"That's fair!" he said, and sat down to draw up his papers. He was evidently a bit of a lawyer—a gombeen man must be—and he knew the practical matters of law affecting things in which he was himself interested. His memorandum of agreement was, so far as I could judge, quite complete, and as concise as possible. He designated the land sold, and named the price which was to be paid into the account in his name in the Galway Bank before twelve o'clock noon on September 27th, or which might be paid in at an earlier date, with the deduction of two per cent, per annum as discount—in which case the receipt was to be given in full, and an undertaking to give possession at the appointed time, namely Wednesday, October 27th, at twelve o'clock noon.

We both signed the memorandum, he having sent the old woman who came up from the village to cook for him for the old schoolmaster to witness the signatures. I arranged that when I should have seen my solicitor and have had the deed properly drafted, I would see him again. I then came away, and got back at the hotel a little while before Dick arrived.

Dick was in great spirits; his experiment with the bog had been quite successful. The cutting had advanced so far that the clay wall hemming in the bog was actually weakened, and with a mining cartridge, prepared for the purpose, he had blown up the last bit of bank remaining. The bog had straightway begun to pour into the opening, not merely from the top, but simultaneously to the whole depth of the cutting.

"The experience of that first half-hour of the rush," went on Dick, "was simply invaluable. I do wish you had been there, old fellow. It was in itself a lesson on bogs and their reclamation."

It just suited my purpose that he should do all the talking at present, so I asked him to explain all that happened. He went on:

"The moment the cartridge exploded the whole of the small clay bank remaining was knocked to bits and was carried away by the first rush. There had evidently been a considerable accumulation of water just behind the bank; and at the first rush this swept through the cutting and washed it clean. Then the bog at the top, and the water in the middle, and the ooze below all struggled for the opening. I could see that the soft part of the bog actually floated. Naturally the water got away first. The bog proper, which was floating, jammed in the opening, and the ooze began to drain out below it. Of course, this was only the first rush; it will be running for days before things begin to settle; and then we shall be able to make some openings in the bog and see if my theories are tenable, in so far as the solidification is concerned. I am only disappointed in one thing."

"What is that?"

"That it will not enlighten us much regarding the bog at Shleenanaher, for I cannot find any indication here of a shelf of rock such as I imagine to be at the basis of the Shifting Bog. If I had had time I would like to have made a cutting into some of the waste where the bog had originally been. I dare say that Joyce would let me try now if I asked him."

I had my own fun out of my answer:

"Oh, I'm sure he will; but even if he won't let you now, he may be inclined to in a month or two, when things have settled down a bit."

His answer startled me.

"Do you know, Art, I fear it's quite on the cards that in a month or two there may be some settling down there that may be serious for some one?"

"How do you mean?"

"Simply this: that I am not at all satisfied about Murdock's house. There is every indication of it being right in the track of the bog in case it should shift again; and I would not be surprised if that hollow where it stands was right over the deepest part of the natural reservoir, where the rock slopes into the ascending stratum. This wet weather looks bad, and already the bog has risen somewhat. If the rain lasts, I wouldn't like to live in that house after five or six weeks."

A thought struck me: "Did you tell this to Murdock?"

"Certainly; the moment the conviction was in my mind."

"When was that now—-just for curiosity?"

"Last night, before I came away."

A light began to dawn on me as to Murdock's readiness to sell the land. I did not want to have to explain anything, so I did not mention the subject of my purchase, but simply asked Dick:

"And what did our upright friend say?"

"He said, in his own sweet manner, that it would last as long as he wanted it, and that after that it might go to hell—and me too, he added, with a thoughtfulness that was all his own."

When I went to my room that night I thought over the matter. For good or ill I had bought the property, and there was no going back now; indeed, I did not wish to go back, for I thought that it would be a fine opportunity for Dick to investigate the subject. If we could succeed in draining the bog and reclaiming it, it would be a valuable addition to the property.

That night I arranged to go over on the following day to

Galway, my private purpose being to consult a solicitor; and I wrote to my bankers in London, directing that an amount something over the sum required to effect my purchase should be lodged forthwith to an account to be opened for me at the Galway Bank.

Next day, I drove to Galway, and there, after a little inquiry, found a solicitor, Mr. Caicy, of whom every one spoke well. I consulted him regarding the purchase. He arranged to do all that was requisite, and to have the deed of purchase drawn. I told him that I wished the matter kept a profound secret. He agreed to meet my wishes in this respect, even to the extent that when he should come to Carnaclif to make the final completion with Murdock, he would pretend not to know me. We parted on the best of terms, after I had dined with him, and had consumed my share of a couple of bottles of as fine old port as is to be had in all the world.

Next day I returned to Carnaclif in the evening and met Dick. Everything had gone right during the two days. Dick was in great spirits; he had seen his Norah during the day, and had exchanged salutations with her. Then he had gone to Knock-nacar, and had seen a great change in the bog, which was already settling down into a more solid form. I simply told him I had been to Galway to do some banking and other business. It was some consolation to me in the midst of my own unhappiness to know that I was furthering the happiness of my friend.

On the third day from this Mr. Caicy was to be over with the deed, and the following day the sale was to be completed, I having arranged with the bank to transfer on that day the purchase money for the sale to the account of Mr. Murdock. The two first days I spent mainly on Knocknacar, going over each day ostensibly to look at the progress made in draining the bog, but in reality in the vain hope of seeing my Unknown.

Each time I went, my feet turned naturally to the hilltop; but on each visit I felt only a renewal of my sorrow and disappointment. I walked on each occasion to and from the hill, and on the second day, which was Sunday, went in the morning and sat on the top many hours, in the hope that some time during the day, it being a holiday, she might be able to find her way there once again.

When I got to the top the chapel bells were ringing in all the parishes below me to the west, and very sweetly and peacefully the sounds came through the bright crisp September air. And in some degree the sound brought peace to my soul, for there is so large a power in even the aspirations and the efforts of men towards good, that it radiates to unmeasurable distance. The wave theory that rules our knowledge of the distribution of light and sound may well be taken to typify, if it does not control, the light of divine love and the beating in unison of human hearts.

I think that during these days I must have looked, as well as felt, miserable; for even Andy did not make any effort to either irritate or draw me. On the Sunday evening, when I was on the strand behind the hotel, he lounged along, in his own mysterious fashion, and after looking at me keenly for a few moments, came up close, and said to me in a grave, pitying half-whisper:

"Don't be afther breakin' yer harrt, yer 'an'r. Divil mend the fairy girrul! Shure, isn't she vanished intirely? Mark me now, there's no sahtisfaction at all, at all, in them fairy girruls. Faix, but I wouldn't like to see a fine young gintleman like yer 'an'r, become like Yeoha, the Sigher, as they called him in the ould times."

"And who might that gentleman be, Andy?" I asked, with what appearance of cheerful interest I could muster up.

"Begor, it's a prince he was that married onto a fairy girrul, what wint an' was tuk off be a fairy man what lived in the same mountain as she done herself. Shure, thim fairy girruls has mostly a fairy man iv their own somewheres, that they love betther nor they does mortials. Jist you take me advice, Master Art, fur ye might do worsen go an' take a luk at Miss Norah, an' ye'll soon forget the fairies. There's a rale girrul av ye like!"

I was too sad to make any angry reply, and before I could think of any other kind, Andy lounged away whistling softly— for he had, like many of his class, a very sweet whistle—the air of "Savourneen Deelish."

The following day Mr. Caicy turned up at the hotel according to his promise. He openly told Mrs. Keating, of whom he had often before been a customer, that he had business with Mr. Murdock. He was, as usual with him, affable to all, "passing the time of day" with the various inhabitants of all degrees, and, as if a stranger, entering into conversation with me as we sat at lunch in the coffee-room. When we were alone he whispered to me that all was ready; that he had made an examination of the title, for which Murdock had sent him all the necessary papers, and that the deed was complete and ready to be signed. He told me he was going over that day to Knockcalltecrore, and would arrange that he would be there the next day, and that he would take care to have someone to witness the signatures.

On the following morning, when Dick went off with Andy to Knocknacar, and Mr. Caicy drove over to Knockcalltecrore, where I also shortly took my way on another car.

We met at Murdock's house. The deed was duly completed, and Mr. Caicy handed over to Murdock the letter from the bank where the lodgement had been made.

The land was now mine; and I was to have possession on the 27th of October. Mr. Caicy took the deed with him, and with it took also instructions to draw out a deed making the property over to Richard Sutherland. He went straight away to Galway; while I, in listless despair, wandered out on the hill-side to look at the view.

## Chapter 10

### In the Cliff Fields

I went along the mountain-side until I came to the great ridge of rocks which, as Dick had explained to me, protected the lower end of Murdock's farm from the westerly wind. I climbed to the top to get a view, and then found that the ridge was continuous, running as far as the Snake's Pass where I had first mounted it. Here, however, I was not, as then, above the sea, for I was opposite what they had called the Cliff Fields, and a very strange and beautiful sight it was.

Some hundred and fifty feet below me was a plateau of seven or eight acres in extent, and some two hundred and fifty feet above the sea. It was sheltered on the north by a high wall of rock like that I stood on, serrated in the same way, as the strata ran in similar layers. In the centre there rose a great rock, with a flat top some quarter of an acre in extent. The whole plateau, save this one bare rock, was a mass of verdure. It was watered by a small stream which fell through a deep, narrow cleft in the rocks, where the bog drains itself from Murdock's present land. The after-grass was deep, and there were many clumps of trees and shrubs—none of them of considerable height except a few great stone-pines which towered aloft and dared the fury of the western breeze. But not all the beauty of the scene could hold my eyes, for seated on the rocky table in the centre, just as I had seen her on the hilltop at Knocknacar, sat a girl to all intents the ditto of my unknown.

My heart gave a great bound, and in the tumult of hope that awoke within my breast the whole world seemed filled with sunshine. For an instant I almost lost my senses; my knees shook, and my eyes grew dim. Then came a horrible suspense and doubt. It was impossible to believe that I should see my Unknown here when I least expected to see her. And then came the man's desire of action.

I do not know how I began. To this day I cannot make out whether I took a bee-line for that isolated table of rock, and from where I was slid or crawled down the face of the rock, or whether I made a detour to the same end. All I can recollect is that I found myself scrambling over some large bowlders, and then passing through the deep, heavy grass at the foot of the rock.

Here I halted to collect my thoughts: a moment sufficed. I was too much in earnest to need any deliberation, and there was no choice of ways. I only waited to be sure that I would not create any alarm by unnecessary violence.

Then I ascended the rock. I did not make more noise than I

could help, but I did not try to come silently. She had evidently heard steps, for she spoke without turning round.

"Am I wanted?" Then, as I was passing across the plateau, my step seemed to arouse her attention; for at a bound she leaped to her feet, and turned with a glad look that went through the shadow of my soul, as the sunshine strikes through the mist.

"Arthur!" She almost rushed to meet me, but stopped suddenly, for an instant grew pale, and then a red flush crimsoned her face and neck. She put up her hands before her face, and I could see the tears drop through her fingers.

As for myself, I was half dazed. When I saw that it was indeed my Unknown a wild joy leaped to my heart; and then came the revulsion from my long pent-up sorrow and anxiety; and as I faltered out, "At last! at last!" the tears sprang unbidden to my eyes. There is, indeed, a dry-eyed grief, but its corresponding joy is as often smitten with sudden tears.

In an instant I was by her side, and had her hand in mine. It was only for a moment, for she withdrew it with a low cry of maidenly fear; but in that moment of gentle, mutual pressure a whole world had passed, and we knew that we loved.

We were silent for a time, and then we sat together on a bowlder, she edging away from me shyly.

What matters it of what we talked? There was not much to say—nothing that was new—the old, old story that has been told since the days when Adam, waking, found that a new joy had entered into his life. For those whose feet have wandered in Eden there is no need to speak; for those who are yet to tread the hallowed ground there is no need either—for in the fullness of time their knowledge will come.

It was not till we had sat some time that we exchanged any sweet words: they were sweet, although to any ne but ourselves they would have seemed the most absurd and soulless commonplaces.

We spoke, and that was all. It is of the nature of love that it can from airy nothings win its own celestial food.

Presently I said—and I pledge my word that this was the first speech that either of us had made, beyond the weather and the view, and such lighter topics:

"Won't you tell me your name? I have so longed to know it, all these weary days."

"Norah—Norah Joyce. I thought you knew."

This was said with a shy lifting of the eyelashes, which were as suddenly and as shyly dropped again.

"Norah!" As I spoke the word—and my whole soul was in its speaking—the happy blush overspread her face again. "Norah! What a sweet name—Norah! No, I did not know it; if I had known it, when I missed you from the hilltop at Knocknacar, I should have sought you here."

Somehow her next remark seemed to chill me:

"I thought you remembered me, from that night when father came home with you?"

There seemed some disappointment that I had so forgotten.

"That night," I said, "I did not see you at all. It was so dark that I felt like a blind man; I only heard your voice."

"I thought you remembered my voice."

The disappointment was still manifest. Fool that I was!—that voice, once heard, should have sunk into my memory forever.

"I thought your voice was familiar when I heard you on the hilltop; but when I saw you, I loved you from that moment; and then every other woman's voice in the world went, for me, out of existence!" She half arose, but sat down again, and the happy blush once more mantled her cheek. I felt that my peace was made. "My name is Arthur." Here a thought struck me—struck me for the first time, and sent through me a thrill of unutterable delight: the moment she had seen me she had mentioned my name—all unconsciously, it is true, but she had mentioned it. I feared, however, to alarm her by attracting her attention to it as yet, and went on: "Arthur Severn—but I think you know it."

"Yes; I heard it mentioned up at Knocknacar."

"Who by?"

"Andy, the driver. He spoke to my aunt and me when we were driving down, the day after we—after we met on the hilltop the last time."

Andy! And so my jocose friend knew all along! Well, wait! I must be even with him! "Your aunt?"

"Yes; my aunt Kate. Father sent me up to her, for he knew it would distress me to see all our things moved from our dear old home—all my mother's things. And father would have been distressed to see me grieved, and I to see him. It was kind of him; he is always so good to me."

"He is a good man, Norah—I know that; I only hope he won't hate me."

"Why?" This was said very faintly.

"For wanting to carry off his daughter. Don't go, Norah. For God's sake, don't go! I shall not say anything you do not wish; but if you only knew the agony I have been in since I saw you last—when I thought I had lost you—you would pity me—indeed you would! Norah, I love you! No! you must listen to me—you must! I want you to be my wife-—I shall love and honour you all my life! Don't refuse me, dear; don't draw back—for I love you!—I love you!"

There, it was all out. The pent-up waters find their own course. For a minute, at least, Norah sat still. Then she turned to me very gravely, and there were tears in her eyes:

"Oh, why did you speak like that, sir? why did you speak like that? Let me go!—let me go! You must not try to detain me!" I stood back, for we had both risen. "I am conscious of your good intention—of the honour you do me—but I must have time to think. Goodbye!"

She held out her hand. I pressed it gently—I dared not do more—true love is very timid at times! She bowed to me, and moved off.

A sudden flood of despair rushed over me—the pain of the days when I thought I had lost her could not be soon forgotten, and I feared that I might lose her again.

"Stay, Norah! stay one moment!" She stopped and turned round. "I may' see you again, may I not? Do not be cruel! May I not see you again?"

A sweet smile lit up the perplexed sadness of her face. "You may meet me here tomorrow evening, if you will," and she was gone.

Tomorrow evening! Then there was hope; and with gladdened heart I watched her pass across the pasture and ascend a path over the rocks. Her movements were incarnate grace; her beauty and her sweet presence filled the earth and air. When she passed from my sight, the sunlight seemed to pale and the warm air to grow chill.

For a long while I sat on that table rock, and my thoughts were of heavenly sweetness—all, save one which was of earth—one brooding fear that all might not be well—some danger I did not understand.

And then I too arose, and took my way across the plateau, and climbed the rock, and walked down the boreen on my way for Carnaclif

And then, and for the first time, did a thought strike me—one which for a moment made my blood run cold—Dick!

Aye, Dick! What about him? It came to me with a shudder, that my happiness—if it should be my happiness—must be based on the pain of my friend. Here, then, there was perhaps a clew to Norah's strange gravity! Could Dick have made a proposal to her? He admitted having spoken to her. Why should he, too, not have been impulsive? Why should it not be that he, being the first to declare himself, had got a favourable answer, and that now Norah was not free to choose?

How I cursed the delay in finding her; how I cursed and found fault with everyone and everything! Andy, especially, came in for my ill-will. He, at any rate, knew that my unknown of the hilltop at Knocknacar was none other than Norah.

And yet, stay! who but Andy persisted in turning my thoughts to Norah, and more than once suggested my paying a visit to Shleenanaher to see her? No; Andy must be acquitted at all points; common justice demanded that. Who, then, was I to blame? Not Andy—not Dick, who was too noble and too loyal a friend to give any cause for such a thought. Had he not asked me at the

130

first if the woman of my fancy was not this very woman; and had he not confessed his own love only when I answered him that it was not? No; Dick must be acquitted from blame.

Acquitted from blame! Was that justice? At present he was in the position of a wronged man, and it was I who had wronged him, in ignorance certainly, but still the wrong was mine. And now what could I do? Should I tell Dick? I shrank from such a thing; and as yet there was little to tell. Not till tomorrow evening should I know my fate; and might not that fate be such that it would be wiser not to tell Dick of it? Norah had asked for time to consider my offer. If it should be that she had already promised Dick, and yet should have taken time to consider another offer, would it be fair to tell Dick of such hesitation, even though the result was a loyal adherence to her promise to him? Would such be fair either to him or to her? No; he must not be told—as yet, at all events.

How, then, should I avoid telling him, in case the subject should crop up in the course of conversation? I had not told him of any of my late visits to Knockcalltecrore, although, God knows! they were taken not in my own interest, but entirely in his; and now an explanation seemed impossible.

Thus revolving the situation in my mind as I walked along, I came to the conclusion that the wisest thing I could do was to walk to some other place and stay there for the night. Thus I might avoid questioning altogether. On the morrow I could return to Carnaclif, and go over to Shleenanaher at such a time that I might cross Dick on the way, so that I might see Norah and get her answer without anyone knowing of my visit. Having so made up my mind, I turned my steps towards Roundwood, and when I arrived there in the evening sent a wire to Dick:

"Walked here, very tired; sleep here tonight; probably return tomorrow."

The long walk did me good, for it made me thoroughly tired, and that night, despite my anxiety of mind, I slept well—I went to

The next day I arrived at Carnaclif about mid-day. I found

that Dick had taken Andy to Knockcalltecrore. I waited until it was time to leave, and then started off. About half a mile from the foot of the boreen I went and sat in a clump of trees, where I could not be seen, but from which I could watch the road, and presently saw Dick passing along on Andy's car. When they had quite gone out of sight, I went on my way to the Cliff Fields.

I went with mingled feelings: there was hope, there was joy at the remembrance of yesterday, there was expectation that I would see her again—even though the result might be unhappiness—there was doubt, and there was a horrible haunting dread. My knees shook, and I felt weak as I climbed the rocks. I passed across the field and sat on the table-rock.

Presently she came to join me. With a queenly bearing she passed over the ground, seeming to glide rather than to walk. She was very pale, but as she drew near I could see in her eyes a sweet calm.

I went forward to meet her, and in silence we shook hands. She motioned to the bowlder, and we sat down. She was less shy than yesterday, and seemed in many subtle ways to be, though not less girlish, more of a woman.

When we sat down I laid my hand on hers and said—and I felt that my voice was hoarse:

"Well?"

She looked at me tenderly, and said, in a sweet, grave voice:

"My father has a claim on me that I must not overlook. He is all alone; he has lost my mother, and my brother is away, and is going into a different sphere of life from us. He has lost his land that he prized and valued, and that has been ours for a long, long time; and now that he is sad and lonely, and feels that he is growing old, how could I leave him? He that has always been so good and kind to me all my life!" Here the sweet eyes filled with tears. I had not taken away my hand, and she had not removed hers; this negative of action gave me hope and courage.

"Norah! answer me one thing: is there any other man between your heart and me?"

"Oh, no! no!" Her speech was impulsive; she stopped as suddenly as she began. A great weight seemed lifted from my heart, and yet there came a qualm of pity for my friend. Poor Dick! poor Dick!

Again we were silent for a minute. I was gathering courage for another question.

"Norah!"—I stopped; she looked at me.

"Norah, if your father had other objects in life, which would leave you free, what would be your answer to me?"

"Oh, do not ask me! do not ask me!" Her tone was imploring; but there are times when manhood must assert itself, even though the heart be torn with pity for woman's weakness. I went on:

"I must, Norah, I must! I am in torture till you tell me! Be pitiful to me! Be merciful to me! Tell me, do you love me? You know I love you, Norah. O God! how I love you! The world has but one being in it for me; and you are that one! With every fibre of my being—with all my heart and soul—I love you! Won't you tell me, then, if you love me?"

A flush as rosy as dawn came over her face, and timidly she asked me, "Must I answer? Must I?"

"You must, Norah!"

"Then, I do love you! God help us both! but I love you! I love you!" and tearing away her hand from mine, she put both hands before her face and burst into a passionate flood of tears.

There could be but one ending to such a scene. In an instant she was in my arms. Her will and mine went down before a sudden flood of passion that burst upon us both. She hid her face upon my breast, but I raised it tenderly, and our lips met in one long, loving, passionate kiss.

We sat on the bowlder, hand in hand, and whispering confessed to each other, in the triumph of our love, all those little secrets of the growth of our affection that lovers hold dear. That final separation, which had been spoken of but a while ago, was kept out of sight by mutual consent; the dead would claim its dead soon enough. Love lives in the present, and in the sunshine finds its joy.

Well, the men of old knew the human heart when they fixed upon the butterfly as the symbol of the soul; for the rainbow is but sunshine through a cloud, and love, like the butterfly, takes the colours of the rainbow on its airy wings!

Long we sat in that beauteous spot. High above us towered the everlasting rocks; the green of Nature's planting lay beneath our feet; and far off the reflection of the sunset lightened the dimness of the soft twilight over the wrinkled sea.

We said little as we sat hand in hand; but the silence was a poem, and the sound of the sea and the beating of our hearts were "hymns of praise to Nature and to Nature's God.

We spoke no more of the future; for now that we knew that we were each beloved, the future had but little terror for us. We were content.

When we had taken our last kiss, and parted beneath the shadow of the rock, I watched her depart through the gloaming to her own home; and then, I too, took my way. At the foot of the boreen I met Murdock, who looked at me in a strange manner, and merely growled some reply to my salutation.

I felt that I could never meet Dick tonight. Indeed, I wished to see no human being, and so I sat for long on the crags above the sounding sea; and then wandered down to the distant beach. To and fro I went all the night long, but ever in sight of the Hill, and ever and anon coming near to watch the cottage where Norah slept.

In the early morning, I took my way to Roundwood, and going to bed, slept until late in the day.

When I woke I began to think of how I could break my news to Dick. I felt that the sooner it was done the better. At first I had a vague idea of writing to him from where I was, and explaining all to him; but this, I concluded, would not do; it seemed too cowardly a way to deal with so true and loyal a friend. I would go now and await his arrival at Carnaclif, and tell him all, at the earliest moment when I could find an opportunity.

I drove to Carnaclif, and waited his coming impatiently, for I intended, if it were not too late, to afterwards drive over to

Shleenanaher, and see Norah—or at least the house she was in.

Dick arrived a little earlier than usual, and I could see from the window that he was grave and troubled. When he got down from the car he asked if I were in, and being answered in the affirmative, ordered dinner to be put on the table as soon as possible, and went up to his room.

I did not come down until the waiter came to tell me that dinner was ready. Dick had evidently waited also, and followed me downstairs. When he came into the room, he said heartily:

"Holloa, Art, old fellow, welcome back! I thought you were lost," and shook hands with me warmly.

Neither of us seemed to have much appetite, but we pretended to eat, and sent away plates full of food, cut up into the smallest proportions. When the apology for dinner was over, Dick offered me a cigar, lit his own, and said:

"Come out for a stroll on the sand, Art; I want to have a chat with you." I could feel that he was making a great effort to appear hearty, but there was a hollowness about his voice, which was not usual. As we went through the hall, Mrs. Keating handed me my letters, which had just arrived.

We walked out on the wide stretch of fine hard sand, which lies westwards from Carnaclif when the tide is out, and were a considerable distance from the town before a word was spoken. Dick turned to me, and said:

"Art, what does it all mean?"

I hesitated for a moment, for I hardly knew where to begin. The question, so comprehensive and so sudden, took me aback. Dick went on:

"Art, two things I have always believed, and I won't give them up without a struggle. One is that there are very few things that, no matter how strange or wrong they look, won't bear explanation of some kind; and the other is that an honourable man does not grow crooked in a moment. Is there anything, Art, that you would like to tell me?"

"There is, Dick. I have a lot to tell; but won't you tell me what you wish me to speak about?" I was just going to tell him all, but it suddenly occurred to me that it would be wise to know something of what was amiss with him first.

"Then I shall ask you a few questions. Did you not tell me that the girl you were in love with was not Norah Joyce?"

"I did; but I was wrong. I did not know it at the time; I only found it out, Dick, since I saw you last."

"Since you saw me last! Did you not then know that I loved Norah Joyce, and that I was only waiting a chance to ask her to marry me?"

"I did." I had nothing to add here; it came back to me that I had spoken and acted all along without a thought of my friend.

"Have you not of late paid many visits to Shleenanaher; and have you not kept such visits quite dark from me?"

"I have, Dick."

"Did you keep me ignorant on purpose?"

"I did. But those visits were made entirely on your account." I stopped, for a look of wonder and disgust spread over my companion's face.

"On my account! on my account! And was it, Arthur Severn, on my account that you asked, as I presume you did, Norah Joyce to marry you—I take it for granted that your conduct was honourable, to her at any rate—the woman whom I had told you I loved, and that I wished to marry, and that you assured me that you did not love, your heart being fixed on another woman? I hate to speak so, Art, but I have had black thoughts, and am not quite myself. Was this all on my account?" It was a terrible question to answer, and I paused. Dick went on:

"Was it on my account that you, a rich man, purchased the home that she loved; while, I, a poor one, had to stand by and see her father despoiled day by day, and, because of my poverty, had to go on with a hateful engagement, which placed me in a false position in her eyes?"

Here I saw daylight. I could answer this scathing question.

"It was, Dick, entirely on your account." He drew away from me, and stood still, facing me in the twilight as he spoke:

"I should like you to explain, Mr. Severn, for your own sake, a statement like that."

Then I told him, with simple earnestness, all the truth. How I had hoped to further his love, since my own seemed so hopeless; how I had bought the land, intending to make it over to him, so that his hands might be strong to woo the woman he loved; how this and nothing else had taken me to Shleenanaher; and that while there I had learned that my own unknown love and Norah were one and the same; of my proposal to her—and here I told him humbly how in the tumult of my own passion I had forgotten his—whereat he shrugged his shoulders—and of my long anxiety till her answer was given. I told him that I had stayed away the first night at Roundwood, lest I should be betrayed into any speech which would lack in loyalty to him as well as to her. And then I told him of her decision not to leave her father, touching but lightly on the confession of her love, lest I should give him needless pain; I did not dare to avoid it lest I should mislead him to his further harm. When I had finished he said, softly:

I thought a moment, and then remembered that I had in my pocket the letters which had been handed to me at the hotel, and that among them there was one from Mr. Caicy at Galway. This letter I took out and handed to Dick.

"There is a letter unopened. Open it and it may tell you something. I know my word will suffice you; but this is in justice to us both."

Dick took the letter and broke the seal. He read the letter from Caicy, and then holding up the deed so that the dying light of the west should fall on it, read it. The deed was not very long. When he finished it he stood for a moment with his hands down by his sides; then he came over to me, and laying his hands, one of which grasped the deed, on my shoulders, said:

"Thank God, Art, there need be no bitterness between me and thee! All is as you say; but oh, old fellow"—and here he laid his head on my shoulder and sobbed—"my heart is broken! All the light has gone out of my life!"

His despair was only for a moment. Recovering himself as

quickly as he had been overcome, he said:

"'Never mind, old fellow, only one of us must suffer; and, thank God! my secret is with you alone; no one else in the wide world even suspects. She must never know. Now tell me all about it; don't fear that it will hurt me. It will be something to know that you are both happy. By the way, this had better be torn up; there is no need of it now!" Having torn the paper across, he put his arm over my shoulder as he used to do when we were boys; and so we passed into the gathering darkness.

Thank God for loyal and royal manhood! Thank God for the heart of a friend that can suffer and remain true! And thanks, above all, that the lessons of tolerance and forgiveness, taught of old by the Son of God, are now and then remembered by the sons of men.

## Chapter 11

### Un Mauvais Quart d'Heure

When we were strolling back to the hotel Dick said to me:

"Cheer up, old fellow! You needn't be the least bit down-hearted. Go soon and see Joyce. He will not stand in the girl's way, you may be sure. He is a good fellow, and loves Norah dearly—who could help it?" He stopped for a moment here, and choked a great sob, but went on bravely:

"It is only like her to be willing to sacrifice her own happiness; but she must not be let do that. Settle the matter soon. Go tomorrow to see Joyce. I shall go up to Knocknacar instead of working with Murdock; it will leave the coast clear for you." Then we went into the hotel, and I felt as if a great weight had been removed.

When I was undressing I heard a knock. "Come in," I called, and Dick entered. Dear old fellow! I could see that he had been wrestling with himself, and had won. His eyes were red, but there was a noble manliness about him which was beyond description.

"Art," said he, "I wanted to tell you something, and I thought it ought to be told now. I wouldn't like the night to close on any wrong impression between you and me. I hope you feel that my suspicion about fair play and the rest of it is all gone."

"I do, old fellow, quite."

"Well, you are not to get thinking of me as in any way wronged in the matter, either by accident or design. I have been going over the whole matter to try and get the heart of the mystery; and I think it only fair to say that no wrong could be done to me. I never spoke a single word to Norah in my life, nor did she to me. Indeed, I have seen her but seldom, though the first time was enough to finish me. Thank God, we have found out the true state of affairs before it was too late.

"It might have been worse, old lad, it might have been worse! I don't think there's any record—even in the novels—of a man's life being wrecked over a girl he didn't know. We don't get hit to death at sight, old boy. It's only skin-deep this time, and though skin-deep hurts the most, it doesn't kill. I thought I would tell you what I had worked out, for I knew we were such old friends that it would worry you and mar your happiness to think I was wretched. I hope, and I honestly expect, that by tomorrow I shall be all right, and able to enjoy the sight of both your happiness—as, please God, I hope such is to be."

We wrung each other's hands, and I believe that from that moment we were closer friends than ever. As he was going out, Dick turned to me, and said:

"It is odd about the legend, isn't it? The Snake is in the Hill still, if I am not mistaken. He told me all about your visits and the sale of the land to you, in order to make mischief. But his time is coming; St. Patrick will lift that crozier of his before long."

"But the Hill holds us all," said I; and as I spoke there was an ominous feeling over me. "We're not through yet; but it will be all right now."

The last thing I saw was a smile on his face as he closed the door.

The next morning Dick started for Knocknacar. It had been arranged the night before that he should go on Andy's car, as I preferred walking to Shleenanaher. I had more than one reason for so doing, but that which I kept in the foreground of my own mind— and which I almost persuaded myself was the chief, if not the only reason—was that I did not wish to be troubled with Andy's curiosity and impertinent badinage. My real and secret reason, however, was that I wished to be alone so that I might collect my thoughts, and acquire courage for what the French call *un mauvais quart d'heure*.[1]

In all classes of life, and under all conditions, this is an ordeal eminently to be dreaded by young men. No amount of reason is of the least avail to them; there is some horrible, lurking, un-known possibility which may defeat all their hopes, and may, in addition, add the flaming aggravation of making them ap-pear ridiculous. I summed up my own merits, and, not being a fool, found considerable ground for hope. I was young, not bad-looking, Norah loved me; I had no great bogie of a past se-cret or misdeed to make me feel sufficiently guilty to fear a just punishment falling upon me; and, considering all things, I was in a social position and of wealth beyond the dreams of a peasant— howsoever ambitious for his daughter he might be.

And yet I walked along those miles of road that day with my heart perpetually sinking into my boots, and harassed with a vague dread which made me feel at times an almost irresistible inclination to run away. I can only compare my feelings, when I drew in sight of the hill-top, with those which animate the mind of a young child when coming in sight of the sea in order to be dipped for the first time.

There is, however, in man some wholesome fear of running away, which at times either takes the place of resolution, or else initiates the mechanical action of guiding his feet in the right direction—of prompting his speech and regulating his move-ments. Otherwise no young man, or very few at least, would ever face the ordeal of asking the consent of the parents of his *inamorata*. Such a fear stood to me now; and with a seeming boldness I approached Joyce's house. When I came to the gate I

1. An unpleasant fifteen minutes.

saw him in the field not far off, and went up to speak to him.

Even at that moment, when the dread of my soul was greatest, I could not but recall an interview which I had had with Andy that morning, and which was not of my seeking, but of his.

After breakfast I had been in my room, making myself as smart as I could, for, of course, I hoped to see Norah, when I heard a knock at the door, timid but hurried. When I called to "come in," Andy's head appeared; and then his whole body was by some mysterious wriggle conveyed through the partial opening of the door. When within, he closed it, and, putting a finger to his lip, said, in a mysterious whisper:

"Masther Art!"

"Well, Andy, what is it?"

"Whisper me now! Shure, I don't want to see yer 'an'r so onasy in yer mind."

I guessed what was coming, so interrupted him, for I was determined to get even with him.

"Now, Andy, if you have any nonsense about your 'Miss Norah,' I don't want to hear it."

"Whisht, surr; let me shpake. I mustn't kape Misther Dick waitin'. Now take me advice, an' take a luk out to Shleenanaher. Ye may see some wan there what ye don't ixpect." This was said with a sly mysteriousness impossible to describe.

"No, no, Andy," said I, looking as sad as I could. "I can see no one there that I don't expect."

"They do say, surr, that the fairies does take quare shapes; and your fairy girrul may have gone to Shleenanaher. Fairies may want to take the wather like mortials."

"Take the water, Andy! What do you mean?"

"What do I mane! why what the quality does call say-bathin'. An', maybe, the fairy girrul has gone too!"

"Ah, no, Andy," said I, in as melancholy a way as I could, "my fairy girl is gone. I shall never see her again."

Andy looked at me very keenly; and then a twinkle came in his eye, and he said, slapping his thigh:

"Begor, but I believe yer 'an'r is cured. Ye used to be that melancholy that, bedad, it's meself what was gettin' sarious about ye; an' now it's only narvous ye are. Well, if the fairy is gone, why not see Miss Norah? Sure wan sight iv her 'd cure all the fairy spells what iver was cast. Go now, yer 'an'r, an' see her this day!"

I said with decision, "No, Andy, I will not go today to see Miss Norah. I have something else to do."

"Oh, very well!" said he with simulated despondency. "If yer 'an'r won't, of course ye won't; but ye're wrong. At any rate, if ye're in the direction iv Shleenanaher, will ye go an' see th' ould man? Musha, but I'm thinkin' it's glad he'd be to see yer 'an'r."

Despite all I could do, I felt blushing up to the roots of my hair. Andy looked at me quizzically, and said oracularly, and with sudden seriousness:

"Begor! if yer fairy girrul is turned into a fairy complately, an' has flew away from ye, maybe ould Joyce too'd become a leprachaun! Hould him tight whin ye catch him! Remimber, wid leprachauns, if ye wance let thim go ye may niver git thim agin. But if ye hould thim tight, they must do whatsumiver ye wish. So they do say—but maybe I'm wrong—I'm intherfarin' wid a gintleman as was bit be a fairy, and knows more nor mortials does about thim. There's the masther callin'. Goodbye, surr, an' good luck!" and with a grin at me over his shoulder, Andy hurried away. I muttered to myself:

"If anyone is a fairy, my bold Andy, I think I can name him. You seem to know everything!"

This scene came back to me with renewed freshness. I could not but feel that Andy was giving me some advice. He evidently knew more than he pretended; indeed, he must have known all along of the identity of my Unknown of Knocknacar with Norah. He now also evidently knew of my knowledge on the subject; and he either knew or guessed that I was off to see Joyce on the subject of his daughter.

In my present state of embarrassment, his advice was a distinct light. He knew the people, and Joyce especially; he also saw some danger to my hopes, and showed me a way to gain my object. I knew already that Joyce was a proud man, and I could quite conceive that he was an obstinate one; and I knew from general experience of life that there is no obstacle so difficult to surmount as the pride of an obstinate man. With all the fervour of my heart I prayed that, on this occasion, his pride might not in any way be touched or arrayed against me.

When I saw him I went straight towards him, and held out my hand. He seemed a little surprised, but took it. Like Bob Acres, I felt my courage oozing out of the tips of my fingers,[2] but with the remnant of it threw myself into the battle:

"Mr. Joyce, I have come to speak to you on a very serious subject."

"A sarious subject! Is it concarnin' me?"

"It is."

"Go on. More throuble, I suppose?"

"I hope not, most sincerely. Mr. Joyce, I want to have your permission to marry your daughter." If I had suddenly turned into a bird and flown away, I do not think I could have astonished him more. For a second or two he was speechless, and then said, in an unconscious sort of way:

"Want to marry me daughter!"

"Yes, Mr. Joyce. I love her very dearly. She is a pearl among women; and if you will give your permission, I shall be the happiest man on earth. I can quite satisfy you as to my means. I am well to do; indeed, as men go, I am a rich man."

"Aye, sir, I don't doubt. I'm contint that you are what you say. But you never saw me daughter, except that dark night when you took me home."

"Oh yes, I have seen her several times, and spoken with her; but, indeed I only wanted to see her once to love her."

"Ye have seen her, and she never tould me! Come wid me!" He beckoned me to come with him, and strode at a rapid pace to his cottage, opened the door, and motioned me to go in. I entered the room—which was both kitchen and living-room—

2. The allusion is to Richard Brinsley Sheridan's *The Rivals*. Bob Acres was a coward whose "courage always oozed out at his finger ends."

to which he pointed. He followed.

As I entered, Norah, who was sewing, saw me and stood up. A rosy blush ran over her face; then she grew as white as snow as she saw the stern face of her father close behind me. I stepped forward, and took her hand; when I let it go, her arm fell by her side.

"Daughter"—Joyce spoke very sternly, but not unkindly— "do you know this gentleman?"

"Yes, father."

"He tells me that you and he have met several times. Is it thrue?"

"Yes, father, but—"

"Ye never tould me! How was that?"

"It was by accident we met."

"Always be accident?" Here I spoke:

"Always by accident—on her part." He interrupted me:

"Yer pardon, young gentleman. I wish me daughter to answer me! Shpeak, Norah!"

"Always, father, except once, and then I came to give a message—yes! it was a message, although from myself."

"What missage?"

"Oh father, don't make me speak! We are not alone. Let me tell you alone. I am only a girl, and it is hard to speak."

His voice had a tear in it, for all its sternness, as he answered:

"It is on a subject that this gentleman has spoke to me about— as mayhap he has spoke to you."

"Oh, father!"—she took his hand, which he did not withdraw, and, bending over, kissed it and hugged it to her breast— oh, father, what have I done that you should seem to mistrust me? You have always trusted me; trust me now, and don't make me speak till we are alone!"

I could not be silent any longer. My blood began to boil, that she I loved should be so distressed, whatsoever the cause, and at the hands of whomsoever, even her father.

"Mr. Joyce, you must let me speak! You would speak yourself to save pain to a woman you loved." He turned to tell me to be

144

silent, but suddenly stopped. I went on: "Norah"—he winced as I spoke her name—"is entirely blameless. I met her quite by chance at the top of Knocknacar when I went to see the view. I did not know who she was—I had not the faintest suspicion; but from that moment I loved her. I went next day, and waited all day in the chance of seeing her; I did see her, but again came away in ignorance even of her name. I sought her again, day after day, day after day, but could get no word of her; for I did not know who she was, or where she came from. Then, by chance, and after many weary days, again I saw her in the Cliff Fields below, three days ago. I could no longer be silent, but told her that I loved her, and asked her to be my wife. She asked a while to think, and left me, promising to give me an answer on the next evening. I came again, and I got my answer."

Here Norah, who was sobbing, with her face turned away, looked round, and said:

"Hush! hush! You must not let father know. All the harm will be done!" Her father answered in a low voice:

"All that could be done is done already, daughter. Ye never tould me!"

"Sir, Norah is worthy of all esteem. Her answer to me was that she could not leave her father, who was all alone in the world." Norah turned away again, but her father's arm went round her shoulder. "She told me I must think no more of her; but, sir, you and I, who are men, must not let a woman, who is dear to us both make such a sacrifice." Joyce's face was somewhat bitter as he answered me:

"Ye think pretty well of yerself, young sir, whin ye consider it a sacrifice for me daughter to shtay wid the father, who loves her, and who she loves. There was never a shadda on her life till ye came." This was hard to hear, but harder to answer, and I stammered as I replied:

"I hope I am man enough to do what is best for her, even if it were to break my heart. But she must marry some time; it is the lot of the young and beautiful." Joyce paused a while, and his look grew very tender as he made answer, softly:

"Aye, thrue, thrue! The young birds lave the nist in due say-son—that's only natural." This seemed sufficient concession for the present; but Andy's warning rose before me, and I spoke:

"Mr. Joyce, God knows I don't want to add one drop of bitterness to either of your lives! Only tell me that I may have hope, and I am content to wait and to try to win your esteem and Norah's love."

The father drew his daughter closer to him, and with his other hand stroked her hair, and said, while his eyes filled with tears:

"Ye didn't wait for me esteem to win her love." Norah threw herself into his arms and hid her face on his breast. He went on:

"We can't undo what is done. If Norah loves ye—and it seems to me that she does—do I shpeak thrue, daughter?" The girl raised her face bravely, and looked in her father's eyes:

"Yes! father." A thrill of wild delight rushed through me. As she dropped her head again, I could see that her neck had

*"The colour of the budding rose's crest."*[3]

"Well, well," Joyce went on, "ye are both young yit. God knows what may happen in a year! Lave the girl free a bit to choose. She has not met many gentlemen in her time, and she may desave herself Me darlin', whativer is for your good shall be done, plase God!"

"And am I to have her in time?" The instant I had spoken I felt that I had made a mistake; the man's face grew hard as he turned to me:

"I think for me daughter, sir, not for you. As it is, her happiness seems to be mixed up with yours—lucky for ye. I suppose ye must meet now and thin; but ye must both promise me that ye'll not meet widout me lave, or, at laste, me knowin' it. We're not gentlefolk, sir, and we don't undherstand their ways. If ye were of Norah's and me own kind, I mightn't have to say the same; but ye're not."

---

3. Lord Byron, *Don Juan*. Canto VI (slightly misquoted).

Things were now so definite that I determined to make one I more effort to fix a time when my happiness might be certain, so I asked:

"Then if all be well, and you agree—as please God you shall when you know me better—when may I claim her?"

When he was face to face with a definite answer Joyce again grew stern. He looked down at his daughter and then up at me, and said, stroking her hair:

"Whin the threasure of Knockcalltecrore is found, thin ye may claim her if ye will, an' I'll freely let her go." As he spoke, there came before my mind the strong idea that we were all in the power of the Hill—that it held us; however, as lightly as I could I spoke:

"Then I would claim her now!"

"What do ye mane?"—this was said half anxiously, half fiercely.

"The threasure of Knockcalltecrore is here; you hold her in your arms!" He bent over her:

"Aye, the threasure sure enough—the threasure ye would rob me of." Then he turned to me, and said sternly, but not unkindly:

"Go, now; I can't bear more at prisent, and even me daughter may wish to be for a while alone wid me." I bowed my head and turned to leave the room; but as I was going out, he called me back:

"Shtay! Afther all, the young is only young. Ye seem to have done but little harm—if any." He held out his hand; I grasped it closely, and from that instant it seemed that our hearts warmed to each other. Then I felt bolder, and stepping to Norah took her hand—she made no resistance—and pressed it to my lips, and went out silently. I had hardly left the door when Joyce came after me.

"Come agin in an hour," he said, and went in and shut the door.

Then I wandered to the rocks and climbed down the rugged path into the Cliff Fields. I strode through the tall grass and the

147

weeds, rank with the continuous rain, and gained the table rock. I climbed it, and sat where I first had met my love, after I had lost her; and, bending, I kissed the ground where her feet had rested. And then I prayed as fervent a prayer as the heart of a lover can yield, for every blessing on the future of my beloved; and made high resolves that whatsoever might befall, I would so devote myself that, if a man's efforts could accomplish it, her feet should never fall on thorny places.

I sat there in a tumult of happiness. The air was full of hope, and love, and light; and I felt that in all the wild glory and fullness of nature the one unworthy object was myself.

When the hour was nearly up I went back to the cottage; the door was open, but I knocked on it with my hand. A tender voice called to me to come in, and I entered.

Norah was standing up in the centre of the room. Her face was radiant, although her sweet eyes were bright with recent tears; and I could see that in the hour which I had passed on the rock, the hearts of the father and the child had freely spoken. The old love between them had taken a newer and fuller and more conscious life—based, as God has willed it with the hearts of men, on the parent's sacrifice of self for the happiness of the child.

Without a word I took her in my arms. She came without bashfulness and without fear; only love and trust spoke in every look and every moment. The cup of our happiness was full to the brim; and it seemed as though God saw, and, as of old with His completed plan of the world, was satisfied that all was good.

We sat, hand in hand, and told again and again the simple truths that lovers tell; and we built bright mansions of future hope. There was no shadow on us, except the shadow that slowly wrapped the earth in the wake of the sinking sun. The long, level rays of sunset spread through the diamond panes of the lattice, grew across the floor, and rose on the opposite wall; but we did not heed them until we heard Joyce's voice behind us:

"I have been thinkin' all the day, and I have come to believe that it is a happy day for us all, sir. I say, though she is my daughter, that the man that won her heart should be a proud man, for it is a heart of gold. I must give her to ye. I was sorry at the first, but I do it freely now. Ye must guard and kape, and hould her as the apple of your eye. If ye should ever fail or falter, remimber that ye took a great thrust in takin' her from me that loved her much, and in whose heart she had a place—not merely for her own sake, but for the sake of the dead that loved her." He faltered a moment, but then coming over, put his hand in mine, and while he held it there, Norah put her arm around his neck, and laying her sweet head on his broad, manly breast, said softly:

"Father, you are very good, and I am very, very happy!" Then she took my hand and her father's together, and said to me:

"Remember, he is to be as your father, too; and that you owe him all the love and honour that I do!"

"Amen!" I said, solemnly; and we three wrung each other's hands.

Before I went away, I said to Joyce:

"You told me I might claim her when the treasure of the Hill was found. Well, give me a month, and perhaps, if I don't have the one you mean, I may have another." I wanted to keep, for the present, the secret of my purchase of the old farm, so as to make a happy surprise when I should have actual possession.

"What do ye mane?" he said.

"I shall tell you when the month is up," I answered; "or if the treasure is found sooner—but you must trust me till then."

Joyce's face looked happy as he strolled out, evidently leaving me a chance of saying goodbye alone to Norah; she saw it too, and followed him.

"Don't go, father," she said. At the door she turned her sweet face to me, and with a shy look at her father, kissed me, and blushed rosy red.

"That's right, me girl," said Joyce, "honest love is without shame! Ye need never fear to kiss your lover before me."

Again we stayed talking for a little while. I wanted to say goodbye again; but this last time I had to give the kiss myself. As I looked back from the gate, I saw father and daughter standing close together; he had his arm round her shoulder, and the dear head that I loved lay close on his breast, as they both waved me farewell.

I went back to Carnaclif, feeling as though I walked on air; and my thoughts were in the heaven that lay behind my footsteps as I went, though before me on the path of life.

## CHAPTER 12

### BOG-FISHING AND SCHOOLING

When I got near home I met Dick, who had strolled out to meet me. He was looking much happier than when I had left him in the morning. I really believe that now that the shock of his own disappointment had passed, he was all the happier that my affair had progressed satisfactorily. I told him all that had passed, and he agreed with the advice given by Joyce, that for a little while, nothing should be said about the matter. We walked together to the hotel, I hurrying the pace somewhat, for it had begun to dawn upon me that I had eaten but little in the last twenty-four hours. It was prosaic, but true: I was exceedingly hungry. Joy seldom interferes with the appetite; it is sorrow or anxiety which puts it in deadly peril.

When we got to the hotel we found Andy waiting outside the door. He immediately addressed me:

"Och, musha, but it's the sad man I am this day! Here's Masther Art giv over intirely to the fairies. An' it's leprachaun catchin' he has been onto this blissed day. Luk at him! isn't it full iv sorra he is? Give up the fairies, Masther Art—do thry an' make him, Misther Dick—an' take to fallin' head over ears in love wid some nice young girrul. Sure, Miss Norah herself, bad as she is, 'd be betther nor none at all, though she doesn't come up to Masther Art's rulin'."

This latter remark was made to Dick, who immediately asked him:

"What is that, Andy?"

"Begor, yer 'an'r, Masther Art has a quare kind iv a girrul in his eye intirely, wan he used to be lukin' for on the top iv

Knocknacar— the fairy girrul, yer 'an'r," he added to me in an explanatory manner. "I suppose, yer 'an'r," turning to me, "ye haven't saw her this day?"

"I saw nobody to answer your description, Andy; and I fear I wouldn't know a fairy girl if I saw one," said I, as I passed into the house followed by Dick, while Andy, laughing loudly, went round to the back of the house, where the bar was.

That was, for me at any rate, a very happy evening. Dick and I sat up late and smoked, and went over the ground that we had passed, and the ground that we were, please God, to pass in time. I felt grateful to the dear old fellow, and spoke much of his undertakings, both at Knocknacar and at Knockcalltecrore. He told me that he was watching carefully the experiment at the former place as a guide to the latter. After some explanations, he said:

"There is one thing there which rather disturbs me. Even with the unusual amount of rain which we have had lately, the flow or drain of water from the bog is not constant; it does not follow the rains as I expected. There seems to be some process of silting, or choking, or damming up the walls of what I imagine to be the different sections or reservoirs of the bog. I cannot make it out, and it disturbs me; for if the same process goes on at Knockcalltecrore, there might be any kind of unforeseen disaster in case of the shifting of the bog.

"I am not at all easy about the way Murdock is going on there. Ever since we found the indication of iron in the bog itself, he has taken every occasion when I am not there to dig away at one of the clay banks that jut into it. I have warned him that he is doing a very dangerous thing, but he will not listen. Tomorrow, when I go up, I shall speak to him seriously. He went into Galway with a cart the night before last, and was to return by tomorrow morning. Perhaps he has some game on. I must ascertain what it is."

Before we parted for the night we had arranged to go together in the morning to Knockcalltecrore, for, of course, I had made up my mind that each day should see me there.

In the morning, early, we drove over. We left Andy, as usual,

151

in the boreen at the foot of the hill, and walked up together. I left Dick at Murdock's gate, and then hurried as fast as my legs could carry me to Joyce's.

Norah must have had wonderful ears. She heard my footsteps in the lane, and when I arrived at the gate she was there to meet me. She said, "Good-morning," shyly, as we shook hands. For an instant she evidently feared that I was going to kiss her there in the open, where someone might see; but almost as quickly she realized that she was safe so far, and we went up to the cottage together. Then came my reward; for, when the door was closed, she put her arms round my neck as I took her in my arms, and our lips met in a sweet, long kiss. Our happiness was complete. Anyone who has met the girl he loved the day after his engagement to her can explain why or how—if any explanation be required.

Joyce was away in the fields. We sat hand in hand, and talked for a good while; but I took no note of time.

Suddenly Norah looked up. "Hush!" she said. "There is a step in the boreen; it is your friend, Mr. Sutherland." We sat just a little further apart and let go hands. Then the gate clicked, and even I heard Dick's steps as he quickly approached. He knocked at the door; we both called out "Come in" simultaneously, and then looked at each other and blushed. The door opened and Dick entered. He was very pale, but in a couple of seconds his pallor passed away. He greeted Norah cordially, and she sweetly bade him welcome. Then he turned to me:

"I am very sorry to disturb you, old fellow, but would you mind coming down to Murdock's for a bit? There is some work which I wish you to give me a hand with."

I started up and took my hat, whispered goodbye to Norah, and went with him. She did not come to the door; but from the gate I looked back and saw her sweet face peeping through the diamond pane of the lattice.

"What is it, Dick?" I asked, as we went down the lane.

"A new start today. Murdock evidently thinks we have got on the track of something. He went into Galway for a big grapnel; and now we are making an effort to lift it—whatever 'it' is—out of the bog."

"By Jove!" said I, "things are getting close."

"Yes," said Dick. "And I am inclined to think he is right. There is most probably a considerable mass of iron in the bog. We have located the spot, and are only waiting for you, so as to be strong enough to make a cast."

When we got to the edge of the bog we found Murdock standing beside a temporary jetty, arranged out of a long plank, with one end pinned to the ground, and the centre supported on a large stone, placed on the very edge of the solid ground, where a rock cropped up. Beside him was a very large grappling-iron, some four feet wide, attached to a coil of strong rope. When we came up, he saluted me in a half surly manner, and we set to work, Dick saying, as we began:

"Mr. Severn, Mr. Murdock has asked us to help in raising something from the bog. He prefers to trust us, whom he knows to be gentlemen, than to let his secret be shared in with anyone else."

Dick got out on the end of the plank, holding the grapnel and a coil of the rope in his hand, while the end of the coil was held by Murdock.

I could see from the appearance of the bog that someone had been lately working at it, for it was all broken about as though to make a hole in it, and a long pole that lay beside where I stood was covered with wet and slime.

Dick poised the grapnel carefully and then threw it out. It sank into the bog, slowly at first, but then more quickly; an amount of rope ran out which astonished me, for I knew that the bog must be at least so deep.

Suddenly the run of the rope ceased, and we knew that the grapnel had gone as far as it could. Murdock and I then held the rope, and Dick took the pole and poked, and beat a passage for it through the bog up to the rock where we stood. Then he too joined us, and we all began to pull.

For a few feet we pulled in the slack of the rope. Then there was a little more resistance for some three or four feet, and we knew that the grapnel was dragging on the bottom. Suddenly there was a check, and Murdock gave a suppressed shout:

"We have got it! I feel it! Pull away for your lives!"

We kept a steady pull on the rope. At first there was simply a dead weight, and in my own mind I was convinced that we had caught a piece of projecting rock. Murdock would have got unlimited assistance and torn out of the bog whatever it was that we had got hold of, even if he had to tear up the rocks by the roots; but Dick kept his head, and directed a long steady pull.

There was a sudden yielding, and then again resistance. We continued to pull, and then the rope began to come, but very slowly, and there was a heavy weight attached to it. Even Dick was excited now. Murdock shut his teeth, and scowled like a demon: it would have gone hard with anyone who came then between him and his prize. As for myself, I was in a tumult. In addition to the natural excitement of the time, there rose to my memory Joyce's words: "When the treasure is found you may claim her if you will," and, although the need for such an occasion passed away with his more free consent, the effect that they had at the time produced on me remained in my mind.

Here, then, was the treasure at last; its hiding for a century in the bog had come to an end.

We pulled and pulled. Heavens! how we tugged at that rope. Foot after foot it came up through our hands, wet and slimy, and almost impossible to hold. Now and again it slipped from each of us in turns a few inches, and a muttered "Steady, steady," was all the sound heard. It took all three of us to hold the weight, and so no one could be spared to make an effort to further aid us by any mechanical appliance. The rope lay beside us in seemingly an endless coil. I began to wonder if it would ever end. Our breath began to come quickly, our hands were cramped. There came a new and more obstinate resistance. I could not account for it. Dick cried out:

"It is under the roots of the bog; we must now take it up straight. Can you two hold on for a moment, and I shall get on the plank." We nodded, breath was too precious for unnecessary speech.

Dick slacked out after we had got our feet planted for a steady resistance. He then took a handful of earth, and went out on the plank a little beyond the centre and caught the rope. When he held it firmly with his clay-covered hands, he said:

"Come now, Art. Murdock, you stay and pull." I ran to him, and, taking my hands full of earth, caught the rope also.

The next few minutes saw a terrible struggle. Our faces were almost black with the rush of blood in stooping and lifting so long and so hard, our hands and backs ached to torture, and we were almost in despair, when we saw the bog move just under us. This gave us new courage and new strength, and with redoubled effort we pulled at the rope.

Then up through the bog came a large mass. We could not see what it was, for the slime and the bog covered it solidly; but with a final effort we lifted it. Each instant it grew less weighty as the resistance of the bog was overcome, and the foul slimy surface fell back into its place and became tranquil. When we lifted and pulled the mass on the rock bank, Murdock rushed forward in a frenzied manner, and shouted to us:

"Kape back! Hands off! It's mine, I say, all mine! Don't dar even to touch it, or I'll do ye a harrum! Here, clear off! This is my land! Go!" and he turned on us with the energy of a madman and the look of a murderer.

I was so overcome with my physical exertions that I had not a word to say, but simply, in utter weariness, threw myself upon the ground; but Dick, with what voice he could command, said:

"You're a nice grateful fellow to men who have helped you. Keep your find to yourself, man alive; we don't want to share. You must know that as well as I do, unless your luck has driven you mad.

Handle the thing yourself, by all means. Faugh! how filthy it is!" and he too sat down beside me.

It certainly was most filthy. It was a shapeless, irregular mass, but made solid with rust and ooze and the bog surface through which it had been dragged. The slime ran from it in a stream; but its filth had no deterring power for Murdock, who threw himself down beside it and actually kissed the nauseous mass, as he murmured:

"At last, at last, me threasure! All me own!"

Dick stood up with a look of disgust on his handsome face.

"Come away, Art; it's too terrible to see a man degraded to this pitch. Leave the wretch alone with his god." Murdock turned to us, and said with savage glee:

"No, shtay—shtay an' see me threasure! It'll make ye happy to think of afther. An' ye can tell Phelim Joyce what I found in me own land—the land what I tuk from him." We stayed.

Murdock took his spade and began to remove the filth and rubbish from the mass; and in a very few moments his discovery proclaimed itself.

There lay before us a rusty iron gun-carriage. This was what we had dragged with so much effort from the bottom of the bog; and beside it Murdock sat down with a scowl of black disappointment.

"Come away," said Dick. "Poor devil, I pity him! It is hard to find even a god of that kind worthless." And so we turned and left Murdock sitting beside the gun-carriage and the slime, with a look of baffled greed which I hope never to see on any face again.

We went to a brook at the foot of the Hill, Andy being by this time in the sheebeen about half a mile off There we cleansed ourselves as well as we could from the hideous slime and filth of the bog, and then walked to the top of the hill to let the breeze freshen us up a bit if possible. After we had been there for a while, Dick said:

"Now, Art, you had better run back to the cottage. Miss Joyce will be wondering what has become of you all this time, and may be frightened." It was so strange to hear her—Norah, my Norah—called "Miss Joyce," that I could not help smiling, and blushing while I smiled. Dick noticed and guessed the cause. He laid his hand on my shoulder, and said:

"You will hear it often, old lad. I am the only one of all your friends privileged to hear of her by the name you knew her by at first. She goes now into your class and among your own circle; and, by George! she will grace it too—it or any circle—and they will naturally give to her folk the same measure of courtesy that they mete to each other. She is Miss Joyce—until she shall be Mrs. Arthur Severn!"

What a delicious thrill the very thought sent through me! I went up to the cottage, and on entering found Norah still alone. She knew that I was under promise not to tell anything of Murdock's proceedings, but noticing that I was not so tidy as before—for my cleansing at the brook-side was a very imperfect one—went quietly and got a basin with hot water, soap, and a towel, and clothes-brush, and said I must come and be made very tidy.

That toilet was to me a sweet experience, and is a sweet remembrance now. It was so wifely in its purpose and its method that I went through it in a languorous manner, like one in a delicious dream. When, with a blush, she brought me her own brush and comb and began to smooth my hair, I was as happy as it is given to a man to be. There is a peculiar sensitiveness in their hair to some men, and to have it touched by hands that they love is a delicious sensation. When my toilet was complete Norah took me by the hand and made me sit down beside her. After a pause, she said to me with a gathering blush:

"I want to ask you something."

"And I want to ask you something," said I. "Norah, dear, there is one thing I want much to ask you."

She seemed to suspect or guess what I was driving at, for she said:

"You must let me ask mine first."

"No, no," I replied, "you must answer me; and then, you know, you will have the right to ask what you like."

"But I do not want any right."

"Then it will be all the more pleasure to me to give a favour—if there can be any such from me to you."

157

Masculine persistence triumphed—men are always more selfish than women—and I asked my question.

"Norah, darling, tell me when will you be mine—my very own? When shall we be married?"

The love-light was sweet in her eyes as she answered me with a blush that made perfect the smile on her lips:

"Nay, you should have let me ask my question first."

Why so, dearest?"

"Because, dear, I am thinking of the future. You know, Arthur, that I love you, and that whatever you wish I would and shall gladly do; but you must think for me too. I am only a peasant girl—"

"Peasant!" I laughed. "Norah, you are the best lady I have ever seen! Why, you are like a queen—what a queen ought to be!"

"I am proud and happy, Arthur, that you think so; but still I am only a peasant. Look at me—at my dress. Yes, I know you like it, and I shall always prize it because it found favour in your eyes." She smiled happily, but went on:

"Dear, I am speaking very truly. My life and surroundings are not yours. You are lifting me to a higher grade in life, Arthur, and I want to be worthy of it and of you. I do not want any of your family or your friends to pity you and say, 'Poor fellow, he has made a sad mistake. Look at her manners; she is not of us.' I could not bear to hear or to know that such was said—that any one should have to pity the man I love, and to have that pity because of me. Arthur, it would break my heart."

As she spoke the tears welled up in the deep dark eyes and rolled unchecked down her cheeks. I caught her to my breast with the sudden instinct of protection, and cried out:

"Norah, no one on earth could say such a thing of you—you who would lift a man, not lower him. You could not be ungraceful if you tried; and as for my family and friends, if there is one who will not hold out both hands to you and love you, he or she is no kin or friend of mine."

"But, Arthur, they might be right. I have learned enough to

know that there is so much more to learn—that the great world you live in is so different from our quiet, narrow life here. Indeed, I do not mean to be nervous as to the future, or to make any difficulties; but, dear, I should like to be able to do all that is right and necessary as your wife. Remember, that when I leave here I shall not have one of my own kin or friends to tell me anything—from whom I could ask advice. They do not themselves even know what I might want— not one of them all. Your world and mine, dear, are so different—as yet."

"But, Norah, shall I not be always by your side to ask?" I felt very superior and very strong, as well as very loving, as I spoke.

"Yes, yes; but oh, Arthur, can you not understand? I love you so that I would like to be, even in the eyes of others, all that you could wish. But, dear, you must understand and help me here. I cannot reason with you. Even now I feel my lack of knowledge, and it makes me fearful. Even now"—her voice died away in a sob, and she hid her beautiful eyes with her hand.

"My darling, my darling!" I said to her passionately, all the true lover in me awake, "tell me what it is that you wish, so that I may try to judge with all my heart."

"Arthur, I want you to let me go to school—to a good school for a while—a year or two before we are married. Oh, I should work so hard! I should try so earnestly to improve, for I should feel that every hour of honest work brought me higher and nearer to your level!"

My heart was more touched than even my passion gave me words to tell; and I tried, and tried hard, to tell her what I felt, and in my secret heart a remorseful thought went up: "What have I done in my life to be worthy of so much love?"

Then, as we sat hand in hand, we discussed how it was to be done, for that it was to be done we were both agreed. I had told her that we should so arrange it that she should go for awhile to Paris, and then to Dresden, and finish up with an English school. That she could learn languages, and that among them would be Italian; but that she would not go to Italy until we went together—on our honeymoon. She bent her head and listened in silent happiness; and when I spoke of our journey together to Italy, and how we would revel in old-world beauty—in the softness and light and colour of that magic land—the delicate porcelain of her shell-like ear became tinged with pink, and I bent over and kissed it. And then she turned and threw herself on my breast, and hid her face.

As I looked I saw the pink spread downward and grow deeper and deeper, till her neck and all became flushed with crimson. And then she put me aside, rose up, and with big brave eyes looked me full in the face through all her deep embarrassment, and said to me:

"Arthur, of course I don't know much of the great world, but I suppose it is not usual for a man to pay for the schooling of a lady before she is his wife, whatever might be arranged between them afterwards. You know that my dear father has no money for such a purpose as we have spoken of, and so if you think it is wiser, and would be less hardly spoken of in your family, I would marry you before I went—if—if you wished it. But we would wait till after I came from school to—to—to go to Italy," and while the flush deepened almost to a painful degree, she put her hands before her face and turned away.

Such a noble sacrifice of her own feelings and her own wishes— and although I felt it in my heart of hearts I am sure none but a woman could fully understand it—put me upon my mettle, and it was with truth I spoke:

"Norah, if anything could have added to my love and esteem for you, your attitude to me in this matter has done it. My darling, I shall try hard all my life to be worthy of you, and that you may never, through any act of mine, decline for a moment from the standard you have fixed. God knows I could have no greater pride or joy than that this very moment I should call you my wife. My dear, my dear, I shall count the very hours until that happy time shall come! But all shall be as you wish. You will go to the schools we spoke of, and your father shall pay for them. He will not refuse, I know, and what is needed he shall have. If there be any way that he would prefer—that suits your wishes—

it shall be done. More than this, if he thinks it right, we can be married before you go, and you can keep your own name until my time comes to claim you."

"No, no, Arthur! When once I shall bear your name I shall be too proud of it to be willing to have any other. But I want, when I do bear it, to bear it worthily—I want to come to you as I think your wife should come."

"My dear, dear Norah—my wife to be—all shall be as you wish."

Here we heard the footsteps of Joyce approaching.

"I had better tell him," she said.

When he came in she had his dinner ready. He greeted me warmly.

"Won't ye stay?" he said. "Don't go unless ye wish to."

"I think, sir, Norah wants to have a chat with you when you have had your dinner."

Norah smiled a kiss at me as I went out. At the door I turned and said to her:

"I shall be in the Cliff Fields in case I am wanted."

I went there straightway, and sat on the table rock in the centre of the fields, and thought and thought. In all my thoughts there was no cloud. Each day, each hour, seemed to reveal new beauties in the girl I loved, and I felt as if all the world were full of sunshine, and all the future of hope; and I built new resolves to be worthy of the good fortune which had come upon me.

It was not long before Norah came to me, and said that she had told her father, and that he wished to speak with me. She said that he quite agreed about the school, and that there would be no difficulty made by him on account of any false pride about my helping in the task. We had but one sweet minute together on the rock, and one kiss; and then, hand in hand, we hurried back to the cottage, and found Joyce waiting for us, smoking his pipe.

Norah took me inside, and, after kissing her father, came shyly and kissed me also, and went out. Joyce began:

"Me daughter has been tellin' me about the plan of her goin' to school, an' her an' me's agreed that it's the right thing to do. Of coorse, we're not of your class, an' if ye wish for her it is only right an' fair that she should be brought up to the level of the people that she's goin' into. It's not in me own power to do all this for her, an' although I didn't give her the schoolin' that the quality has, I've done already more nor min like me mostly does. Norah knows more nor any girl about here.

"An' as ye're to have the benefit of yer wife's schoolin', I don't see no rayson why ye shouldn't help in it. Mind ye this, if I could see me way to do it meself, I'd work me arms off before I'd let you or anyone else come between her an' me in such a thing. But it'd be only a poor kind of pride that'd hurt the poor child's feelin's, an' mar her future; an' so it'll be as ye both wish. Ye must find out the schools an' write me about them when ye go back to London." I jumped up and shook his hand.

"Mr. Joyce, I am more delighted than I can tell you; and I promise, on my honour, that you shall never in your life regret what you have done."

"I'm sure of that—Mr.—Mr.—"

"Call me Arthur."

"Well—I must do it someday—Arthur. An' as to the matther that Norah told me ye shpoke of—that, if I'd wish it, ye'd be married first. Well, me own mind an' Norah's is the same: I'd rather that she come to you as a lady at wance, though, God knows, it's a lady she is in all ways I iver see one in me life—barrin' the clothes."

"That's true, Mr. Joyce; there is no better lady in all the land."

"Well, that's all settled. Ye'll let me know in good time about the schools, won't ye? An' now I must get back to me work," and he passed out of the house, and went up the hillside.

Then Norah came back, and with joy I told her that all had been settled; and somehow, we seemed to have taken another step up the ascent that leads from earth to heaven, and that all feet may tread which are winged with hope.

Presently Norah sent me away for a while, saying that she had

162

some work to do, as she expected both Dick and myself to come back to tea with them; and I went off to look for Dick.

I found him with Murdock. The latter had got over his disappointment, and had evidently made up his mind to trust to Dick's superior knowledge and intelligence. He was feverishly anxious to continue his search, and when I came up we held a long discussion as to the next measure to be taken. The afternoon faded away in this manner before Murdock summed up the matter thus:

"The chist was carried on the gun-carriage, and where wan is th' other is not far off. The min couldn't have carried the chist far, from what ould Moynahan sez. His father saw the min carryin' the chist only a wee bit." Dick said:

"There is one thing, Murdock, that I must warn you about. You have been digging in the clay bank by the edge of the bog. I told you before how dangerous this is; now, more than ever, I see the danger of it. It was only today that we got an idea of the depth of the bog, and it rather frightens me to think that with all this rain falling, you should be tampering with what is more important to you than even the foundations of your house. The bog has risen far too much already, and you have only to dig perhaps one spadeful too much in the right place and you'll have a torrent that will sweep away all you have.

"I have told you that I don't like the locality of your house down in the hollow. If the bog ever moves again, God help you! You seem also to have been tampering with the stream that runs into the Cliff Fields. It is all very well for you to try to injure poor Joyce more than you have done—and that's quite enough, God knows!— but here you are actually imperilling your own safety. That stream is the safety valve of the bog, and if you continue to dam up that cleft in the rock you will have a terrible disaster. Mind, now, I warn you seriously against what you are doing. And, besides, you do not even know for certain that the treasure is here. Why, it may be anywhere on the mountain, from the brook below the boreen to the Cliff Fields. Is the off chance worth the risk you run?" Murdock started when he mentioned the Cliff Fields, and then said suddenly: "If ye're afraid ye can go. I'm not."

"Man alive!" said Dick, "why not be afraid if you see cause for fear? I don't suppose I'm a coward any more than you are, but I can see a danger, and a very distinct one, from what you are doing. Your house is directly in the track in which the bog has shifted at any time this hundred years; and if there should be another movement, I would not like to be in the house when the time comes."

"All right," he returned, doggedly, "I'll take me chance; and I I'll find the threasure, too, before many days is over!"

"Well, but be reasonable also, or you may find your death."

"Well, if I do that's me own luk out. Ye may find yer death first."

"Of course I may, but I see it my duty to warn you. The weather these last few weeks back has been unusually wet. The bog is rising as it is. As a matter of fact, it is nearly a foot higher now than it was when I came here first; and yet you are doing what must help to rise it higher still, and are weakening its walls at the same time." He scowled at me as he sullenly answered:

"Well, all I say is I'll do as I like wid me own. I wouldn't give up me chance iv findin' the threasure now—no, not for God himself!"

"Hush, man; hush!" said Dick sternly, as we turned away. "Do not tempt him, but be warned in time!"

"Let him look out for himself, an' I'll look out for meself," he answered with a sneer. "I'll find the threasure, an', if need be, in spite iv God an' iv the Divil too!"

## CHAPTER 13

### MURDOCH'S WOOING

I think it was a real pleasure to Dick to get Norah's message that he was expected to tea that evening. Like the rest of his sex, he was not quite free from vanity; for when I told him, his first act was to look down at himself ruefully, and his first words were:

"But I say, old lad, look at the mess I'm in! and these clothes are not much, anyhow."

"Never mind, Dick, you are as good as I am."

"Oh, well," he laughed, "if you'll do, I suppose I needn't mind. We're both pretty untidy. No, begad!" he added, looking me all over, "you're not out of the perpendicular with regard to cleanliness, anyhow. I say, Art, who's been tidying you up? Oh, I see!—forgive me, old lad—and quite natural, too! Miss Joyce should see you blush, Art! Why, you are as rosy as a girl!"

"Call her 'Norah,' Dick; it is more natural, and I am sure she will like it better. She is to look on you as a brother, you know."

"All right, Art," he answered, heartily, "but you must manage it for me, for I think I should be alarmed to do so unless I got a lead; but it will come easy enough after the first go off. Remember, we both always thought of her as 'Norah.'"

We went down towards the brook and met with Andy, who had the car all ready for us.

"Begor yer 'an'rs," said he, "I thought yez was lost intirely, or that the fairies had carried yez off, both iv yez this time"—this with a sly look at me, followed by a portentous wink to Dick; "an' I'm thinkin' it's about time fur somethin' to ate. Begor, but me stummick is cryin' out that me throat is cut!"

"You're quite right, Andy, as to the fact," said Dick, "but you are a little antecedent."

"An' now what's that, surr? Begor, I niver was called that name afore. Shure, an' I always thry to be dacent; divvle a man but can tell ye that. Antidacent, indeed! Well, now, what nixt?"

"It means, Andy, that we are going to be carried off by the fairies, and to have some supper with them too; and that you are to take this half-crown, and go over to Mother Kelligan's, and get her to try to dissipate that unnatural suspicion of capital offence wreaked on your thoracic region. Here, catch! and see how soon you can be off."

"Hurroo! Begor, yer 'an'r, it's the larned gintleman y' are! Musha! but ye ought to be a counsillor intirely. Gee-up, ye ould corn-crake!" and Andy was off at full speed.

When we had got rid of him, Dick and I went down to the brook and made ourselves look as tidy as we could. At least Dick did; for, as to myself, I purposely disarranged my hair—unknown to Dick— in the hope that Norah would take me in hand again, and that I might once more experience the delicious sensation of a toilet aided by her sweet fingers.

Young men's ideas, however, are very crude; no one who knew either the sex or the world would have fallen into such an absurd hope. When I came in with Dick, Norah—in spite of some marked hints, privately and secretly given to her—did not make either the slightest remark on my appearance or the faintest suggestion as to improving it.

She had not been idle in the afternoon. The room, which was always tidy, was as prettily arranged as the materials would allow. There were some flowers and flag-leaves and grasses tastefully placed about, and on the table in a tumbler was a bunch of scarlet poppies. The tablecloth, although of coarse material, was as white as snow, and the plates and cups, of common white and blue, were all that was required.

When Joyce came in from his bedroom, where he had been tidying himself, he looked so manly and handsome in his dark frieze coat with horn buttons, his wide, unstarched shirt-collar, striped waistcoat, and cord breeches, with gray stockings, that I felt quite proud of him. There was a natural grace and dignity about him which suited him so well, that I had no wish to see him other than a peasant. He became the station, and there was no pretence. He made a rough kind of apology to us both:

"I fear ye'll find things a bit rough, compared with what you're accustomed to, but I know ye'll not mind. We have hardly got settled down here yit; and me sisther, who always fixes with us, is away with me other sisther that is sick, so Norah has to fare by herself; but, gentlemen both—you, Mr. Sutherland, and you, Arthur—you're welcome."

We sat down to table, and Norah insisted on doing all the attendance herself. I wanted to help her, and, when she was taking up a plate of cakes from the hearth, stooped beside her and said:

"May not I help, Norah? Do let me!"

"No—no, dear," she whispered. "Don't ask me now—I'm a little strange yet—another time. You'll be very good, won't you, and help me not to feel awkward?"

Needless to say, I sat at table for the rest of the meal and feasted my eyes on my darling, while, in common with the others, I enjoyed the good things placed before us. But when she saw that I looked too long and too lovingly, she gave me such an imploring glance from her eloquent eyes, that for the remainder of the time I restrained both the ardour of my glance and its quantity within modest bounds.

Oh, but she was fair and sweet to look upon! Her dark hair was plainly combed back and coiled modestly round her lovely head. She had on her red petticoat and chintz body, that she knew I admired so much; and on her breast she wore a great scarlet poppy, whose splendid colour suited well with her dark and noble beauty. At the earliest opportunity, when tea was over, I whispered to her:

"My darling, how well the poppy suits you. How beautiful you are. You are like the Goddess of Sleep!" She put her finger to her lips with a happy smile, as though to forbid me to pay compliments— before others. I suppose the woman has never yet been born—and never shall be—who would not like to hear her praises from the man she loves.

I had eaten potato-cakes before, but never such as Norah had made for us; possibly they seemed so good to me because I knew that her hands had made them. The honey, too, was the nicest I had tasted—for it was made by Norah's bees. The butter was perfect—for it was the work of her hands!

I do not think that a happier party ever assembled round a tea-table. Joyce was now quite reconciled to the loss of his daughter, and was beaming all over; and Dick's loyal nature had its own reward, for he too was happy in the happiness of those he loved—or else I was, and am, the most obtuse fool, and he the most consummate actor, that has been. As for Norah and myself, I know we were happy—as happy as it is given to mortals to be.

When tea was over, and Norah fetched her father's pipe and lighted it for him, she said to me with a sweet blush, as she called me by my name for the first time before a stranger:

"I suppose, Arthur, you and Mr. Sutherland would like your own cigars best; but if you care for a pipe there are some new ones here," and she pointed them out. We lit our cigars, and sat round the fire; for in this damp weather the nights were getting a little chilly. Joyce sat on one side of the fire and Dick on the other. I sat next to Dick, and Norah took her place between her father and me, sitting on a little stool beside her father and leaning her head against his knees, while she took the hand that was fondly laid over her shoulder and held it in her own. Presently, as the gray autumn twilight died away, and as the light from the turf-fire rose and fell, throwing protecting shadows, her other hand stole towards my own, which was waiting to receive it; and we sat silent for a spell, Norah and I in an ecstasy of quiet happiness.

By-and-by we heard a click at the latch of the gate, and firm, heavy footsteps coming up the path. Norah jumped up and peeped out of the window.

"Who is it, daughter?" said Joyce.

"Oh father, it is Murdock! What can he want?"

There was a knock at the door. Joyce rose up, motioning to us to sit still, laid aside his pipe, and went to the door and opened it. Every word that was spoken was perfectly plain to us all.

"Good-evenin', Phelim Joyce."

"Good-evenin'. You want me?"

"I do." Murdock's voice was fixed and firm, as of one who has made up his mind.

"What is it?"

"May I come in? I want to shpake to ye particular."

"No, Murtagh Murdock. Whin a man comes undher me roof by me own consint, I'm not free wid him to spake me mind the

same as whin he's outside. Ye haven't thrated me well, Murdock,
Ye've been hard wid me; and there's much that I can't forgive!"

"Well! if I did, ye gev me what no other man has ever gave
me yit widout repintin' it sore. Ye sthruck me a blow before all
the people, an' I didn't strike ye back."

"I did, Murtagh; an' I'm sorry for it. That blow has been
hangin' on me conscience iver since. I would take it back if I
could; God knows that is thrue. Much as ye wronged me, I don't
want such a thing as that to remimber when me eyes is closin'.
Murtagh Murdock, I take it back, an' gladly. Will ye let me?"

"I will—on wan condition."

"What is it?"

"That's what I've kem here to shpake about; but I'd like to
go in."

"No, ye can't do that—not yit, at any rate, till I know what
ye want. Ye must remimber, Murtagh, that I've but small rayson
to thrust ye."

"Well, Phelim, I'll tell ye, tho' it's mortial hard to name it
shtandin' widout the door like a thramp. I'm a warrum man; I've
a power iv money put by, an' it brings me in much."

"I know! I know!" said the other bitterly. "God help me! but
I know too well how it was gother up."

"Well, niver mind that now; we all know that. Anyhow, it is
gother up. An' them as finds most fault wid the manes, mayhap
'd be the first to get hould iv it av they could. Well, anyhow, I'm
warrum enough to ask any girrul in these parts to share it wid
me. There's many min and weemin between this and Galway,
that'd like to talk over the fortin iv their daughter wid Murtagh
Murdock, for all he's a gombeen man."

As he spoke the clasp of Norah's hand and mine grew closer.
I could feel in her clasp both a clinging, as for protection, and a
restraining power on myself Murdock went on:

"But there's none of thim girls what I've set me harrt on—
except wan!" He paused. Joyce said, quietly:

"An' who, now, might that be?"

"Yer own daughther, Norah Joyce!" Norah's hand restrained

169

me as I was instinctively rising.

"Go on!" said Joyce, and I could notice that there was a suppressed passion in his voice.

"Well, I've set me harrt on her; and I'm willin' to settle a fortin on her, on wan condition."

"And what, now, might that be?"—the tone was of veiled sarcasm.

"She'll have all the money that I settle on her to dale wid as she likes—that is, the intherest iv it—as long as she lives; an' I'm to have the Cliff Fields that is her's, as me own to do what I like wid, an' that them an' all in them belongs to me." Joyce paused a moment before answering:

"Is that all ye have to say?" Murdock seemed nonplussed, but after a slight pause he answered:

"Yis."

"An' ye want me answer?"

"Iv coorse!"

"Thin, Murtagh Murdock, I'd like to ask ye for why me daughter would marry you or the like of you? Is it because that yer beauty d take a young girl's fancy—you, that's known as the likest thing to a divil in these parts? Or is it because of yer kind nature? You that tried to ruin her own father, and that drove both her and him out of the home she was born in, and where her poor mother died! Is it because yer characther is respicted in the counthry wheriver yer name is known?—" Here Murdock interrupted him:

"I tould ye it's a warrum man I am"—he spoke decisively, as if his words were final—"an' I can, an' will, settle a fortin on her." Joyce answered slowly, and with infinite scorn:

"Thank ye Mr. Murtagh Murdock, but me daughter is not for sale!"

There was a long pause. Then Murdock spoke again, and both suppressed hate and anger were in his voice:

"Ye had bether have a care wid me. I've crushed ye wance, an' I'll crush ye agin! Ye can shpake scornful yerself, but mayhap the girrul would give a different answer."

"Then, ye had better hear her answer from herself. Norah! Come here, daughter; come here!"

Norah rose, making an imperative sign to me to keep my seat, and with the bearing of an empress passed across to the door and beside her father. She took no notice whatever of her wooer.

"What is it, father?"

"Now, Murdock, spake away! Say what ye have to say; an' take yer answer from her own lips." Murdock spoke with manifest embarrassment:

"I've been tellin' yer father that I'd like ye for me wife."

"I've heard all you said."

"An' yer answer?"

"My father has answered for me."

"But I want me answer from yer own lips. My, but it's the handsome girrul ye are this night!"

"My answer is 'No!'" and she turned to come back.

"Shtay!" Murdock's voice was nasty, so nasty that instinctively I stood up. No person should speak like that to the woman I loved. Norah stopped. "I suppose ye won't luk at me because ye have a young shpark on yer hands. I'm no fool, an' I know why ye've been down in the fields! I seen yez both more nor wance; an' I'm makin' me offer knowin' what I know. I don't want to be too hard on ye, an' I'll say nothin' if ye don't dhrive me to. But remimber ye're in me power; an' ye've got to plase me in wan way or another. I knew what I was doin' whin I watched ye wid yer young shpark! Ye didn't want yer father to see him nigh the house! Ye'd better be careful, the both of ye. If ye don't intind to marry me, well, ye won't; but mind how ye thrate me or shpake to me, here or where there's others by; or be th'Almighty, I'll send the ugly whisper round the counthry about ye—"

Flesh and blood could not stand this. In an instant I was out in the porch and ready to fly at his throat; but Norah put her arm between us.

"Mr. Severn," she said, in a voice which there was no gainsaying, "my father is here. It is for him to protect me here, if any protection is required from a thing like that!" The scorn of her voice made even Murdock wince, and seemed to cool both Joyce and myself, and also Dick, who now stood beside us.

Murdock looked from one to another of us for a moment in amazement, and then, with a savage scowl, as though he were looking who and where to strike with venom, he fixed on Norah—God forgive him!

"An' so ye have him at home already, have ye! An' yer father present, too, an' a witness. It's the sharp girrul ye are, Norah Joyce, but I suppose this wan is not the first." I restrained myself simply because Norah's hand was laid on my mouth. Murdock went on:

"An' so ye thought I wanted ye for yerself! Oh no! It's no bankrup's daughther for me; but I may as well tell ye why I wanted ye. It was because I've had in me hands, wan time or another, ivery inch iv this mountain, bit be bit, all except the Cliff Fields; and thim I wanted for purposes iv me own—thim as knows why, has swore not to tell"—this with a scowl at Dick and me. "But I'll have thim yit; an' have thim, too, widout thinkin' that me wife likes sthrollin' there wid sthrange min!"

Here I could restrain myself no longer; and to my joy on the instant—and since then whenever I have thought of it—Norah withdrew her hand as if to set me free. I stepped forward, and with one blow fair in the lips knocked the foul-mouthed ruffian head over heels. He rose in an instant, his face covered with blood, and rushed at me. This time I stepped out, and with an old foot-ball trick, taking him on the breastbone with my open hand, again tumbled him over.

He arose livid—but this time his passion was cold—and standing some yards off, said, while he wiped the blood from his face:

"Wait; ye'll be sorry yit ye shtruck that blow! Aye, ye'll both be sorry—sad an' sorry—an' for shame that ye don't reckon on. Wait!" I spoke out:

"Wait! yes, I shall wait, but only till the time comes to punish you. And let me warn you to be careful how you speak of this lady. I have shown you already how I can deal with you personally; next time—if there be a next time—" Here Murdock interrupted *sotto voce:*

"There'll be a next time; don't fear! Be God, but there will!" I went on:

"I shall not dirty my hands with you, but I shall have you in jail for slander."

"Jail me, is it?" he sneered. "We'll see. An' so ye think ye're going to marry a lady, whin ye make an honest woman iv Norah Joyce, do ye? Luk at her! an' it's a lady ye're goin' to make iv her, is it? An' thim hands iv hers, wid the marks iv the milkin' an' the shpade onto them. My! but they'll luk well among the quality, won't they?" I was going to strike him again, but Norah laid her hand on my arm; so, smothering my anger as well as I could, I said:

"Don't dare to speak ill of people whose shoes you are not worthy to black; and be quick about your finishing your work at Shleenanaher, for you've got to go when the time is up. I won't have the place polluted by your presence a day longer than I can help."

Norah looked wonderingly at me and at him, for he had given a manifest start. I went on:

"And as for these hands"—I took Norah's hands in mine—"perhaps the time may come when you will pray for the help of their honest strength—pray with all the energy of your dastard soul! But whether this may be or not, take you care how you cross her path or mine again, or you shall rue it to the last hour of your life. Come, Norah, it is not fit that you should contaminate your eyes or your ears with the presence of this wretch!" and I led her in. As we went I heard Joyce say:

"An' listen to me: niver you dare to put one foot across me mearin' again, or I'll take the law into me own hands!" Then Dick spoke:

"And hark you, Mr. Murdock: remember that you have to deal with me also in any evil that you attempt!" Murdock turned on him savagely:

"'As for you, I dismiss ye from me imploymint. Ye'll niver set foot on me land agin! Away wid ye!"

"Hurrah!" shouted Dick. "Mr. Joyce, you're my witness that he has discharged me, and I am free." Then he stepped down from the porch, and said to Murdock, in as exasperating a way as he could:

"And, dear Mr. Murdock, wouldn't it be a pleasure to you to have it out with me here, now? Just a simple round or two, to see which is the best man? I am sure it would do you good—and me too. I can see you are simply spoiling for a fight. I promise you that there will be no legal consequences if you beat me, and if I beat you I shall take my chance. Do let me persuade you! Just one round;" and he began to take off his coat. Joyce, however, stopped him, speaking gravely:

"No, Mr. Sutherland, not here; and let me warn ye, for ye're a younger man nor me, agin such anger. I sthruck that man wance, an' it's sorry I am for that same! No; not that I'm afeered of him"— answering the query in Dick's face—"but because, for a full-grown man to sthrike in anger is a sarious thing. Arthur there sthruck not for himself, but for an affront to his wife that's promised, an' he's not to be blamed." Norah here took my arm and held it tight; "but I say, wid that one blow that I've sthruck since I was a lad on me mind, Never sthrike a blow in anger all yer life long, unless it be to purtect one ye love.'" Dick turned to him, and said, heartily:

"You're quite right, Mr. Joyce, and I'm afraid I acted like a cad. Here, you clear off! Your very presence seems to infect better men than yourself, and brings them something nearer to your level. Mr. Joyce, forgive me; I promise I'll take your good lesson to heart."

They both came into the room; and Norah and I looking out of the window—my arm being around her—saw Murdock pass down the path and out at the gate.

We all took our places once again around the fire. When we sat down Norah instinctively put her hands behind her, as if to hide them—that ruffian's words had stung her a little; and as I looked, without, however, pretending to take any notice,

I ground my teeth. But with Norah such an ignoble thought could be but a passing one. With a quick blush she laid her hand open on my knee, so that, as the firelight fell on it, it was shown in all its sterling beauty. I thought the opportunity was a fair one, and I lifted it to my lips and said:

"Norah, I think I may say a word before your father and my friend. This hand—this beautiful hand," and I kissed it again, "is dearer to me a thousand times, because it can do, and has done, honest work; and I only hope that in all my life I may be worthy of it." I was about to kiss it yet again, but Norah drew it gently away. Then she shifted her stool a little, and came closer to me. Her father saw the movement, and said simply:

"Go to him, daughter. He is worth it—he sthruck a good blow for ye this night." And so we changed places, and she leaned her head against my knee; her other hand—the one not held in mine—rested on her father's knee.

There we sat and smoked, and talked for an hour or more. Then Dick looked at me and I at him, and we rose. Norah looked at me lovingly as we got our hats. Her father saw the look, and said:

"Come, daughter; if you're not tired, suppose we see them down the boreen."

A bright smile and a blush came in her face; she threw a shawl over her head, and we went all together. She held her father's arm and mine; but by-and-by the lane narrowed, and her father went in front with Dick, and we two followed.

Was it to be wondered at, if we did lag a little behind them, and if we spoke in whispers? Or, if now and again, when the lane curved and kindly bushes projecting threw dark shadows, our lips met?

When we came to the open space before the gate we found Andy. He pretended to see only Dick and Joyce, and saluted them.

"Begor, but it's the fine night, it is, Misther Dick, though more betoken the rain is comin' on agin soon. A fine night, Misther Joyce; and how's Miss Norah?—God bless her! Musha!

175

but it's sorry I am that she didn't walk down wid ye this fine night! An' poor Masther Art—I suppose the fairies has got him agin?" Here he pretended to just catch sight of me. "Yer 'an'r, but it's the sorraful man I was; shure, an' I thought ye was tuk aff be the fairies—or, mayhap, it was houldin' a leprachaun that ye wor. An' my! but there's Miss Norah, too, comin' to take care iv her father! God bless ye. Miss Norah, acushla, but it's glad I am to see ye!"

"And I'm always glad to see you, Andy," she said, and shook hands with him.

Andy took her aside, and said, in a *staccato* whisper intended for us all:

"Musha! Miss Norah, dear, may I ax ye somethin?"

"Indeed you may, Andy. What is it?"

"Well, now, it's throubled in me mind I am about Masther Art—that young gintleman beyant ye, talkin' t' yer father;" the hypocritical villain pointed me out, as though she did not know me. I could see in the moonlight the happy smile on her face as she turned towards me.

"Yes; I see him," she answered.

"Well, Miss Norah, the fairies got him on the top iv Knock-nacar, and ivir since he's been wandherin' round lukin' fur wan iv thim. I thried to timpt him away be tellin' him iv nice girruls iv these parts—real girruls, not fairies. But he's that obstinate he wouldn't luk at wan iv thim—no, nor listen to me, ayther."

"Indeed!" she said, her eyes dancing with fun.

"An', Miss Norah, dear, what kind iv a girrul d'ye think he wanted to find?"

"I don't know, Andy. What kind?"

"Oh, begor! but it's meself can tell ye! Shure, it's a long, yalla, dark girrul, shtreaky—like—like he knows what—not quite a faymale nagur, wid a rid petticoat, an' a quare kind iv an eye!"

"Oh, Andy!" was all she said, as she turned to me smiling.

"Get along, you villain!" said I, and I shook my fist at him in fun; and then I took Norah aside, and told her what the "quare kind iv an eye" was that I had sought—and found.

Then we two said "Goodnight" in peace, while the others in front went through the gate. We took—afterwards—a formal and perfectly decorous farewell, only shaking hands all round, before Dick and I mounted the car. Andy started off at a gallop, and his "Git up, ye ould corn-crake!" was lost in our shouts of "Goodbye!" as we waved our hats. Looking back, we saw Norah's hands waving as she stood with her father's arm around her, and her head laid back against his shoulder, while the yellow moonlight bathed them from head to foot in a sea of celestial light.

And then we sped on through the moonlight and the darkness alike, for the clouds of the coming rain rolled thick and fast across the sky.

But for me the air was all aglow with rosy light, and the car was a chariot flying swiftly to the dawn!

## Chapter 14

### A Trip to Paris

The next day was Sunday; and after church I came over early to Knockcalltecrore, and had a long talk with Norah about her school project. We decided that the sooner she began the better—she because, as she at first alleged, every month of delay made school a less suitable place for her—I because, as I took care not only to allege but to reiterate, as the period had to be put in, the sooner it was begun the sooner it would end, and so the sooner would my happiness come.

Norah was very sweet, and shyly told me that if such was my decided opinion, she must say that she too had something of the same view.

"I do not want you to be pained, dear, by any delay," she said, "made by your having been so good to me; and I love you too well to want myself to wait longer than is necessary;" an admission that was an intoxicating pleasure to me.

We agreed that our engagement was, if not to be kept a secret, at least not to be spoken of unnecessarily. Her father was to tell her immediate relatives, so that there would not be any gossip at her absence, and I was to tell one or two of my own connections—for I had no immediate relatives—and perhaps one or two friends who were rather more closely connected with me than those of my own blood. I asked to be allowed to tell also my solicitor, who was an old friend of my father's, and who had always had more than merely professional relations with me. I had reasons of my own for telling him of the purposed change in my life, for I had important matters to execute through him, so as to protect Norah's future in case my own death should occur before the marriage was to take place. But of this, of course, I did not tell her.

We had a happy morning together, and when Joyce came in we told him of the conclusion we had arrived at. He fully acquiesced; and then, when he and I were alone, I asked him if he would prefer to make the arrangements about the schools himself or by some solicitor he would name, or that should all be done by my solicitor. He told me that my London solicitor would probably know what to do better than anyone in his own part of the world; and we agreed that I was to arrange it with him.

Accordingly I settled with Norah that the next day but one I should leave for London, and that when I had put everything on a satisfactory footing I should return to Carnaclif, and so be for a little longer able to see my darling. Then I went back to the hotel to write my letters in time for the post.

That afternoon I wrote to my solicitor, Mr. Chapman, and asked him to have inquiries made, without the least delay, as to what was the best school in Paris to which to send a young lady, almost grown up, but whose education had been neglected. I added that I should be myself in London within two days of my letter, and would hope to have the information.

That evening I had a long talk on affairs with Dick, and opened to him a project I had formed regarding Knockcalltecrore. This was that I should try to buy the whole of the mountain, right away from where the sandy peninsula united it to the main-land, for evidently it had ages ago been an isolated sea-girt rock-bound island. Dick knew that already we held a large part of it—Norah the Cliff Fields, Joyce the upper land on the sea side, and myself the part that I had already bought from Murdock. He quite fell in with the idea, and as we talked it over he grew more and more enthusiastic.

"Why, my dear fellow," he said, as he stood up and walked about the room, "it will make the most lovely residence in the world, and will be a fine investment for you. Holding long leases, you will easily be able to buy the freehold, and then every penny spent will return manifold. Let us once be able to find the springs that feed the bog, and get them in hand, and we can make the place a paradise. The springs are evidently high up on the Hill, so that we can not only get water for irrigating and ornamental purposes, but we can get power also!

"Why, you can have electric light, and everything else you like, at the smallest cost. And if it be, as I suspect, that there is a streak of limestone in the Hill, the place might be a positive mine of wealth as well! We have not lime within fifty miles, and if once we can quarry the stone here we can do anything. We can build a harbour on the south side, which would be the loveliest place to keep a yacht in that ever was known—quite big enough for anything in these parts—as safe as Portsmouth, and of fathomless depth."

"Easy, old man!" I cried, for the idea made me excited too.

"But I assure you, Art, I am within the truth."

"I know it, Dick; and now I want to come to business."

"Eh! how do you mean?" he said, looking puzzled.

Then I told him of the school project, and that I was going to London after another day to arrange it. He was delighted, and quite approved.

"It is the wisest thing I ever heard of!" was his comment. "But how do you mean about business?" he asked.

"Dick, this has all to be done; and it needs someone to do it. I am not a scientist nor an engineer, and this project wants the aid of both, or of one man who is the two. Will you do it for me—and for Norah?"

He seemed staggered for a moment, but said heartily:

"That I will; but it will take some time."

"We can do it within two years," I answered, "and that is the time that Norah will be away. It will help to pass it;" and I sighed.

"A long time, indeed, but oh, what a time, Art! Just fancy what you are waiting for; there need be no unhappy moment, please God, in all those months."

Then I made him a proposition, to which he, saying that my offer was too good, at first demurred. I reasoned with him, and told him that the amount was little to me, as, thanks to my great aunt, I had more than I ever could use; and that I wanted to make Norah's country-home a paradise on earth, so far as love and work and the means at command could do it; that it would take up all Dick's time, and keep him for the whole period from pursuing his studies; and that he would have to be manager as well as engineer, and would have to buy the land for me. I told him also my secret hope that in time he would take all my affairs in hand and manage everything for me.

"Buying the land will, I fancy, be easy enough," he said. "Two of the farms are in the market now, and all round here land is literally going a-begging. However, I shall take the matter in hand at once, and write you to London, in case there should be anything before you get back." And thus we settled that night that I was, if possible, to buy the whole mountain. I wrote by the next post to Mr. Caicy, telling him that I had a project of purchase in hand, and that Mr. Sutherland would do everything for me during my absence, and that whatever he wished was to be done. I asked him to come over and see Dick before the week was out.

The next day I spoke to Joyce, and asked him if he would care to sell me the lease of the land he now held. He seemed rejoiced at the chance of being able to get away.

"I will go gladly, though, sure enough, I'll be sad for awhile to lave the shpot where I was born, and where I've lived all me life. But whin Norah is gone—an' sure she'll never be back, for

I'm thinkin' that after her school ye'll want to get married at once—"

"That we shall!" I interrupted.

"An' right enough too. But widout her the place will be that lonesome that I don't think I could a-bear it! Me sister'll go over to Knocknacar to live wid me married sister there, that'll be only too happy to have her with her; and I'll go over to Glasgow, where Eugene is at work. The boy wants me to come, and whin I wrote and tould him of Norah's engagement, he wrote at once askin' me to lave the Hill and come to him. He says that before the year is out he hopes to be able to keep himself—and me, too, if we should want it; an' he wrote such a nice letter to Norah—but the girl will like to tell ye about that herself. I can't sell ye the Cliff Fields meself, for they belong to Norah; but if ye like to ask her I'm sure she'll make no objection."

"I should be glad to have them," I said, "but all shall be hers in two years."

And then and there we arranged for the sale of the property. I made Joyce the offer; he accepted at once, but said it was more than it was worth.

"No," said I, "I shall take the chance. I intend to make improvements."

Norah did not make any objection to her father selling the Cliff Fields. She told me that as I wanted to have them, I might, of course; but she hoped I would never sell the spot, as it was very dear to her. I assured her that in this, as in all other matters, I would do as she wished, and we sealed the assurance with—never mind; we sealed it.

I spent the afternoon there, for it was to be my last afternoon with Norah until I came back from Paris. We went down for a while to the Cliff Fields, and sat on the table rock and talked over all our plans. I told her I had a scheme regarding Knockcalltecrore, but that I did not wish to tell her about it, as it was to be a surprise. It needed a pretty hard struggle to be able to keep her in the dark even to this extent—there is nothing more sweet to young lovers than to share a secret. She knew that my wishes were all for her, and was content.

When we got back to the cottage I said goodbye. This naturally took some time—a first goodbye always does—and went home to get my traps packed ready for an early start in the morning, more especially as I wished, when in Galway, to give Mr. Caicy instructions as to transferring the two properties— Norah's and her father's.

When Dick came home he and I had a long talk on affairs, and I saw that he thoroughly understood all about the purchase of the whole mountain. Then we said goodnight, and I retired.

I did not sleep very well. I think I was too happy; and out of the completeness of my happiness there seemed to grow a fear—some dim, haunting dread of a change—something which would reverse the existing order of things. And so in dreams the Drowsy God played at ball with me: now throwing me to a dizzy height of joy, and then, as I fell swiftly through darkness, arresting my flight into the nether gloom with some new sweet hope. It seemed to me that I was awake all the night; and yet I knew I must have slept, for I had distinct recollections of dreams in which all the persons and circumstances lately present to my mind were strangely jumbled together.

The jumble was kaleidoscopic; there was an endless succession of its phases, but the pieces all remained the same. There were moments when all seemed aglow with rosy light, and hard on them others horrid with the gloom of despair or fear; but in all the dominating idea was the mountain standing against the sunset, always as the embodiment of the ruling emotion of the scene, and always Norah's beautiful eyes shone upon me. I seemed to live over again in isolated moments all the past weeks; but in such a way that the legends and myths and stories of Knockcalltecrore which I had heard were embodied in each moment. Thus, Murdock had always a part in the gloomy scenes, and got inextricably mixed up with the King of the Snakes. They freely exchanged personalities, and at one time I could see the Gombeen Man defying St. Patrick, while at another the Serpent seemed to be struggling with Joyce, and, after twisting round the mountain, being only beaten off by a mighty blow from Norah's father, rushing to the sea through the Shleenanaher.

Towards morning, as I suppose the needs of the waking day became more present to my mind in the gradual process of awakening, the bent of my thoughts began to be more practical; the Saint and His Majesty of the Serpents began to disappear, and the two dim cuirassiers, who, with the money-chest, had through the earlier hours of the night been passing far athwart my dreams, appearing and disappearing equally mysteriously, took a more prominent, or, perhaps, a more real part.

Then I seemed to see Murdock working in a grave, whose sides were ever crumbling in as he frantically sought the treasure-chest, while the gun-carriage, rank with the slime of the bog, was high above him on the brink of the grave, projected blackly against the yellow moon. Every time this scene in its myriad variations came round, it changed to one where the sides of the grave began to tumble in, and Murdock in terror tried to scream out, but could make no sound, nor could he make any effort to approach Norah, whose strong hands were stretched out to aid him.

With such a preparation for waking, is it any wonder that I suddenly started broad awake, with a strong sense of something forgotten, and found that it was four o'clock, and time to get ready for my journey? I did not lose any time, and after a hot cup of tea, which the cheery Mrs. Keating had herself prepared for me, was on my way under Andy's care to Recess, where we were to meet the "long-car" to Galway.

Andy was, for a wonder, silent, and as I myself felt in a most active frame of mind, this rather gave me an opportunity for some amusement. I waited for a while to see if he would suggest any topic in his usual style; but as there was no sign of a change, 1 began:

"You are very silent today, Andy. You are sad. What is it?"

"I'm thinkin'."

"So I thought, Andy. But who are you thinking of?"

"Faix, I'm thinkin' iv poor Miss Norah there wid ne'er a bhoy

183

on the flure at all, at all; an' iv the fairy girrul at Knocknacar—the poor craythur waitin' for some kind iv a leprachaun to come back to her. They do say, yer 'an'r, that the fairies is mighty fond iv thim leprachauns intirely. Musha! but it's a quare thing that weemen of all natures thinks a power more iv minkind what is hard to be caught nor iv them that follys them an' is had aisy!"

"Indeed, Andy." I felt he was getting on dangerous ground, and thought it would be as well to keep him to generalities if I could.

"Shure, they do tell me so; that the girruls, whether fairies or weemin, is more fond iv lukin' out fur leprachauns, or min, if that's their kind, than the clargy is iv killin' the divil—an' they've bin at him fur thousands iv years, an' him not turned a hair."

"Well, Andy, isn't it only natural, too? If we look at the girls and make love to them, why shouldn't they have a turn too, poor things, and make love to us? Now you would like to have a wife, I know; only that you're too much afraid of any woman."

"Thrue for ye! But shure an' how could I go dhrivin' about the counthry av I had a wife iv me own in wan place? It's meself that's welkim everywhere, jist because any wan iv the weemen might fear I'd turn the laugh on her whin I got her home; but a car-dhriver can no more shpake soft to only wan girrul nor he can dhrive his car in his own shanty."

"Well, but, Andy, what would you do if you were to get married?"

"Faix, surr, an' the woman must settle that whin she comes. But, begor, it's not for a poor man like me—nor for the likes iv me—that the fairies does be keepin' their eyes out. I tell yer 'an'r that poor min isn't iv much account anyhow! Shure, poverty is the worst iv crimes; an' there's no hidin' it like th' others. Patches is saw a mighty far way off; and, shure enough, they're more frightfuller nor even the polis!"

"By George, Andy," said I, "I'm afraid you're a cynic."

"A cynic, surr; an', faix, what sin am I up to now?"

"You say poverty is a crime."

"Begor, but it's worse! Most crimes is forgave afther a bit;

an' the law is done wid ye whin ye're atin' yer skilly. But there's some people—aye! an' lashins iv thim too—what'd rather see ye in a good shute iv coffin than in a bad shute iv clothes!"

"Why, Andy, you're quite a philosopher!"

"Bedad, that's quare; but whisper me now, surr, what kind iv a thing's that?"

"Well, it's a very wise man—one who loves wisdom."

"Begor, yer 'an'r, lovin' girruls is more in my shtyle; but I thought maybe it was some new kind iv a Protestan'."

"Why a Protestant?"

"Sorra wan iv me knows! I thought maybe they can believe even less nor the ould wans."

Andy's method of theological argument was quite too difficult for me, so I was silent; but my companion was not. He, however, evidently felt that theological disquisition was no more his *forte* than my own, for he instantly changed to another topic:

"I'll be goin' back to Knockcalltecrore tomorra, yer 'an'r. I've been tould to call fur Mr. Caicy, th' attorney—savin' yer prisence— to take him back to Carnaclif. Is there any missage ye'd like to send to any wan?" He looked at me so slyly that his meaning was quite obvious.

"Thanks, Andy, but I think not, unless you tell Mr. Dick that we have had a pleasant journey this morning."

"Nothin' but that?—to nobody?"

"Who to, for instance, Andy?"

"There's Miss Norah, now. Shure girruls is always fond iv gettin' missages, an' most iv all from people what they're not fond iv!"

"Meaning me?"

"Oh yis, oh yis, if there's wan more nor another what she hates the sight iv, it's yer 'an'r. Shure didn't I notice it in her eye ere yistherday night, beyant at the boreen gate? Faix, but it's a nice eye Miss Norah has. Now, yer 'an'r, wouldn't an eye like that be betther for a young gintleman to luk into, than the quare eye iv yer fairy girrul—the wan that ye wor lukin' for, an' didn't find?"

185

The sly way in which Andy looked at me as he said this was quite indescribable. I have seen sly humour in the looks of children where the transparent simplicity of their purpose was a foil to their manifest intention to pretend to deceive. I have seen the arch glances of pretty young women when their eyes contradicted with resistless force the apparent meaning of their words; but I have never seen any slyness which could rival that of Andy. However, when he had spoken as above, he seemed to have spent the last bolt in his armoury; and for the remainder of the drive to Recess he did not touch again on the topic, or on a kindred one.

When I was in the hotel porch waiting the arrival of the long-car, Andy came up to me:

"What day will I be in Galway for yer 'an'r?"

"How do you mean, Andy? I didn't tell you I was coming back."

Andy laughed a merry, ringing laugh.

"Begor, yer 'an'r, d'ye think there's only wan way iv tellin' things? Musha! but spache'd be a mighty precious kind iv a thing if that was the way."

"But, Andy, is not speech the way to make known what you wish other people to know?"

"Ah, go to God! I'd like to know if ye take it for granted whin ask a girrul a question an' she says 'no', that she manes it, or that she intends ayther that ye should think she manes it. Faix, it'd be a harrd wurrld to live in, if that was so; an' there'd be mighty few widdys in it ayther!"

"Why widows, Andy?"

"Shure, isn't wives the shtuff that widdys is made iv?"

"Oh, I see. I'm learning, Andy—I'm getting on."

"Yis, yer 'an'r. Ye haven't got on the long cap now, but I'm afeerd it's only a leather medal ye'd get as yit. Niver mind, surr! Here's the long-car comin'; an' whin ye tellygraph to Misther Dick to sind me over to Galway fur to bring ye back, I'll luk up Miss Norah an' ax her to condescind to give ye some lessons in the differ betwixt yes' an' no' as shpoke by girruls. I'm

186

tould now, it's a mighty intherestin' kind iv a shtudy for a young gintleman."

There was no answering this Parthian shaft.

"Goodbye, Andy," I said, as I left a sovereign in his hand.

"Good luck, yer 'an'r; though what's the use iv wishin' luck to a man, whin the fairies is wid him?"

The last thing I saw was Andy waving his ragged hat as we passed the curve of the road round the lake before Recess was hidden from our view.

When I got to Galway I found Mr. Caicy waiting for me. He was most hearty in his welcome, and told me that as there was nearly an hour to wait before the starting of the Dublin express, he had luncheon on the table, and that we could discuss our business over it. We accordingly adjourned to his house, and after explaining to him what I wanted done with regard to the purchase of the property at Knockcalltecrore, I told him that Dick knew all the details, and would talk them over with him when he saw him on the next evening.

I began my eastward journey with my inner man in a most comfortable condition. Indeed, I concluded that there was no preparation for a journey like a bottle of "Sneyd's 47"[1] between two. I got to Dublin in time for the night mail, and on the following morning walked into Mr. Chapman's office at half-past ten o'clock.

He had all the necessary information for me; indeed, his zeal and his kindness were such that then and there I opened my heart to him, and was right glad that I had done so when I felt the hearty grasp of his hand as he wished me joy and all good fortune. He was, of course, on the side of prudence. He was my own lawyer and my father's friend, and it was right and fitting that he should be. But it was quite evident that in the background of his musty life there was some old romance—musty old attorneys always have romances—so at least say the books. He entered heartily into my plan, and suggested that, if I chose, he would come with me to see the school and the schoolmis-

1. A type of claret.

187

tress in Paris.

"It will be better, I am sure," he said, "to have an old man like myself with you, and who can in our negotiations speak for her father. Indeed, my dear boy, from being so old a friend of your father's, and having no children of my own, I have almost come to look on you as my son, so it will not be much of an effort to regard Miss Norah as my daughter. The schoolmistress will, in the long-run, be better satisfied with my standing *in loco parentis* than with yours." It was a great relief to me to find my way thus smoothed, for I had half expected some objection or remonstrance on his part. His kind offer was, of course, accepted, and the next morning found us in Paris.

We went to see the school and the schoolmistress. All was arranged as we wished. Mr. Chapman did not forget that Norah wished to have all the extra branches of study, or that I wished to add all that could give a charm to her life. The schoolmistress opened her eyes at the total of Norah's requirements, which Mr. Chapman summed up as "all extras"—the same including the use of a saddle-horse, and visits to the opera and such performances as should be approved of, under the special care and with the special accompaniment of Madame herself.

I could see that for the coming year Norah's lines would lie in pleasant places in so far as Madame Lepecheaux could accomplish it. The date of her coming was to be fixed by letter, and as soon as possible.

Mr. Chapman had suggested that it might be well to arrange with Madame Lepecheaux that Norah should be able to get what clothes she might require, and such matters as are wanted by young ladies of the position which she was entering. The genial French woman quite entered into the idea, but insisted that the representative of Norah's father should come with her to the various *magasins*[2] and himself make arrangements. He could not refuse; and as I was not forbidden by the unsuspecting lady, I came too.

These matters took up some time, and it was not until the

---

2. Stores

fifth day after I had left Connemara that we were able to start on our return journey. We left at night, and after our arrival in the early morning, went, as soon as we had breakfasted, to Mr. Chapman's office to get our letters.

I found two. The first I took to the window to read, where I was hidden behind a curtain, and where I might kiss it without being seen; for although the writing was strange to me—for I had never seen her handwriting—I knew that it was from Norah.

Do any of us who arrive at middle life ever attempt to remember our feelings on receiving the first letter from the woman or the man of our love? Can there come across the long expanse of commonplace life, strewn as it is with lost beliefs and shattered hopes, any echo, any after-glow, of that time, any dim recollection of the thrill of pride and joy that flashed through us at such a moment? Can we rouse ourselves from the creeping lethargy of the contented acceptance of things, and feel the generous life-blood flowing through us once again?

I held Norah's letter in my hand, and it seemed as though with but one more step I should hold my darling herself in my arms. I opened her letter most carefully; anything that her hands had touched was sacred to me. And then her message—the message of her heart to mine—sent direct and without intermediary, reached me:

My Dear Arthur,—I hope you had a good journey, and that you enjoyed your trip to Paris. Father and I are both well, and we have had excellent news of Eugene, who has been promoted to more important work. We have seen Mr. Sutherland every day. He says that everything is going just as you wish it. Mr. Murdock has taken old Bat Moynahan to live with him since you went; they are always together, and Moynahan seems to be always drunk. Father thinks that Mr. Murdock has some purpose on foot, and that it cannot be a good one. We shall all be glad to see you soon again. I am afraid this letter must seem very odd to you; but you know I am not accustomed to writing letters. You must believe one thing: that whatever I say to you, I feel and believe with all my heart. I got your letters, and I cannot tell you what pleasure they gave me, or how I treasure them. Father sends his love and duty. What could I send that words could carry? I may not try yet. Perhaps I shall be more able to do what I wish when I know more.

Norah.

The letter disappointed me. Was any young man ever yet satisfied with written words, when his medium had hitherto been rosy lips, with the added commentary of loving eyes? And yet, when I look back on that letter from a peasant girl, without high education or knowledge of the world, and who had possibly never written a letter before except to her father or brother, or a girl friend, and but few even of these—when I read in every word its simplicity and truth, and recognise the *arrière pensée of* that simple phrase, "Whatever I say to you I feel and think with all my heart," I find it hard to think that any other letter that she or anyone else could have written, could have been more suitable, or could have meant more.

When I had read Norah's letter over a few times, and feared that Mr. Chapman would take humorous notice of my absorption, I turned to the other letter, which I knew was from Dick. I brought this from the window to the table, beside which I sat to read it, Mr. Chapman being still deep in his own neglected correspondence.

I need not give his letter in detail. It was long and exhaustive, and told me accurately of every step taken and everything accomplished since I had seen him. Mr. Caicy had made his appearance, as arranged, and the two had talked over and settled affairs. Mr. Caicy had lost no time, and fortune had so favoured him that he found that nearly all the tenants on the east side of the hill wished to emigrate, and so were anxious to realize on their holdings.

The estate from which they held was in bankruptcy; and as a sale was then being effected, Mr. Caicy had purchased the estate, and then made arrangements for all who wished to purchase to do so on easy terms from me.

The net result was, that when certain formalities should be complied with, and certain moneys paid, I should own the whole of Knockcalltecrore and the land immediately adjoining it, together with certain other parcels of land in the neighbourhood. There were other matters of interest also in his letter. He told me that Murdock, in order to spite and injure Joyce, had completed the damming up of the stream which ran from his land into the Cliff Fields by blocking with great stones the narrow chine in the rocks through which it fell; that this, coupled with the continuous rains had made the bog rise enormously, and that he feared much there would be some disaster.

His fear was increased by what had taken place at Knocknacar. Even here the cuttings had shown some direful effects of the rain; the openings, made with so much trouble, had become choked, and as a consequence the bog had risen again, and had even spread downwards on its original course. Alarmed by these things, Dick had again warned Murdock of the danger in which he stood from the position of his house; and further, from tampering with the solid bounds of the bog itself. Murdock had not taken his warnings in good part—not any better than usual—and the interview had, as usual, ended in a row.

Murdock had made the quarrel the occasion of ventilating his grievance against me for buying the whole mountain, for by this time it had leaked out that I was the purchaser. His language, Dick said, was awful. He cursed me and all belonging to me. He cursed Joyce and Norah, and Dick himself, and swore to be revenged on us all, and told Dick that he would balk me of finding the treasure, even if I were to buy up all Ireland, and if he had to peril his soul to forestall me. Dick ended his description of his proceedings characteristically: "In fact, he grew so violent, and said such insulting things of you and others, that I had to give him a good sound thrashing."

"Others"—that meant Norah, of course—good old Dick! It was just as well for Mr. Murdock's physical comfort, and for the peace of the neighbourhood, that I did not meet him then and there; for, under these favouring conditions, there would have been a continuance of his experiences under the hands of Dick Sutherland.

Then Dick went on to tell me at greater length what Norah had conveyed in her letter—that, since I had left, Murdock had taken Bat Moynahan to live with him, and kept him continually drunk; that the two of them were evidently trying to locate the whereabouts of the treasure; and that, whenever they thought they were not watched, they trespassed on Joyce's land, to get near a certain part of the bog.

"I mean to watch them the first dark night," wrote Dick, at the close of his letter; "for I cannot help thinking that there is some devilment on foot. I don't suppose you care much for the treasure— you've got a bigger treasure from Knockcalltecrore than ever was hidden in it by men—but, all the same, it is yours after Murdock's time is up; and, as the guardian of your interest, I feel that I have a right to do whatever may be necessary to protect you. I have seen, at times, Murdock give such a look at Moynahan out of the corners of his eyes—when he thought no one was looking—that, upon my soul, I am afraid he means—if he gets the chance—to murder the old man, after he has pumped him of all he knows. I don't want to accuse a man of such an intention, without being able to prove it, and of course have said nothing to a soul; but I shall be really more comfortable in my mind when the man has gone away."

By the time I had finished the letter, Mr. Chapman had run through his correspondence—vacation business was not much in his way—and we discussed affairs.

The settlement of matters connected with my estate, and the purchase of Knockcalltecrore, together with the making of certain purchases—including a ring for Norah—kept me a few days in London; but at length all was complete, and I started on my trip to the west of Ireland. Before leaving, I wrote to Norah that I would be at Knockcalltecrore on the morning of the 20th of October; and also to Dick, asking him to see that Andy was sent to meet me at Galway on the morning of the 19th, for I preferred rather to have the drive in solitude than to be subjected to the interruptions of chance fellow-passengers.

At Dublin Mr. Caicy met me, as agreed; and together we went to various courts, chambers, offices, and banks, completing the purchase with all the endless official formalities and eccentricities habitual to a country whose administration has traditionally adopted and adapted every possible development of all belonging to red-tape.

At last, however, all was completed; and very early the next morning Mr. Caicy took his seat in the Galway express, in a carriage with the owner of Knockcalltecrore, to whom he had been formally appointed Irish law agent.

The journey was not a long one, and it was only twelve o'clock when we steamed into Galway. As we drew up at the platform, I saw Dick, who had come over to meet me. He was, I thought, looking a little pale and anxious; but as he did not say anything containing the slightest hint of any cause for such a thing, I concluded that he wished to wait until we were alone. This, however, was not to be for a little while; for Mr. Caicy had telegraphed to order lunch at his house, and thither we had to repair. We walked over, although Andy, who was in waiting outside the station, grinning from ear to ear, offered to "rowl our 'an'rs over in half a jiffey."

Lunch over, and our bodies the richer for some of Mr. Caicy's excellent port, we prepared to start. Dick took occasion to whisper to me:

"Some time on the road propose to walk for a bit, and send on the car. I want a talk with you alone without making a mystery."

"All right, Dick. Is it a serious matter?"

"Very serious."

# CHAPTER 15

## A Midnight Treasure-Hunt

When, some miles on our road, we came to a long stretch of moorland, I told Andy to stop till we got off. This being done, I told him to go on and wait for us at the next house, as we wished to have a walk.

"The nixt house?" queried Andy, "the very nixt house? Must it be that same?"

"No, Andy," I answered, "the next after that will do equally well, or the third, if it is not too far off. Why do you want to change?"

"Well, yer 'an'r, to tell ye the thruth, there's a girrul at the house beyant what thinks it's a long time on the road I am widout doin' anythin' about settlin' down, an' that it's time I asked her fortin, anyhow. Musha! but it's afeerd I am to shtop there, fur maybe she'd take advantage iv me whin she got me all alone, an' me havin' to wait there till yez come. An' me so soft-hearted, that maybe I'd say too much or too little."

"Why too much or too little?"

"Faix, if I said too much I might be settled down before the month was out; an' if I said too little I might have a girrul lukin' black at me iv'ry time I dhruv by. The house beyant it is a public, an' shure I know I'm safe there anyhow—if me dhrouth'll only hould out!"

I took the hint, and Andy spun my shilling in the air as he drove off. Dick and I walked together, and when he was out of earshot I said:

"Now, old fellow, we are alone. What is it?"

"It's about Murdock."

"Not more than you told me in your letter, I hope. I owe you a good turn for that thrashing you gave him!"

"Oh, that was nothing; it was a labour of love. What I want to speak of is a much more serious affair."

"Nothing to touch Norah, I hope?" I said, anxiously.

"This individual thing is not, thank God! But everything

194

which that ruffian can do to worry her, or any of us, will be done. We'll have to watch him closely."

"What is this new thing?"

"It is about old Moynahan. I am in serious doubt and anxiety as to what I should do. At present I have only suspicion to go on, and not the faintest shadow of proof, and I really want help and advice." "Tell me all about it."

"I shall, exactly as I remember it; and when I have told you, you may be able to draw some conclusion which can help us."

"Go on; but remember I am, as yet, in ignorance of what it is all about. You must not take any knowledge on my part for granted."

"I'll bear it in mind. Well, you remember what I said in my letter, that I had a suspicion of Murdock, and intended watching him?" I nodded. "Two nights after I had written that, the evening was dark and wet—just the weather I would have chosen myself had I had any mysterious purpose on hand. As soon as it got dark I put on my black water-proof and fishing-boots and a sou'wester,[1] and then felt armed for any crouching or lying down that might be required. I waited outside Murdock's house in the lane-way, where I could see from the shadows on the window that both men were in the house. I told you that old Bat Moynahan had taken up his residence entirely with the Gombeen Man—"

"And that he was always drunk."

"Exactly. I see you understand the situation. Presently I heard a stumble on the stone outside the porch, and peeping in through the hedge I saw Murdock holding up old Moynahan. Then he shut the door and they came down the path. The wind was by this time blowing pretty strongly, and made a loud noise in the hedge-rows, and bore in the roar of the surf. Neither of the men could hear me, for I took care as I followed them to keep on the leeward side, and always with something between us. Murdock did not seem to have the slightest suspicion that any one was even on the hillside, let alone listening, and he did

---

1. A waterproof hat with a broad brim behind to protect the neck

not even lower his tone as he spoke. Moynahan was too drunk to either know or care how loud he spoke, and indeed both had to speak pretty loud in order to be heard through the sound of the growing storm.

The rain fell in torrents, and the men passed down the boreen stumbling and slipping. I followed on the other side of the hedge, and I can tell you I felt grateful to the original Mackintosh, or Golosh, or whatever was the name of the Johnny who invented the water-proof. When they had reached the foot of the hill, they went on the road which curves round by the south-east, and I managed to scramble through the fir wood without losing sight of them. When they came to the bridge over the stream, where it runs out on the north side of the peninsula, they turned up on the far bank. I slipped over the bridge behind them, and got on the far side of the fringe of alders. Here they stopped and sheltered for a while, and as I was but a few feet from them I heard every word which passed. Murdock began by saying to Moynahan:

"'Now, keep yer wits about ye, if ye can. Ye'll get lashins iv dhrink whin we get back, but remimber ye promised to go over the ground where yer father showed ye that the Frinchmin wint wid the gun-carriage an' the horses. Where was it now that he tuk ye?' Moynahan evidently made an effort to think and speak:

"It was just about this shpot wheer he seen thim first. They crast over the sthrame—there wor no bridge thin nigher nor Galway—an' wint up the side iv the hill sthraight up.'

"Now, couldn't ye folia the way yer father showed ye? Jist think. It's all dark, and there's nothin' that ye know to confuse ye—no threes what has growed up since thin. Thry an' remimber, an' ye'll have lashins iv dhrink this night, an' half the goold whin we find it.'

"'I can go. I can show the shpot. Come on.' He made a sudden bolt down into the river, which was running unusually high. The current almost swept him away; but Murdock was beside him in a moment, crying out:

"'Go an; the wather isn't deep! don't be afeerd! I'm wid ye.'
When I heard this, I ran around and across the bridge, and was
waiting behind the hedge on the road when they came up again.
The two men went up the Hill straight for perhaps a hundred
yards, I still close to them; then Moynahan stopped:

"'Here's about the shpot me father tould me that he seen
the min whin the moon shone out. Thin they went aff beyant,'
and he pointed to the south. The struggle through the stream
had evidently sobered him somewhat, for he spoke much more
clearly.

"'Come on thin,' cried Murdock, and they moved off.

"'Here's wheer they wint to, thin,' said Moynahan, as he
stopped on the south side of the Hill—as I knew it to be from
the louder sound of the surf which was borne in by the western
gale. Here they wor, jist about here, an' me father wint away to
hide from thim beside the big shtone at the Shleenanaher so that
they wouldn't see him.' Then he paused, and went on in quite a
different voice:

"'There, now I've tould ye enough for wan night. Come
home, for it's chilled to the harrt I am, an' shtarved wid the
cowld. Come home; I'll tell no more this night.' The next sound
I heard was the popping of a cork, and then the voice of Murdock in a cheery tone:

"'Here, take a sup of this, ould man. It's chilled we both are,
an' cramped wid cowld. Take a good dhraw, ye must want it
if ye're as bad as I am!' The gurgle that followed showed that
he had obeyed orders; this was confirmed within an incredibly
short time by his voice as he spoke again.

"'Me father hid there beyant. Come on.' We all, each in his
own way, moved down to the Shleenanaher, and stood there.
Moynahan spoke first.

"'From here, he seen them jist over the ridge iv the hill. I
can go there now; come on.' He hurried up the slope, Murdock
holding on to him. I followed, now crouching low, for there was
but little shelter here. Moynahan stopped and said:

"'It was just here.'

197

"'How do ye know?' asked Murdock, doubtfully.

"'How do I know! Hasn't me father been over the shpot wid me a score iv times; aye, an' a hundhred times afore that be himself. It was here, I tell ye, that he seen the min wid the gun-carriage for the last time. Do ye want to arguey it?'

"'Not me,' said Murdock; and as he spoke I saw him stoop, for as I was at the time lying on the ground, I could see his outline against the dark sky. He was looking away from me, and as I looked, too, I could see him start as he whispered to himself:

"'Be God, but it's thrue! There's the gun-carriage.' There it was, Art, true enough before my eyes, not ten feet away on the edge of the bog. Moynahan went on:

"'Me father told me that the mountain was different at that time; the bog only kem down about as low as this. Musha! but it's the quare lot it has shifted since thin!' There was a pause, broken by Murdock, who spoke in a hoarse, hard voice:

"'An' where did he see them nixt?' Moynahan seemed to be getting drunker and drunker, as was manifest in his later speech; his dose of whiskey had no doubt been a good one.

"'He seen them next to the north beyant—higher up towards Murdock's house.'

"'Towards Murdock's house! Ye mane Joyce's.'

"'No, I mane Black Murdock's; the wan he had before he robbed Joyce. But, begor, he done himself! It's on Joyce's ground the money is. He's a naygur, anyhow—Black Murdock, the Gombeen—bloody end to him!' and he relapsed into silence. I could hear Murdock grind his teeth; then, after a pause, he spoke as the bottle popped again.

"'Have a sup; it'll kape out the cowld.' Moynahan took the bottle.

"'Here's death and damnation to Black Gombeen!' and the gurgling was heard again.

"'Come, now, show me the shpot where yer father last saw the min!' Murdock spoke authoritatively, and the other responded mechanically, and ran rather than walked, along the side of the Hill. Suddenly he stopped.

"'Here's the shpot!' he said, and incontinently tumbled down.

"'Git up! Wake up!' shouted Murdock in his ear. But the whiskey had done its work; the man slept, breathing heavily and stentoriously, heedless of the storm and the drenching rain. Murdock gathered a few stones and placed them together; I could hear the sound as they touched each other. Then he, too, took a pull at the bottle, and sat down beside Moynahan. I moved off a little, and when I came to a whin bush [2] got behind it for a little shelter, and raising myself, looked round. We were quite close to the edge of the bog, about half-way between Joyce's house and Murdock's, and well in on Joyce's land. I was not satisfied as to what Murdock would do, so I waited.

"Fully an hour went by without any stir, and then I heard Murdock trying to awaken old Moynahan. I got down on the ground again and crawled over close to them. I heard Murdock shake the old man, and shout in his ear; presently the latter awoke, and the Gombeen Man gave him another dose of whiskey. This seemed to revive him a little as well as to complete his awakening.

"'Musha, but it's cowld I am!' he shivered.

"'Begor it is. Git up and come home,' said Murdock, and he dragged the old man to his feet.

"'Hould me up, Murtagh,' said the latter; 'I'm that cowld I can't shtand, an' me legs is like shtones: I can't feel them at all, at all!'

"'All right,' said the other; walk on a little bit—sthraight—as ye're goin' now; I'll just shtop to cork the bottle.'

"From my position I could see their movements, and as I am a living man, Art, I saw Murdock turn him with his face to the bog, and send him to walk straight to his death!"

"Good God, Dick, are you quite certain?"

"I haven't the smallest doubt on my mind. I wish I could have, for it's a terrible thing to remember. That attempt to murder in the dark and the storm, comes between me and sleep. Moreover,

---

2. A spiny evergreen shrub with yellow flowers, also called furze or gorse.

Murdock's action the instant after showed only too clearly what he intended. He turned quickly away, and I could hear him mutter as he moved past me on his way down the Hill:

"'He'll not throuble me now, curse him! an' his share won't be required,' and then he laughed a low, horrible laugh, slow and harsh, and as though to himself; and I heard him say:

"'An' whin I do get the chist, Miss Norah, ye'll be the nixt!'"

My blood began to boil as I heard of the villain's threat. "Where is he Dick? He must deal with me for that."

"Steady, Art, steady!" and Dick laid his hand on me.

"Go on," I said.

"I couldn't go after him, for I had to watch Moynahan, whom I followed close, and I caught hold of as soon as I thought Murdock was too far to see me. I was only just in time, for as I touched him he staggered, lurched forward, and was actually beginning to sink in the bog. It was at one of those spots where the rock runs sheer down into the morass. It took all my strength to pull him out, and when I did get him on the rock he sank down again into his drunken sleep. I thought the wisest thing I could do was to go to Joyce's for help; and as, thanks to my experiments with the magnets all those weeks, I knew the ground fairly well, I was able to find my way—although the task was a slow and difficult one.

"When I got near I saw a light at the window. My rubber boots, I suppose, and the plash of the falling rain dulled my footsteps, for as I drew near I could see that a man was looking in at the window, but he did not hear me. I crept up behind the hedge and watched him. He went to the door and knocked—evidently not for the first time; then the door was opened, and I could see Joyce's figure against the light that came from the kitchen.

"'Who's there? What is it?' he asked. Then I heard Murdock's voice.

"'I'm lukin' for poor ould Moynahan. He was out on the Hill in the evenin', but he hasn't kem home, an' I'm anxious about him, for he had a sup in him, an' I fear he may have fallen into the bog. I've been out lukin' for him, but I can't find him. I thought he might have kem in here.'

"'No, he has not been here. Are you sure he was on the Hill?'

"Well, I thought so; but what ought I to do? I'd be thankful if ye'd advise me. Be-the-way, what o'clock might it be now?'

"Norah, who had joined her father, ran in and looked at the clock.

"'It is just ten minutes past twelve,' she said.

"'I don't know what's to be done,' said Joyce. 'Could he have got to the sheebeen?'

"'That's a good idea. I suppose I'd betther go there an' Ink afther him. Ye see, I'm anxious about him, for he's been livin' wid me, an' if anythin' happened to him, people might say I done it!'

"'That's a queer thing for him to say,' said Norah to her father.

"Murdock turned on her at once.

"Quare thing—no more quare than the things they'll be sayin' about you before long.'

"'What do you mean?' said Joyce, coming out.

"'Oh, nawthin', nawthin'! I must look for Moynahan.' And without a word he turned and ran. Joyce and Norah went into the house. When Murdock had quite gone I knocked at the door, and Joyce came out like a thunder-bolt.

"'I've got ye now, ye ruffian!' he shouted. 'What did ye mean to say to me daughter?' But by this time I stood in the light, and he recognized me.

"'Hush!' I said; 'let me in quietly;' and when I passed in we shut the door. Then I told them that I had been out on the mountain, and had found Moynahan. I told them both that they must not ask me any questions, or let on to a soul that I had told them anything— that much might depend on it; for I thought, Art, old chap, that they had better not be mixed up in it, however the matter might end. So we all three went out with a lantern, and I brought them to where the old man was asleep. We lifted him, and between us carried him to the house; Joyce and I undressed him and put him in bed, between warm blankets. Then I came away and went over to Mrs. Kelligan's, where I slept in a chair before the fire.

"The next morning when I went up to Joyce's I found that Moynahan was all right—that he hadn't even got a cold, but that he remembered nothing whatever about his walking into the bog. He had even expressed his wonder at seeing the state his clothes were in. When I went into the village I found that Murdock had been everywhere and had told everyone of his fears about Moynahan. I said nothing of his being safe, but tried quietly to arrange matters so that

I might be present when Murdock should set his eyes for the first time on the man he had tried to murder. I left him with a number of others in the sheebeen, and went back to bring Moynahan, but found, when I got to Joyce's that he had already gone back to Murdock's house. Joyce had told him, as we had arranged, that when Murdock had come asking for him he had been alarmed, and had gone out to look for him; had found him asleep on the hillside, and had brought him home with him. As I found that my scheme of facing Murdock with his victim was frustrated, I took advantage of Murdock's absence to remove the stones which he had placed to mark the spot where the treasure was last seen.

I found them in the form of a cross, and moving them, replaced them at a spot some distance lower down the line of the bog. I marked the place, however, with a mark of my own—four stones put widely apart at the points of a letter Y—the centre marking the spot where the cross had been. Murdock returned to his house not long after, and within a short time ran down to tell that Moynahan had found his way home, and was all safe. They told me that he was then white and scared-looking." Here Dick paused:

"Now, my difficulty is this: I know he tried to murder the man, but I am not in a position to prove it. No man could expect

202

his word to be taken in such a matter and under such circumstances. And yet I am morally certain that he intends to murder him still. What should I do? To take any preventive steps would involve making the charge which I cannot prove. As yet neither of the men has the slightest suspicion that I am concerned in the matter in any way, or that I even know of it. Now, may I not be most useful by keeping a watch and biding my time?"

I thought a moment, but there seemed to be only one answer.

"You are quite right, Dick. We can do nothing just at present. We must keep a sharp lookout, and get some tangible evidence of his intention—something that we can support, and then we can take steps against him. As to the matter of his threat to harm Norah, I shall certainly try to bring that out in a way we can prove, and then he shall have the hottest corner he ever thought of in his life."

"Quite right that he should have it, Art; but we must think of her too. It would not do to have her name mixed up with any gossip. She will be going away very shortly, I suppose, and then his power to hurt her will be nil. In the mean time everything must be done to guard her."

"I shall get a dog—a good savage one, this very day; that ruffian must not be able to even get near the house again—" Dick interrupted me.

"Oh, I quite forgot to tell you about that. The very day after that night I got a dog and sent it up. It is the great mastiff that Meldon, the dispensary doctor, had—the one that you admired so much. I specially asked Norah to keep it for you, and train it to be always with her. She promised that she would always feed him herself and take him about with her. I am quite sure she understood that he was to be her protector."

"Thank you, Dick," I said, and I am sure he knew I was grateful.

By this time we had come near the house outside which the car stood. Andy was inside, and evidently did not expect our coming so soon, for he sat with a measure of stout half emptied before him on the table, and on each of his knees sat a lady—one evidently the mother of the other. As we appeared in the door-way he started up.

"Be the powdhers, there's the masther! Git up, acushla!"— this to the younger woman, for the elder had already jumped up. Then to me:

"Won't ye sit down, yer 'an'r. There's only the wan chair, so ye see the shifts we're dhruv to, whin there's three iv us. I couldn't put Mrs. Dempsey from off iv her own shtool, an' she wouldn't sit on me knee alone—the dacent woman—so we had to take the girrul on too. They all sit that way in these parts!" The latter statement was made with brazen openness and shameless effrontery. I shook my finger at him:

"Take care, Andy. You'll get into trouble one of these days."

"Into throuble, for a girrul sittin' on me knee! Begor, the Govermint'll have to get up more coorts and more polis if they want to shtop that ould custom. An' more betoken, they'll have to purvide more shtools, too. Mrs. Dempsey, whin I come round agin, mind ye kape a govermint shtool for me. Here's the masther wouldn't let any girrul sit on anywan's knee. Begor, not even the quality nor the fairies! All right, yer 'an'r, the mare's quite ready. Goodbye, Mrs. Dempsey. Don't forgit the shtool—an' wan, too, for Biddy! Gee up, ye ould corn-crake!" and so we resumed our journey.

As we went along Dick gave me all details regarding the property which he and Mr. Caicy had bought for me. Although I had signed deeds and papers without number, and was owner in the present or in future of the whole Hill, I had not the least idea of either

the size or disposition of the estate. Dick had been all over it, and was able to supply me with every detail. As he went on he grew quite enthusiastic—everything seemed to be even more favourable than he had at first supposed. There was plenty of clay; and he suspected that in two or three places there was pottery clay, such as is found chiefly in Cornwall. There was any amount of water; and when we should be able to control the whole Hill and regulate matters as we wished, the supply would enable us to do anything in the way of either irrigation or ornamental development. The only thing we lacked, he said, was limestone, and he had a suspicion that limestone was to be found somewhere on the Hill.

"I cannot but think," said he, "that there must be a streak of limestone somewhere. I cannot otherwise account for the subsidence of the lake on the top of the Hill. I almost begin to think that that formation of rock to which the Snake's Pass is due runs right through the Hill, and that we shall find that the whole top of it has similar granite cliffs, with the hollow between them possibly filled in with some rock of one of the later formations. However, when we get possession I shall make accurate search.

"I tell you, Art, it will well repay the trouble if we can find it. A limestone quarry here would be pretty well as valuable as a gold mine. Nearly all these promontories on the western coast of Ireland are of slate or granite, and here we have not got lime within thirty miles. With a quarry on the spot, we can not only build cheap and reclaim our own bog, but we can supply five hundred square miles of country with the rudiments of prosperity, and at a nominal price compared with what they pay now."

Then he went on to tell me of the various arrangements effected—how those who wished to emigrate were about to do so, and how others who wished to stay were to have better farms given them on what we called "the main-land"; and how he had devised a plan for building houses for them—good solid stone houses, with proper offices and farmyards. He concluded what seemed to me like a somewhat modified daydream:

"And if we can find the limestone—well, the improvements can all be done without costing you a penny; and you can have around you the most prosperous set of people to be found in the country."

In such talk as this the journey wore on till the evening came upon us. The day had been a fine one—one of those rare sunny days in a wet autumn. As we went I could see everywhere the signs of the continuous rains. The fields were sloppy and sodden, and the bottoms were flooded; the bogs were teeming with water; the roads were washed clean—not only the mud but even the sand having been swept away, and the road-metal was everywhere exposed. Often, as we went along, Dick took occasion to illustrate his views as to the danger of the shifting of the bog at Knockcalltecrore by the evidence around us of the destructive power of the continuous rain.

When we came to the mountain gap where we got our first and only view of Knockcalltecrore from the Gal way road, Andy reined in the mare, and turned to me, pointing with his whip.

"There beyant, yer 'an'r, is Knockcalltecrore—the Hill where the threasure is. They do say that a young English gintleman has bought up the Hill, an' manes to git the threasure for himself. Begor, perhaps he has found it already. Here, gee up, ye ould corn-crake! What the divil are ye kapin' the quality waitin' for?" and we sped down the road.

The sight of the Hill filled me with glad emotion, and I do not think that it is to be wondered at. And yet my gladness was as followed by an unutterable gloom—a gloom that fell over me the instant after my eyes took in the well-known Hill struck by the falling sunset from the west. It seemed to me that all had been so happy and so bright and so easy for me, that there must be in store some terrible shock or loss to make the balance even, and to reduce my satisfaction with life to the level above which man's happiness may not pass.

There was a curse on the Hill! I felt it and realized it at that moment for the first time. I suppose I must have shown something of my brooding fear in my face, for Dick, looking round at me after a period of silence, said suddenly:

"Cheer up, Art, old chap! Surely you, at any rate, have no cause to be down on your luck. Of all men that live, I should think you ought to be about the very happiest."

"That's it, old fellow," I answered. "I fear that there must be something terrible coming. I shall never be quite happy till Norah and all of us are quite away from the Hill."

"What on earth do you mean? Why, you have just bought

the whole place."

"It may seem foolish, Dick; but the words come back to me and keep ringing in my ears: The mountain holds, and it holds tight." Dick laughed.

"Well, Art, it is not my fault, or Mr. Caicy's, if you don't hold it tight. It is yours now, every acre of it; and, if I don't mistake, you are going to make it in time—and not a long time either—into the fairest bower to which the best fellow ever brought the fairest lady! There now, Art, isn't that a pretty speech?"

Dick's words made me feel ashamed of myself, and I made an effort to pull myself together, which lasted until Dick and I said goodnight.

## CHAPTER 16

### A GRIM WARNING

I cannot say the night was a happy one. There were moments when I seemed to lose myself and my own anxieties in thoughts of Norah and the future, and such moments were sweet to look back on—then as they are now; but I slept only fitfully and dreamt frightfully.

It was natural enough that my dreams should centre around Knockcalltecrore; but there was no good reason why they should all be miserable or terrible. The Hill seemed to be ever under some uncomfortable or unnatural condition. When my dreams began, it was bathed in a flood of yellow moonlight, and at its summit was the giant Snake, the jewel of whose crown threw out an unholy glare of yellow light, and whose face and form kept perpetually changing to those of Murtagh Murdock.

I can now, with comparatively an easy effort, look back on it all, and disentangle or give a reason for all the phases of my thought. The snake "wid side whishkers" was distinctly suggested the first night I heard the legend at Mrs. Kelligan's; the light from the jewel was a part of the legend itself; and so on with every fact and incident. Presently, as I dreamed, the whole Mountain seemed to writhe and shake as though the great Snake was circling round it, deep under the earth; and again this movement changed into the shifting of the bog. Then through dark shadows that lay athwart the Hill I could see the French soldiers, with their treasure-chest, pass along in dusky, mysterious silence, and vanish in the hillside.

I saw Murdock track them; and, when they were gone, he and old Moynahan—who suddenly and mysteriously appeared beside him—struggled on the edge of the bog, and, with a shuddering wail, the latter threw up his arms and sank slowly into the depths of the morass. Again Norah and I were wandering together, when suddenly Murdock's evil face, borne on a huge serpent body, writhed up beside us; and in an instant Norah was whirled from my side and swept into the bog, I being powerless to save her or even help her.

The last of all my dreams was as follows: Norah and I were sitting on the table rock in the Cliff Fields; all was happy and smiling around us. The sun shone and the birds sang, and as we sat hand in hand the beating of our hearts seemed a song also. Suddenly there was a terrible sound—half a roar, as of an avalanche, and half a fluttering sound, as of many great wings. We clung together in terror, waiting for the portent which was at hand. Ami then over the cliff poured the whole mass of the bog, foul-smelling, foetid, terrible, and of endless might. Just as it was about to touch us, and as I clasped Norah to me, so that we might die together, and while her despairing cry was in my ear, the whole mighty mass turned into loathsome, writhing snakes, sweeping into the sea!

I awoke with a scream which brought nearly everyone in the hotel into my bedroom. Dick was first, and found me standing on the floor, white and drunk with terror.

"What is it, old fellow? Oh, I see, only a nightmare! Come on; he's all right; it's only a dream!" and almost before I had realized that the waking world and not the world of shadows was around me, the room was cleared and I was alone. I lit a candle and put on some clothes; as it was of no use trying to sleep again after such an experience, I got a book and resolutely set to reading. The effort was successful, as such efforts always are, and

I quite forgot the cause of my disturbance in what I read. Then the matter itself grew less interesting.

There was a tap at my door. I started awake. It was broad daylight, and the book lay with crumpled leaves beside me on the floor. It was a message to tell me that Mr. Sutherland was waiting breakfast for me. I called out that I would be down in a few minutes, which promise I carried out as nearly as was commensurate with the requirements of the tub and the toilet. I found Dick awaiting me; he looked at me keenly as I came in, and then said, heartily:

"I see your nightmare has not left any ill effects. I say, old chap, it must have been a whopper—a regular Derby winner among nightmares—worse than Andy's old corn-crake. You yelled fit to wake the dead. I would have thought the contrast between an ordinary night and the day you are going to have would have been sufficient to satisfy any one without such an addition to its blackness." Then he sung out in his rich voice:

*"Och, Jewel, kape dhramin' that same till ye die,*
*For bright mornin' will give dirty night the black lie."*

We sat down to breakfast, and I am bound to say, from the trencher experience of that meal, that there is nothing so fine as an appetiser for breakfast as a good preliminary nightmare.

We drove off to Knockcalltecrore. When we got to the foot of the hill we stopped as usual. Andy gave me a look which spoke a lot, but he did not say a single word—for which forbearance I owed him a good turn. Dick said:

"I want to go round to the other side of the hill, and shall cross over the top. I shall look you up, if I may, at Joyce's about two o'clock."

"All right," I said; "we shall expect you," and I started up the hill.

When I got to the gate and opened it there was a loud, deep barking, which, however, was instantly stilled. I knew that Norah had tied up the mastiff, and I went to the door. I had no need to knock; for as I came near it opened, and in another instant

209

Norah was in my arms. She whispered in my ear when I had kissed her:

"I would like to have come out to meet you, but I thought you would rather meet me here." Then, as we went into the sitting-room, hand in hand, she whispered again:

"Aunt has gone to buy groceries, so we are all alone. You must tell me all about everything."

We sat down close together, still hand in hand, and I told her all that we had done since I had left. When I had finished the Paris part of the story, she put up her hands before her face, and I could see the tears drop through her fingers.

"Norah, Norah, don't cry, my darling! What is it?"

"Oh, Arthur, I can't help it! It is so wonderful—more than all I ever longed or wished for!" Then she took her hands away, and put them in mine, and looked me bravely in the face, with her eyes half laughing and half crying, and her cheeks wet, and said:

"Arthur, you are the Fairy Prince! There is nothing that I can wish for that you have not done—even my dresses are ready by your sweet thoughtfulness. It needs an effort, dear, to let you do all this, but I see it is quite right: I must be dressed like one who is to be your wife. I shall think I am pleasing you afresh every time I put one of them on; but I must pay for them myself. You know I am quite rich now. I have all the money you paid for the Cliff Fields; father says it ought to go in such things as will fit me for my new position, and will not hear of taking any of it."

"He is quite right, Norah, my darling, and you are quite right, too; all shall be just as you wish. Now tell me all about everything since I went away."

"May I bring in Turco? he is so quiet with me; and he must learn to know you and love you, or he won't be any friend of mine." She looked at me lovingly, and went and brought in the mastiff, by whom I was forthwith received into friendship.

That was indeed a happy day. We had a family consultation about the school; the time of beginning was arranged, and there was perfect accord among us. As Dick and I drove back through the darkness, I could not but feel that, even if evil were looming ahead of us, at least some of us had experienced what it is to be happy.

It had been decided that after a week's time—on the 28th of October—Norah was to leave for school. Her father was to bring her as far as London, and Mr. Chapman was to take her over to Paris. This was Joyce's own wish. He said:

"'Twill be betther for ye, darlin', to go widout me. Ye'll have quite enough to do for a bit to keep even wid the girls that have been reared in betther ways nor you, widout me there to make little iv ye"

"But, father," she remonstrated, "I don't want to appear any different from what I am. And I am too fond of you, and too proud of you, not to want to appear as your daughter."

Her father stroked her hair gently as he answered: "Norah, my darlin', it isn't that. Ye've always been the good and dutiful daughter to me; an' in all your pretty life there's not wan thing I wish undone or unsaid. But I'm older than you, daughter, an' I know more iv the world; an' what I say is best for ye—now, and in yer future. I'm goin' to live wid Eugene; an' afther a while I suppose I, too, 'll be somethin' different from what I am. An' thin, whin I've lived a while in a city, and got somethin' of city ways, I'll come an' see ye, maybe. Ye must remimber that it's not only of you we've to think, but of th' other girls in the school. I don't want to have any of them turnin' up their noses at ye; that's not the way to get the best out iv school, my dear; for I suppose school is like everywhere else in the world: the higher ye're able to hould yer head, the more others'll look up to ye."

His words were so obviously true, that not one of us had a word to say, and the matter was acquiesced in *nem. con.*[1] I myself got leave to accompany the party as far as London, but not beyond. It was further arranged that Joyce should take his daughter to Galway to get some clothes for her—just enough to take her to Paris—and that when in Paris she should have a full outfit under the direction of Madame Lepecheaux. They were to leave on Friday, so as to have the Saturday in Galway; and as Norah

---

1. Without dissent.

211

wanted to say goodbye on the Sunday to old school-fellows and friends in the convent, they would return on Monday, the 25th of October.

Accordingly, on the morning after next, Joyce took a letter for me to Mr. Caicy, who was to pay to him whatever portion of the purchase-money of his land he should require, and whom I asked to give all possible assistance in whatever matters either he or Norah might desire. I would have dearly liked to have gone myself with them, but the purpose and the occasion were such that I could not think of offering to go. On the day fixed they left on the long car from Carnaclif. They started in torrents of rain, but were as well wrapped up as the resources of Dick and myself would allow.

When they had gone Dick and I drove over to Knockcalltecrore. Dick wished to have an interview with Murdock, regarding his giving up possession of the land on the 27th, as arranged.

We left Andy as usual at the foot of the Hill, and went up to Murdock's house. The door was locked; and although we knocked several times, we could get no answer. We came away, therefore, and went up the Hill, as Dick wished me to see where, according to old Moynahan, was the last place at which the Frenchmen had been seen. As we went on and turned the brow of the mound, which lay straight up—for the bog-land lay in a curve round its southern side—we saw before us two figures at the edge of the bog. They were those of Murdock and old Moynahan. When we saw who they were, Dick whispered to me:

"They are at the place to which I changed the mark, but are still an Joyce's land."

They were working just as Dick and I had worked with Murdock, when we had recovered the gun-carriage, and were so intent on the work at which they toiled with feverish eagerness that they did not see us coming; and it was only when we stood close beside them that they were conscious of our presence. Murdock turned at once with a scowl and a sort of snarl. When he saw who it was he became positively livid with passion, and at once began to bombard us with the foulest vituperation. Dick pressed my arm, as a hint to keep quiet and leave the talking to him, and I did nothing; but he opposed the Gombeen Man's passion with an unruffled calm. Indeed, he seemed to me to want even to exasperate Murdock to the last degree. When the latter paused for a second for breath, he quietly said:

"Keep your hair on, Murdock, and just tell me quietly why you are trespassing; and why, and what, you are trying to steal from this property?"

Murdock made no answer, so Dick went on:

"Let me tell you that I act for the owner of this land, who bought it as it is, and I shall hold you responsible for your conduct. I don't want to have a row needlessly, so if you go away quietly, and promise to not either trespass here again, or try to steal anything, I shall not take any steps. If not, I shall do as the occasion demands."

Murdock answered him with the most manifestly intentional insolence:

"You! ye tell me to go away! I don't ricognize ye at all. This land belongs to me frind, Mr. Joyce, an' I shall come on it whin I like; and do as I like. Whin me frind tells me not to come here, I shall shtay away. Till then I shall do as I like."

Said Dick:

"You think that will do to bluff me because you know Joyce is away for the clay, and that, in the mean time, you can do what you want, and perhaps get out of the bog some property that does not belong to you. I shall not argue with you anymore; but I warn you that you will have to answer for your conduct."

Murdock and Moynahan continued their pulling at the rope. We waited till the haul was over, and saw that the spoil on this occasion was a part of the root of a tree. Then, when both men were sitting exhausted beside it, Dick took out his note-book, and began to make notes of everything. Presently he turned to Murdock, and said:

"Have you been fishing, Mr. Murdock? What a strange booty you have brought up! It is really most kind of you to be aiding to secure the winter firing for Mr. Joyce and my friend. Is there anything but bog-wood to be found here?"

Murdock's reply was a curse and a savage scowl; but old Moynahan joined in the conversation:

"Now, I tould ye, Murtagh, that we wur too low down."

"Shut up!" shouted the other, and the old man shrank back as if he had been struck. Dick looked down, and seemed to be struck by the cross of loose stones at his feet, and said:

"Dear me! that is very strange—a cross of stones! It would almost seem as if it were made here to mark something; but yet"—here he lifted one of the stones—"it cannot have been long here; the grass is fresh under the stones." Murdock said nothing, but clinched his hands and ground his teeth. Presently, however, he sent Moynahan back to his house to get some whiskey. When the latter was out of earshot, Murdock turned to us, and said:

"An' so ye think to baffle me, do ye? Well, I'll have that money out if I have to wade in yer blood. I will, by the livin' God!" and he burst into a string of profanities that made us shudder.

He was in such deadly earnest that I felt a pity for him, and said impulsively:

"Look here, if you want to get it out, you can have a little more time if you like, if only you will conduct yourself properly. I don't want to be bothered looking for it. Now, if you'll only behave decently, and be something like a civilized being, I'll give you another month if you want it."

Again he burst out at me with still more awful profanities. He didn't want any of my time. He'd take what time he liked. God himself—and he particularized the persons of the Trinity—couldn't balk him, and he'd do what he liked; and if I crossed his path it would be the worse for me! And, as for others, that he would send the hard word round the country about me and my leman.[2] I couldn't be always knocking the ruffian down, so I turned away and called to Dick.

"Coming," said Dick, and he walked up to Murdock and

---

2. Sweetheart or lover.

214

knocked him down. Then, as the latter lay dazed on the grass, he followed me.

"Really," he said, apologetically, "the man wants it. It will do him good."

Then we went back to Carnaclif

These three days were very dreary ones for me; we spent most of the time walking over Knockcalltecrore and making plans for the future. But, without Norah, the place seemed very dreary.

We did not go over on the Monday, as we knew that Joyce and Norah would not get home until late in the evening, and would be tired. Early, however, on the day after—Tuesday—we drove over. Joyce was out, and Dick left me at the foot of the boreen, so when I got to the house I found Norah alone.

The dear girl showed me her new dresses with much pride; and presently going to her room put on one of them, and came back to let me see how she looked. Her face was covered with blushes. Needless to say that I admired the new dress, as did her father, who just then came in.

When she went away to take off the dress Joyce beckoned me outside. When we got away from the house he turned to me; his face was very grave, and he seemed even more frightened than angry.

"There's somethin' I was tould while I was away that I think ye ought to know."

"Go on, Mr. Joyce."

"Somebody has been sayin' hard things about Norah."

"About Norah! Surely there is nobody mad enough or bad enough to speak evil of her."

"There's wan." He turned as he spoke, and looked instinctively in the direction of Murdock's house.

"Oh, Murdock, as he threatened. What did he say?"

"Well, I don't know. I could only get it that somebody was sayin' somethin', an' that it would be well to have things so that no wan could say anythin' that we couldn't prove. It was a frind tould me; and that's all he would tell. Mayhap he didn't know

215

any more himself; but I knew him to be a frind."

"And it was a friendly act, Mr. Joyce. I have no doubt that Murdock has been sending round wicked lies about us all. But, thank God, in a few days we will be all moving, and it doesn't matter much what he can do."

"No, it won't matter much in wan way, but he's not goin', all the same, to throw dirt on me child. If he goes on I'll folly him up."

"He won't go on, Mr. Joyce. Before long, he'll be out of the neighbourhood altogether. To tell you the truth, I have bought the whole of his land, and I get possession of it tomorrow; and then I'll never let him set foot here again. When once he is out of this he will have too much other wickedness on hand to have time to meddle with us."

"That's thrue enough. Well, we'll wait an' see what happens; but we'll be mighty careful all the same."

"Quite right," I said, "we cannot be too careful in such a matter." Then we went back to the house, and met Norah coming into the room in her red petticoat, which she knew I liked. She whispered to me, oh, so sweetly:

"I thought, dear, you would like me to be the old Norah, today. It is our last day together in the old way." Then hand in hand we went down to the Cliff Fields, and sat on the table rock for the last time, and feasted our eyes on the glorious prospect, while we told each other our bright dreams of the future.

In the autumn twilight we came back to the house. Dick had, in the mean time, come in, and we both stayed for tea. I saw that Dick had something to tell me, but he waited until we were going home before he spoke.

It was a sad parting with Norah that night; for it was the last day together before she went off to school. For myself, I felt that whatever might be in the future—and I hoped for much—it was the last time that I might sit by the firelight with the old Norah. She, too, was sad, and when she told me the cause of her sadness I found that it was the same as my own.

"But oh, Arthur, my darling, I shall try—I shall try to be worthy of my great good-fortune—and of you," she said, as she put her arms round my neck, and leaning her head on my bosom, began to cry.

"Hush, Norah. Hush, my darling!" I said; "you must not say such things to me—you, who are worthy of all the good gifts of life. Oh, my dear, my dear! I am only fearful that you may be snatched away from me by some terrible misfortune; I shall not be happy till you are safely away from the shadow of this fateful mountain, and are beginning your new life."

"Only one more day," she said. "Tomorrow we must settle up everything—and I have much to do for father—poor father, how good he is to me! Please God, Arthur, we shall be able some day to repay him for all his goodness to me." How inexpressibly sweet it was to me to hear her say "we" shall be able, as she nestled up close to me.

Ah, that night! Ah, that night!—the end of the day when, for the last time, I sat on the table rock with the old Norah that I loved so well. It almost seemed as if Fate, who loves the keen contrasts of glare and gloom, had made on purpose that day so bright, and of such flaw less happiness.

As we went back to Carnaclif, Dick told me what had been exercising his mind all the afternoon. When he had got to the bog he found that it had risen so much that he thought it well to seek the cause. He had gone at once to the place where Murdock had dammed up the stream that ran over into the Cliff Fields, and had found that the natural position of the ground had so far aided his efforts that the great stones thrown into the chine had become solidified with the rubbish by the new weight of the risen bog into a compact mass, and unless some heroic measure, such as blowing up the dam, should be taken, the bog would continue to rise until it should flow over the lowest part of the solid banks containing it.

"As sure as we are here, Art," he said, "that man will do himself to death. I am convinced that if the present state of things goes on, with the bog at its present height, and with this terrible rainfall, there will be another shifting of the bog, and then, God

217

help him; and, perhaps, others too! I told him of the danger, and explained it to him; but he only laughed at me and called me a fool and a traitor; that I was doing it to prevent him getting his treasure—his treasure, forsooth! And then he went again into those terrible blasphemies, so I came away; but he is a lost man, and I don't see how we can stop him." I said, earnestly:

"Dick, there's no danger to them—the Joyces—is there?"

"No," he answered, "not the slightest; their house is on the rock high over the spot, and quite away from any possible danger."

Then we relapsed into silence, as we each tried to think out a solution.

That night it rained more heavily than ever. The downfall was almost tropical—as it can be on the west coast—and the rain on the iron roof of the stable behind the hotel sounded like thunder; it was the last thing in my ears before I went to sleep.

That night again I kept dreaming—dreaming in the same nightmare fashion as before. But although the working of my imagination centred round Knockcalltecrore and all it contained, and although I suffered dismal tortures from the hideous dreams of ruin and disaster which afflicted me, I did not on this occasion arouse the household. In the morning, when we met, Dick looked at my pale face and said:

"Dreaming again, Art! Well, please God, it's all nearly over now. One more day, and Norah will be away from Knockcalltecrore."

The thought gave me much relief. The next morning—on Thursday, the 28th of October—we should be on our way to Galway *en route* for London, while Dick would receive on my behalf possession of the property which I had purchased from Murdock. Indeed, his tenure ended at noon this very day; but we thought it wiser to postpone taking possession until after Norah had left. Although Norah's departure meant a long absence from the woman I loved, I could not regret it, for it was after all but a long road to the end I wished for. The two years would soon be over. And then—and then life would begin in real earnest, and along its paths of sorrow as of joy Norah and I should walk with equal steps.

Alas for dreaming! The dreams of the daylight are often more delusive than even those born of the glamour of moonlight or starlight, or of the pitchy darkness of the night.

It had been arranged that we were not on this day to go over to Knockcalltecrore, as Norah and her father wanted the day together. Miss Joyce, Norah's aunt, who usually had lived with them, was coming back to look after the house. So after breakfast Dick and I smoked and lounged about, and went over some business matters, and we arranged many things to be done during my absence. The rain still continued to pour down in a perfect deluge; the roadway outside the hotel was running like a river, and the windswept the rain-clouds so that the drops struck like hail. Every now and again, as the gusts gathered in force, the rain seemed to drive past like a sheet of water; and looking out of the window we could see dripping men and women trying to make headway against the storm. Dick said to me:

"If this rain holds on much longer it will be a bad job for Murdock. There is every fear that if the bog should break under the flooding he will suffer at once. What an obstinate fool he is! he won't take any warning. I almost feel like a criminal in letting him go to his death, ruffian though he is; and yet what can one do? We are all powerless if anything should happen." After this he was silent. I spoke the next:

"Tell me, Dick, is there any earthly possibility of any harm coming to Joyce's house in case the bog should shift again? Is it quite certain that they are all safe?"

"Quite certain, old fellow. You may set your mind at rest on that score. In so far as the bog is concerned, she and her father are in no danger. The only way they could run any risk of danger would be by their going to Murdock's house, or by being by chance lower down on the Hill, and I do not think that such a thing is likely to happen."

This set my mind more at ease, and while Dick sat down to write some letters I continued to look at the rain.

By-and-by I went down to the tap-room, where there were always a lot of peasants, whose quaint speech amused and interested me. When I came in one of them, whom I recognized as one of our navvies at Knocknacar, was telling something, for the others all stood round him. Andy was the first to see me, and said, as I entered:

"Yell have to go over it all agin, Mike. Mere's his 'an'r, that is just death on to bogs—an' the like," he added, looking at me slyly.

"What is it?" I asked.

"Oh, not much, yer 'an'r, except that the bog up at Knocknacar has run away intirely. Whin the wather rose in it, the big cuttin' we med tuk it all out, like butthermilk out iv a jug. Begor, there never was seen such a flittin' since the wurrld begun! An', more betoken, the quare part iv it is that it hasn't left the bit iv a hole behind it at all, but it's all mud an' wather at the prisint minit."

I knew this would interest Dick exceedingly, so I went for him. When he heard it he got quite excited, and insisted that we should go off to Knocknacar at once. Accordingly Andy was summoned, the mare was harnessed, and, with what protection we could get in the way of wraps, we went off to Knocknacar through the rain-storm.

As we went along we got some idea of the damage done, and being done, by the wonderful rainfall. Not only the road was like a river, and the mountain streams were roaring torrents, but in places the road was flooded to such a dangerous depth that we dared not have attempted the passage only that, through our repeated journeys, we all knew the road so well.

However, we got at last to Knocknacar, and there found that the statement we heard was quite true. The bog had been flooded to such a degree that it had burst out through the cutting which we had made, and had poured in a great stream over all the sloping moorland on which we had opened it. The brown bog and black mud lying all over the stony space looked like one of the lava streams which mark the northern side of Vesuvius. Dick went most carefully all over the ground wherever we could venture, and took quite a number of notes. Indeed, the day was beginning to draw in when, dripping and chilled, we prepared for our return journey through the rain. Andy had not been wasting his time in the sheebeen, and was in one of his most jocular humours; and when we, too, were fortified with steaming hot punch, we were able to listen to his fun without wanting to kill him.

On the journey back, Dick, when Andy allowed him speech, explained to me the various phenomena which we had noticed. When we got back to the hotel it was night. Had the weather been fine we might have expected a couple more hours of twilight; but with the mass of driving clouds overhead, and the steady downpour of rain, and the fierce rush of the wind, there was left to us not the slightest suggestion of day.

We went to bed early, for I had to rise by daylight for our journey on the morrow. After lying awake for some time listening to the roar of the storm and the dash of the rain, and wondering if it were to go on forever, I sank into a troubled sleep.

It seemed to me that all the nightmares which had individually afflicted me during the last week returned to assail me collectively on the present occasion. I was a sort of Mazeppa in the world of dreams. Again and again the fatal Hill and all its mystic and terrible associations haunted me; again the snakes writhed around and took terrible forms; again she I loved was in peril; again Murdock seemed to arise in new forms of terror and wickedness; again the lost treasure was sought under terrible conditions; and once again I seemed to sit on the table rock with Norah, and to see the whole mountain rush down on us in a dread avalanche, and turn to myriad snakes as it came; and again Norah seemed to call to me, "Help! help! Arthur, save me! save me!" And again, as was most natural, I found myself awake on the floor of my room—though this time I did not scream— wet and quivering with some nameless terror, and with Norah's despairing cry in my ears.

But even in the first instant of my awakening I had taken

a resolution which forthwith I proceeded to carry into effect. These terrible dreams, whencesoever they came, must not have come in vain; the grim warning must not be despised. Norah was in danger, and I must go to her at all hazards.

I threw on my clothes and went and woke Dick. When I told him my intention he jumped up at once and began to dress, while I ran down-stairs and found Andy, and set him to get out the car at once.

"Is it goin' out agin in the shtorm ye are? Begor, ye'd not go widout some rayson, an' I'm not the bhoy to be behind whin ye want me. I'll be ready, yer 'an'r, in two skips iv a dead salmon;" and Andy proceeded to make, or rather complete, his toilet, and hurried out to the stable to get the car ready. In the mean time Dick had got two lanterns and a flask, and showed them to me.

"We may as well have them with us. We do not know what we may want in this storm."

It was now past one o'clock, and the night was pitchy dark. The rain still fell, and high overhead we could hear the ceaseless rushing of the wind. It was a lucky thing that both Andy and the mare knew the road thoroughly, for otherwise we never could have got on that night. As it was, we had to go much more slowly than we had ever gone before.

I was in a perfect fever. Every second's delay seemed to me like an hour. I feared—nay more, I had a deep conviction—that some dreadful thing was happening, and I had over me a terrible dread that we should arrive too late.

## CHAPTER 17

### THE CATASTROPHE

As we drew closer to the mountain, and recognized our whereabouts by the various landmarks, my dread seemed to grow. The night was now well on, and there were signs of the storm abating; occasionally the wind would fall off a little, and the rain beat with less dreadful violence. In such moments some kind of light would be seen in the sky—or, to speak more correctly, the darkness would be less complete—and then the new squall which followed would seem by contrast with the calm to smite us with renewed violence. In one of these lulls we saw for an instant the mountain rise before us, its bold outline being shown darkly against a sky less black.

But the vision was swept away an instant after by a squall and a cloud of blinding rain, leaving only a dreadful memory of some field for grim disaster. Then we went on our way even more hopelessly; for earth and sky, which in that brief instant we had been able to distinguish, were now hidden under one unutterable pall of gloom.

On we went slowly. There was now in the air a thunderous feeling, and we expected each moment to be startled by the lightning's flash or the roar of heaven's artillery. Masses of mist or sea-fog now began to be borne landward by the passing squalls. In the time that elapsed between that one momentary glimpse of Knockcalltecrore and our arrival at the foot of the boreen a whole lifetime seemed to me to have elapsed, and in my thoughts and harrowing anxieties I recalled—as drowning men are said to do before death—every moment, every experience since I had first come within sight of the western sea. The blackness of my fears seemed only a carrying inward of the surrounding darkness, which was made more pronounced by the flickering of our lanterns, and more dread by the sounds of the tempest with which it was laden.

When we stopped in the boreen Dick and I hurried up the Hill, while Andy, with whom we left one of the lanterns, drew the horse under the comparative shelter of the windswept alders which lined the entrance to the lane. He wanted a short rest before proceeding to Mrs. Kelligan's, where he was to stop the remainder of the night, so as to be able to come for us in the morning.

As we came near Murdock's cottage Dick pressed my arm.

"Look!" he called to me, putting his mouth to my ear so that I could hear him, for the storm swept the Hill fiercely here, and a special current of wind came whirling up through the Shleen-anaher. "Look! he is up even at this hour. There must be some villany afloat!"

When we got up a little farther he called to me again in the same way.

"The nearest point of the bog is here; let us look at it." We diverged to the left, and in a few minutes were down at the edge of the bog.

It seemed to us to be different from what it had been. It was raised considerably above its normal height, and seemed quivering all over in a very strange way. Dick said to me, very gravely:

"We are just in time. There's something going to happen here."

"Let us hurry to Joyce's," I said, "and see if all is safe there."

"We should warn them first at Murdock's," he said. "There may not be a moment to lose." We hurried back to the boreen, and ran on to Murdock's, opened the gate, and ran up the path. We knocked at the door, but there was no answer. We knocked more loudly still, but there came no reply.

"We had better make certain," said Dick; and I could hear him more easily now, for we were in the shelter of the porch. We opened the door, which was only on the latch, and went in. In the kitchen a candle was burning, and the fire on the hearth was blazing, so that it could not have been long since the inmates had left. Dick wrote a line of warning in his pocket-book, tore out the leaf, and placed it on the table where it could not fail to be seen by anyone entering the room. We then hurried out, and up the lane to Joyce's.

As we drew near we were surprised to find a light in Joyce's window also. I got to the windward side of Dick, and shouted to him:

"A light here also; there must be something strange going on." We hurried as fast as we could up to the house. As we drew close the door was opened, and through a momentary lull we heard the voice of Miss Joyce, Norah's aunt:

"Is that you, Norah?"

"No," I answered.

"Oh, is it you, Mr. Arthur? Thank God, ye've come! I'm in

such terror about Phelim and Norah. They're both out in the shtorm, an' I'm nigh disthracted about them."

By this time we were in the house, and could hear each other speak, although not too well even here, for again the whole force of the gale struck the front of the house, and the noise was great.

"Where is Norah? Is she not here?"

"Oh no, God help us! Wirrastru, wirrastru!" The poor woman was in such a state of agitation and abject terror that it was with some difficulty we could learn from her enough to understand what had occurred. The suspense of trying to get her to speak intelligibly was agonizing, for now every moment was precious; but we could not do anything or make any effort whatever until we had learned all that had occurred. At last, however, it was conveyed to us that early in the evening Joyce had gone out to look after the cattle, and had not since returned.

Late at night old Moynahan had come to the door half drunk, and had hiccoughed a message that Joyce had met with an accident, and was then in Murdock's house. He wanted Norah to go to him there, but Norah only was to go and no one else. She had at once suspected that it was some trap of Murdock's for some evil purpose, but still she thought it better to go, and accordingly called to Turco,[1] the mastiff, to come with her, she remarking to her aunt, "I am safe with him, at any rate." But Turco did not come. He had been restless and groaning for an hour before, and now on looking for him they had found him dead.

This helped to confirm Norah's suspicions, and the two poor women were in an agony of doubt as to what they should do. While they were discussing the matter Moynahan had returned, this time even drunker than before, and repeated his message, but with evident reluctance. Norah had accordingly set to work to cross-examine him, and after a while he admitted that Joyce was not in Murdock's house at all—that he had been sent with the message and told when he had delivered it to go away to

---

1. The text of the first edition reads "Hector" here, but as the dog was referred to as "Turco" in the preceding chapter, the name has been changed here for consistency.

Mother Kelligan's, and not to ever tell anything whatever of the night's proceedings, no matter what might happen or what might be said.

When he had admitted this much he had been so overcome with fright at what he had done that he began to cry and moan, and say that Murdock would kill him for telling on him. Norah had told him he could remain in the cottage where he was if he would tell her where her father was, so that she could go to look for him; but that he had sworn most solemnly that he did not know, but that Murdock knew, for he told him that there would be no chance of seeing him at his own house for hours yet that night.

This had determined Norah that she would go out herself, although the storm was raging wildly, to look for her father. Moynahan, however, would not stay in the cottage, as he said he would be afraid to, unless Joyce himself were there to protect him; for if there were no one but women in the house Murdock would come and murder him and throw his body in the bog, as he had often threatened. So Moynahan had gone out into the night by himself, and Norah had shortly after gone out also, and from that moment she—Miss Joyce—had not set eyes on her, and feared that some harm had happened.

This the poor soul told us in such an agony of dread and grief that it was pitiful to hear her, and we could not but forgive the terrible delay. I was myself in deadly fear, for every kind of harrowing possibility rose before me as the tale was told. It was quite evident that Murdock was bent on some desperate scheme of evil; he either intended to murder Norah or to compromise her in some terrible way. I was almost afraid to think of the subject. It was plain to me that by this means he hoped not only to gratify his revenge, but to get some lever to use against us, one and all, so as to secure his efforts in searching for the treasure. In my rage against the cowardly hound I almost lost sight of the need of thankfulness for one great peril avoided.

However, there was no time at present for further thought—action, prompt and decisive, was vitally necessary. Joyce was absent—we had no clew to where he could be. Norah was alone on the mountain, and with the possibility of Murdock assailing her, for he, too, was abroad, as we knew from the fact of his being away from his house.

We lost not a moment, but went out again into the storm. We did not, however, take the lantern with us, as we found by experience that its occasional light was in the long-run an evil, as we could not by its light see any distance, and the gray of the coming dawn was beginning to show through the abating storm, with a faint indication that before long we should have some light.

We went down the Hill westward until we came near the bog, for we had determined to make a circuit of it as our first piece of exploration, since we thought that here lay the most imminent danger. Then we separated, Dick following the line of the bog downward while I went north, intending to cross at the top and proceed down the farther side. We had agreed on a signal, if such could be heard through the storm, choosing the Australian "coo-ee," which is the best sound to travel known.

I hurried along as fast as I dared, for I was occasionally in utter darkness. Although the morning was coming with promise of light, the sea windswept inland masses of swiftly-driving mist, which, while they encompassed me, made movement not only difficult and dangerous, but at times almost impossible. The electric feeling in the air had become intensified, and each moment I expected the thunderstorm to burst. Every little while I called, "Norah! Norah!" in the vain hope that, while returning from her search for her father, she might come within the sound of my voice. But no answering sound came back to me, except the fierce roar of the storm, laden with the wild dash of the breakers hurled against the cliffs and the rocks below.

Even then, so strangely does the mind work, the words of the old song, "The Pilgrim of Love,"[2] came mechanically to my

---

2. A popular 19th century song which began "Orinthia my beloved, I call in vain." The song would also figure significantly in another Irish work, George Bernard Shaw's *The Apple Cart* (1930)

memory, as though I had called "Orinthia" instead of "Norah":

*"Till with 'Orinthia' all the rocks resound."*

On, on I went, following the line of the bog, till I had reached the northern point, where the ground rose and began to become solid. I found the bog here so swollen with rain that I had to make a long detour so as to get round to the western side. High up on the Hill there was, I knew, a rough shelter for the cattle; and as it struck me that Joyce might have gone here to look after his stock, and that Norah had gone hither to search for him, I ran up to it. The cattle were there, huddled together in a solid mass behind the sheltering wall of sods and stones. I cried out as loudly as I could from the windward side, so that my voice would carry:

"Norah! Norah! Joyce! Joyce! Are you there? Is anyone there?" There was a stir among the cattle and one or two low "moos" as they heard the human voice, but no sound from either of those I sought; so I ran down again to the farther side of the bog. I knew now that neither Norah nor her father could be on this point of the hill, or they would have heard my voice; and as the storm came from the west, I made a zigzag line going east to west as I followed down the bog so that I might have a chance of being heard should there be any one to hear. When I got near to the entrance to the Cliff Fields I shouted as loudly as I could, "Norah! Norah!" but the wind took my voice away as it would sweep thistles down, and it was as though I made the effort but no voice came, and I felt awfully alone in the midst of a thick pall of mist.

On, on I went, following the line of the bog. Lower down there was some shelter from the storm, for the great ridge of rocks here rose between me and the sea, and I felt that my voice could be heard farther off. I was sick at heart and chilled with despair, till I felt as if the chill of my soul had extended even to my blood; but on I went with set purpose, the true doggedness of despair.

As I went I thought I heard a cry through the mist—Norah's

voice. It was but an instant, and I could not be sure whether my ears indeed heard, or if the anguish of my heart had created the phantom of a voice to deceive me. However, be it what it might, it awoke me like a clarion; my heart leaped and the blood surged in my brain till I almost became dizzy. I listened to try if I could distinguish from what direction the voice had come.

I waited in agony. Each second seemed a century, and my heart beat like a trip-hammer. Then again I heard the sound— faint, but still clear enough to hear. I shouted with all my power, but once again the roar of the wind overpowered me; however, I ran on towards the voice.

There was a sudden lull in the wind—a blaze of lightning lit up the whole scene, and, some fifty yards before me, I saw two figures struggling at the edge of the rocks. In that welcome glance, infinitesimal though it was, I recognized the red petticoat which, in that place and at that time, could be none other than Norah's. I shouted as I leaped forward; but just then the thunder broke overhead, and in the mighty and prolonged roll every other sound faded into nothingness, as though the thunder-clap had come on a primeval stillness. As I drew near to where I had seen the figures, the thunder rolled away, and through its vanishing sound I heard distinctly Norah's voice:

"Help! help! Arthur! Father! help! help!" Even in that wild moment my heart leaped, that of all names, she called on mine the first.—Whatever men may say, Love and Jealousy are near kinsmen! I shouted in return as I ran, but the wind took my voice away; and then I heard her voice again, but fainter than before:

"Help! Arthur—father! Is there no one to help me now?" And then the lightning flashed again, and in the long jagged flash we saw each other, and I heard her glad cry before the thunder-clap drowned all else. I had seen that her assailant was Murdock, and I rushed at him, but he had seen me too, and before I could lay hands on him he had let her go, and with a mighty oath which the roll of the thunder drowned, he struck her to the earth and ran.

I raised my poor darling, and, carrying her a little distance, placed her on the edge of the ridge of rocks beside us, for by the light in the sky, which grew paler each second, I saw that a stream of water rising from the bog was flowing towards us. She was unconscious; so I ran to the stream and dipped my hat full of water to bring to revive her. Then I remembered the signal of finding her, and putting my hands to my lips I sounded "coo-ee" once, twice. As I stood I could see Murdock running to his house, for every instant it seemed to grow lighter, and the mist to disperse. The thunder had swept away the rain-clouds, and let in the light of the coming dawn.

But even as I stood there—and I had not delayed an unnecessary second—the ground under me seemed to be giving way. There was a strange shudder or shiver below me, and my feet began to sink. With a wild cry—for I felt that the fatal moment had come, that the bog was moving, and had caught me in its toils—I threw myself forward towards the rock. My cry seemed to arouse Norah like the call of a trumpet. She leaped to her feet, and in an instant seemed to realize my danger, and rushed towards me. When I saw her coming I shouted to her:

"Keep back! keep back." But she did not pause an instant, and the only words she said were:

"I am coming, Arthur, I am coming!"

Half-way between us there was a flat-topped piece of rock, which raised its head out of the surrounding bog. As she struggled towards it, her feet began to sink, and a new terror for her was added to my own. But she did not falter a moment, and, as her lighter weight was in her favour, with a great effort she gained it. In the mean time I struggled forward. There was between me and the rock a clump of furze-bushes; on these I threw myself, and for a second or two they supported me. Then even these began to sink with me, for faster and faster, with each succeeding second, the earth seemed to liquify and melt away.

Up to now I had never realized the fear, or even the possibility, of death to myself; hitherto all my fears had been for Norah. But now came to me the bitter pang which must be for each of the children of men on whom Death has laid his icy hand. That this dread moment had come there was no doubt; nothing short of a miracle could save me.

No language could describe the awful sensation of that melting away of the solid earth; the most dreadful nightmare would be almost a pleasant memory compared with it.

I was now only a few feet from the rock whose very touch meant safety to me, but it was just beyond my reach. I was sinking to my doom! I could see the horror in Norah's eyes as she gained the rock and struggled to her feet.

But even Norah's love could not help me; I was beyond the reach of her arms, and she no more than I could keep a foothold on the liquifying earth. Oh, that she had a rope and I might be saved! Alas! she had none; even the shawl that might have aided me had fallen off in her struggle with Murdock.

But Norah had, with her woman's quick instinct, seen a way to help me. In an instant she had torn off her red petticoat of heavy homespun cloth and thrown one end to me. I clutched and caught it with a despairing grasp, for by this time only my head and hands remained above the surface.

"Now, O God, for strength!" was the earnest prayer of her heart; and my thought was:

"Now for the strong hands that that other had despised!"

Norah threw herself backward with her feet against a projecting piece of the rock, and I felt that if we could both hold out long enough I was saved.

Little by little I gained! I drew closer and closer to the rock! Closer! closer still! till with one hand I grasped the rock itself, and hung on, breathless, in blind desperation. I was only just able to support myself, for there was a strange dragging power in the viscous mass that held me, and greatly taxed my strength, already exhausted in the terrible struggle for life. The bog was beginning to move! But Norah bent forward, kneeling on the rock, and grasped my coat-collar in her strong hands. Love and despair lent her additional strength, and with one last great effort she pulled me upward, and in an instant more I lay on the rock safe and in her arms.

During this time, short as it was, the morning had advanced, and the cold gray mysterious light disclosed the whole slope before us, dim in the shadow of the Hill. Opposite to us, across the bog, we saw Joyce and Dick watching us, and between the gusts of wind we faintly heard their shouts.

To our right, far down the Hill, the Shleenanaher stood out boldly, its warder rocks struck by the gray light falling over the hilltop. Nearer to us, and something in the same direction, Murdock's house rose, a black mass in the centre of the hollow.

But as we looked around us, thankful for our safety, we grasped each other more closely, and a low cry of fear emphasized Norah's shudder, for a terrible thing began to happen.

The whole surface of the bog, as far as we could see it in the dim light, became wrinkled, and then began to move in little eddies, such as one sees in a swollen river. It seemed to rise and rise till it grew almost level with where we were, and instinctively we rose to our feet and stood there awe-struck, Norah clinging to me, and with our arms round each other.

The shuddering surface of the bog began to extend on every side to even the solid ground which curbed it, and with relief we saw that Dick and Joyce stood high up on a rock. All things on its surface seemed to melt away and disappear as though swallowed up. This silent change or demoralization spread down in the direction of Murdock's house, but when it got to the edge of the hollow in which the house stood, it seemed to move as swiftly forward as water leaps down a cataract.

Instinctively we both shouted a warning to Murdock—he, too, villain though he was, had a life to lose. He had evidently felt some kind of shock or change, for he came rushing out of the house full of terror. For an instant he seemed paralyzed with fright as he saw what was happening. And it was little wonder; for in that instant the whole house began to sink into the earth—to sink as a ship founders in a stormy sea, but without the violence and turmoil that marks such a catastrophe. There was something more terrible, more deadly, in that silent, causeless destruction than in the devastation of the earthquake or the hurricane.

The wind had now dropped away; the morning light struck full over the Hill, and we could see clearly. The sound of the waves dashing on the rocks below, and the booming of the distant breakers filled the air, but through it came another sound, the like of which I had never heard, and the like of which I hope, in God's providence, I shall never hear again: a long, low gurgle, with something of a sucking sound—something terrible, resistless, and with a sort of hiss in it, as of seething waters striving to be free.

Then the convulsion of the bog grew greater; it almost seemed as if some monstrous living thing was deep under the surface and writhing to escape.

By this time Murdock's house had sunk almost level with the bog. He had climbed on the thatched roof, and stood there looking towards us, and stretching forth his hands as though in supplication for help. For a while the superior size and buoyancy of the roof sustained it, but then it too began slowly to sink. Murdock knelt, and clasped his hands in a frenzy of prayer.

And then came a mighty roar and a gathering rush. The side of the Hill below us seemed to burst. Murdock threw up his arms; we heard his wild cry as the roof of the house, and he with it, was in an instant sucked below the surface of the heaving mass.

Then came the end of the terrible convulsion. With a rushing sound, and the noise of a thousand waters falling, the whole bog swept, in waxes of gathering size and with a hideous writhing, down the mountain-side to the entrance of the Shleenanaher— struck the portals with a sound like thunder, and piled up to a vast height. And then the millions of tons of slime and ooze, and bog and earth, and broken rock swept through the Pass into the sea.

Norah and I knelt down, hand in hand, and with full hearts thanked God for having saved us from so terrible a doom.

The waves of the torrent rushing by us at first came almost

level with us; but the stream diminished so quickly, that in an incredibly short time we found ourselves perched on the top of a high jutting rock, standing sharply up from the sloping sides of a deep ravine, where but a few minutes before the bog had been. Carefully we climbed down, and sought a more secure place on the base of the ridge of rocks behind us. The deep ravine lay below us, down whose sides began to rattle ominously, here and there, masses of earth and stones deprived of their support below where the torrent had scoured their base.

Lighter and lighter grew the sky over the mountain, till at last one red ray shot up like a crack in the vault of heaven, and a great light seemed to smite the rocks that glistened in their coat of wet. Across the ravine we saw Joyce and Dick beginning to descend, so as to come over to us. This aroused us, and we shouted to them to keep back and waved our arms to them in signal; for we feared that some landslip or some new outpouring of the bog might sweep them away, or that the bottom of the ravine might be still only treacherous slime.

They saw our gesticulations, if they did not hear our voices, and held back. Then we pointed up the ravine, and signalled them that we would move up the edge of the rocks. This we proceeded to do, and they followed on the other side, watching us intently. Our progress was slow, for the rocks were steep and difficult, and we had to keep eternally climbing up and descending the serrated edges, where the strata lapped over each other; and besides we were chilled and numbed with cold.

At last, however, we passed the corner where was the path down to the Cliff Fields, and turned eastward up the Hill. Then in a little while we got well above the ravine, which here grew shallower, and could walk on more level ground. Here we saw that the ravine ended in a deep cleft, whence issued a stream of water. And then we saw hurrying up over the top of the cleft Joyce and Dick.

Up to now Norah and I had hardly spoken a word. Our hearts were too full for speech; and, indeed, we understood each other, and could interpret our thoughts by a subtler language than that formulated by man.

In another minute Norah was clasped in her father's arms. He held her close, and kissed her, and cried over her; while Dick wrung my hand hard. Then Joyce left his daughter, and came and flung his arms round me, and thanked God that I had escaped; while Norah went up to Dick, and put her arms round him, and kissed him as a sister might.

We all went back together as fast as we could; and the sun that rose that morning rose on no happier group, despite the terror and the trouble of the night. Norah walked between her father and me, holding us both tightly, and Dick walked on my other side with his arm in mine. As we came within sight of the house, we met Miss Joyce, her face gray with anxiety. She rushed towards us, and flung her arms round Norah, and the two women rocked each other in their arms; and then we all kissed her—even Dick, to her surprise. His kiss was the last, and it seemed to pull her together; for she perked up, and put her cap straight—a thing which she had not done for the rest of us. Then she walked beside us, holding her brother's hand.

We all talked at once, and told the story over and over again of the deadly peril I had been in, and how Norah had saved my life; and here the brave girl's fortitude gave way. She seemed to realize all at once the terror and the danger of the long night, and suddenly her lips grew white, and she would have sunk down to the ground, only that I had seen her faint coming and had caught her and held her tight. Her dear head fell over on my shoulder, but her hands never lost their grasp of my arm.

We carried her down towards the house as quickly as we could; but before we had got to the door she had recovered from her swoon, and her first look when her eyes opened was for me, and the first word she said was:

"Arthur! Is he safe?"

And then I laid her in the old armchair by the hearth-place, and took her cold hands in mine, and kissed them and cried over them— which I hoped vainly that no one saw.

Then Miss Joyce, like a true housekeeper, stirred herself, and the flames roared up the chimney, and the slumbering kettle on the chain over the fire woke and sang again; and it seemed like magic, for all at once we were all sipping hot whiskey punch, and beginning to feel the good effects of it.

Then Miss Joyce hurried away Norah to change her clothes, and Dick and I went with Joyce, and we all rigged ourselves out with whatever came to hand; and then we came back to the kitchen and laughed at each other's appearance. We found Miss Joyce already making preparations for breakfast, and succeeding pretty well, too.

And then Norah joined us, but she was not the least grotesque; she seemed as though she had just stepped out of a bandbox—she seemed so trim and neat, with her gray jacket and her Sunday red petticoat. Her black hair was coiled in one glorious roll round her noble head, and there was but one thing which I did not like, and which sent a pang through my heart—a blue and swollen bruise on her ivory forehead where Murdock had struck her that dastard blow! She saw my look and her eyes fell, and when I went to her and kissed the wound and whispered to her how it pained me, she looked up at me and whispered so that none of the others could hear:

"Hush! hush! Poor soul, he has paid a terrible penalty; let us forget as we forgive." And then I took her hands in mine and stooped to kiss them, while the others all smiled happily as they looked on; but she tried to draw them away, and a bright blush dyed her cheeks as she murmured to me:

"No, no, Arthur! Arthur dear, not now! I only did what any one would do for you!" and the tears rushed to her eyes.

"I must, Norah," said I, "I must, for I owe these brave hands my life!" and I kissed them and she made no more resistance. Her father's voice and words sounded very true as he said:

"Nay, daughter, it is right that he should kiss those hands this blessed mornin', for they took a true man out of the darkness of the grave!"

And then my noble old Dick came over too, and he raised those dear hands reverently to his lips, and said, very softly:

"For he is dear to us all!"

By this time Miss Joyce had breakfast well under way, and one and all we thought that it was time we should let the brightness of the day and the lightness of our hearts have a turn; and Joyce said heartily:

"Come now! Come now! Let us sit down to breakfast; but first let us give thanks to Almighty God that has been so good to us, and let us forgive that poor wretch that met such a horrible death. Rest to his soul!"

We were all silent for a little bit, for the great gladness of our hearts, that came through the terrible remembrance thus brought home to us, was too deep for words. Norah and I sat hand in hand, and between us was but one heart and one soul and one thought—and all were filled with gratitude.

When once we had begun breakfast in earnest a miniature babel broke out. We had each something to tell and much to hear; and for the latter reason we tacitly arranged, after the first outbreak, that each should speak in turn.

Miss Joyce told us of the terrible anxiety she had been in ever since she had seen us depart, and how every sound, great or small—even the gusts of wind that howled down the chimney and made the casements rattle—had made her heart jump into her mouth, and brought her out to the door to see if we or any of us were coming. Then Dick told us how, on proceeding down the eastern side of the bog, he had diverged so as to look in at Murdock's house to see if he were there, but had found only old Moynahan lying on the floor in a state of speechless drunkenness, and so wet that the water running from his clothes had formed a pool of water on the floor.

He had evidently only lately returned from wandering on the hillside. Then as he was about to go on his way, he had heard, as he thought, a noise lower down the Hill, and on going towards it had met Joyce carrying a sheep which had its leg broken, and which he told him had been blown off a steep rock on the south side of the Hill. Then they two had kept together, after Dick had told him of our search for Norah, until we had seen them in the coming gray of the dawn.

Next Joyce took up the running, and told us how he had been working on the top of the mountain when he saw the signs of the storm coming so fast that he thought it would be well to look after the sheep and cattle, and see them in some kind of shelter before the morning. He had driven all the cattle which were up high on the hill into the shelter where I had found them, and then had gone down the southern shoulder of the hill, placing all the sheep and cattle in places of shelter as well as he could, until he had come across the wounded one, which he took on his shoulders to bring it home, but which had since been carried away in the bursting of the bog. He finished by reminding me jocularly that I owed him something for his night's work, for the stock was now all mine.

"No," said I, "not for another day. My purchase of your ground and stock was only to take effect from afternoon of the 28th, and we are now only at the early morning of that day; but at any rate I must thank you for the others," for I had a number of sheep and cattle which Dick had taken over from the other farmers whose land I had bought.

Then I told over again all that had happened to me. I had to touch on the blow which Norah had received, but I did so as lightly as I could; and when I said "God forgive him!" they all added softly, "Amen!"

Then Dick put in a word about poor old Moynahan:

"Poor old fellow, he is gone also. He was a drunkard, but he wasn't all bad. Perhaps he saved Norah last night from a terrible danger. His life, mayhap, may leaven the whole lump of filth and wickedness that went through the Shleenanaher into the sea last night!"

We all said "Amen" again, and I have no doubt that we all meant it with all our hearts.

Then I told again of Norah's brave struggle, and how, by her courage and her strength, she took me out of the very jaws of a terrible death. She put one hand before her eyes—for I held the other close in mine—and through her fingers dropped her welling tears.

We sat silent for a while, and we felt that it was only right and fitting when Joyce came round to her and laid his hand on her head and stroked her hair as he said:

"Ye have done well, daughter—ye have done well!"

## Chapter 18

### The Fulfilment

When breakfast was finished, Dick proposed that we should go now and look in the full daylight at the effect of the shifting of the bog. I suggested to Norah that perhaps she had better not come as the sight might harrow her feelings, and, besides, that she would want some rest and sleep after her long night of terror and effort. She point-blank refused to stay behind, and accordingly we all set out, having now had our clothes dried and changed, leaving only Miss Joyce to take care of the house.

The morning was beautiful and fresh after the storm. The deluge of rain had washed everything so clean that already the ground was beginning to dry, and as the morning sun shone hotly there was in the air that murmurous hum that follows rain when the air is still. And the air was now still—the storm seemed to have spent itself, and away to the west there was no sign of its track, except that the great Atlantic rollers were heavier and the surf on the rocks rose higher than usual.

We took our way first down the Hill, and then westward to the Shleenanaher, for we intended, under Dick's advice, to follow, if possible, up to its source the ravine made by the bog. When we got to the entrance of the Pass we were struck with the vast height to which the bog had risen when its mass first struck the portals. A hundred feet overhead there was the great brown mark, and on the sides of the Pass the same mark was visible, declining quickly as it got seaward and the Pass widened, showing the track of its passage to the sea.

We climbed the rocks and looked over. Norah clung close to me, and my arm went round her and held her tight as we peered over and saw where the great waves of the Atlantic struck the rocks three hundred feet below us, and were for a quarter of a mile away still tinged with the brown slime of the bog.

We then crossed over the ravine, for the rocky bottom was here laid bare, and so we had no reason to fear water-holes or pitfalls. A small stream still ran down the ravine and, shallowing out over the shelf of rock, spread all across the bottom of the Pass, and fell into the sea—something like a miniature of the Staubach Fall, as the water whitened in the falling.

We then passed up on the west side of the ravine, and saw that the stream which ran down the centre was perpetual—a live stream, and not merely the drainage of the ground where the bog had saturated the earth. As we passed up the Hill we saw where the side of the slope had been torn bodily away, and the great chasm where once the house had been which Murdock took from Joyce, and so met his doom. Here there was a great pool of water—and, indeed, all throughout the ravine were places where the stream broadened into deep pools, and again into shallow pools w here it ran over the solid bed of rock. As we passed up Dick hazarded an explanation or a theory:

"Do you know it seems to me that this ravine or valley was once before just as it is now? The stream ran down it and out at the Shleenanaher just as it does now. Then by some landslips, or a series of them, or by a falling tree, the passage became blocked, and the hollow became a lake, and its edges grew rank with boggy growth; and then, from one cause and another—the falling in of the sides, or the rush of rain-storms carrying down the detritus of the mountain and perpetually washing down particles of clay from the higher levels—the lake became choked up; and then the lighter matter floated to the top, and by time and vegetable growth became combined.

"And so the whole mass grew cohesive and floated on the water and slime below. This may have occurred more than once. Nay, moreover, sections of the bog may have become segregated or separated by some similarity of condition affecting its parts, or by some formation of the ground, as by the valley narrowing in parts between walls of rock so that the passage could be easily choked. And so solid earth formed to be again softened and demoralized by the latter mingling with the less solid mass above it. It is possible, if not probable, that more than once, in the countless ages that have passed, this ravine has been as we see it, and again as it was but a few hours ago."

No one had anything to urge against this theory, and we all proceeded on our way.

When we came to the place where Norah had rescued me, we examined the spot most carefully, and again went over the scene and the exploit. It was almost impossible to realize that this great rock, towering straight up from the bottom of the ravine, had, at the fatal hour, seemed only like a tussock rising from the bog. When I had climbed to the top I took my knife and cut a cross on the rock, where my brave girl's feet had rested, to mark the spot.

Then we went on again. Higher up the Hill we came to a place where, on each side, a rocky promontory with straight, deep walls, jutted into the ravine, making a sort of narrow gateway or gorge in the valley. Dick pointed it out.

"See, here is one of the very things I spoke of that made the bog into sections, or chambers, or tanks, or whatever we should call them. More than that, here is an instance of the very thing I hinted at before—that the peculiar formation of the Snake's Pass runs right through the Hill. If this be so—but we shall see later on."

On the other side was, we agreed, the place where old Moynahan had said the Frenchmen had last been seen. Dick and I were both curious about the matter, and we agreed to cross the ravine and make certain, for if it were the spot, Dick's mark of the stones in the Y shape would be a proof. Joyce and Norah both refused to let us go alone, so we all went up a little farther, where the sides of the rock sloped on each side, and where we could pass safely, as the bed was rock and quite smooth, with the stream flowing over it in a thin sheet.

When we got to the bottom, Joyce, who was looking round, said suddenly:

"What is that like a square block behind the high rock on the other side?" He went over to it, and an instant after gave a great cry, and turned and beckoned to us. We all ran over; and there before us, in a crescent-shaped nook at the base of the lofty rock, lay a wooden chest. The top was intact, but one of the lower corners was broken, as though with a fall; and from the broken aperture had fallen out a number of coins, which we soon found to be of gold.

On the top of the chest we could make out the letters R. F. in some metal, discoloured and corroded with a century of slime, and on its ends were great metal handles, to each of which something white was attached. We stooped to look at them, and then Norah, with a low cry, turned to me and laid her head on my breast, as though to shut out some horrid sight. Then we investigated the mass that lay there.

At each end of the chest lay a skeleton, the fleshless fingers grasping the metal handle. We recognized the whole story at a glance, and our hats came off.

"Poor fellows," said Dick; "they did their duty nobly; they guarded their treasure to the last." Then he went on: "See, they evidently stepped into the bog, straight off the rock, and were borne down at once, holding tight to the handles of the chest they carried—or, stay"—and he stooped lower and caught hold of something—"see how the bog can preserve. This leather strap attached to the handles of the chest each had round his shoulder, and so, willy nilly, they were dragged to their doom. Never mind, they were brave fellows all the same, and faithful ones; they never let go the handles; look, their dead hands clasp them still. France should be proud of such sons. It would make a noble coat of arms, this treasure-chest sent by freemen to aid others, and with two such supporters!"

We looked at the chest and the skeletons for a while, and then Dick said:

"Joyce, this is on your land—for it is yours till tomorrow—and you may as well keep it; possession is nine points of the law, and if we take the gold out, the Government can only try to claim it. But if they take it, we may ask in vain." Joyce answered:

"Take it I will, an' gladly; but not for meself. The money was sent for Ireland's good, to help them that wanted help, an' plase God, I'll see it doesn't go asthray now."

Dick's argument was a sensible one, and straightway we wrenched the top off the chest, and began to remove the gold; but we never stirred the chest or took away those skeleton hands from the handles which they grasped.

It took us all, carrying a good load each, to bring the money to Joyce's cottage. We locked it in a great oak chest, and warned Miss Joyce not to say a word about it. I told Miss Joyce that if Andy came for me he was to be sent on to us, explaining that we were going back to the top of the new ravine.

We followed it up farther, till we reached a point much higher up on the Hill, and at last came to the cleft in the rock w hence the stream issued. The floor here was rocky, and, it being so, we did not hesitate to descend, and even to enter the chine. As we did so, Dick turned to me.

"Well, it seems to me that the mountain is giving up its secrets today. We have found the Frenchmen's treasure, and now we may expect, I suppose, to find the lost crown. By George, though, it is strange! They said the Snake became the Shifting Bog, and that it went out by the Shleenanaher, as we saw the bog did."

When we got well into the chine we began to look about us curiously. There was something odd—something which we did not expect. Dick was the most prying, and certainly the most excited of us all. He touched some of the rock and then almost shouted: "Hurrah! this a day of discoveries!—Hurrah! hurrah!"

"Now, Dick, what is it?" I asked—myself in a tumult, for his enthusiasm, although we did not know the cause, excited us all.

"Why, man, don't you see? This is what we have wanted all along."

"What is? Speak out, man dear! We are all in ignorance." Dick laid his hand impressively on the rock.

"Limestone! There is a streak of it here, right through the mountain; and, moreover, look, look! This is not all Nature's work; these rocks have been cut in places by the hands of men." We all got very excited, and hurried up the chine; but the rocks now joined over our heads, and all was dark beyond, and the chine became a cave.

"Has anyone a match? We must have a light of some kind here," said Joyce.

"There is the lantern in the house. I shall run for it. Don't stir until I get back," I cried; and I ran out and climbed the side of the ravine, and got to Joyce's house as soon as I could. My haste and impetuosity frightened Miss Joyce, who called in terror:

"Is there anything wrong—not an accident I hope?"

"No, no; we only want to examine a rock, and the place is dark. Give us the lantern—quick—and some matches."

"Aisy, aisy, alanna!" she said. "The rock won't run away."

I took the lantern and matches and ran back. When we had lit the lantern, Norah suggested that we should be very careful, as there might be foul air about. Dick laughed at the idea.

"No foul air here, Norah; it was full of water a few hours ago," and, taking the lantern, he went into the narrow opening. We all followed, Norah clinging tightly to me. The cave widened as we entered, and we stood in a moderate-sized cavern, partly natural and partly hollowed out by rough tools. Here and there were inscriptions in strange character, formed by straight vertical lines something like the old telegraph signs, but placed differently.

"Ogham!—one of the oldest and least known of writings," said Dick, when the light fell on them as he raised the lantern.

At the far end of the cave was a sort of slab or bracket, formed of a part of the rock carven out. Norah went towards it, and called us to tier with a loud cry. We all rushed over, and Dick threw the light of the lantern on her; and then exclamations of wonder burst from us also.

In her hand she held an ancient crown of strange form. It was composed of three pieces of flat gold joined all along one edge, like angle-iron, and twisted delicately. The gold was wider and the curves bolder in the centre, from which they were fined away to the ends and then curved into a sort of hook. In the centre was set a great stone, that shone with the yellow light of a topaz, but with a fire all its own.

Dick was the first to regain his composure, and, as usual, to speak.

"The Lost Crown of Gold!—the crown that gave the Hill its name, and was the genesis of the story of St. Patrick and the King of the Snakes. Moreover, see, there is a scientific basis for the legend. Before this stream cut its way out through the limestone, and made this cavern, the waters were forced upward to the lake at the top of the Hill, and so kept it supplied; but when its channel was cut here—or a way opened for it by some convulsion of nature, or the rending asunder of these rocks—the lake fell away."

He stopped, and I went on:

"And so, ladies and gentlemen, the legend is true: that the Lost Crown would be discovered when the water of the lake was found again."

"Begor, that's thrue, anyhow!" said the voice of Andy in the entrance. "Well, yer 'an'r, iv all the sthrange things what iver happened, this is the most shtrangest! Fairies isn't in it this time, at all, at all!"

I told Andy something of what had happened, including the terrible deaths of Murdock and Moynahan, and sent him off to tell the head-constable of police, and anyone else he might see. I told him also of the two skeletons found beside the chest.

Andy was off like a rocket. Such news as he had to tell would not come twice in a man's lifetime, and would make him famous through all the countryside. When he was gone we decided that we had seen all that was worthwhile, and agreed to go back to the house, where we might be on hand to answer all queries regarding the terrible occurrences of the night. When we got outside the cave, and had ascended the ravine, I noticed that the crown in Norah's hands had now none of the yellow glare of the jewel, and feared the latter had been lost. I said to her:

"Norah, dear, have you dropped the jewel from the crown?"

She held it up, startled, to see; and then we all wondered again, for the jewel was still there, but it had lost its yellow colour, and shone with a white light, something like the lustre of a pearl seen in the midst of the flash of diamonds. It looked like some kind of uncut crystal, but none of us had ever seen anything like it.

We had hardly got back to the house when the result of Andy's mission began to be manifested. Every soul in the countryside seemed to come pouring in to see the strange sights at Knockcalltecrore. There was a perfect babel of sounds; and every possible and impossible story, and theory, and conjecture was ventilated at the top of the voice of every one, male and female.

The head-constable was one of the first to arrive. He came into the cottage, and we gave him all the required details of Murdock's and Moynahan's death, which he duly wrote down, and then went off with Dick to go over the ground.

Presently there was a sudden silence among the crowd outside, the general body of which seemed to continue as great as ever from the number of new arrivals, despite the fact that a large number of those present had followed Dick and the head-constable in their investigation of the scene of the catastrophe. The silence was as odd as noise would have been under ordinary circumstances, so I went to the door to see what it meant. In the porch I met Father Ryan, who had just come from the scene of the disaster. He shook me warmly by the hand, and said loudly, so that all those around might hear:

"Mr. Severn, I'm real glad and thankful to see ye this day. Praise be to God, that watched over ye last night, and strengthened the arms of that brave girl to hold ye up." Here Norah came to join us; and he took her warmly by both hands, while the people cheered.

"My, but we're all proud of ye! Remember that God has given a great mercy through your hands, and ye both must thank him all the days of your life. And those poor men that met their death so horribly—poor Moynahan, in his drunken slumber. Men, it's a warning to ye all. Whenever ye may be tempted to take a glass too much, let the fate of that poor soul rise up before ye and forbid ye to go too far. As for that unhappy Murdock, may God forgive him and look lightly an' his sins! I told him what he should expect—that the fate of Ahab and Jezebel would be his. For Ahab coveted the vineyard of his neighbour Naboth, and as Jezebel wrought evil to aid him to his desire, so this man hath coveted his neighbour's goods and wrought evil to ruin him. And now behold his fate, even as the fate of Ahab and Jezebel! He went without warning and without rites, and no man knows where his body lies. The fishes of the sea have preyed on him, even as the dogs on Jezebel." Here Joyce joined us, and he turned to him:

"And do you, Phelim Joyce, take to heart the lesson of God's goodness! Ye thought when yer land and yer house was taken that a great wrong was done ye, and that God had deserted ye; and yet so inscrutable are his ways that these very things were the salvation of ye and all belonging to ye. For in his stead you and yours would have been swept in that awful avalanche into the sea."

And now the head-constable returned with Dick, and the priest went out. I took the former aside and asked him if there would be any need for Norah to remain, as there were other witnesses to all that had occurred. He told me that there was not the slightest need. Then he went away, after telling the people that we all had had a long spell of trouble and labour, and would want to be quiet and have some rest. And so, with a good feeling and kindness of heart which I have never seen lacking in this people, they melted away; and we all came within the house, and shut the door, and sat round the fire to discuss what should be done. Then and there we decided that the very next day Norah should start with her father, for the change of scene would do her good, and take her mind off the terrible experiences of last night.

So that day we rested. The next morning Andy was to drive Joyce and Norah and myself off to Galway, *en route* for London and Paris.

In the afternoon Norah and I strolled out together for one last look at the beautiful scene from our table rock in the Cliff Fields. Close as we had been hitherto, there was now a new bond between us; and when we were out of sight of prying eyes—on the spot where we had first told our loves, I told her of my idea of the new-bond. She hung down her head, but drew closer to me as I told her how much more I valued my life since she had saved it for me, and how I should in all the two years that were to come try hard that every hour should be such as she would like me to have passed.

"Norah, dear," I said, "the bar you place on our seeing each other in all that long time will be hard to bear, but I shall know that I am enduring for your sake." She turned to me, and with earnest eyes looked lovingly into mine as she said:

"Arthur, dear Arthur, God knows I love you! I love you so well that I want to come to you, if I can, in such a way that I may never do you discredit; and I am sure that when the two years are over— and, indeed, they will not go lightly for me— you will not be sorry that you have made the sacrifice for me. Dear, I shall ask you when we meet on our wedding morning if you are satisfied."

When it was time to go home we rose up, and—it might have been that the evening was chilly—a cold feeling came over me, as though I still stood in the shadow of the fateful Hill. And there in the Cliff Fields I kissed Norah Joyce for the last time.

The two years sped quickly enough, although my not being able to see Norah at all was a great trial to me. Often and often I felt tempted almost beyond endurance to go quietly and hang round where she was so that I might get even a passing glimpse of her; but I felt that such would not be loyal to my dear girl. It was hard not to be able to tell her, even now and again, how I loved her; but it had been expressly arranged—and wisely enough too—that I should only write in such a manner as would pass, if necessary, the censorship of the schoolmistress.

"I must be," said Norah to me, "exactly as the other girls are, and, of course, I must be subject to the same rules." And so it was that my letters had to be of tempered warmth, which caused me now and again considerable pain.

My dear girl wrote to me regularly, and although there was not any of what her schoolmistress would call "love" in her letters, she always kept me posted in all her doings; and with every letter it was borne in on me that her heart and feelings were unchanged.

I had certain duties to attend to with regard to my English property, and this kept me fairly occupied.

Each few months I ran over to the Knockcalltecrore, which Dick was transforming into a fairy-land. The discovery of the limestone had, as he had conjectured, created possibilities in the way of building and of water-works of which at first we had not dreamed. The new house rose *on* the table rock in the Cliff Fields. A beautiful house it was, of red sandstone with red tiled roof and quaint gables, and jutting windows and balustrades of carven stone. The whole Cliff Fields were laid out as exquisite gardens, and the murmur of water was everywhere. None of this I ever told Norah in my letters, as it was to be a surprise to her.

On the spot where she had rescued me we had reared a great stone—a monolith—whereon a simple legend told the story of a woman's strength and bravery. Round its base were sculptured the history of the mountain, from its legend of the King of Snakes down to the lost treasure and the rescue of myself. This was all carried out under Dick's eye. The legend on the stone was:

*Norah Joyce a Brave Woman*
*On This Spot*
*By Her Courage and Devotion*
*Saved a Man's Life.*

At the end of the first year Norah went to another school at Dresden for six months; and then, by her own request to Mr.

Chapman, was transferred to an English school at Brighton, one justly celebrated among Englishwomen.

These last six months were very, very long to me; for as the time drew near when I might claim my darling the suspense grew very great, and I began to have harrowing fears lest her love might not have survived the long separation and the altered circumstances.

I heard regularly from Joyce. He had gone to live with his son Eugene, who was getting along well, and was already beginning to make a name for himself as an engineer. By his advice his father had taken a subsection of the great ship canal, then in progress of construction, and with the son's know ledge and his own shrewdness and energy was beginning to realize what to him was a fortune. So that the purchase-money of Shleenanaher, which formed his capital, was used to a good purpose.

At last the long period of waiting came to an end. A month before Norah's school was finished, Joyce went to Brighton to see her, having come to visit me beforehand. His purpose and mine was to arrange all about the wedding, which we wanted to be exactly as she wished. She asked her father to let it be as quiet as possible, with absolutely no fuss—no publicity, and in some quiet place where no one knew us.

"Tell Arthur," she said, "that I should like it to be somewhere near the sea, and where we can get easily on the Continent."

I fixed on Hythe, which I had been in the habit of visiting occasionally, as the place where we were to be married. Here, high over the sea level, rises the grand old church where the bones of so many brave old Norsemen rest after a thousand years. The place was so near to Folkestone that, after the wedding and an informal breakfast, we could drive over to catch the mid-day boat. I lived the requisite time in Hythe, and complied with all the formalities.

I did not see my darling until we met in the church-porch, and then I gazed on her with unstinted admiration. Oh, what a peerless beauty she was! Every natural grace and quality seemed developed to the full. Every single grace of womanhood was there; every subtle manifestation of high-breeding; every stamp of the highest culture. There was no one in the porch—for those with me delicately remained in the church when they saw me go out to meet my bride—and I met her with a joy unspeakable. Joyce went in and left her with me a moment—they had evidently arranged to do so—but when we were quite alone she said to me, with a very serious look:

"Mr. Severn, before we go into the church answer me one question—answer me truthfully, I implore you!" A great fear came upon me that at the last I was to suffer the loss of her I loved—that at the moment when the cup of happiness was at my lips it was to be dashed aside; and it was with a hoarse voice and a beating heart I answered:

"I shall speak truly, Norah. What is it?" She said, very demurely:

"Mr. Severn, are you satisfied with me?" I looked up and caught the happy smile in her eyes, and for answer took her in my arms to kiss her; but she said:

"Not yet, Arthur, not yet. What would they say? And, besides, it would be unlucky." So I released her, and she took my arm, and as we came up the aisle together I whispered to her:

"Yes, my darling! Yes, yes, a thousand times! The time has been long, long; but the days were well spent." She looked at me with a glad, happy look as she murmured in my ear:

"We shall see Italy soon, dear, together. I am so happy!" and she pinched my arm.

That was a very happy wedding, and as informal as it was happy. As Norah had no bridesmaid, Dick, who was to have been my best man, was not going to act; but when Norah knew this she insisted on it, and said, sweetly:

"I should not feel I was married properly unless Dick took his place. And as to my having no bridesmaid, all I can say is, if we had half so good a girl friend, she would be here, of course."

This settled the matter, and Dick, with his usual grace and energy carried out the best man's chief duty of taking care of his principal's hat.

There were only our immediate circle present: Joyce and Eugene, Miss Joyce (who had come all the way from Knocknacar), Mr. Chapman, and Mr. Caicy (who had also come over from Galway specially). There was one other old friend also present, but I did not know it until I came out of the vestry, after signing the register, with my wife on my arm.

There, standing modestly in the background, and with a smile as manifest as a ten-acre field, was none other than Andy—Andy, so well-dressed and smart that there was really nothing to distinguish him from any other man in Hythe. Norah saw him first, and said, heartily:

"Why, there is Andy! How are you, Andy?" and held out her hand. Andy took it in his great fist, and stooped and kissed it as if it had been a saint's hand and not a woman's:

"God bless and keep ye, Miss Norah darlin', an' the Virgin and the saints watch over ye both!" Then he shook hands with me.

"Thank you, Andy," we said, both together, and then I beckoned Dick and whispered to him.

We went back to breakfast in my rooms, and sat down as happy a party as could be, the only one not quite comfortable at first being Andy. He and Dick both came in quite hot and flushed. Dick pointed to him:

"He's an obstinate, truculent villain, is Andy! Why, I had to almost fight him to make him come in. Now, Andy, no running away; it is Miss Norah's will." And Andy subsided bashfully into a seat. It was fully several minutes before he either smiled or winked. We had a couple of hours to pass before it became time to leave for Folkestone; and when breakfast was over, one and then another said a few kindly words. Dick opened the ball by speaking most beautifully of our own worthiness, and of how honestly and honourably each had won the other, and of the long life and happiness that lay, he hoped and believed, before us. Then Joyce spoke a few manly words of love for his daughter and his pride in her. The tears were in his eyes when he said how his one regret in life was that her dear mother had to look down from Heaven her approval on this day, instead of sharing it among us as the best of mothers and the best of women. Then Norah turned to him and laid her head on his breast and cried a little—not unhappily, but happily, as a bride should cry at leaving those she loves for one she loves better still.

Of course both the lawyers spoke, and Eugene said a few words bashfully. I was about to reply to them all, when Andy got up and crystallized the situation in a few words.

"Miss Norah an' yer 'an'r, I'd like, if I might make so bould, to say a wurrd fur all the men and weemen in Ireland that ayther iv yez iver kem across. I often heerd iv fairies, an' Masther Art knows well how he hunted wan from the top iv Knocknacar to the top iv Knockcalltecrore, and I won't say a wurrd about the kind iv a fairy he wanted to find—not even in her quare kind iv an eye—bekase I might be overlooked, as the masther was; and, more betoken, since I kem here Masther Dick has tould me that I'm to be yer 'an'r's Irish coachman.

"Hurroo! an' I might get evicted from that same houldin' fur me impidence in tellin'' tales iv the Masther before he was married; but I'll promise yez both that there'll be no man from the Giant's Causeway to Cape Clear what'll thry, an' thry hardher, to make yer feet walk an' yer wheels rowl in aisy ways than meself. I'm takin' a liberty, I know, be sayin' so much, but plase God, ye'll walk yer ways wid honour an' wid peace, believin' in aich other an' in God; an' may he bless ye both, an' yer childher, and yer childher's childher to folly ye. An' if iver ayther iv yez wants to shtep into glory over a man's body, I hope ye'll not look past poor ould Andy Sullivan!"

Andy's speech was quaint, but it was truly meant, for his heart was full of quick sympathy, and the honest fellow's eyes were full of tears as he concluded.

Then Miss Joyce's health was neatly proposed by Mr. Chapman and responded to in such a way by Mr. Caicy that Norah whispered to me that she would not be surprised if aunt took up her residence in Galway before long.

And now the hour was come to say goodbye to all friends.

253

We entered our carriage and rolled away, leaving behind us waving hands, loving eyes, and hearts that beat most truly.

And the great world lay before us with all the possibilities of happiness that men and women may win for themselves. There was never a cloud to shadow our sunlit way; and we felt that we were one.

# The Watter's Mou'

## CHAPTER 1

It threatened to be a wild night. All day banks of sea-fog had come and gone, sweeping on shore with the south-east wind, which is so fatal at Cruden Bay, and indeed all along the coast of Aberdeenshire, and losing themselves in the breezy expanses of the high uplands beyond. As yet the wind only came in puffs, followed by intervals of ominous calm; but the barometer had been falling for days, and the sky had on the previous night been streaked with great "mare's-tails" running in the direction of the dangerous wind. Up to early morning the wind had been south-westerly, but had then "backed" to south-east; and the sudden change, no less than the backing, was ominous indeed. From the waste of sea came a ceaseless muffled roar, which seemed loudest and most full of dangerous import when it came through the mystery of the driving fog.

Whenever the fog-belts would lift or disperse, or disappear inland before the gusts of wind, the sea would look as though swept with growing anger; for though there were neither big waves as during a storm, nor a great swell as after one, all the surface of the water as far as the eye could reach was covered with little waves tipped with white. Closer together grew these waves as the day wore on, the angrier ever the curl of the white water where they broke. In the North Sea it does not take long for the waves to rise; and all along the eastern edge of Buchan it was taken for granted that there would be wild work on the coast before the night was over.

In the little lookout house on the top of the cliff over the tiny harbour of Port Erroll the coastguard on duty was pacing rapidly to and fro. Every now and again he would pause, and lifting a field-glass from the desk, sweep the horizon from Girdleness at the south of Aberdeen, when the lifting of the mist would let him see beyond the Scaurs, away to the north, where the high cranes of the Blackman quarries at Murdoch Head seemed to cleave the sky like gigantic gallows-trees.

He was manifestly in high spirits, and from the manner in which, one after another, he looked again and again at the Martini-Henry rifle in the rack, the navy revolver stuck muzzle down on a spike, and the cutlass in its sheath hanging on the wall, it was easy to see that his interest arose from something connected with his work as a coastguard. On the desk lay an open telegram smoothed down by his hard hands, with the brown envelope lying beside it. It gave some sort of clue to his excitement, although it did not go into detail. "Keep careful watch tonight; run expected; spare no efforts; most important."

William Barrow, popularly known as Sailor Willy, was a very young man to be a chief boatman in the preventive service, albeit that his station was one of the smallest on the coast. He had been allowed, as a reward for saving the life of his lieutenant, to join the coast service, and had been promoted to chief boatman as a further reward for a clever capture of smugglers, wherein he had shown not only great bravery, but much ability and power of rapid organisation.

The Aberdeen coast is an important one in the way of guarding on account of the vast number of fishing-smacks which, during the season, work from Peterhead up and down the coast, and away on the North Sea right to the shores of Germany and Holland. This vast coming and going affords endless opportunities for smuggling; and, despite of all vigilance, a considerable amount of "stuff" finds its way to the consumers without the formality of the Custom House. The fish traffic is a quick traffic, and its returns come all at once, so that a truly enormous staff would be requisite to examine adequately the thousand fish-smacks which use the harbour of Peterhead, and on Sundays pack its basins with a solid mass of boats.

The coast-line for some forty miles south is favourable for this illicit traffic. The gneiss and granite formations broken up by every convulsion of nature, and worn by the strain and toil of ages into every conceivable form of rocky beauty, offers an endless variety of narrow creeks and bays where the daring, to whom the rocks and the currents and the tides are known, may find secret entrance and speedy exit for their craft. This season the smuggling had been chiefly of an overt kind—that is, the goods had been brought into the harbour amongst the fish and nets, and had been taken through the streets under the eyes of the unsuspecting Customs officers. Some of these takes were so large, that the authorities had made up their minds that there must be a great amount of smuggling going on.

The secret agents in the German, Dutch, Flemish, and French ports were asked to make extra exertions in discovering the amount of the illicit trade, and their later reports were of an almost alarming nature. They said that really vast amounts of tobacco, brandy, rum, silks, laces, and all sorts of excisable commodities were being secretly shipped in the British fishing-fleet; and as only a very small proportion of this was discovered, it was manifest that smuggling to a large extent was once more to the fore.

Accordingly precautions were doubled all along the east coast frequented by the fishing-fleets. Not only were the coastguards warned of the danger and cautioned against devices which might keep them from their work at critical times, but they were apprised of every new shipment as reported from abroad. Furthermore, the detectives of the service were sent about to parts where the men were suspected of laxity—or worse.

Thus it was that Sailor Willy, with the experience of two promotions for cause, and with the sense of responsibility which belonged to his office, felt in every way elated at the possibility of some daring work before him. He knew, of course, that a similar telegram had been received at every station on the coast, and that the chance of an attempt being made in Cruden Bay or its surroundings was a small one; but he was young and brave and hopeful, and with an adamantine sense of integrity to support him in his work. It was unfortunate that his comrade was absent, ill in the hospital at Aberdeen, and that the strain at present on the service, together with the men away on annual training and in the naval manoeuvres, did not permit of a substitute being sent to him. However, he felt strong enough to undertake any amount of duty—he was strong enough and handsome enough to have a good opinion of himself, and too brave and too sensible to let his head be turned by vanity.

As he walked to and fro there was in the distance of his mind—in that dim background against which in a man's mind a woman's form finds suitable projection—some sort of vague hope that a wild dream of rising in the world might be some time realised. He knew that every precaution in his power had been already taken, and felt that he could indulge in fancies without detriment to his work. He had signalled the coastguard at Whinnyfold on the south side of the Bay, and they had exchanged ideas by means of the signal language.

His appliances for further signalling by day or night were in perfect order, and he had been right over his whole boundary since he had received the telegram seeing that all things were in order. Willy Barrow was not one to leave things to chance where duty was concerned.

His daydreams were not all selfish. They were at least so far unselfish that the results were to be shared with another; for Willy Barrow was engaged to be married. Maggie MacWhirter was the daughter of an old fisherman who had seen days more prosperous than the present. He had once on a time owned a fishing-smack, but by degrees he had been compelled to borrow on her, till now, when, although he was nominal owner, the boat was so heavily mortgaged that at any moment he might lose his entire possession.

That such an event was not unlikely was manifest, for the mortgagee was no other than Solomon Mendoza of Hamburg and Aberdeen, who had changed in like manner the ownership of a hundred boats, and who had the reputation of being as remorseless as he was rich. MacWhirter had long been a widower, and Maggie since a little girl had kept house for her father and her two brothers, Andrew and Neil. Andrew was twenty-seven—six years older than Maggie—and Neil had just turned twenty. The elder brother was a quiet, self-contained, hard-working man, who now and again manifested great determination, though generally at unexpected times; the younger was rash, impetuous, and passionate, and though in his moments of quiescence more tender to those he cared for than was usual with men of his class, he was a never-ending source of anxiety to his father and his sister. Andrew, or Sandy as he was always called, took him with consistent quietness.

The present year, although a good one in the main, had been but poor for MacWhirter's boat. Never once had he had a good take of fish—not one-half the number of crans of the best boat; and the season was so far advanced, and the supply had been so plentiful, that a few days before, the notice had been up at Peterhead that after the following week the buyers would not take any more herring.

This notice naturally caused much excitement, and the whole fishing industry determined to make every effort to improve the shining hours left to them. Exertions were on all sides redoubled, and on sea and shore there was little idleness. Naturally the smuggling interest bestirred itself too; its chance for the year was in the rush and bustle and hurry of the coming and going fleet, and anything held over for a chance had to be ventured now or left over for a year—which might mean indefinitely.

Great ventures were therefore taken by some of the boats; and from their daring the authorities concluded that either heavy bribes were given, or else that the goods were provided by others than the fishermen who undertook to run them. A few important seizures, however, made the men wary; and it was understood from the less frequent but greater importance of the seizures, that the price for "running" had greatly gone up. There was much passionate excitement amongst those who were found out and their friends, and a general wish to discover the informers. Some of the smuggling fishermen at first refused to pay the fines until they were told who had informed. This position being unsupportable, they had instead paid the fines and cherished hatred in their hearts.

Some of the more reckless and turbulent spirits had declared their intention of avenging themselves on the informers when they should be known. It was only natural that this feeling of rage should extend to the Customs officers and men of the preventive service, who stood between the unscrupulous adventurers and their harvest; and altogether matters had become somewhat strained between the fishermen and the authorities.

The Port Erroll boats, like those from Collieston, were all up at Peterhead, and of course amongst them MacWhirter's boat the *Sea Gull* with her skipper and his two sons. It was now Friday night, and the boats had been out for several days, so that it was pretty certain that there would be a full harbour at Peterhead on the Saturday. A marriage had been arranged to take place this evening between Thomas Keith of Boddam and Alice MacDonald, whose father kept the public-house The Jamie Fleeman on the northern edge of the Erroll estate. Though the occasion was to be a grand one, the notice of it had been short indeed. It was said by the bride's friends that it had been fixed so hurriedly because the notice of the closing of the fishing season had been so suddenly given out at Peterhead.

Truth to tell, some sort of explanation was necessary, for it was only on Wednesday morning that word had been sent to the guests, and as these came from all sorts of places between Peterhead and Collieston, and taking a sweep of some ten miles inland, there was need of some preparation. The affair was to top all that had ever been seen at Port Erroll, and as The Jamie Fleeman was but a tiny place—nothing, in fact, but a wayside public-house—it was arranged that it was to take place in the new barn and storehouses Matthew Beagrie had just built on the inner side of the sandhills, where they came close to the

Water of Cruden.

Throughout all the east side of Buchan there had for some time existed a wonder amongst the quiet-going people as to the strange prosperity of MacDonald. His public-house had, of course, a practical monopoly; for as there was not a licensed house on the Erroll estate, and as his was the nearest house of call to the port, he naturally got what custom there was going. The fishermen all along the coast for some seven or eight miles went to him either to drink or to get their liquor for drinking elsewhere; and not a few of the Collieston men on their Saturday journey home from Peterhead and their Sunday journey out there again made a detour to have a glass and a chat and a pipe, if time permitted, with "Tammas Mac"—for such was his sobriquet.

To the authorities he and his house were also sources of interest; for there was some kind of suspicion that some of the excellent brandy and cigars which he dispensed had arrived by a simpler road than that through the Custom House. It was at this house, in the good old days of smuggling, that the coastguards used to be entertained when a run was on foot, and where they slept off their drunkenness whilst the cargoes were being hidden or taken inland in the ready carts. Of course all this state of things had been altered, and there was as improved a decorum amongst the smugglers as there was a sterner rule and discipline amongst the coastguards. It was many a long year since Philip Kennedy met his death at Kirkton at the hands of the exciseman Anderson. Comparatively innocent deception was now the smugglers' only wile.

Tonight the whole countryside was to be at the wedding, and the dance which was to follow it; and for this occasion the lion was to lie down with the lamb, for the coastguards were bidden to the feast with the rest. Sailor Willy had looked forward to the dance with delight, for Maggie was to be there, and on the Billy Ruffian, which had been his last ship, he had been looked on as the best dancer before the mast. If there be any man who shuns a dance in which he knows he can shine, and at which his own particular girl is to be present, that man is not to be found in the Royal Naval Marine, even amongst those of them who have joined in the preventive service. Maggie was no less delighted, although she had a source of grief which for the present she had kept all to herself. Her father had of late been much disturbed about affairs. He had not spoken of them to her, and she did not dare to mention the matter to him; for old MacWhirter was a closemouthed man, and did not exchange many confidences even with his own children.

But Maggie guessed at the cause of the sadness—of the down-bent head when none were looking; the sleepless nights and the deep smothered groans which now and again marked his heavy sleep told the tale loudly enough to reach the daughter's ears. For the last few weeks, whenever her father was at home, Maggie had herself lain awake listening, listening, in increasing agony of spirit, for one of these half moans or for the sound of the tossing of the restless man. He was as gentle and kind to his daughter as ever; but on his leaving the last time there had been an omission on his part which troubled her to the quick. For the first time in his life he had not kissed her as he went away.

On the previous day Sailor Willy had said he would come to the wedding and the dance if his duties should permit him; and, when asked if he could spare a few rockets for the occasion, promised that he would let off three Board of Trade rockets, which he could now deal with as it was three months since he had used any. He was delighted at the opportunity of meeting the fisherfolk and his neighbours; for his officers had impressed on him the need of being on good terms with all around him, both for the possibility which it would always afford him of knowing how things were going on, and for the benefit of the rocket-service whenever there might be need of willing hands and hearts to work with him, for in the Board of Trade rocket-service much depends on voluntary aid. That very afternoon he had fixed the rockets on the wall of the barn with staples, so that he could fire them from below with a slow match, which he fixed ready.

When he had got the telegram he had called in to Maggie and told her if he did not come to fetch her she was to go on to the wedding by herself, and that he would try to join her later. She had appeared a little startled when he told her he might not be present; but after a pause smiled, and said she would go, and that he was not to lose any time coming when he was free.

Now that every arrangement was complete, and as he had between puffs of the sea-fog got a clean sweep of the horizon and saw that there was no sail of any kind within sight, he thought he might have a look through the village and keep in evidence so as not to create any suspicion in the minds of the people. As he went through the street he noticed that nearly every house door was closed—all the women were at the new barn. It was now eight o'clock, and the darkness, which is slow of coming in the North, was closing in.

Down by the barn there were quite a number of carts, and the horses had not been taken out, though the wedding was not to be till nine o'clock, or perhaps even later; for Mrs MacDonald had taken care to tell her friends that Keith might not get over from Boddam till late. Willy looked at the carts carefully—some idea seemed to have struck him. Their lettering shewed them to be from all parts round, and the names mostly of those who had not the best reputation. When his brief survey was finished he looked round and then went swiftly behind the barn so that no one might see him. As he went he muttered reflectively:

"Too many light carts and fast horses—too much silence in the barn—too little liquor going, to be all safe. There's something up here tonight." He was under the lee of the barn and looked up where he had fixed the rockets ready to fire. This gave him a new idea.

"I fixed them low so as to go over the sandhills and not be noticeable at Collieston or beyond. They are now placed up straight and will be seen for fifty miles if the weather be clear."

It was too dark to see very clearly, and he would not climb up to examine them lest he should be noticed and his purpose of acquiring information frustrated; but then and there he made

263

up his mind that Port Erroll or its neighbourhood had been the spot chosen for the running of the smuggled goods. He determined to find out more, and straightaway went round to the front and entered the room.

## CHAPTER 2

As soon as Sailor Willy was seen to enter, a large part of the gathering looked relieved, and at once began to chat and gabble in marked contrast to their previous gloom and silence. Port Erroll was well represented by its womankind, and by such of its men as were not away at the fishing; for it was the intention to mask the smuggling scheme by an assemblage at which all the respectability would be present. There appeared to be little rivalry between the two shoemakers, MacPherson and Beagrie, who chatted together in a corner, the former telling his companion how he had just been down to the lifeboat-house to see, as one of the Committee, that it was all ready in case it should be wanted before the night was over. Lang John and Lang Jim, the policemen of the place, looked sprucer even than usual, and their buttons shone in the light of the many paraffin lamps as if they had been newly burnished. Mitchell and his companions of the salmon fishery were grouped in another corner, and Andrew Mason was telling Mackay, the new flesher, whose shed was erected on the edge of the burn opposite John Reid's shop, of a great crab which he had taken that morning in a pot opposite the Twa Een.

But these and nearly all the other Port Erroll folk present were quiet, and their talk was of local interest; the main clack of tongues came from the many strange men who stood in groups near the centre of the room and talked loudly. In the midst of them was the bridegroom, more joyous than any, though in the midst of his laughter he kept constantly turning to look at the door. The minister from Peterhead sat in a corner with the bride and her mother and father—the latter of whom, despite his constant laughter, had an anxious look on his face. Sailor Willy was greeted joyously, and the giver of the feast and the bridegroom each rose, and, taking a bottle and glass, offered him a drink.

"To the bride", said he; but seeing that no one else was drinking, he tapped the bridegroom on the shoulder, "Come, drink this with me, my lad!" he added. The latter paused an instant and then helped himself from MacDonald's bottle. Willy did not fail to notice the act, and holding out his glass said:

"Come, my lad, you drink with me! Change glasses in old style!" An odd pallor passed quickly across the bridegroom's face, but MacDonald spoke quickly:

"Tak it, mon, tak it!" So he took the glass, crying "No heeltaps", threw back his head, and raised the glass. Willy threw back his head too, and tossed off his liquor, but, as he did so, took care to keep a sharp eye on the other, and saw him, instead of swallowing his liquor, pour it into his thick beard. His mind was quite made up now. They meant to keep him out of the way by fair means or foul.

Just then two persons entered the room, one of them, James Cruickshank of the Kilmarnock Arms, who was showing the way to the other, an elderly man with a bald head, keen eyes, a ragged grey beard, a hooked nose, and an evil smile. As he entered MacDonald jumped up and came over to greet him.

"Oh! Mr Mendoza, this is braw! We hopit tae see ye the nicht, but we were that feared that ye wadna come."

"*Mein Gott*, but why shall I not come—on this occasion of all—the occasion of the marriage of the daughter of *mein* goot frient, Tam Smack? And moreovers when I bring these as I haf promise. For you, *mein* frient Keith, this cheque, which one week you cash, and for you, my tear Miss Alice, these so bright necklace, which you will wear, ant which will sell if so you choose."

As he spoke he handed his gifts to the groom and bride. He then walked to the corner where Mrs Mac sat, exchanging a keen look with his host as he did so. The latter seemed to have taken his cue and spoke out at once.

"And now, reverend sir, we may proceed—all is ready." As he spoke the bridal pair stood up, and the friends crowded round. Sailor Willy moved towards the door, and just as the parson opened his book, began to pass out. Tammas Mac immediately spoke to him:

"Ye're no gangin', Sailor Willy? Sure ye'll wait and see Tam Keith marrit on my lass?"

He instantly replied: "I must go for a while. I have some things to do, and then I want to try to bring Maggie down for the dance!" and before anything could be said, he was gone.

The instant he left the door he slipped round to the back of the barn, and running across the sandhills to the left, crossed the wooden bridge, and hurrying up the roadway by the cottage on the cliff gained the watch-house. He knew that none of the company in the barn could leave till the service was over, with the minister's eye on them, without giving cause for after suspicion; and he knew, too, that as there were no windows on the south side of the barn, nothing could be seen from that side. Without a moment's delay he arranged his signals for the call for aid; and as the rockets whizzed aloft, sending a white glare far into the sky, he felt that the struggle had entered on its second stage.

The night had now set in with a darkness unusual in August. The swaithes of sea-mist whirled in by the wind came fewer and fainter, and at times a sudden rift through the driving clouds showed that there was starlight somewhere between the driving masses of mist and gloom. Willy Barrow once more tried all his weapons and saw that all his signals were in order. Then he strapped the revolver and the cutlass in his belt, and lit a dark lantern so that it might be ready in case of need. This done, he left the watch-house, locking the door behind him, and, after looking steadily across the Bay to the Scaurs beyond, turned and walked northward towards the Watter's Mou'.

Between the cliff on the edge of this and the watch-house there was a crane used for raising the granite boulders quarried below, and when he drew near this he stopped instinctively and called out, "Who is there?" for he felt, rather than saw, some presence. "It is only me, Willy," came a soft voice, and a woman drew a step nearer through the darkness from behind the shaft of the crane.

"Maggie! Why, darling, what brings you here? I thought you were going to the wedding!"

"I knew ye wadna be there, and I wanted to speak wi' ye"- this was said in a very low voice.

"How did you know I wouldn't be there?—I was to join you if I could."

"I saw Bella Cruickshank hand ye the telegram as ye went by the Post Office, and—and I knew there would be something to keep ye. O Willy, Willy! why do ye draw awa frae me?" for Sailor Willy had instinctively loosened his arms which were round her and had drawn back—in the instant his love and his business seemed as though antagonistic. He answered with blunt truthfulness:

"I was thinking, Maggie, that I had no cause to be making love here and now. I've got work, mayhap, tonight!"

"I feared so, Willy—I feared so!" Willy was touched, for it seemed to him that she was anxious for him, and answered tenderly:

"All right, dear! All right! There's no danger—why, if need be, I am armed," and he slipped his hand on the butt of the revolver in his belt. To his surprise Maggie uttered a deep low groan, and turning away sat on the turf bank beside her, as though her strength was failing her. Willy did not know what to say, so there was a space of silence. Then Maggie went on hurriedly:

"Oh my God! it is a dreadfu' thing to lift yer han' in sic a deadly manner against yer neighbours, and ye not knowing what woe ye mau cause." Willy could answer this time:

"Ah, lass! it's hard indeed, and that's the truth. But that's the very reason that men like me are put here that can and will do their duty no matter how hard it may be."

Another pause, and then Maggie spoke again. Willy could not see her face, but she seemed to speak between gasps for breath.

"Ye're lookin' for hard wark the nicht?"

"I am!—I fear so."

"I can guess that that telegram tellt ye that some boats would try to rin in somewhere the nicht."

"Mayhap, lass. But the telegrams are secret, and I must not speak of what's in them."

After a long pause Maggie spoke again, but in a voice so low that he could hardly hear her amid the roar of the breaking waves which came in on the wind:

"Willy, ye're not a cruel man!—ye wadna, if ye could help it, dae harm to them that loved ye, or work woe to their belongin's?"

"My lass! that I wouldn't." As he answered he felt a horrible sinking of the heart. What did all this mean? Was it possible that Maggie, too, had any interest in the smuggling? No, no! a thousand times no! Ashamed of his suspicion he drew closer and again put his arm around her in a protecting way. The unexpected tenderness overcame her, and, bursting into tears, she threw herself on Willy's neck and whispered to him between her sobs:

"O Willy, Willy! I'm in sic sair trouble, and there's nane that I can speak to. Nae! not ane in the wide warld."

"Tell me, darling; you know you'll soon be my wife, and then I'll have a right to know all!"

"Oh, I canna! I canna! I canna!" she said, and taking her arms from around his neck she beat her hands wildly together. Willy was something frightened, for a woman's distress touches a strong man in direct ratio to his manliness. He tried to soothe her as though she were a frightened child, and held her tight to him.

"There! there! my darling. Don't cry. I'm here with you, and you can tell me all your trouble." She shook her head; he felt the movement on his breast, and he went on:

"Don't be frightened, Maggie; tell me all. Tell me quietly, and mayhap I can help ye out over the difficult places." Then he remained silent, and her sobs grew less violent; at last she raised her head and dashed away her tears fiercely with her hand. She dragged herself away from him: he tried to stop her, but she said:

"Nae, nae, Willy dear; let me speak it in my ain way. If I canna trust ye, wha can I trust? My trouble is not for mysel." She paused, and he asked:

"Who, then, is it for?"

"My father and my brothers." Then she went on hurriedly, fearing to stop lest her courage should fail her, and he listened in dead silence, with a growing pain in his heart.

"Ye ken that for several seasons back our boat has had bad luck—we took less fish and lost mair nets than any of the boats; even on the land everything went wrong. Our coo died, and the shed was blawn doon, and then the blight touched the potatoes in our field. Father could dae naething, and had to borrow money on the boat to go on with his wark; and the debt grew and grew, till now he only owns her in name, and we never ken when we may be sold up. And the man that has the mortgage isn't like to let us off or gie time!"

"Who is he? His name?" said Willy hoarsely.

"Mendoza—the man frae Hamburg wha lends to the boats at Peterhead."

Willy groaned. Before his eyes rose the vision of that hard, cruel, white face that he had seen only a few minutes ago, and again he saw him hand over the presents with which he had bought the man and woman to help in his wicked scheme. When Maggie heard the groan her courage and her hope arose. If her lover could take the matter so much to heart all might yet be well, and in the moment all the womanhood in her awoke to the call. Her fear had broken down the barriers that had kept back her passion, and now the passion came with all the force of a virgin nature. She drew Willy close to her—closer still—and whispered to him in a low sweet voice, that thrilled with emotion:

"Willy, Willy, darlin'; ye wouldna see harm come to my father—my father, my father!" and in a wave of tumultuous, voluptuous passion she kissed him full in the mouth. Willy felt for the moment half dazed. Love has its opiates that soothe and stun even in the midst of their activity. He clasped Maggie close

269

in his arms, and for a moment their hearts beat together and their mouths breathed the same air. Then Willy drew back, but Maggie hung limp in his arms. The silence which hung in the midst of nature's tumult broke its own spell. Willy realised what and where he was: with the waves dashing below his feet and the night wind laden with drifting mist wreathing around him in the darkness, and whistling amongst the rocks and screaming sadly through the ropes and stays of the flagstaff on the cliff. There was a wild fear in his heart and a burning desire to know all that was in his sweetheart's mind.

"Go on, Maggie! go on!" he said. Maggie roused herself and again took up the thread of her story—this time in feverish haste. The moment of passion had disquieted and disturbed her. She seemed to herself to be two people, one of whom was new to her, and whom she feared, but woman-like, she felt that as she had begun so much she go on; and thus her woman's courage sustained her.

"Some weeks ago, father began to get letters frae Mr Mendoza, and they aye upset him. He wrote answers and sent them away at once. Then Mr Mendoza sent him a telegram frae Hamburg, and he sent a reply—and a month ago father got a telegram telling him to meet him at Peterhead. He was very angry at first and very low-spirited after; but he went to Peterhead, and when he cam back he was very still and quite pale. He would eat naething, and went to bed although it was only seven o'clock. Then there were more letters and telegrams, but father answered nane o' them—sae far as I ken—and then Mr Mendoza cam to our hoose.

"Father got as pale as a sheet when he saw him, and then he got red and angry, and I thocht he was going to strike him; but Mr Mendoza said not to frichten his daughter, and father got quiet and sent me oot on a message to the Nether Mill. And when I cam back Mr Mendoza had gone, and father was sitting with his face in his hands, and he didna hear me come in. When I spoke, he started up and he was as white as a sheet, and then he mumbled something and went into his room. And ever since then he hardly spoke to any one, and seemed to avoid me a'thegither.

"When he went away the last time he never even kissed me. And so, Willy—so, I fear that that awfu' Mr Mendoza has made him dae something that he didna want to dae, and it's all breaking my heart!" and again she laid her head on her lover's breast and sobbed. Willy breathed more freely; but he could not be content to remain in doubt, and his courage was never harder tried than when he asked his next question.

"Then, Maggie, you don't know anything for certain?"

"Naething, Willy—but I fear."

"But there may be nothing, after all!" Maggie's hopes rose again, for there was something in her lover's voice which told her that he was willing to cling to any straw, and once again her woman's nature took advantage of her sense of right and wrong. "Please God, Willy, there may be naething! but I fear much that it may be so; but we must act as if we didna fear. It wadna dae to suspect poor father without some cause. You know, Willy, the Earl has promised to mak him the new harbourmaster. Old Forgie is bedridden now, and when winter comes he'll no even be able to pretend to work, so the Earl is to pension him, and father will get the post and hae the hoose by the harbour, and you know that every one's sae glad, for they a'respect father."

"Ay, lass," interrupted Willy, "that's true; and why, then, should we—you and me, Maggie—think he would do ill to please that damned scoundrel, Mendoza?"

"Indeed, I'm thinkin' that it's just because that he is respeckit that Mendoza wants him to help him. He kens weel that nane would suspeck father, and—"here she clipped her lover close in her arms once again, and her breath came hot in his face till it made him half drunk with a voluptuous intoxication—"he kens that father, my father, would never be harmt by my lover!"

Even then, at the moment when the tragedy of his life seemed to be accomplished, when the woman he loved and honoured seemed to be urging him to some breach of duty, Willy Barrow could not but feel that some responsibility for her action rested on him. That first passionate kiss, which had seemed to unlock the very gates of her soul—in which she had yielded herself to him—had some mysterious bond or virtue like that which abides in the wedding ring. The Maggie who thus acted was his Maggie, and in all that came of it he had a part.

But his mind was made up; nothing—not Maggie's kisses or Maggie's fears—would turn him from his path of duty, and strong in this resolution he could afford to be silent to the woman in his arms. Maggie instinctively knew that silence could now be her best weapon, and said no word as they walked towards the guard-house, Willy casting keen looks seawards, and up and down the coast as they went. When they were so close that in its shelter the roar of the surf seemed muffled, Maggie again nestled close to her lover, and whispered in his ear as he looked out over Cruden Bay:

"The *Sea Gull* comes hame the nicht!" Willy quivered, but said nothing for a time that seemed to be endless. Then he answered—"They'll find it hard to make the Port tonight. Look! the waves are rolling high and the wind is getting up. It would be madness to try it." Again she whispered to him:

"Couldna she rin in somewhere else—there are other openings besides Port Erroll in Buchan!" Willy laughed the laugh of a strong man who knew well what he said:

"Other openings! Ay, lass, there are other openings; but the coble isn't built that can run them this night. With a south-east gale, who would dare to try? The Bullers, or Robies Haven, or Dunbuy, or Twa Havens, or Lang Haven, or The Watter's Mou'—why, lass, they'd be in matches on the rocks before they could turn their tiller or slack a sail."

She interrupted him, speaking with a despairing voice:

"Then ye'll no hae to watch nane o' them the nicht?"

"Nay, Maggie. Port Erroll is my watch tonight; and from it I won't budge."

"And the Watter's Mou'?" she asked, "it that no safe wi'oot watch? it's no far frae the Port." Again Willy laughed his arrogant, masculine laugh, which made Maggie, despite her trouble, admire him more than ever, and he answered:

"The Watter's Mou'? To try to get in there in this wind would be to court sudden death. Why, lass, it would take a man all he knew to get out from there, let alone get in, in this weather! And then the chances would be ten to one that he'd be dashed to pieces on the rocks beyond," and he pointed to where a line of sharp rocks rose between the billows on the south side of the inlet.

Truly it was a fearful-looking place to be dashed on, for the great waves broke on the rocks with a loud roaring, and even in the semi-darkness they could see the white lines as the waters poured down to leeward in the wake of the heaving wave. The white cluster of rocks looked like a ghostly mouth opened to swallow whatever might come in touch. Maggie shuddered; but some sudden idea seemed to strike her, and she drew away from her lover for a moment, and looked towards the black cleft in the rocks of which they could just see the top from where they stood—the entrance to the Watter's Mou'.

And then with one long, wild, appealing glance skyward, as though looking a prayer which she dared not utter even in her heart, Maggie turned towards her lover once more. Again she drew close to him, and hung around his neck, and said with many gasps and pauses between her words:

"If the *Sea Gull* should come in to the Port the nicht, and if ony attempt that ye feared should tak you away to Whinnyfold or to Dunbuy so that you might be a bit—only a wee bit—late to search when the boat cam in—"

She stopped affrighted, for Willy put her from him to arm's length, not too gently either, and said to her so sternly that each word seemed to smite her like the lash of a whip, till she shrunk and quivered and cowered away from him:

"Maggie, lass! What's this you're saying to me? It isn't fit for you to speak or me to hear! It's bad enough to be a smuggler, but what is it that you would make of me? Not only a smuggler, but a perjurer and a traitor too. God! am I mistaken? Is it you, Maggie, that would make this of me? Of me! Maggie MacWhirter, if this be your counsel, then God help us both! you are no fit wife for me!" In an instant the whole truth dawned on Maggie of what a thing she would make of the man she loved, whom she had loved at the first because he was strong and brave and true. In the sudden revulsion of her feelings she flung herself on her knees beside him, and took his hand and held it hard, and despite his efforts to withdraw it, kissed it wildly in the humility of her self-abasement, and poured out to him a passionate outburst of pleading for his forgiveness, of justification of herself, and of appeals to his mercy for her father.

"Oh Willy, Willy! dinna turn frae me this nicht! My heart is sae fu' o' trouble that I am nigh mad! I dinna ken what to dae nor where to look for help! I think, and think, and think, and everywhere there is nought but dark before me, just as there is blackness oot ower the sea, when I look for my father. And noo when I want ye to help me—ye that are all I hae, and the only ane on earth that I can look tae in my wae and trouble—I can dae nae mair than turn ye frae me! Ye that I love! oh, love more than my life or my soul! I must dishonour and mak ye hate me! Oh, what shall I dae? What shall I dae? What shall I dae?" and again she beat the palms of her hands together in a paroxysm of wild despair, whilst Willy looked on with his heart full of pain and pity, though his resolution never flinched.

And then through the completeness of her self-abasement came the pleading of her soul from a depth of her nature even deeper than despair. Despair has its own bravery, but hope can sap the strongest resolution. And the pleadings of love came from the depths of that Pandora's box which we call human nature.

"O Willy, Willy! forgie me—forgie me! I was daft to say what I did! I was daft to think that ye would be so base!—daft to think that I would like you to so betray yoursel! Forgie me, Willy, forgie me, and tak my wild words as spoken not to ye but to the storm that maks me fear sae for my father! Let me tak it a' back, Willy darlin'—Willy, my Willy; and dinna leave me desolate here with this new shadow ower me!" Here, as she kissed his hand again, her lover stooped and raised her in his strong arms and held her to him. And then, when she felt herself in a position of security, the same hysterical emotion came sweeping up in her brain and her blood—the same self-abandonment to her lover overcame her—and the current of her thought once again turned to win from him something by the force of her woman's wile and her woman's contact with the man.

"Willy," she whispered, as she kissed him on the mouth and then kissed his head on the side of his neck, "Willy, ye have forgien me, I ken—and I ken that ye'll harm father nae mair than ye can help—but if—"

What more she was going to say she hardly knew herself. As for Willy, he felt that something better left unsaid was coming, and unconsciously his muscles stiffened till he held her from him rather than to him. She, too, felt the change, and held him closer—closer still, with the tenacity induced by a sense of coming danger. Their difficulty was solved for them, for just on the instant when the suggestion of treachery to his duty was hanging on her lips, there came from the village below, in a pause between the gusts of wind, the fierce roar of a flying rocket.

Up and up and up, as though it would never stop—up it rose with its prolonged screech, increasing in sound at the first till it began to die away in the aerial heights above, so that when the explosion came it seemed to startle a quietude around it. Up in the air a thousand feet over their heads the fierce glitter of the falling fires of red and blue made a blaze of light which lit up the coast-line from the Scaurs to Dunbuy, and with an instinctive intelligence Willy Barrow took in all he saw, including the many men at the little port below, sheltering under the sea-wall from the sweeping of the waves as they looked out seawards. Instinctively also he counted the seconds till the next rocket should be fired—one, two, three; and then another roar and another blaze of coloured lights.

And then another pause, of six seconds this time! and then the third rocket sped aloft with its fiery message. And then the darkness seemed blacker than ever, and the mysterious booming of the sea to grow louder and louder as though it came through silence. By this time the man and the woman were apart no less in spirit than physically. Willy, intent on his work, was standing outside the window of the guard-house, whence he could see all around the Bay and up and down the coast, and at the same time command the whole of the harbour. His feet were planted wide apart, for on the exposed rock the sweep of the wind was strong, and as he raised his arm with his field-glass to search the horizon the wind drove back his jacket and showed the butt of his revolver and the hilt of his cutlass.

Maggie stood a little behind him, gazing seawards, with no less eager eyes, for she too expected what would follow. Her heart seemed to stand still though her breath came in quick gasps, and she did not dare to make a sound or to encroach on the business-like earnestness of the man. For full a minute they waited thus, and then far off at sea, away to the south, they saw a faint blue light, and then another and another, till at the last three lights were burning in a row. Instantly from the town a single rocket went up—not this time a great Board of Trade rocket, laden with coloured fire, but one which left a plain white track of light behind it.

Willy gazed seawards, but there was no more sign from the far-off ship at sea; the signal, whatever it was, was complete. The coastguard was uncertain as to the meaning, but to Maggie no explanation was necessary. There, away at sea, tossed on the stormy waters, was her father. There was danger round him, but a greater danger on the shore—every way of entrance was barred by the storm—save the one where, through his fatal cargo, dishonour lay in wait for him. She seemed to see her duty clear before her, and come what might she meant to do it: her father must be warned. It was with a faint voice indeed that she now spoke to her lover:

"Willy!"

His heart was melted at the faltering voice, but he feared she was trying some new temptation, so, coldly and hardly enough, he answered:

"What is it, lass?"

276

"Willy, ye wadna see poor father injured?"

"No, Maggie, not if I could help it. But I'd have to do my duty all the same."

"And we should a' dae oor duty—whatever it might be—at a' costs?"

"Ay, lass—at all costs!" His voice was firm enough now, and there was no mistaking the truth of its ring. Maggie's hope died away. From the stern task which seemed to rise before her over the waste of the black sea she must not shrink. There was but one more yielding to the weakness of her fear, and she said, so timidly that Willy was startled, the voice and manner were so different from those he had ever known:

"And if—mind I say 'if', Willy—I had a duty to dae and it was fu' o' fear and danger, and ye could save me frae it, wad ye?" As she waited for his reply, her heart beat so fast and so heavily that Willy could hear it: her very life, she felt, lay in his answer. He did not quite understand the full import of her words and all that they implied, but he knew that she was in deadly earnest, and he felt that some vague terror lay in his answer; but the manhood in him rose to the occasion—Willy Barrow was of the stuff of which heroes are made—and he replied:

"Maggie, as God is above us, I have no other answer to give! I don't know what you mean, but I have a shadow of fear! I must do my duty whatever comes of it!" There was a long pause, and then Maggie spoke again, but this time in so different a voice that her lover's heart went out to her in tenfold love and passion, with never a shadow of doubt or fear.

"Willy, tak me in your arms—I am not unworthy, dear, though for a moment I did falter!" He clasped her to him, and whispered when their lips had met:

"Maggie, my darling, I never loved you like now. I would die for you if I could do you good."

"Hush, dear, I ken it weel. But your duty is not only for yoursel, and it must be done! I too hae a duty to dae—a grave and stern ane!"

"What is it? Tell me, Maggie dear!"

"Ye maunna ask me! Ye maun never ken! Kiss me once again, Willy, before I go—for oh, my love, my love! it may be the last!"

Her words were lost in the passionate embrace which followed. Then, when he least expected it, she suddenly tore herself away and fled through the darkness across the field which lay between them and her home, whilst he stood doggedly at his watch looking out for another signal between sea and shore.

## Chapter 3

When she got to the far side of the field, Maggie, instead of turning to the left, which would have brought her home, went down the sloping track to the right, which led to the rustic bridge crossing the Back Burn near the Pigeon Tower. Thence turning to the right she scrambled down the bank beside the ruined barley-mill, so as to reach the little plots of sea-grass—islands, except at low tide—between which the tide rises to meet the waters of the stream.

The whole situation of Cruden is peculiar. The main stream, the Water of Cruden, runs in a south-easterly direction, skirts the sandhills, and, swirling under the stone bridge, partly built with the ruins of the old church which Malcolm erected to celebrate his victory over Sueno, turns suddenly to the right and runs to sea over a stony bottom. The estuary has in its wash some dangerous outcropping granite rocks, nearly covered at high tide, and the mouth opens between the most northerly end of the sandhills and the village street, whose houses mark the slope of the detritus from the rocks.

Formerly the Water of Cruden, instead of taking this last turn, used to flow straight on till it joined the lesser stream known as the Back Burn, and together the streams ran seawards. Even in comparatively recent years, in times of flood or freshet, the spate broke down or swept over the intervening tongue of land, and the Water of Cruden took its old course seaward. This course is what is known as the Watter's Mou'. It is a natural cleft—formed by primeval fire or earthquake or some sort of natural convulsion—which runs through the vast mass of red granite which forms a promontory running due south.

Water has done its work as well as fire in the formation of the gully as it now is, for the drip and flow and rush of water that mark the seasons for countless ages have completed the work of the pristine fire. As one sees this natural mouth of the stream in the rocky face of the cliff, it is hard to realise that Nature alone has done the work.

At first the cleft runs from west to east, and broadens out into a wide bay of which on one side a steep grassy slope leads towards the new castle of Slains, and on the other rises a sheer bank, with tufts of the thick grass growing on the ledges, where the earth has been blown. From this the cleft opens again between towering rocks like what in America is called a canon and tends seaward to the south between precipices two hundred feet high, and over a bottom of great boulders exposed at low water towards the northern end.

The precipice to the left or eastward side is twice rent with great openings, through which, in time of storm, the spray and spume of the easterly gale piling the great waves into the Castle Bay are swept. These openings are, however, so guarded with masses of rock that the force of the wildest wave is broken before it can leap up the piles of boulders which rise from their sandy floors. At the very mouth the cleft opens away to the west, where the cliff falls back, and seaward of which rise great masses of black frowning rock, most of which only show their presence at high water by the angry patches of foam which even in calm weather mark them—for the current here runs fast. The eastern portal is composed of a giant mass of red granite, which, from its overhanging shape, is known as "the Ship's Starn". It lies somewhat lower than the cliff of which it is a part, being attached to it by a great sloping shelf of granite, over which, when the storm is easterly, the torrent of spray sent up by the dashing waves rolls down to join the foamy waves in the Watter's Mou'.

Maggie knew that close to the Barley Mill, safe from the onset of the waves—for the wildest waves that ever rise lose their force fretting and churning on the stony sides and bottom of the Watter's Mou'—was kept a light boat belonging to her brother, which he sometimes used when the weather was fine and he wanted to utilise his spare time in line fishing. Her mind was made up that it was her duty to give her father warning of what awaited him on landing—if she could. She was afraid to think of the danger, of the myriad chances against her success; but, woman-like, when once the idea was fixed in her mind she went straight on to its realisation.

Truly, thought of any kind would have been an absolute barrier to action in such a case, for any one of the difficulties ahead would have seemed sufficient. To leave the shore at all on such a night, and in such a frail craft, with none but a girl to manage it; then to find a way, despite storm and current, out to the boat so far off at sea; and finally, to find the boat she wanted at all in the fret of such a stormy sea—a wilderness of driving mist—in such a night, when never a star even was to be seen: the prospect might well appal the bravest.

But to think was to hesitate, and to hesitate was to fail. Keeping her thoughts on the danger to her father, and seeing through the blackness of the stormy night his white, woe-laden face before her, and hearing through the tumult of the tempest his sobs as on that night when her fear for him began to be acute, she set about her work with desperate energy. The boat was moored on the northern side of the largest of the little islands of sea-grass, and so far in shelter that she could get all in readiness. She set the oars in their places, stepped the mast, and rigged the sail ready to haul up.

Then she took a small spar of broken wood and knotted to it a piece of rope, fastening the other end of the rope, some five yards long, just under the thwarts near the centre of the boat, and just a little forward on the port side. The spar she put carefully ready to throw out of the boat when the sweep of the wind should take her sail—for without some such strain as it would afford, the boat would probably heel over. Then she guided the boat in the shallow water round the little island till it was stern on to the sea side. It was rough work, for the rush and recoil of the waves beat the boat back on the sandy bank or left her now and again dry till a new wave lifted her.

All this time she took something of inspiration from the darkness and the roar of the storm around her. She was not yet face to face with danger, and did not realise, or try to realise, its magnitude. In such a mystery of darkness as lay before, above, and around her, her own personality seemed as nought. Truly there is an instinct of one's own littleness which becomes consciously manifest in the times when Nature puts forth her might. The wind swept up the channel of the Watter's Mou' in great gusts, till the open bay where she stood became the centre of an intermittent whirlwind. The storm came not only from the Mouth itself, but through the great gaps in the eastern wall. It drove across the gully till high amongst the rocks overhead on both sides it seemed now and again to scream as a living thing in pain or anger.

Great sheets of mist appeared out of the inky darkness beyond, coming suddenly as though like the great sails of ships driving up before the wind. With gladness Maggie saw that the sheets of fog were becoming fewer and thinner, and realised that so far her dreadful task was becoming possible. She was getting more inspired by the sound and elemental fury around her. There was in her blood, as in the blood of all the hardy children of the northern seas, some strain of those study Berserkers who knew no fear, and rode the very tempest on its wings with supreme bravery. Such natures rise with the occasion, and now, when the call had come, Maggie's brave nature answered it.

It was with a strong, almost an eager, heart that she jumped into the boat, and seizing the oars, set out on her perilous course. The start was difficult, for the boat was bumping savagely on the sand; but, taking advantage of a big wave, two or three powerful strokes took her out into deeper water. Here, too, there was shelter, for the cliffs rose steeply; and when she had entered the elbow of the gully and saw before her the whole length of the Watter's Mou', the drift of the wind took it over her head, and she was able to row in comparative calmness under the shadow of the cliffs.

A few minutes took her to the first of the openings in the eastern cliff, and here she began to feel the full fury of the storm. The opening itself was sheer on each side, but in the gap between was piled a mass of giant boulders, the work of the sea at its wildest during the centuries of stress. On the farther side of these the waves broke, and sent up a white cloud of spume that drove instantly into the darkness beyond. Maggie knew that here her first great effort had to be made, and lending her strength pulled the boat through the turmoil of wind and wave.

As she passed the cleft, driven somewhat more out into the middle of the channel, she caught, in a pause between the rush of the waves, a glimpse of the lighted windows of the castle on the cliff. The sight for an instant unnerved her, for it brought into opposition her own dreadful situation, mental and physical, with the happy faces of those clustered round the comforting light. But the reaction was helpful, for the little jealousy which was at the base of the idea was blotted out by the thought of that stem and paramount duty which she had undertaken. Not seldom in days gone by had women like her, in times of test and torment, taken their way over the red-hot ploughshares under somewhat similar stress of mind.

She was now under the shelter of the cliff, and gaining the second and last opening in the rocky wall: as the boat advanced the force of the waves became greater, for every yard up the Watter's Mou' the fretting of the rocky bottom and sides had broken their force. This was brought home to her roughly when the breaking of a coming wave threw a sheet of water over her as she bent to her oars. Chop! chop! went the boat into the trough of each succeeding wave, till it became necessary to bale out the boat or she might never even get started on her way. This done she rowed on, and now came to the second opening in the cliff.

This was much wilder than the first, for outside of it, to the east, the waves of the North Sea broke in all their violence, and with the breaking of each a great sheet of water came drifting over the wall of piled up boulders. Again Maggie kept out in the channel, and, pulling with all her might, passed again into the shelter of the cliff. Here the water was stiller, for the waves were breaking directly behind the sheltering cliff, and the sound of them was heard high overhead in the rushing wind.

Maggie drew close to the rock, and, hugging it, crept on her outward way. There was now only one danger to come, before her final effort. The great shelf of rock inside the Ship's Starn was only saved from exposure by its rise on the outer side; but here, happily, the waves did not break, they swept under the overhanging slope on the outer side, and then passed on their way; the vast depth of the water outside was their protection within. Now and then a wave broke on the edge of the Ship's Starn, and then a great wall of green water rose and rushed down the steep slope, but in the pause between Maggie passed along; and now the boat nestled on the black water, under the shelter of the very outermost wall of rock. The Ship's Starn was now her last refuge.

As she hurriedly began to get the sail ready she could hear the whistling of the wind round the outer side of the rock and overhead. The black water underneath her rose and fell, but in some mysterious eddy or backwater of Nature's forces she rested in comparative calm on the very edge of the maelstrom. By contrast with the darkness of the Watter's Mou' between the towering walls of rock, the sea had some mysterious light of its own, and just outside the opening on the western side she could see the white water pouring over the sunken rocks as the passing waves exposed them, till once more they looked like teeth in the jaws of the hungry sea.

And now came the final struggle in her effort to get out to open water. The moment she should pass beyond the shelter of the Ship's Starn the easterly gale would in all probability drive her straight upon the outer reef of rocks amongst those angry jaws, where the white teeth would in an instant grind her and her boat to nothingness. But if she should pass this last danger she should be out in the open sea and might make her way to save her father. She held in her mind the spot whence she had seen the answering signal to the rockets, and felt a blind trust that God would help her in her difficulty. Was not God pleased with self-sacrifice? What could be better for a maid than to save her father from accomplished sin and the discovery which made sin so bitter to bear? *Greater love hath no man than this, that a man lay down his life for his friend.*

Besides there was Sailor Willy! Had not he—even he—doubted her; and might she not by this wild night's work win back her old place in his heart and his faith? Strong in this new hope, she made careful preparation for her great effort. She threw overboard the spar and got ready the tiller. Then having put the sheet round the thwart on the starboard side, and laid the loose end where she could grasp it whilst holding the tiller, she hoisted the sail and belayed the rope that held it. In the eddy of the storm behind the sheltered rock the sail hung idly for a few seconds, and in this time she jumped to the stern and held the tiller with one hand and with the other drew the sheet of the sail taut and belayed it.

An instant after, the sail caught a gust of wind and the boat sprang, as though a living thing, out toward the channel. The instant the shelter was past the sail caught the full sweep of the easterly gale, and the boat would have turned over only for the strain from the floating spar line, which now did its part well. The bow was thrown round towards the wind, and the boat began rushing through the water at a terrific pace. Maggie felt the coldness of death in her heart; but in that wild moment the bravery of her nature came out. She shut her teeth and jammed the tiller down hard, keeping it in place against her thigh, with the other leg pressed like a pillar against the side of the boat.

The little craft seemed sweeping right down on the outer rocks; already she could see the white wall of water, articulated into white lines like giant hairs, rushing after the retreating waves, and a great despair swept over her. But at that moment the rocks on the western side of the Watter's Mou' opened so far that she caught a glimpse of Sailor Willy's lamp reflected through the window of the coastguard hut. This gave her new hope, and with a mighty effort she pressed the tiller harder. The boat sank in the trough of the waves, rose again, the spar caught the rush of the receding wave and pulled the boat's head a point round, and then the outer rock was passed, and the boat, actually touching the rock so that the limpets scraped her side, ran free in the stormy waves beyond.

Maggie breathed a prayer as with trembling hand she unloosed the rope of the floating spar; then, having loosened the sheet, she turned the boat's head south, and, tacking, ran out in the direction where she had seen the signal light of her father's boat.

By contrast with the terrible turmoil amid the rocks, the great waves of the open sea were safety itself. No one to whom the sea is an occupation ever fears it in the open; and this fisher's daughter, with the Viking blood in her veins, actually rejoiced as the cockleshell of a boat, dipping and jerking like an angry horse, drove up and down the swell of the waves. She was a good way out now, and the whole coast-line east and west was opening up to her. The mist had gone by, or, if it lasted, hung amid the rocks inshore; and through the great blackness round she saw the lights in the windows of the castle, the glimmering lights of the village of Cruden, and far off the powerful light at Girdleness blazing out at intervals.

But there was one light on which her eyes lingered fixedly—the dim window of the coastguard's shelter, where she knew that her lover kept his grim watch. Her heart was filled with gladness as she thought that by what she was doing she would keep pain and trouble from him. She knew now, what she had all along in her heart believed, that Sailor Willy would not flinch from any duty however stern and pain-laden to him it might be; and she knew, too, that neither her rugged father nor her passionate young brother would ever forgive him for that duty. But now she would not, could not, think of failing, but gripped the tiller hard, and with set teeth and fixed eyes held on her perilous way.

Time went by hour by hour, but so great was her anxiety that she never noted how it went, but held on her course, tacking again and again as she tried to beat her way to her father through the storm. The eyes of sea folk are not ordinary eyes—they can pierce the darkness wherein the vision of land folk becomes lost or arrested; and the sea and the sky over it, and the coastline, however black and dim—however low-lying or distant—have lessons of their own. Maggie began by some mysterious instinct to find her way where she wanted to go, till little by little the coast-line, save for the distant lights of Girdleness and Boddam, faded out of sight.

Lying as she was on the very surface of the water, she had the horizon rising as it were around her, and there is nearly always some slight sign of light somewhere on the horizon's rim. There came now and again rents in the thick clouding of the stormy sky, and at such moments here and there came patches of lesser darkness like oases of light in the desert of the ebon sea. At one such moment she saw far off to the port side the outline of a vessel well known on the coast, the revenue cutter which was the seaward arm of the preventive service.

And then a great fear came over poor Maggie's heart; the sea was no longer the open sea, for her father was held in the toils of his enemies, and escape seaward became difficult or would be almost impossible, when the coming morn would reveal all the mysteries that the darkness hid. Despair, however, has its own courage, and Maggie was too far in her venture now to dread for more than a passing moment anything which might follow. She knew that the *Sea Gull* lay still to the front, and with a beating heart and a brain that throbbed with the eagerness of hope and fear she held on her course.

The break in the sky which had shown her the revenue cutter was only momentary, and all was again swallowed up in the darkness; but she feared that some other such rent in the cloudy night might expose her father to his enemies. Every moment, therefore, became precious, and steeling her heart and drawing the sheet of her sail as tight as she dared, she sped on into the darkness—on for a time that seemed interminable agony. Suddenly something black loomed up ahead of her, thrown out against the light of the horizon's rim, and her heart gave a great jump, for something told her that the Powers which aid the good wishes of daughters had sent her father out of that wilderness of stormy sea.

With her sea-trained eyes she knew in a few moments that the boat pitching so heavily was indeed the *Sea Gull*. At the same moment someone on the boat's deck saw her sail, and a hoarse muffled murmur of voices came to her over the waves in the gale. The coble's head was thrown round to the wind, and in that stress of storm and chopping sea she beat and buffeted, and like magic her way stopped, and she lay tossing. Maggie realised the intention of the manoeuvre, and deftly swung her boat round till she came under the starboard quarter of the fishing-boat, and in the shadow of her greater bulk and vaster sail, reefed though it was, found a comparative calm. Then she called out:

"Father! It's me—Maggie! Dinna show a licht, but try to throw me a rope."

With a shout in which were mingled many strong feelings, her father leaned over the bulwark, and, with seaman's instinct of instant action, threw her a rope. She deftly caught it, and, making it fast to the bows of her boat, dropped her sail. Then someone threw her another rope, which she fastened round her waist. She threw herself into the sea, and, holding tight to the rope, was shortly pulled breathless on board the *Sea Gull*.

She was instantly the centre of a ring of men. Not only were her father and two brothers on board, but there were no less than six men, seemingly foreigners, in the group.

"Maggie!" said her father, "in God's name, lass, hoo cam ye oot here? Were ye ovrta'en by the storm? God be thankit that ye met us, for this is a wild nicht to be oot on the North Sea by yer lanes."

"Father!" said she, in a hurried whisper in his ear. "I must speak wi' ye alane. There isna a moment to lose!"

"Speak on, lass."

"No' before these strangers, father. I must speak alane!"

Without a word, MacWhirter took his daughter aside, and, amid a muttered dissatisfaction of the strange men, signed to her to proceed. Then, as briefly as she could, Maggie told her father that it was known that a cargo was to be run that night, that the coastguard all along Buchan had been warned, and that she had come out to tell him of his danger.

As she spoke the old man groaned, and after a pause said: "I maun tell the rest. I'm no' the maister here the noo. Mendoza has me in his grip, an' his men rule here!"

"But, father, the boat is yours, and the risk is yours. It is you'll be punished if there is a discovery!"

"That may be, lass, but I'm no' free."

"I feared it was true, father, but I thocht it my duty to come!" Doubtless the old man knew that Maggie would understand fully what he meant, but the only recognition he made of her act of heroism was to lay his hand heavily on her shoulder. Then stepping forward he called the men round him, and in his own rough way told them of the danger. The strangers muttered and scowled; but Andrew and Neil drew close to their sister, and the younger man put his arm around her and pressed her to him. Maggie felt the comfort of the kindness, and laying her head on her brother's shoulder, cried quietly in the darkness. It was a relief to her pent-up feelings to be able to give way if only so far. When MacWhirter brought his tale to a close, and asked: "And now, lads, what's to be done?" one of the strangers, a brawny, heavily-built man, spoke out harshly:

"But for why this? Was it not that this woman's lover was of the guard? In this affair the women must do their best too. This lover of the guard—" He was hotly interrupted by Neil:

"Tisna the part of Maggie to tak a hand in this at a'."

"But I say it is the part of all. When Mendoza bought this man he bought all—unless there be traitors in his housed!"

This roused Maggie, who spoke out quickly, for she feared her brother's passion might brew trouble:

"I hae nae part in this dreadfu' affair. It's no' by ma wish or ma aid that father has embarked in this—this enterprise. I hae naught to dae wi't o' ony kind."

"Then for why are you here?" asked the burly man, with a coarse laugh.

"Because ma father and ma brithers are in danger, danger into which they hae been led, or been forced, by ye and the like o' ye. Do you think it was for pleasure, or, O my God! for profit either, that I cam oot this nicht—an' in that?" and as she spoke she pointed to where the little boat strained madly at the rope which held her. Then MacWhirter spoke out fiercely, so fiercely that the lesser spirits who opposed him were cowed:

"Leave the lass alane, I say! Yon's nane o' her doin'; and if ye be men ye'd honour her that cam oot in sic a tempest for the sake o' the likes o' me—o' us!"

But when the strangers were silent, Neil, whose passion had been aroused, could not be quietened, and spoke out with a growing fury which seemed to choke him:

"So Sailor Willy told ye the danger and then let ye come oot in this nicht! He'll hae to reckon wi' me for that when we get in."

"He telt me naething. I saw Bella Cruickshank gie him the telegram, and I guessed. He doesna ken I'm here—and he maun never ken. Nane must ever ken that a warning cam the nicht to father!"

"But they'll watch for us comin' in."

"We maun rin back to Cuxhaven," said the quiet voice of Andrew, who had not yet spoken."

"But ye canna," said Maggie; "the revenue cutter is on the watch, and when the mornin' comes will follow ye; and besides, hoo can ye get to Cuxhaven in this wind?"

"Then what are we to do, lass?" said her father.

"Dae, father? Dae what ye should dae—throw a' this poison-ous stuff that has brought this ruin owerboard. Lichten yer boat as ye will lighten yer conscience, and come hame as ye went oot!"

The bruly ran swore a great oath.

"Nothing overboard shall be thrown. These belongs not to you but to Mendoza. If they be touched he closes on your boat and ruin it is for you!" Maggie saw her father hesitate, and feared that other counsels might prevail, so she spoke out as by an inspiration. There, amid the surges of the perilous seas, the daughter's heroic devotion and her passionate earnestness made a new calm in her father's life:

"Father, dinna be deceived. Wi' this wind on shore, an' the revenue cutter ootside an' the dawn no' far off ye canna escape. Noo in the darkness ye can get rid o' the danger. Dinna lose a moment. The storm is somewhat lesser just enoo. Throw a' owerboard and come back to yer old self! What if we be ruined? We can work; and shall a' be happy yet!"

Something seemed to rise in the old man's heart and give him strength. Without pause he said with a grand simplicity:

"Ye're reet, lass, ye're reet! Haud up the casks, men, and stave them in!"

Andrew and Neil rushed to his bedding. Mendoza's men protested, but were afraid to intervene, and one after another bales and casks were lifted on deck. The bales were tossed overboard and the heads of the casks stove in till the scuppers were alternately drenched with brandy and washed with the seas.

In the midst of this, Maggie, knowing that if all were to be of any use she must be found at home in the morning, quietly pulled her boat as close as she dared, and slipping down the rope managed to clamber into it. Then she loosed the painter; and the wind and waves took her each instant farther and farther away. The sky over the horizon was brightening every instant, and there was a wild fear in her heart which not even the dull thud of the hammers as the casks were staved in could allay.

She felt that it was a race against time, and her overexcited imagination multiplied her natural fear; her boat's head was to home, steering for where she guessed was the dim light on the cliff, towards which her heart yearned. She hauled the sheets close—as close as she dared, for now speed was everything if she was to get back unseen. Well she knew that Sailor Willy on his lonely vigil would be true to his trust, and that his eagle eye could not fail to note her entry when once the day had broken. In a fever of anxiety she kept her eye on the Girdleness light by which she had to steer, and with the rise and fall of every wave as she swept by them, threw the boat's head a point to the wind and let it fall away again.

The storm had nearly spent itself, but there were still angry moments when the mist was swept in masses before fresh gusts. These, however, were fewer and fewer, and in a little while she ceased to heed them or even to look for them, and at last her eager eye began to discern through the storm the flickering lights of the little port. There came a moment when the tempest poured out the lees of its wrath in one final burst of energy, which wrapped the flying boat in a wraith of mist.

And then the tempest swept onward, shoreward, with the broken mist showing white in the springing dawn like the wings of some messenger of coming peace.

## CHAPTER 4

Matters looked serious enough on the *Sea Gull* when the time came in which rather the darkness began to disappear than the light to appear. Night and day have their own mysteries, and their nascence is as distant and as mysterious as the origin of life. The sky and the waters still seemed black, and the circle in which the little craft lived was as narrow as ever; but here and there in sky and on sea were faint streaks perceptible rather than distinguishable, as though swept thither by the trumpet blast of the messenger of the dawn. Mendoza's men did not stint their curses nor their threats, and Neil with passionate violence so assailed them in return that both MacWhirter and Andrew had to exercise their powers of restraint.

But blood is hot, and the lives of lawless men are prone to make violence a habit; the two elder men were anxious that there should be no extension of the present bitter bickering. As for MacWhirter, his mind was in a whirl and tumult of mixed emotions. First came his anxiety for Maggie when she had set forth alone on the stormy sea with such inadequate equipment. Well the old fisherman knew the perils that lay before her in her effort to win the shore, and his heart was postively sick with anxiety when every effort of thought or imagination concerning her ended in something like despair.

In one way he was happier than he had been for many months; the impending blow had fallen, and though he was ruined it had come in such a time that his criminal intent had not been accomplished. Here again his anxiety regarding Maggie became intensified, for was it not to save him that she had set forth on her desperate enterprise. He groaned aloud as he thought of the price that he might yet have to pay—that he might have paid already, though he knew it not as yet—for the service which had saved him from the after-consequences of his sin.

He dared not think more on the subject, for it would, he feared, madden him, and he must have other work to engross his thoughts. Thus it was that the danger of collision between Neil and Mendoza's men became an anodyne to his pain. He knew that a quarrel among seamen and under such conditions would be no idle thing, for they had all their knives, and with such hot blood on all sides none would hesitate to use them. The whole of the smuggled goods had by now been thrown overboard, the tobacco having gone the last, the bales having been broken up. So heavy had been the cargo that there was a new danger in that the boat was too much lightened.

As Mendoza had intended that force as well as fraud was to aid this venture he had not stuck at trifles. There was no pretence of concealment and even the ballast had made way for cask and box and bale. The Sea Gull had been only partially loaded at Hamburg, but when out of sight of port her cargo had been completed from other boats which had followed, till, when she started for Buchan, she was almost a solid mass of contraband goods. Mendoza's men felt desperate at this hopeless failure of the venture; and as Neil, too, was desperate, in a different way, there was a grim possibility of trouble on board at any minute.

The coming of the dawn was therefore a welcome relief, for it united—if only for a time—all on board to try to avert a common danger.

Lighter and lighter grew the expanse of sea and sky, until over the universe seemed to spread a cool, pearly grey, against which every object seemed to stand starkly out. The smugglers were keenly on the watch, and they saw, growing more clearly each instant out of the darkness, the black, low-lying hull, short funnel, and tapering spars of the revenue cutter about three or four miles off the starboard quarter. The preventive men seemed to see them at the same time, for there was a manifest stir on board, and the cutter's head was changed. Then MacWhirter knew it was necessary to take some bold course of action, for the *Sea Gull* lay between two fires, and he made up his mind to run then and there for Port Erroll.

As the *Sea Gull* drew nearer in to shore the waves became more turbulent, for there is ever a more ordered succession in deep waters than where the onward rush is broken by the undulations of the shore. Minute by minute the dawn was growing brighter, and the shore was opening up. The *Sea Gull,* lightened of her load, could not with safety be thrown across the wind, and so the difficulty of her tacks was increased. The dawn was just shooting its first rays over the eastern sea when the final effort to win the little port came to be made.

The harbour of Port Erroll is a tiny haven of refuge won from the jagged rocks that bound the eastern side of Cruden Bay. It is sheltered on the northern side by the cliff which runs as far as the Watter's Mou', and separated from the mouth of the Water of Cruden, with its waste of shifting sands, by a high wall of concrete. The harbour faces east, and its first basin is the smaller of the two, the larger opening sharply to the left a little way in. At the best of times it is not an easy matter to gain the harbour, for only when the tide has fairly risen is it available at all, and the rapid tide which runs up from the Scaurs makes in itself a difficulty at such times. The tide was now at three-quarters flood, so that in as far as water was concerned there was no difficulty; but the fierceness of the waves which sent up a wall of white water all along the cliffs looked ominous indeed.

As the *Sea Gull* drew nearer to the shore, considerable commotion was caused on both sea and land. The revenue cutter dared not approach so close to the shore, studded as it was with sunken rocks, as did the lighter draughted coble; but her commander evidently did not mean to let this be to the advantage of the smuggler. A gun was fired to attract the authorities on shore, and signals were got ready to hoist.

The crowd of strangers who thronged the little port had instinctively hidden themselves behind rock and wall and boat, as the revelation of the dawn came upon them, so that the whole place presented the appearance of a warren when the rabbits are beginning to emerge after a temporary scare. There were not wanting, however, many who stood out in the open, affecting, with what nonchalance they could, a simple business interest at the little port. Sailor Willy was on the cliff between the guardhouse and the Watter's Mou', where he had kept his vigil all the night long.

As soon as possible after he had sent out his appeal for help the lieutenant had come over from Collieston with a boatman and three men, and these were now down on the quay waiting for the coming of the *Sea Gull*. When he had arrived, and had learned the state of things, the lieutenant, who knew of Willy Barrow's relations with the daughter of the suspected man, had kindly ordered him to watch the cliff, whilst he himself with the men would look after the port. When he had first given the order in the presence of the other coastguards, Willy had instinctively drawn himself up as though he felt that he, too, had come under suspicion, so the lieutenant took the earliest opportunity when they were alone of saying to Willy:

"Barrow, I have arranged your duties as I have done, not by any means because I suspect that you would be drawn by your sympathies into any neglect of duty—I know you too well for that—but simply because I want to spare you pain in case things may be as we suspect!"

Willy saluted and thanked him with his eyes as he turned away, for he feared that the fullness of his heart might betray him. The poor fellow was much overwrought. All night long he had paced the cliffs in the dull routine of his duty, with his heart feeling like a lump of lead, and his brain on fire with fear. He knew from the wildness of Maggie's rush away from him that she was bent on some desperate enterprise, and as he had no clue to her definite intentions he could only imagine. He thought and thought until his brain almost began to reel with the intensity of his mental effort; and as he was so placed, tied to the stake of his duty, that he could speak with no one on the subject, he had to endure alone, and in doubt, the darkness of his soul, tortured alike by hopes and fears, through all the long night. At last, however, the pain exhausted itself, and doubt became its own anodyne. Despair has its calms—the backwaters of fears—where the tired imagination may rest awhile before the strife begins anew.

With joy he saw that the storm was slackening with the coming of the dawn; and when the last fierce gust had swept by him, screaming through the rigging of the flagstaff overhead, and sweeping inland the broken fragments of the mist, he turned to the sea, now of a cool grey with the light of the coming dawn, and swept it far and wide with his glass. With gladness—and yet with an ache in his heart which he could not understand—he realised that there was in sight only one coble—the *Sea Gull*—he knew her well—running for the port, and farther out the hull and smoke, the light spars and swift lines of the revenue cutter, which was evidently following her.

He strolled with the appearance of leisureliness, though his heart was throbbing, towards the cliff right over the little harbour, so that he could look down and see from close quarters all that went on. He could not but note the many strangers dispersed about, all within easy distance of a rush to the quay when the boat should land, or the way in which the lieutenant and his men seemed to keep guard over the whole place. As first the figures, the walls of the port, the cranes, the boats, and the distant headlands were silhouetted in black against the background of grey sea and grey sky; but as the dawn came closer each object began to stand out in its natural proportions.

All kept growing clearer and yet clearer and more and more thoroughly outlined, till the moment came when the sun, shooting over the horizon, set every living thing whose eyes had been regulated to the strain of the darkness and the twilight blinking and winking in the glory of the full light of day.

Eagerly he searched the faces of the crowd with his glass for Maggie, but he could not see her anywhere, and his heart seemed to sink within him, for well he knew that it must be no ordinary cause which kept Maggie from being one of the earliest on the lookout for her father. Closer and closer came the *Sea Gull*, running for the port with a speed and recklessness that set both the smugglers and the preventive men all agog.

Such haste and such indifference to danger sprang, they felt, from no common cause, and they all came to the conclusion that the boat, delayed by the storm, discovered by the daylight, and cut off by the revenue cutter, was making a desperate push for success in her hazard. And so all, watchers and watched, braced themselves for what might come about. Amongst the groups moved the tall figure of Mendoza, whispering and pointing, but keeping carefully hidden from the sight of the coastguards. He was evidently inciting them to some course from which they held back.

Closer and closer came the *Sea Gull*, lying down to the scuppers as she tacked; lightened as she was she made more leeway than was usual to so crank a boat. At last she got her head in the right direction for a run in, and, to the amazement of all who saw her, came full tilt into the outer basin, and, turning sharply round, ran into the inner basin under bare poles. There was not one present, smuggler or coastguard, who did not set down the daring attempt as simply suicidal. In a few seconds the boat stuck on the sandbank accumulated at the western end of the basin and stopped, her bows almost touching the side of the pier.

The coastguards had not expected any such manoeuvre, and

had taken their place on either side of the entrance to the inner basin, so that it took them a few seconds to run the length of the pier and come opposite the boat. The crowd of the smugglers and the smugglers' friends was so great that just as Neil and his brother began to shove out a plank from the bows to step ashore there was so thick a cluster round the spot that the lieutenant as he came could not see what was going on.

Some little opposition was made to his passing through the mass of people, which was getting closer every instant, but his men closed up behind, and together they forced a way to the front before any one from the *Sea Gull* could spring on shore. A sort of angry murmur—that deep undertone which marks the passion of a mass—arose, and the lieutenant, recognising its import, faced round like lightning, his revolver pointed straight in the faces of the crowd, whilst the men with him drew their cutlasses.

To Sailor Willy this appearance of action gave a relief from almost intolerable pain. He was in feverish anxiety about Maggie, but he could do nothing—nothing; and to an active and resolute man this feeling is in itself the worst of pain. His heart was simply breaking with suspense, and so it was that the sight of drawn weapons, in whatever cause, came like an anodyne to his tortured imagination. The flash of the cutlasses woke in him the instinct of action, and with a leaping heart he sprang down the narrow winding path that led to the quay.

Before the lieutenant's pistol the crowd fell back. It was not that they were afraid—for cowardice is pretty well unknown in Buchan—but authority, and especially in arms, has a special force with law-breakers. But the smugglers did not mean going back altogether now that their booty was so close to them, and the two bodies stood facing each other when Sailor Willy came upon the scene and stood beside the officers. Things were looking pretty serious when the resonant voice of MacWhirter was heard:

"What d'ye mean, men, crowdin' on the officers. Stand back, there, and let the coastguards come aboard an they will. There's naught here that they mayn't see."

The lieutenant turned and stepped on the plank—which Neil had by this time shoved on shore—and went on board, followed by two of his men, the other remaining with the boatman and Willy Barrow on the quay. Neil went straight to the officer, and said:

"I want to go ashore at once! Search me an ye will!" He spoke so rudely that the officer was angered, and said to one of the men beside him:

"Put your hands over him and let him go," adding, *sotto voce*, "He wants a lesson in manners!" The man lightly passed his hands over him to see that he had nothing contraband about him, and, being satisfied on the point, stood back and nodded to his officer, and Neil sprang ashore, and hurried off towards the village.

Willy had, by this time, a certain feeling of relief, for he had been thinking, and he knew that MacWhirter would not have been so ready to bring the coastguards on board if he had any contraband with him. Hope did for him what despair could not, for as he instinctively turned his eyes over the waste of angry sea, for an instant he did not know if it were the blood in his eyes or, in reality, the red of the dawn which had shot up over the eastern horizon.

Mendoza's men, having been carefully searched by one of the coastguards, came sullenly on shore and went to the back of the crowd, where their master, scowling and white-faced, began eagerly to talk with them in whispers. MacWhirter and his elder son busied themselves with apparent nonchalance in the needful matters of the landing, and the crowd seemed holding back for a spring. The suspense of all was broken by the incoming of a boat sent off from the revenue cutter, which, driven by four sturdy oarsmen, and steered by the commander himself, swept into the outer basin of the harbour, tossing amongst the broken waves. In the comparative shelter of the wall it turned, and driving into the inner basin pulled up on the slip beyond where the *Sea Gull* lay.

The instant the boat touched, six bluejackets sprang ashore, followed by the commander, and all seven men marched quietly but resolutely to the quay opposite the *Sea Gull's* bow. The oarsmen followed, when they had hauled their boat up on the slip. The crowd now abandoned whatever had been its intention, and fell back looking and muttering thunder.

By this time the lieutenant was satisfied that the coble contained nothing that was contraband, and, telling its master so, stepped on shore just as Neil, with his face white as a sheet, and his eyes blazing, rushed back at full speed. He immediately attacked Sailor Willy:

"What hae ye dune wi' ma sister Maggie?"

He answered as quietly as he could, although there shot through his heart a new pain, a new anxiety:

"I know naught of her. I haven't seen her since last night, when Alice MacDonald was being married. Is she not at home?"

"Dinna ye ken damned weel that she's no'. Why did ye send her oot?" And he looked at him with the menace of murder in his eyes. The lieutenant saw from the looks of the two men that something was wrong, and asked Neil shortly:

"Where did you see her last?" Neil was going to make some angry reply, but in an instant Mendoza stepped forward, and in a loud voice gave instruction to one of his men who had been on board the *Sea Gull* to take charge of her, as she was his under a bill of sale. This gave Neil time to think, and his answer came sullenly:

"Nane o' ye're business—mind yer ain affairs!"

MacWhirter, when he had seen Neil come running back, had realised the worst, and leaned on the taffrail of the boat, groaning. Mendoza's man sprang on board, and, taking him roughly by the shoulder, said:

"Come, clear out here. This boat is to Mendoza; get away!" The old man was so overcome with his feelings regarding Maggie that he made no reply, but quietly, with bent form, stepped on the plank and gained the quay. Willy Barrow rushed forward and took him by the hand and whispered to him:

"What does he mean?"

"He means," said the old man in a low, strained voice, "that for me an' him, an' to warn us she cam oot last nicht in the storm in a wee bit boat, an' that she is no' to her hame!" and he groaned. Willy was smitten with horror. This, then, was Maggie's high and desperate purpose when she left him. He knew now the meaning of those despairing words, and the darkness of the grave seemed to close over his soul. He moaned out to the old man: "She did not tell me she was going. I never knew it. O my God!" The old man, with the protective instinct of the old to the young, laid his hand on his shoulder, as he said to him in a broken voice:

"A ken it, lad! A ken it weel! She tell't me sae hersel! The sin is a' wi' me, though you, puir lad, must e'en bear yer share o' the pain!" The commander said quietly to the lieutenant:

"Looks queer, don't it—the coastguard and the smuggler whispering?"

"All right," came the answer, "I know Barrow; he is as true as steel, but he's engaged to the old man's daughter. But I gather there's something queer going on this morning about her. I'll find out. Barrow," he added, calling Willy to him, "what is it about MacWhirter's daughter?"

"I don't know for certain, sir, but I fear she was out at sea last night." .

"At sea," broke in the commander; "at sea last night—how?"

"She was in a bit fishin'-boat," broke in MacWhirter. "Neighbours, hae ony o' ye seen her this mornin'? 'Twas ma son Andra's boat, that he keeps i' the Downans!"—another name for the Watter's Mou'. A sad silence that left the angry roar of the waves as they broke on the rocks and on the long strand in full possession was the only reply.

"Is the boat back in the Watter's Mou'?" asked the lieutenant sharply.

"No." said a fisherman. "A cam up jist noo past the Barley Mill, an' there's nae boat there."

"Then God help her, an' God forgie me," said MacWhirter,

tearing off his cap and holding up his hands, "for A've killed her—her that sae loved her auld father, that she went oot alane in a bit boat i' the storm i' the nicht to save him frae the consequence o' his sin." Willy Barrow groaned, and the lieutenant turned to him: "Heart, man, heart! God won't let a brave girl like that be lost. That's the lass for a sailor's wife. 'Twill be all right—you'll be proud of her yet!"

But Sailor Willy only groaned despite the approval of his conscience; his words of last night came back to him. "Ye're no fit wife for me!" Now the commander spoke out to MacWhirter:

"When did you see her last?"

"Aboot twa o'clock i' the mornin'."

"Where?"

"Aboot twenty miles off the Scaurs."

"How did she come to leave you?"

"She pulled the boat that she cam in alongside the coble, an' got in by hersel—the last I saw o' her she had hoisted her sail an' was running nor'west . . . But A'll see her nae mair—a's ower wi' the puir, brave lass—an' wi' me, tae, that killed her—a's ower the noo—a's ower!" and he covered his face with his hands and sobbed. The commander said kindly enough, but with a stern gravity that there was no mistaking:

"Do I take it rightly that the girl went out in the storm to warn you?"

"Ay! Puir lass—'twas an ill day that made me put sic a task on her—God forgie me!" and there and then he told them all of her gallant deed.

The commander turned to the lieutenant, and spoke in the quick, resolute, masterful accent of habitual command:

"I shall leave you the bluejackets to help—send your men all out, and scour every nook and inlet from Kirkton to Boddam. Out with all the lifeboats on the coast! And you, men!" he turned to the crowd, "turn out, all of you, to help! Show that there's some man's blood in you, to atone if you can for the wrong that sent this young girl out in a storm to save her father from you and your like!" Here he turned again to the lieutenant,

"Keep a sharp eye on that man—Mendoza, and all his belongings. We'll attend to him later on: I'll be back before night."

"Where are you off to, Commander?"

"I'm going to scour the sea in the track of the storm where that gallant lass went last night. A brave girl that dared what she did for her father's sake is not to be lost without an effort; and, by God, she shan't lack it whilst I hold Her Majesty's command! Boatswain, signal the cutter full steam up—no, you! We mustn't lose time, and the boatswain comes with me. To your oars, men!"

The seamen gave a quick, sharp "Hurrah!" as they sprang to their places, whilst the man of the shore party to whom the order had been given climbed the sea-wall and telegraphed the needful orders; the crowd seemed to catch the enthusiasm of the moment, and scattered right and left to make search along the shore. In a few seconds the revenue boat was tossing on the waves outside the harbour, the men laying to their work as they drove her along, their bending oars keeping time to the swaying body of the commander, who had himself taken the tiller. The lieutenant said to Willy with thoughtful kindness:

"Where would you like to work on the search? Choose which part you will!" Willy instinctively touched his cap as he answered sadly:

"I should like to watch here, sir, if I may. She would make straight for the Watter's Mou'!"

## CHAPTER 5

The search for the missing girl was begun vigorously, and carried on thoroughly and with untiring energy. The Port Erroll lifeboat was got out and proceeded up coast, and a telegram was sent to Kirkton to get out the lifeboat there, and follow up the shore to Port Erroll. From either place a body of men with ropes followed on shore keeping pace with the boat's progress. In the meantime the men of each village and hamlet all along the shore of Buchan from Kirkton to Boddam began a systematic exploration of all the openings on the coast. Of course there were some places where no search could at present be made. The Bullers, for instance, was well justifying its name with the wild turmoil of waters that fretted and churned between its rocky walls, and the neighbourhood of the Twa Een was like a seething caldron.

At Dunbuy, a great sheet of foam, perpetually renewed by the rush and recoil of the waves among the rocks, lay like a great white blanket over the inlet, and effectually hid any flotsam or jetsam that might have been driven thither. But on the high cliffs around these places, on every coign of vantage, sat women and children, who kept keen watch for aught that might develop. Every now and again a shrill cry would bring a rush to the place and eager eyes would follow the pointing hand of the watcher who had seen some floating matter; but in every case a few seconds and a little dispersing of the shrouding foam put an end to expectation. Throughout that day the ardour of the searchers never abated.

Morning had come rosy and smiling over the waste of heaving waters, and the sun rose and rose till its noonday rays beat down oppressively. But Willy Barrow never ceased from his lonely vigil on the cliff. At dinner-time a good-hearted woman brought him some food, and in kindly sympathy sat by him in silence, whilst he ate it. At first it seemed to him that to eat at all was some sort of wrong to Maggie, and he felt that to attempt it would choke him. But after a few mouthfuls the human need in him responded to the occasion, and he realised how much he wanted food. The kindly neighbour then tried to cheer him with a few words of hope, and a many words of Maggie's worth, and left him, if not cheered, at least sustained for what he had to endure.

All day long his glass ranged the sea in endless, ever-baffled hope. He saw the revenue boat strike away at first towards Girdleness, and then turn and go out to where Maggie had left the *Sea Gull*; and then under full steam churn her way northwest through the fretted seas. Now and again he saw boats, far and near, pass on their way; and as they went through that wide belt of sea where Maggie's body might be drifting with the wreckage of her boat, his heart leaped and fell again under stress of hope and despair. The tide fell lower and ever lower, till the waves piling into the estuary roared among the rocks that paved the Watter's Mou'.

Again and again he peered down from every rocky point in fear of seeing amid the turmoil—what, he feared to think. There was ever before his eyes the figure of the woman he loved, spread out rising and falling with the heaving waves, her long hair tossing wide and making an aureole round the upturned white face. Turn where he would, in sea or land, or in the white clouds of the summer sky, that image was ever before him, as though it had in some way burned into his iris.

Later in the afternoon, as he stood beside the crane, where he had met Maggie the night before, he saw Neil coming towards him, and instinctively moved from the place, for he felt that he would not like to meet on that spot, for ever to be hallowed in his mind, Maggie's brother with hatred in his heart. So he moved slowly to meet him, and when he had got close to the flagstaff waited till he should come up, and swept once again the wide horizon with his glass—in vain. Neil, too, had begun to slow his steps as he drew nearer. Slower and slower he came, and at last stood close to the man whom in the morning he had spoken to with hatred and murder in his heart.

All the morning Neil had worked with a restless, feverish actively, which was the wonder of all. He had not stayed with the searching party with whom he had set out; their exhaustive method was too slow for him, and he soon distanced them, and alone scoured the whole coast as far as Murdoch Head. Then in almost complete despair, for his mind was satisfied that Maggie's body had never reached that part of the shore, he had retraced his steps almost at a run, and, skirting the sands of Cruden Bay, on whose wide expanse the beakers still rolled heavily and roared loudly, he glanced among the jagged rocks that lay around Whinnyfold and stretched under the water away to the Scaurs. Then he came back again, and the sense of desolation complete upon him moved his passionate heart to sympathy and pity. It is when the soul within us feels the narrow environments of our selfishness that she really begins to spread her wings.

Neil walked over the sandhills along Cruden Bay like a man in a dream. With a sailor's habit he watched the sea, and now and again had his attention attracted by the drifting masses of seaweed torn from its rocky bed by the storm. In such tossing black masses he sometimes thought Maggie's body might lie, but his instinct of the sea was too true to be long deceived. And then he began to take himself to task. Hitherto he had been too blindly passionate to be able to think of anything but his own trouble; but now, despite what he could do, the woe-stricken face of Sailor Willy would rise before his inner eye like the embodiment or the wraith of a troubled conscience.

When once this train of argument had been started, the remorseless logic which is the mechanism of the spirit of conscience went on its way unerringly. Well he knew it was the ill-doing of which he had a share, and not the duty that Willy owed, that took his sister out alone on the stormy sea. He knew from her own lips that Willy had neither sent her nor even knew of her going, and the habit of fair play which belonged to his life began to exert an influence. The first sign of his change of mind was the tear which welled up in his eye and rolled down his cheek.

"Poor Maggie! Poor Willy!" he murmured to himself, half unconsciously, "A'll gang to him an' tak it a' back!" With this impulse on him he quickened his steps, and never paused till he saw Willy Barrow before him, spy-glass to eye, searching the sea for any sign of his lost love. Then his fears, and the awkwardness which a man feels at such a moment, no matter how poignant may be the grief which underlies it, began to trip him up. When he stood beside Willy Barrow, he said, with what bravery he could:

"I tak it a' back, Sailor Willy! Ye werena to blame! It was oor daein'! Will ye forgie me?" Willy turned and impulsively grasped the hand extended to him. In the midst of his overwhelming pain this was some little gleam of sunshine. He had himself just sufficient remorse to make the assurance of his innocence by another grateful. He knew well that if he had chosen to sacrifice his duty Maggie would never have gone out to sea, and though it did not even occur to him to repent of doing his duty, the mere temptation—the mere struggle against it, made a sort of foothold where flying remorse might for a moment rest.

When the eyes of the two men met, Willy felt a new duty rise within his. He had always loved Neil, who was younger than himself, and was Maggie's brother, and he could not but see the look of anguish in the eyes that were so like Maggie's. He saw there something which in one way transcended his own pain, and made him glad that he had not on his soul the guilt of treachery to his duty. Not for the wide world would he have gazed into Maggie's eyes with such a look as that in his own. And yet—and yet—there came back to him with an over-powering flood of anguish the thought that, though the darkness had mercifully hidden it, Maggie's face, after she had tempted him, had had in it something of the same expression.

It is a part of the penalty of being human that we cannot forbid the coming of thoughts, but it is a glory of humanity that we can wrestle with them and overcome them. Quick on the harrowing memory of Maggie's shame came the thought of Maggie's heroic self-devotion: her true spirit had found a way out of shame and difficulty, and the tribute of the lieutenant, "That's the lass for a sailor's wife!" seemed to ring in Willy's ears. As far as death was concerned, Willy Barrow did not fear it for himself, and how could he feel the fear for another.

Such semblance of fear as had been in his distress was based on the selfishness which is a part of man's love, and in this wild hour of pain and distress became a thing of naught. All this reasoning, all this sequence of emotions, passed in a few seconds, and, as it seemed to him all at once, Willy Barrow broke out crying with the abandon which marks strong men when spiritual pain breaks down the barriers of their pride. Men of Willy's class seldom give way to their emotions. The prose of life is too continuous to allow of any habit of prolonged emotional indulgence; the pendulum swings back from fact to fact and things go on as before. So it was with Sailor Willy.

His spasmodic grief was quick as well as fierce, like an April shower; and in a few seconds he had regained his calm. But the break, though but momentary, had relieved his pent-up feelings, and his heart beat more calmly for it. Then some of the love which he had for Maggie went out to her brother, and as he saw that the pain in his face did not lessen, a great pity overcame him and he tried to comfort Neil.

"Don't grieve, man. Don't grieve. I know well you'd give your heart's blood for Maggie"—he faltered as he spoke her name, but with a great gulp went on bravely: "There's your father—her father, we must try and comfort him. Maggie," here he lifted his cap reverently, "is with God! We, you and I, and all, must so bear ourselves that she shall not have died in vain." To Sailor Willy's tear-blurred eyes, as he looked upward, it seemed as if the great white gull which perched as he spoke on the yard of the flagstaff over his head was in some way an embodiment of the spirit of the lost girl, and, like the lightning phantasmagoria of a dream, there flitted across his mind many an old legend and eerie belief gained among the wolds and barrows of his Yorkshire home.

There was not much more to be said between the men, for they understood each other, and men of their class are not prone to speak more than is required. They walked northwards, and for a long time they stood together on the edge of the cliff, now and again gazing seawards, and ever and anon to where below their feet and falling tide was fretting and churning amongst the boulders at the entrance of the Watter's Mou'.

Neil was unconsciously watching his companion's face and following his thoughts, and presently said, as though in answer to something that had gone before: "Then ye think she'll drift in here, if onywhere?" Willy started as though he had been struck, for there seemed a positive brutality in the way of putting his own secret belief. He faced Neil quickly, but there was nothing in his face of any brutal thought. On the contrary, the lines of his face were so softened that all his likeness to his sister stood out so markedly as to make the heart of her lover ache with a fresh pang—a new sense, not of loss, but of what he had lost. Neil was surprised at the manner of his look, and his mind working back gave him the clue. All at once he broke out:

"O Willy mon, we'll never see her again! Never! never! Till the sea gies up its dead; what can we dae, mon? what can we dae? what can we dae?"

Again there was a new wrench to Sailor Willy's heart. Here were almost Maggie's very words of the night before, spoken in the same despairing tone, in the same spot, and by one who was not only her well-beloved brother, but who was, as he stood in this abandonment of his grief, almost her living image. However, he did not know what to say, and he could do nothing but only bear in stolid patient misery the woes that came upon him. He did all that could be done—nothing—but stood in silent sympathy and waited for the storm in the remorseful young man's soul to pass. After a few minutes Neil recovered somewhat, and, pulling himself together, said to Willy with what bravery he could:

"A'll gang look after father. A've left him ower lang as't is!"

The purpose of Maggie's death was beginning to bear fruit already.

He went across the field straight towards where his father's cottage stood under the brow of the slope towards the Water of Cruden. Sailor Willy watched him go with sadness, for anything that had been close to Maggie was dear to him, and Neil's presence had been in some degree an alleviation of his pain.

During the hours that followed he had one gleam of pleasure—something that moved him strangely in the midst of his pain. Early in the morning the news of Maggie's loss had been taken to the Castle, and all its household had turned out to aid vigorously in the search. In his talk with the lieutenant and his men, and from the frequent conversation of the villagers, the Earl had gathered pretty well the whole truth of what had occurred.

Maggie had been a favourite with the ladies of the Castle, and it was as much on her account as his own that the Mastership of the Harbour had been settled prospectively on MacWhirter. That this arrangement was to be upset since the man had turned smuggler was taken for granted by all, and already rumour and surmise were busy in selecting a successor to the promise. The Earl listened but said nothing.

Later on in the day, however, he strolled up the cliff where Willy paced on guard, and spoke with him. He had a sincere regard and liking for the fine young fellow, and when he saw his silent misery his heart went out to him. He tried to comfort him with hopes, but, finding that there was no response in Willy's mind, confined himself to praise of Maggie. Willy listened eagerly as he spoke of her devotion, her bravery, her noble spirit, that took her out on such a mission; and the words fell like drops of balm on the seared heart of her lover. But the bitterness of his loss was too much that he should be altogether patient, and he said presently:

"And all in vain! All in vain! she lost, and her father ruined, his character gone as well as all his means of livelihood—and all in vain! God might be juster than to let such a death as hers be in vain!"

"No, not in vain!" he answered solemnly, "such a deed as hers is never wrought in vain. God sees and hears, and His hand is strong and sure. Many a man in Buchan for many a year to come will lead an honester life for what she has done; and many a woman will try to learn her lesson in patience and self-devotion. God does not in vain put such thoughts into the minds of His people, or into their hearts the noble bravery to carry them out."

Sailor Willy groaned. "Don't think me ungrateful, my lord," he said, "for your kind words—but I'm half wild with trouble, and my heart is sore. Maybe it is as you say—and yet—and yet the poor lass went out to save her father and here he is, ruined in means, in character, in prospects—for who will employ him now just when he most wants it. Everything is gone—and she gone too that could have helped and comforted him!"

As he spoke there shot through the mind of his comforter a

thought followed by a purpose not unworthy of that ancestor, whose heroism and self-devotion won an earldom with an ox-yoke as its crest, and the circuit of a hawk's flight as its dower. There was a new tone in the Earl's voice as he spoke:

"You mean about the harbour-mastership! Don't let that distress you, my poor lad. MacWhirter has lapsed a bit, but he has always borne an excellent character, and from all I hear he was sorely tempted. And, after all, he hasn't done—at least completed—any offence. Oh!" and here he spoke solemnly, "poor Maggie's warning did come in time. Her work was not in vain, though God help us all! she and those that loved her paid a heavy price for it. But even if MacWhirter had committed the offence, and it lay in my power, I should try to prove that her noble devotion was not without its purpose—or its reward.

"It is true that I might not altogether trust MacWhirter until, at least, such time as by good service he had re-established his character. But I would and shall trust the father of Maggie MacWhirter, that gave her life for him; and well I know that there isn't an honest man or woman in Buchan that won't say the same. He shall be the harbourmaster if he will. We shall find in time that he has reared again the love and respect of all men. That will be Maggie's monument; and a noble one too in the eyes of God and of men!"

He grasped Willy's hand in his own strong one, and the hearts of both men, the gentle and the simple, went out each to the other, and became bound together as men's hearts do when touched with flame of any kind.

When he was alone Willy felt somehow more easy in his mind. The bitterest spirit of all is woe—the futility of Maggie's sacrifice—was gone, exorcised by the hopeful words and kind act of the Earl, and the resilience of his manhood began to act.

And now there came another distraction to his thoughts—an ominous weather change. It had grown colder as the day went on, but now the heat began to be oppressive, and there was a deadly stillness in the air; it was manifest that another storm was at hand. The sacrifice of the night had not fully appeased the storm-gods. Somewhere up in that Northern Unknown, where the Fates weave their web of destiny, a tempest was brewing which would soon boil over. Darker and darker grew the sky, and more still and silent and oppressive grew the air, till the cry of a sea-bird or the beating of the waves upon the rocks came as distinct and separate things, as though having no counterpart in the active world.

Towards sunset the very electricity in the air made all animate nature so nervous that men and women could not sit quiet, but moved restlessly. Susceptible women longed to scream out and vent their feelings, as did the cattle in the meadows with their clamorous lowing, or the birds wheeling restlessly aloft with articulate cries. Willy Barrow stuck steadfastly to his post. He had some feeling—some presentiment that there would soon be a happening—what, he knew not; but, as all his thoughts were of Maggie, it must surely be of her.

It might have been that the thunderous disturbance wrought on a system overtaxed almost beyond human endurance, for it was two whole nights since he had slept. Or it may have been that the recoil from despair was acting on his strong nature in the way that drives men at times to desperate deeds, when they rush into the thick of battle, and, fighting, die. Or it may simply have been that the seaman in him spoke through all the ways and offices of instinct and habit, and that with the foreknowledge of coming stress woke the power that was to combat with it. For great natures of the fighting kind move with their surroundings, and the spirit of the sailor grew with the storm pressure whose might he should have to brave.

Down came the storm in one wild, frenzied burst. All at once the waters seemed to rise, throwing great sheets of foam from the summit of the lifting waves. The wind whistled high and low, and screamed as it swept through the rigging of the flagstaff. Flashes of lightning and rolling thunderclaps seemed to come together, so swift their succession. The rain fell in torrents, so that within a few moments the whole earth seemed one filmy sheet, shining in the lightning flashes that rent the black clouds, and burn and rill and runlet roared with rushing water.

All through the hamlet men and women, even the hardiest, fled to shelter—all save the one who paced the rocks above the Watter's Mou', peering as he had done for many an hour down into the depths below him in the pauses of his seaward glance. Something seemed to tell him that Maggie was coming closer to him. He could feel her presence in the air and the sea; and the memory of that long, passionate kiss, which had made her his, came back, not as a vivid recollection, but as something of the living present.

To and fro he paced between the flagstaff and the edge of the rocks; but each turn he kept further and further from the flagstaff, as though some fatal fascination was holding him to the Watter's Mou'. He saw the great waves come into the cove tumbling and roaring; dipping deep under the lee of the Ship's Starn in wide patches of black, which in the dark silence of their onward sweep stood out in strong contrast to the white turmoil of the churning waters under his feet.

Every now and again a wave greater than all its fellows—what fishermen call the "sailor's wave"—would ride in with all the majesty of resistless power, shutting out for a moment the jagged whiteness of the submerged rocks, and sweeping up the cove as though the bringer of some royal message from the sea.

As one of these great waves rushed in, Willy's heart beat loudly, and for a second he looked around as though for some voice, from whence he knew not, which was calling to him. Then he looked down and saw, far below him, tossed high upon the summit of the wave, a mass that in the gloom of the evening and the storm looker like a tangle of wreckage—spar and sail and rope—twirling in the rushing water round a dead woman, whose white face was set in an aureole of floating hair. Without a word, but with the bound of a panther, Willy Barrow sprang out on the projecting point of rock, and plunged down into the rushing wave whence he could meet that precious wreckage and grasp it tight.

Down in the village the men were talking in groups as the

chance of the storm had driven them to shelter. In the rocket-house opposite the Salmon Fisher's store had gathered a big cluster, and they were talking eagerly of all that had gone by. Presently one of them said:

"Men, oughtn't some o' us to gang abeen the rocks and bide a wee wi' Sailor Willy? The puir lad is nigh daft wi' his loss, an' 'a wee bit companionship wouldna be bad for him." To which a sturdy youth answered as he stepped out:

"A'l go bide wi' him. It must be main lonely for him in the guard-house the nicht. An' when he's relieved, as A hear he is to be, by Michael Watson ower frae Whinnyfold, A'll gang wi' him or tak him hame wi' me. Mither'll be recht glad to thole for him!" and drawing his oilskin closer round his neck he went out in the storm.

As he walked up the path to the cliff the storm seemed to fade away—the clouds broke, and through the wet mist came gleams of fading twilight; and when he looked eastwards from the cliff the angry sea was all that was of storm, for in the sky was every promise of fine weather to come. He went straight to the guard-house and tried to open the door, but it was locked; then he went to the side and looked in. There was just sufficient light to see that the place was empty. So he went along the cliff looking for Willy.

It was now light enough to see all round, for the blackness of the sky overhead had passed, the heavy clouds being swept away by the driving wind; but nowhere could he see any trace of the man he sought. He went all along the cliff up the Watter's Mou', till, following the downward trend of the rock, and splashing a way through the marsh—now like a quagmire, so saturated was it with the heavy rainfall—he came to the shallows opposite the Barley Mill. Here he met a man from The Bullers, who had come along by the Castle, and him he asked if he had seen Willy Barrow on his way.

The decidedly negative answer "A've seen nane. It's nae a night for ony to be oot than can bide wi'in!" made him think that all might not be well with Sailor Willy, and so he went back again on his search, peering into every hole and cranny as he went. At the flagstaff he met some of his companions, who, since the storm had passed, had come to look for weather signs and to see what the sudden tempest might have brought about. When they heard that there was no sign of the coastguard they separated, searching for him, and shouting lest he might have fallen anywhere and hear their voices.

All that night they searched, for each minute made it more apparent that all was not well with him; but they found no sign.

The waves still beat into the Watter's Mou' with violence, for though the storm had passed the sea was a wide-stretching mass of angry waters, and curling white crowned every wave. But with the outgoing tide the rocky bed of the cove broke up the waves, and they roared sullenly as they washed up the estuary.

In the grey of the morning a fisher-boy rushed up to a knot of men who were clustered round the guard-house and called to them:

"There's somethin' wollopin' aboot i' the shallows be the Barley Mill! Come an' get it oot! It looks like some ane!" So there was a rush made to the place. When they got to the islands of sea-grass the ebbing tide had done its work, and stranded the "something" which had rolled amid the shallows.

There, on the very spot whence the boat had set sail on its warning errand, lay its wreckage, and tangled in it the body of the noble girl who had steered it—her brown hair floating wide and twined round the neck of Sailor Willy, who held her tight in his dead arms.

The requiem of the twain was the roar of the breaking waves and the screams of the white birds that circled round the Watter's Mou'.

# The Coming of Abel Behenna

The little Cornish port of Pencastle was bright in the early April, when the sun had seemingly come to stay after a long and bitter winter. Boldly and blackly the rock stood out against a background of shaded blue, where the sky fading into mist met the far horizon. The sea was of true Cornish hue—sapphire, save where it became deep emerald green in the fathomless depths under the cliffs, where the seal caves opened their grim jaws.

On the slopes the grass was parched and brown. The spikes of furze bushes were ashy grey, but the golden yellow of their flowers streamed along the hillside, dipping out in lines as the rock cropped up, and lessening into patches and dots till finally it died away all together where the sea winds swept round the jutting cliffs and cut short the vegetation as though with an ever-working aerial shears. The whole hillside, with its body of brown and flashes of yellow, was just like a colossal yellow-hammer.

The little harbour opened from the sea between towering cliffs, and behind a lonely rock, pierced with many caves and blow-holes through which the sea in storm time sent its thunderous voice, together with a fountain of drifting spume. Hence, it wound westwards in a serpentine course, guarded at its entrance by two little curving piers to left and right. These were roughly built of dark slates placed endways and held together with great beams bound with iron bands. Thence, it flowed up the rocky bed of the stream whose winter torrents had of old cut out its way amongst the hills.

This stream was deep at first, with here and there, where

it widened, patches of broken rock exposed at low water, full of holes where crabs and lobsters were to be found at the ebb of the tide. From amongst the rocks rose sturdy posts, used for warping in the little coasting vessels which frequented the port. Higher up, the stream still flowed deeply, for the tide ran far inland, but always calmly for all the force of the wildest storm was broken below.

Some quarter mile inland the stream was deep at high water, but at low tide there were at each side patches of the same broken rock as lower down, through the chinks of which the sweet water of the natural stream trickled and murmured after the tide had ebbed away. Here, too, rose mooring posts for the fishermen's boats. At either side of the river was a row of cottages down almost on the level of high tide. They were pretty cottages, strongly and snugly built, with trim narrow gardens in front, full of old-fashioned plants, flowering currants, coloured primroses, wallflower, and stonecrop.

Over the fronts of many of them climbed clematis and wisteria. The window sides and door posts of all were as white as snow, and the little pathway to each was paved with light coloured stones. At some of the doors were tiny porches, whilst at others were rustic seats cut from tree trunks or from old barrels; in nearly every case the window ledges were filled with boxes or pots of flowers or foliage plants.

Two men lived in cottages exactly opposite each other across the stream. Two men, both young, both good-looking, both prosperous, and who had been companions and rivals from their boyhood. Abel Behenna was dark with the gypsy darkness which the Phoenician mining wanderers left in their track; Eric Sanson—which the local antiquarian said was a corruption of Sagamanson—was fair, with the ruddy hue which marked the path of the wild Norseman.

These two seemed to have singled out each other from the very beginning to work and strive together, to fight for each other and to stand back to back in all endeavours. They had now put the coping-stone on their Temple of Unity by falling in love with the same girl. Sarah Trefusis was certainly the prettiest girl in Pencastle, and there was many a young man who would gladly have tried his fortune with her, but that there were two to contend against, and each of these the strongest and most resolute man in the port—except the other.

The average young man thought that this was very hard, and on account of it bore no good will to either of the three principals: whilst the average young woman who had, lest worse should befall, to put up with the grumbling of her sweetheart, and the sense of being only second best which it implied, did not either, be sure, regard Sarah with friendly eye. Thus it came, in the course of a year or so, for rustic courtship is a slow process, that the two men and the woman found themselves thrown much together. They were all satisfied, so it did not matter, and Sarah, who was vain and something frivolous, took care to have her revenge on both men and women in a quiet way. When a young woman in her "walking out" can only boast one not-quite-satisfied young man, it is no particular pleasure to her to see her escort cast sheep's eyes at a better-looking girl supported by two devoted swains.

At length there came a time which Sarah dreaded, and which she had tried to keep distant—the time when she had to make her choice between the two men. She liked them both, and, indeed, either of them might have satisfied the ideas of even a more exacting girl. But her mind was so constituted that she thought more of what she might lose, than of what she might gain; and whenever she thought she had made up her mind she became instantly assailed with doubts as to the wisdom of her choice.

Always the man whom she had presumably lost became endowed afresh with a newer and more bountiful crop of advantages than had ever arisen from the possibility of his acceptance. She promised each man that on her birthday she would give him his answer, and that day, the 11th of April, had now arrived. The promises had been given singly and confidentially, but each was given to a man who was not likely to forget. Early in the morning she found both men hovering round her door. Neither had taken the other into his confidence, and each was simply seeking an early opportunity of getting his answer, and advancing his suit if necessary. Damon, as a rule, does not take Pythias with him when making a proposal; and in the heart of each man his own affairs had a claim far above any requirements of friendship.

So, throughout the day, they kept seeing each other out. The position was doubtless somewhat embarrassing to Sarah, and though the satisfaction of her vanity that she should be thus adored was very pleasing, yet there were moments when she was annoyed with both men for being so persistent. Her only consolation at such moments was that she saw, through the elaborate smiles of the other girls when in passing they noticed her door thus doubly guarded, the jealousy which filled their hearts. Sarah's mother was a person of commonplace and sordid ideas, and, seeing all along the state of affairs, her one intention, persistently expressed to her daughter in the plainest of words, was to so arrange matters that Sarah should get all that was possible out of both men.

With this purpose she had cunningly kept herself as far as possible in the background in the matter of her daughter's wooings, and watched in silence. At first Sarah had been indignant with her for her sordid views; but, as usual, her weak nature gave way before persistence, and she had now got to the stage of passive acceptance. She was not surprised when her mother whispered to her in the little yard behind the house:—

"Go up the hillside for a while; I want to talk to these two. They're both red-hot for ye, and now's the time to get things fixed!" Sarah began a feeble remonstrance, but her mother cut her short.

"I tell ye, girl, that my mind is made up! Both these men want ye, and only one can have ye, but before ye choose it'll be so arranged that ye'll have all that both have got! Don't argy, child! Go up the hillside, and when ye come back I'll have it fixed—I see a way quite easy!" So Sarah went up the hillside through the narrow paths between the golden furze, and Mrs. Trefusis joined the two men in the living-room of the little house.

She opened the attack with the desperate courage which is in all mothers when they think for their children, howsoever mean the thoughts may be.

"Ye two men, ye're both in love with my Sarah!"

Their bashful silence gave consent to the barefaced proposition. She went on.

"Neither of ye has much!" Again they tacitly acquiesced in the soft impeachment.

"I don't know that either of ye could keep a wife!" Though neither said a word their looks and bearing expressed distinct dissent. Mrs. Trefusis went on:

"But if ye'd put what ye both have together ye'd make a comfortable home for one of ye—and Sarah!" She eyed the men keenly, with her cunning eyes half shut, as she spoke; then satisfied from her scrutiny that the idea was accepted she went on quickly, as if to prevent argument:

"The girl likes ye both, and mayhap it's hard for her to choose.

Why don't ye toss up for her? First put your money together—ye've each got a bit put by, I know. Let the lucky man take the lot and trade with it a bit, and then come home and marry her. Neither of ye's afraid, I suppose! And neither of ye'll say that he won't do that much for the girl that ye both say ye love!"

Abel broke the silence:

"It don't seem the square thing to toss for the girl! She wouldn't like it herself, and it doesn't seem—seem respectful like to her—" Eric interrupted. He was conscious that his chance was not so good as Abel's, in case Sarah should wish to choose between them:

"Are ye afraid of the hazard?"

"Not me!" said Abel, boldly. Mrs. Trefusis, seeing that her idea was beginning to work, followed up the advantage.

"It is settled that ye put yer money together to make a home for her, whether ye toss for her or leave it for her to choose?"

"Yes," said Eric quickly, and Abel agreed with equal sturdiness.

Mrs. Trefusis' little cunning eyes twinkled. She heard Sarah's step in the yard, and said:

"Well! Here she comes, and I leave it to her." And she went out.

During her brief walk on the hillside Sarah had been trying to make up her mind. She was feeling almost angry with both men for being the cause other difficulty, and as she came into the room said shortly:

"I want to have a word with you both—come to the Flagstaff Rock, where we can be alone." She took her hat and went out of the house up the winding path to the steep rock crowned with a high flagstaff, where once the wreckers' fire basket used to burn. This was the rock which formed the northern jaw of the little harbour. There was only room on the path for two abreast, and it marked the state of things pretty well when, by a sort of implied arrangement, Sarah went first, and the two men followed, walking abreast and keeping step. By this time, each man's heart was boiling with jealousy. When they came to the top of the rock, Sarah stood against the flagstaff, and the two young men stood opposite her. She had chosen her position with knowledge and intention, for there was no room for anyone to stand beside her. They were all silent for a while; then Sarah began to laugh and said:—

"I promised the both of you to give you an answer today. I've been thinking and thinking and thinking, till I began to get angry with you both for plaguing me so; and even now I don't seem any nearer than ever I was to making up my mind." Eric said suddenly:

"Let us toss for it, lass!" Sarah showed no indignation whatever at the proposition; her mother's eternal suggestion had schooled her to the acceptance of something of the kind, and her weak nature made it easy to her to grasp at any way out of the difficulty. She stood with downcast eyes idly picking at the sleeve of her dress, seeming to have tacitly acquiesced in the proposal. Both men instinctively realising this pulled each a coin from his pocket, spun it in the air, and dropped his other hand over the palm on which it lay. For a few seconds they remained thus, all silent; then Abel, who was the more thoughtful of the men, spoke:

"Sarah! Is this good?" As he spoke he removed the upper hand from the coin and placed the latter back in his pocket. Sarah was nettled.

"Good or bad, it's good enough for me! Take it or leave it as you like," she said, to which he replied quickly:

"Nay lass! Aught that concerns you is good enow for me. I did but think of you lest you might have pain or disappointment hereafter. If you love Eric better nor me, in God's name say so, and I think I'm man enow to stand aside. Likewise, if I'm the one, don't make us both miserable for life!" Face to face with a difficulty, Sarah's weak nature proclaimed itself; she put her hands before her face and began to cry, saying—

"It was my mother. She keeps telling me!" The silence which followed was broken by Eric, who said hotly to Abel:

"Let the lass alone, can't you? If she wants to choose this way, let her. It's good enough for me—and for you, too! She's said it now, and must abide by it!" Hereupon Sarah turned upon him in sudden fury, and cried:

"Hold your tongue! What is it to you, at any rate?" and she resumed her crying. Eric was so flabbergasted that he had not a word to say, but stood looking particularly foolish, with his mouth open and his hands held out with the coin still between them. All were silent till Sarah, taking her hands from her face, laughed hysterically and said:

"As you two can't make up your minds, I'm going home!" and she turned to go.

"Stop," said Abel, in an authoritative voice. "Eric, you hold the coin, and I'll cry. Now, before we settle it, let us clearly understand: the man who wins takes all the money that we both have got, brings it to Bristol and ships on a voyage and trades with it. Then he comes back and marries Sarah, and they two keep all, whatever there may be, as the result of the trading. Is this what we understand?"

"Yes," said Eric.

"I'll marry him on my next birthday," said Sarah. Having said it the intolerably mercenary spirit of her action seemed to strike her, and impulsively she turned away with a bright blush. Fire seemed to sparkle in the eyes of both the men. Said Eric: "A year so be! The man that wins is to have one year."

"Toss!" cried Abel, and the coin spun in the air. Eric caught it, and again held it between his outstretched hands.

"Heads!" cried Abel, a pallor sweeping over his face as he spoke. As he leaned forward to look Sarah leaned forward too, and their heads almost touched. He could feel her hair blowing on his cheek, and it thrilled through him like fire. Eric lifted his upper hand; the coin lay with its head up. Abel stepped forward and took Sarah in his arms. With a curse Eric hurled the coin far into the sea. Then he leaned against the flagstaff and scowled at the others with his hands thrust deep in his pockets. Abel whispered wild words of passion and delight into Sarah's ears, and as she listened she began to believe that fortune had rightly interpreted the wishes of her secret heart, and that she loved Abel best.

Presently Abel looked up and caught sight of Eric's face as the last ray of sunset struck it. The red light intensified the natural ruddiness of his complexion, and he looked as though he were steeped in blood. Abel did not mind his scowl, for now that his own heart was at rest he could feel unalloyed pity for his friend. He stepped over, meaning to comfort him, and held out his hand, saying:

"It was my chance, old lad. Don't grudge it me. I'll try to make Sarah a happy woman, and you shall be a brother to us both!"

"Brother be damned!" was all the answer Eric made, as he turned away. When he had gone a few steps down the rocky path he turned and came back. Standing before Abel and Sarah, who had their arms round each other, he said:

"You have a year. Make the most of it! And be sure you're in time to claim your wife! Be back to have your banns up in time to be married on the 11th April. If you're not, I tell you I shall have my banns up, and you may get back too late."

"What do you mean, Eric? You are mad!"

"No more mad than you are, Abel Behenna. You go, that's your chance! I stay, that's mine! I don't mean to let the grass grow under my feet. Sarah cared no more for you than for me five minutes ago, and she may come back to that five minutes after you're gone! You won by a point only—the game may change."

"The game won't change!" said Abel shortly. "Sarah, you'll be true to me? You won't marry till I return?"

"For a year!" added Eric, quickly, "that's the bargain."

"I promise for the year," said Sarah. A dark look came over Abel's face, and he was about to speak, but he mastered himself and smiled.

"I mustn't be too hard or get angry tonight! Come, Eric! We played and fought together. I won fairly. I played fairly all the game of our wooing! You know that as well as I do; and now when I am going away, I shall look to my old and true comrade to help me when I am gone!"

"I'll help you none," said Eric, "So help me God!"

"It was God helped me," said Abel, simply.

"Then let Him go on helping you," said Eric angrily. "The Devil is good enough for me!" and without another word he rushed down the steep path and disappeared behind the rocks.

When he had gone Abel hoped for some tender passage with Sarah, but the first remark she made chilled him.

"How lonely it all seems without Eric!" and this note sounded till he had left her at home—and after.

Early on the next morning Abel heard a noise at his door, and on going out saw Eric walking rapidly away: a small canvas bag full of gold and silver lay on the threshold; on a small slip of paper pinned to it was written:

Take the money and go. I stay. God for you! The Devil for

me! Remember the 11th of April.—Eric Sanson.

That afternoon Abel went off to Bristol, and a week later sailed on the *Star of the Sea* bound for Pahang. His money—including that which had been Eric's—was on board in the shape of a venture of cheap toys. He had been advised by a shrewd old mariner of Bristol whom he knew, and who knew the ways of the Chersonese, who predicted that every penny invested would be returned with a shilling to boot.

As the year wore on Sarah became more and more disturbed in her mind. Eric was always at hand to make love to her in his own persistent, masterful manner, and to this she did not object. Only one letter came from Abel, to say that his venture had proved successful, and that he had sent some two hundred pounds to the bank at Bristol, and was trading with fifty pounds still remaining in goods for China, whither the *Star of the Sea* was bound and whence she would return to Bristol. He suggested that Eric's share of the venture should be returned to him with his share of the profits. This proposition was treated with anger by Eric, and as simply childish by Sarah's mother.

More than six months had since then elapsed, but no other letter had come, and Eric's hopes which had been dashed down by the letter from Pahang, began to rise again. He perpetually assailed Sarah with an "if!" If Abel did not return, would she then many him? If the 11th April went by without Abel being in the port, would she give him over? If Abel had taken his fortune, and married another girl on the head of it, would she marry him, Eric, as soon as the truth were known?

And so on in an endless variety of possibilities. The power of the strong will and the determined purpose over the woman's weaker nature became in time manifest. Sarah began to lose her faith in Abel and to regard Eric as a possible husband; and a possible husband is in a woman's eye different to all other men. A new affection for him began to arise in her breast, and the daily familiarities of permitted courtship furthered the growing affection. Sarah began to regard Abel as rather a rock in the road of her life, and had it not been for her mother's constantly reminding her of the good fortune already laid by in the Bristol Bank she would have tried to have shut her eyes altogether to the fact of Abel's existence.

The 11th April was Saturday, so that in order to have the marriage on that day it would be necessary that the banns should be called on Sunday, 22nd March. From the beginning of that month Eric kept perpetually on the subject of Abel's absence, and his outspoken opinion that the latter was either dead or married began to become a reality to the woman's mind. As the first half of the month wore on Eric became more jubilant, and after church on the 15th he took Sarah for a walk to the Flagstaff Rock. There he asserted himself strongly:

"I told Abel, and you too, that if he was not here to put up his banns in time for the eleventh, I would put up mine for the twelfth. Now the time has come when I mean to do it. He hasn't kept his word"—here Sarah struck in out of her weakness and indecision:

"He hasn't broken it yet!" Eric ground his teeth with anger.

"If you mean to stick up for him," he said, as he smote his hands savagely on the flagstaff, which sent forth a shivering murmur, "well and good. I'll keep my part of the bargain. On Sunday I shall give notice of the banns, and you can deny them in the church if you will. If Abel is in Pencastle on the eleventh, he can have them cancelled, and his own put up; but till then, I take my course, and woe to anyone who stands in my way!" With that he flung himself down the rocky pathway, and Sarah could not but admire his Viking strength and spirit, as, crossing the hill, he strode away along the cliffs towards Bude.

During the week no news was heard of Abel, and on Saturday Eric gave notice of the banns of marriage between himself and Sarah Trefusis. The clergyman would have remonstrated with him, for although nothing formal had been told to the neighbours, it had been understood since Abel's departure that on his return he was to marry Sarah; but Eric would not discuss the question.

"It is a painful subject, sir," he said with a firmness which the parson, who was a very young man, could not but be swayed by. "Surely there is nothing against Sarah or me. Why should there be any bones made about the matter?" The parson said no more, and on the next day he read out the banns for the first time amidst an audible buzz from the congregation. Sarah was present, contrary to custom, and though she blushed furiously enjoyed her triumph over the other girls whose banns had not yet come. Before the week was over she began to make her wedding dress. Eric used to come and look at her at work and the sight thrilled through him. He used to say all sorts of pretty things to her at such times, and there were to both delicious moments of love-making.

The banns were read a second time on the 29th, and Eric's hope grew more and more fixed, though there were to him moments of acute despair when he realised that the cup of happiness might be dashed from his lips at any moment, right up to the last. At such times he was full of passion—desperate and remorseless-and he ground his teeth and clenched his hands in a wild way as though some taint of the old Berserker fury of his ancestors still lingered in his blood. On the Thursday of that week he looked in on Sarah and found her, amid a flood of sunshine, putting finishing touches to her white wedding gown. His own heart was full of gaiety, and the sight of the woman who was so soon to be his own so occupied, filled him with a joy unspeakable, and he felt faint with a languorous ecstasy. Bending over he kissed Sarah on the mouth, and then whispered in her rosy ear—

"Your wedding dress, Sarah! And for me!" As he drew back to admire her she looked up saucily, and said to him—

"Perhaps not for you. There is more than a week yet for Abel!" and then cried out in dismay, for with a wild gesture and a fierce oath Eric dashed out of the house, banging the door behind him. The incident disturbed Sarah more than she could have thought possible, for it awoke all her fears and doubts and indecision afresh. She cried a little, and put by her dress, and to soothe herself went out to sit for a while on the summit of the Flagstaff Rock. When she arrived she found there a little group anxiously discussing the weather. The sea was calm and the sun bright, but across the sea were strange lines of darkness and light, and close in to shore the rocks were fringed with foam, which spread out in great white curves and circles as the currents drifted. The wind had backed, and came in sharp, cold puffs. The blowhole, which ran under the Flagstaff Rock, from the rocky bay without to the harbour within, was booming at intervals, and the seagulls were screaming ceaselessly as they wheeled about the entrance of the port.

"It looks bad," she heard an old fisherman say to the coastguard. "I seen it just like this once before, when the East Indiaman *Coromandel* went to pieces in Dizzard Bay!" Sarah did not wait to hear more. She was of a timid nature where danger was concerned, and could not bear to hear of wrecks and disasters. She went home and resumed the completion of her dress, secretly determined to appease Eric when she should meet him with a sweet apology—and to take the earliest opportunity of being even with him after her marriage.

The old fisherman's weather prophecy was justified. That night at dusk a wild storm came on. The sea rose and lashed the western coasts from Skye to Scilly and left a tale of disaster everywhere. The sailors and fishermen of Pencastle all turned out on the rocks and cliffs and watched eagerly. Presently, by a flash of lightning, a *ketch* was seen drifting under only a jib about half-a-mile outside the port. All eyes and all glasses were concentrated on her, waiting for the next flash, and when it came a chorus went up that it was the *Lovely Alice*, trading between Bristol and Penzance, and touching at all the little ports between.

"God help them!" said the harbour-master, "for nothing in this world can save them when they are between Bude and Tintagel and the wind on shore!" The coastguards exerted themselves, and, aided by brave hearts and willing hands, they brought the rocket apparatus up on the summit of the Flagstaff Rock. Then they burned blue lights so that those on board might see the harbour opening in case they could make any effort to reach it.

They worked gallantly enough on board; but no skill or strength of man could avail.

Before many minutes were over the *Lovely Alice* rushed to her doom on the great island rock that guarded the mouth of the port. The screams of those on board were fairly borne on the tempest as they flung themselves into the sea in a last chance for life. The blue lights were kept burning, and eager eyes peered into the depths of the waters in case any face could be seen; and ropes were held ready to fling out in aid. But never a face was seen, and the willing arms rested idle. Eric was there amongst his fellows. His old Icelandic origin was never more apparent than in that wild hour. He took a rope, and shouted in the ear of the harbour-master:

"I shall go down on the rock over the seal cave. The tide is running up, and someone may drift in there!"

"Keep back, man!" came the answer. "Are you mad? One slip on that rock and you are lost: and no man could keep his feet in the dark on such a place in such a tempest!"

"Not a bit," came the reply. "You remember how Abel Behenna saved me there on a night like this when my boat went on the Gull Rock. He dragged me up from the deep water in the seal cave, and now someone may drift in there again as I did," and he was gone into the darkness. The projecting rock hid the light on the Flagstaff Rock, but he knew his way too well to miss it. His boldness and sureness of foot standing to him, he shortly stood on the great round-topped rock cut away beneath by the action of the waves over the entrance of the seal cave, where the water was fathomless.

There he stood in comparative safety, for the concave shape of the rock beat back the waves with their own force, and though the water below him seemed to boil like a seething cauldron, just beyond the spot there was a space of almost calm. The rock, too, seemed here to shut off the sound of the gale, and he listened as well as watched. As he stood there ready, with his coil of rope poised to throw, he thought he heard below him, just beyond the whirl of the water, a faint, despairing cry. He echoed it with a shout that rang out into the night. Then he waited for the flash of lightning, and as it passed flung his rope out into the darkness where he had seen a face rising through the swirl of the foam. The rope was caught, for he felt a pull on it, and he shouted again in his mighty voice:

"Tie it round your waist, and I shall pull you up." Then when he felt that it was fast he moved along the rock to the far side of the sea cave, where the deep water was something stiller, and where he could get foothold secure enough to drag the rescued man on the overhanging rock. He began to pull, and shortly he knew from the rope taken in that the man he was now rescuing must soon be close to the top of the rock. He steadied himself for a moment, and drew a long breath, that he might at the next effort complete the rescue. He had just bent his back to the work when a flash of lightning revealed to each other the two men—the rescuer and the rescued.

Eric Sanson and Abel Behenna were face to face—and none knew of the meeting save themselves; and God.

On the instant a wave of passion swept through Eric's heart. All his hopes were shattered, and with the hatred of Cain his eyes looked out. He saw in the instant of recognition the joy in Abel's face that his was the hand to succour him, and this intensified his hate. Whilst the passion was on him he started back, and the rope ran out between his hands. His moment of hate was followed by an impulse of his better manhood, but it was too late.

Before he could recover himself, Abel encumbered with the rope that should have aided him, was plunged with a despairing cry back into the darkness of the devouring sea.

Then, feeling all the madness and the doom of Cain upon him, Eric rushed back over the rocks, heedless of the danger and eager only for one thing—to be amongst other people whose living noises would shut out that last cry which seemed to ring still in his ears. When he regained the Flagstaff Rock the men surrounded him, and through the fury of the storm he heard the harbour-master say:—

"We feared you were lost when we heard a cry! How white you are! Where is your rope? Was there anyone drifted in?"

"No one," he shouted in answer, for he felt that he could never explain that he had let his old comrade slip back into the sea, and at the very place and under the very circumstances in which that comrade had saved his own life. He hoped by one bold lie to set the matter at rest for ever. There was no one to bear witness—and if he should have to carry that still white face in his eyes and that despairing cry in his ears for evermore—at least none should know of it. "No one," he cried, more loudly still. "I slipped on the rock, and the rope fell into the sea!" So saying he left them, and, rushing down the steep path, gained his own cottage and locked himself within.

The remainder of that night he passed lying on his bed-dressed and motionless—staring upwards, and seeming to see through the darkness a pale face gleaming wet in the lightning, with its glad recognition turning to ghastly despair, and to hear a cry which never ceased to echo in his soul.

In the morning the storm was over and all was smiling again, except that the sea was still boisterous with its unspent fury. Great pieces of wreck drifted into the port, and the sea around the island rock was strewn with others. Two bodies also drifted into the harbour—one the master of the wrecked ketch, the other a strange seaman whom no one knew.

Sarah saw nothing of Eric till the evening, and then he only looked in for a minute. He did not come into the house, but simply put his head in through the open window.

"Well, Sarah," he called out in a loud voice, though to her it did not ring truly, "is the wedding dress done? Sunday week, mind! Sunday week!"

Sarah was glad to have the reconciliation so easy; but, wom-anlike, when she saw the storm was over and her own fears groundless, she at once repeated the cause of offence.

"Sunday so be it," she said, without looking up, "if Abel isn't there on Saturday!" Then she looked up saucily, though her heart was full of fear of another outburst on the part of her impetuous

330

lover. But the window was empty; Eric had taken himself off, and with a pout she resumed her work. She saw Eric no more till Sunday afternoon, after the banns had been called the third time, when he came up to her before all the people with an air of proprietorship which half-pleased and half-annoyed her.

"Not yet, mister!" she said, pushing him away, as the other girls giggled. "Wait till Sunday next, if you please—the day after Saturday!" she added, looking at him saucily. The girls giggled again, and the young men guffawed. They thought it was the snub that touched him so that he became as white as a sheet as he turned away. But Sarah, who knew more than they did, laughed, for she saw triumph through the spasm of pain that overspread his face.

The week passed uneventfully; however, as Saturday drew nigh Sarah had occasional moments of anxiety, and as to Eric he went about at night-time like a man possessed. He restrained himself when others were by, but now and again he went down amongst the rocks and caves and shouted aloud. This seemed to relieve him somewhat, and he was better able to restrain himself for some time after. All Saturday he stayed in his own house and never left it. As he was to be married on the morrow, the neighbours thought it was shyness on his part, and did not trouble or notice him. Only once was he disturbed, and that was when the chief boatman came to him and sat down, and after a pause said:

"Eric, I was over in Bristol yesterday. I was in the ropemaker's getting a coil to replace the one you lost the night of the storm, and there I saw Michael Heavens of this place, who is salesman there. He told me that Abel Behenna had come home the week ere last on the *Star of the Sea* from Canton, and that he had lodged a sight of money in the Bristol Bank in the name of Sarah Behenna. He told Michael so himself—and that he had taken a passage on the *Lovely Alice* to Pencastle. Bear up, man," for Eric had with a groan dropped his head on his knees, with his face between his hands. "He was your old comrade, I know, but you couldn't help him. He must have gone down with the rest that awful night. I thought I'd better tell you, lest it might come some other way, and you might keep Sarah Trefusis from being frightened. They were good friends once, and women take these things to heart. It would not do to let her be pained with such a thing on her wedding-day!" Then he rose and went away, leaving Eric still sitting disconsolately with his head on his knees.

"Poor fellow!" murmured the chief boatman to himself; "he takes it to heart. Well, well! right enough! They were true comrades once, and Abel saved him!"

The afternoon of that day, when the children had left school, they strayed as usual on half-holidays along the quay and the paths by the cliffs. Presently some of them came running in a state of great excitement to the harbour, where a few men were unloading a coal *ketch*, and a great many were superintending the operation. One of the children called out:

"There is a porpoise in the harbour mouth! We saw it come through the blow hole! It had a long tail, and was deep under the water!"

"It was no porpoise," said another; "it was a seal; but it had a long tail! It came out of the seal cave!" The other children bore various testimony, but on two points they were unanimous—it, whatever "it" was, had come through the blow-hole deep under the water, and had a long, thin tail—a tail so long that they could not see the end of it. There was much unmerciful chaffing of the children by the men on this point, but as it was evident that they had seen something, quite a number of persons, young and old, male and female, went along the high paths on either side of the harbour-mouth to catch a glimpse of this new addition to the fauna of the sea, a long-tailed porpoise or seal.

The tide was now coming in. There was a slight breeze, and the surface of the water was rippled so that it was only at moments that anyone could see clearly into the deep water. After a spell of watching a woman called out that she saw something moving up the channel, just below where she was standing. There was a stampede to the spot, but by the time the crowd had gathered the breeze had freshened, and it was impossible to see with any distinctness below the surface of the water.

On being questioned the woman described what she had seen, but in such an incoherent way that the whole thing was put down as an effect of imagination; had it not been for the children's report she would not have been credited at all. Her semi-hysterical statement that what she saw was "like a pig with the entrails out" was only thought anything of by an old coast-guard, who shook his head but did not make any remark. For the remainder of the daylight this man was seen always on the bank, looking into the water, but always with disappointment manifest on his face.

Eric arose early on the next morning—he had not slept all night, and it was a relief to him to move about in the light. He shaved himself with a hand that did not tremble, and dressed himself in his wedding clothes. There was a haggard look on his face, and he seemed as though he had grown years older in the last few days. Still there was a wild, uneasy light of triumph in his eyes, and he kept murmuring to himself over and over again:

"This is my wedding-day! Abel cannot claim her now—living or dead!—living or dead! Living or dead!" He sat in his arm-chair, waiting with an uncanny quietness for the church hour to arrive. When the bell began to ring he arose and passed out of his house, closing the door behind him. He looked at the river and saw that the tide had just turned.

In the church he sat with Sarah and her mother, holding Sarah's hand tightly in his all the time, as though he feared to lose her. When the service was over they stood up together, and were married in the presence of the entire congregation; for no one left the church. Both made the responses clearly—Eric's being even on the defiant side. When the wedding was over Sarah took her husband's arm, and they walked away together, the boys and younger girls being cuffed by their elders into a decorous behaviour, for they would fain have followed close behind their heels.

The way from the church led down to the back of Eric's cottage, a narrow passage being between it and that of his next neighbour. When the bridal couple had passed through this the remainder of the congregation, who had followed them at a little distance, were startled by a long, shrill scream from the bride. They rushed through the passage and found her on the bank with wild eyes, pointing to the river bed opposite Eric Sanson's door.

The falling tide had deposited there the body of Abel Behenna stark upon the broken rocks. The rope trailing from its waist had been twisted by the current round the mooring post, and had held it back whilst the tide had ebbed away from it. The right elbow had fallen in a chink in the rock, leaving the hand outstretched toward Sarah, with the open palm upward as though it were extended to receive hers, the pale drooping fingers open to the clasp.

All that happened afterwards was never quite known to Sarah Sanson. Whenever she would try to recollect there would come a buzzing in her ears and a dimness in her eyes, and all would pass away. The only thing that she could remember of it at all—and this she never forgot—was Eric's breathing heavily, with his face whiter than that of the dead man, as he muttered under his breath:

"Devil's help! Devil's faith! Devil's price!"

# Buried Treasures

## 1
### THE OLD WRECK

Mr Stedman spoke.

'I do not wish to be too hard on you; but I will not, I cannot
consent to Ellen's marrying you till you have sufficient means
to keep her in comfort. I know too well what poverty is. I saw
her poor mother droop and pine away till she died, and all from
poverty. No, no, Ellen must be spared that sorrow at all events.'

'But, sir, we are young. You say you have always earned your
living. I can do the same and I thought'—this with a flush—'I
thought that if I might be so happy as to win Ellen's love that
you might help us.'

'And so I would, my dear boy; but what help could I give? I
find it hard to keep the pot boiling as it is, and there is only Ellen
and myself to feed. No, no, I must have some certainty for Ellen
before I let her leave me. Just suppose anything should happen
to me'—

'Then, sir, what could be better than to have someone to look
after Ellen—someone with a heart to love her as she should be
loved, and a pair of hands to be worked to the bone for her
sake.'

'True, boy; true. But still it cannot be. I must be certain of
Ellen's future before I trust her out of my own care. Come now,
let me see you with a hundred pounds of your own, and I shall
not refuse to let you speak to her. But mind, I shall trust to your
honour not to forestall that time.'

335

'It is cruel, sir, although you mean it in kindness. I could as easily learn to fly as raise a hundred pounds with my present opportunities. Just think of my circumstances, sir. If my poor father had lived all would have been different; but you know that sad story.'

'No, I do not. Tell it to me.'

'He left the Gold Coast after spending half his life there toiling for my poor mother and me. We knew from his letter that he was about to start for home, and that he was coming in a small sailing vessel, taking all his savings with him. But from that time to this he has never been heard of.'

'Did you make inquiries?'

'We tried every means, or rather poor mother did, for I was too young, and we could find out nothing.'

'Poor boy. From my heart I pity you; still I cannot change my opinion. I have always hoped that Ellen would marry happily. I have worked for her, early and late, since she was born, and it would be mistaken kindness to let her marry without sufficient provision for her welfare.'

Robert Hamilton left Mr Stedman's cottage in great dejection. He had entered it with much misgiving, but with a hope so strong that it brightened the prospect of success. He went slowly along the streets till he got to his office, and when once there he had so much work to do that little time was left him for reflection until his work for the day was over. That night he lay awake, trying with all the intentness of his nature to conceive some plan by which he might make the necessary sum to entitle him to seek the hand of Ellen Stedman: but all in vain. Scheme after scheme rose up before him, but each one, though born of hope, quickly perished in succession.

Gradually his imagination grew in force as the real world seemed to fade away; he built bright castles in the air and installed Ellen as their queen. He thought of all the vast sums of money made each year by chances, of old treasures found after centuries, new treasures dug from mines, and turned from mills and commerce. But all these required capital—except the old treasures—and this source of wealth being a possibility, to it his thoughts clung as a man lost in mid-ocean clings to a spar-clung as he often conceived that his poor father had clung when lost with all his treasure far at sea.

'Vigo Bay, the Schelde, already giving up their long-buried spoil,' so thought he. 'All round our coasts lie millions lost, hidden but for a time. Other men have benefited by them—why should not I have a chance also?' And then, as he sunk to sleep the possibility seemed to become reality, and as he slept he found treasure after treasure, and all was real to him, for he knew not that he dreamt.

He had many dreams. Most of them connected with the finding of treasures, and in all of them Ellen took a prominent place. He seemed in his dreams to renew his first acquaintance with the girl he loved, and when he thought of the accident that brought them together, it might be expected that the sea-shore was the scene of many of his dreams. The meeting was in this wise: One holiday, some three years before, he had been walking on the flat shore of the 'Bull,' when he noticed at some distance off a very beautiful young girl, and set to longing for some means of making her acquaintance. The means came even as he wished. The wind was blowing freely, and the girl's hat blew off and hurried seawards over the flat shore. He ran after it and brought it back: and from that hour the two had, after their casual acquaintance had been sanctioned by her father, became fast friends.

Most of his dreams of the night had faded against morning, but one he remembered.

He seemed to be in a wide stretch of sand near the hulk of a great vessel. Beside him lay a large iron-bound box of great weight, which he tried in vain to lift. He had by a lever just forced it through a hole in the side of the ship, and it had fallen on the sand and was sinking. Despite all he could do, it still continued to go down into the sand, but by slow degrees. The mist was getting round him, shutting out the moonlight, and from far he could hear a dull echoing roar muffled by the fog, and the air seemed laden with the clang of distant bells. Then the air became instinct with the forms of life, and amid them floated the form of Ellen, and with her presence the gloom and fog and darkness were dispelled, and the sun rose brightly on the instant, and all was fair and happy.

Next day was Sunday, and so after prayers he went for a walk with his friend, Tom Harrison.

They directed their steps towards Dollymount, and passing across the bridge, over Crab Lake, found themselves on the North Bull. The tide was 'black' out, and when they crossed the line of low bent-covered sand-hills, or *dunnes* as they are called in Holland, a wide stretch of sand intersected with shallow tidal streams lay before them, out towards the mouth of the bay. As they looked, Robert's dream of the night before flashed into his memory, and he expected to see before him the hulk of the old ship. Presently Tom remarked:

'I do not think I ever saw the tide so far out before. What an immense stretch of sand there is. It is a wonder there is no rock or anything of the kind all along this shore.'

'There is one,' said Robert, pointing to where, on the very edge of the water, rose a little mound, seemingly a couple of feet at most, over the level of the sand.

'Let us go out to it,' said Tom, and accordingly they both took off their boots and stockings, and walked over the wet sand, and forded the shallow streams till they got within a hundred yards of the mound. Suddenly Tom called out: 'It is not a rock at all; it is a ship, bottom upwards, with the end towards us, and sunk in the sand.'

Robert's heart stood still for an instant.

What if this should be a treasure-ship, and his dream prove prophetic? In an instant more he shook aside the fancy and hurried on.

They found that Tom had not been mistaken. There lay the hulk of an old ship, with just its bottom over the sand. Close round it the ebb and flow of the tide had worn a hole like the moat round an old castle; and in this pool small fishes darted about, and lazy crabs sidled into the sand.

Tom jumped the narrow moat, and stood balanced on the keel, and a hard task he had to keep his footing on the slippery seaweed. He tapped the timbers with his stick, and they gave back a hollow sound. 'The inside is not yet choked up,' he remarked.

Robert joined him, and walked all over the bottom of the ship, noticing how some of the planks, half rotten with long exposure, were sinking inwards.

After a few minutes Tom spoke—

'I say, Bob, suppose that this old ship was full of money, and that you and I could get it out.'

'I have just been thinking the same.'

'Suppose we try,' said Tom and he commenced to endeavour to prize up the end of a broken timber with his stick. Robert watched him for some minutes, and when he had given up the attempt in despair, spoke—

'Suppose we do try, Tom. I have a very strange idea. I had a curious dream last night, and this old ship reminds me of it.'

Tom asked Robert to tell the dream. He did so, and when he had finished, and had also confided his difficulty about the hundred pounds, Tom remarked—

'We'll try the hulk, at any rate. Let us come some night and cut a hole in her and look. It might be worth our while; it will be a lark at any rate.'

He seemed so interested in the matter that Robert asked him the reason.

'Well, I will tell you,' he said. 'You know Tomlinson. Well, he told me the other day that he was going to ask Miss Stedman to marry him. He is well off—comparatively, and unless you get your chance soon you may be too late. Don't be offended at me for telling you. I wanted to get an opportunity.'

'Thanks, old boy,' was Robert's answer, as he squeezed his hand. No more was spoken for a time. Both men examined the hulk carefully, and then came away, and sat again on a sand hill.

Presently a coastguard came along, with his telescope under his arm. Tom entered into conversation with him about the wreck.

'Well, sir,' he said, 'that was afore my time here. I've been here only about a year, and that's there a matter o' fifteen year or thereabouts. She came ashore here in the great storm when the *Mallard* was lost in the Scillies. I've heerd tell'—

Robert interrupted him to ask—

'Did anyone ever try what was in her?'

'Well, sir, there I'm out. By rights there should, but I've bin told that about then there was a lawsuit on as to who the shore belonged to. The ship lay in the line between the Ballast Board ground and the Manor ground, or whatever it is, and so nothin' could be done till the suit was ended, and when it was there weren't much use lookin' for anything, for she was settled nigh as low as she is now, and if there ever was anything worth havin' in her the salt water had ruined it long ago.

'Then she was never examined?' said Tom.

'Most like not, sir; they don't never examine little ships like her—if she was a big one we might,' and the coastguard departed.

When he was gone Tom said, 'By Jove, he forgot to say on whose ground she is,' and he ran after him to ask the question. When he came back he said, 'It's all right; it belongs to Sir Arthur Forres.'

After watching for some time in silence Robert said, 'Tom, I have very strange thoughts about this. Let us get leave from Sir Arthur—he is, I believe, a very generous man—and regularly explore.'

'Done,' said Tom, and, it being now late, they returned to town.

## 2

### Wind and Tide

Robert and Tom next day wrote a letter to Sir Arthur Forres asking him to let them explore the ship, and by return of post got a kind answer, not only granting the required permission, but making over the whole ship to them to do what they pleased with. Accordingly they held a consultation as to the best means of proceeding, and agreed to commence operations as soon as possible, as it was now well on in December, and every advance of winter would throw new obstacles in their way.

Next day they bought some tools, and brought them home in great glee. It often occurred to both of them that they were setting out on the wildest of wild-goose chases, but the novelty and excitement of the whole affair always overcame their scruples. The first moonlight night that came they took their tools, and sallied out to Dollymount to make the first effort on their treasure ship. So intent were they on their object that their immediate surroundings did not excite their attention.

It was not, therefore, till they arrived at the summit of the sand hill, from which they had first seen the hulk, that they discovered that the tide was coming in, and had advanced about half way. The knowledge was like a cold bath to each of them, for here were all their hopes dashed to the ground, for an indefinite time at least. It might be far into the winter time—perhaps months—before they could get a union of tide, moonlight, and fair weather, such as alone could make their scheme practicable. They had already tried to get leave from office, but so great was the press of business that their employer told them that unless they had special business, which they could name, he could not dispense with their services. To name their object would be to excite ridicule, and as the whole affair was but, based on a chimera they were of course silent.

They went home sadder than they had left it, and next day, by a careful study of the almanac, made out a list of the nights which might suit their purpose—if moon and weather proved favourable. From the fact of their living in their employer's house their time was further curtailed, for it was an inflexible rule that by twelve o'clock everyone should be home. Therefore, the only nights which could suit were those from the 11th to the 15th December, on which there would be low water between the hours of seven and eleven. This would give them on each night about one hour in which to work, for that length of time only was the wreck exposed between the ebbing and flowing tides.

They waited in anxiety for the 11th December, the weather continued beautifully fine, and nearly every night the two friends walked to view the scene of their future operations. Robert was debarred from visiting Ellen by her father's direction, and so was glad to have some object of interest to occupy his thoughts whilst away from her.

As the time wore on, the weather began to change, and Robert and Tom grew anxious. The wind began to blow in short sharp gusts, which whirled the sodden dead leaves angrily about exposed corners, and on the seaboard sent the waves shorewards topped with angry crests. Misty clouds came drifting hurriedly over the sea, and at times the fog became so thick that it was hardly possible to see more than a few yards ahead, still the young men continued to visit their treasure every night. At first, the coastguards had a watchful eye on them, noticing which they unfolded their purpose and showed Sir Arthur's letter making the ship over to their hands.

The sailors treated the whole affair as a good joke, but still promised to do what they could to help them, in the good-humoured way which is their special charm. A certain fear had for some time haunted the two friends—a fear which neither of them had ever spoken out. From brooding so much as they did on their adventure, they came to think, or rather to feel, that the ship which for fifteen years had been unnoticed and untouched in the sand, had suddenly acquired as great an interest in the eyes of all the world as of themselves.

Accordingly, they thought that some evil-designing person might try to cut them out of their adventure by forestalling them in searching the wreck. Their fear was dispelled by the kindly promise of the coastguards not to let anyone meddle with the vessel without their permission.

As the weather continued to get more and more broken, the very disappointment of their hopes, which the break threatened served to enlarge those hopes, and when on the night of the tenth they heard a wild storm howling round the chimneys, as they lay in bed, each was assured in his secret heart that the old wreck contained such a treasure as the world had seldom seen.

Seven o'clock next night saw them on the shore of the Bull looking out into the pitchy darkness. The wind was blowing so strongly inshore that the waves were driven high beyond their accustomed line at the same state of the tide, and the channels were running like mill-dams. As each wave came down over the flat shore it was broke up into a mass of foam and spray, and the wind swept away the spume until on shore it fell like rain. Far along the sandy shore was heard the roaring of the waves, hoarsely bellowing, so that hearing the sound we could well imagine how the district got its quaint name.

On such a night it would have been impossible to have worked at the wreck, even could the treasure-seekers have reached it, or could they have even found it in the pitchy darkness. They waited some time, but seeing that it was in vain, they sadly departed homeward, hoping fondly that the next evening would prove more propitious.

Vain were their hopes. The storm continued for two whole days, for not one moment of which, except between the pauses of the rushing or receding waves, was the wreck exposed. Seven o'clock each night saw the two young men looking over the sand-hills, waiting in the vain hope of a chance of visiting the vessel, hoping against hope that a sudden calm would give the opportunity they wished. When the storm began to abate their hopes were proportionally raised, and on the morning of the 14th when they awoke and could not hear the wind whistling through the chimneys next their attic, they grew again sanguine of success.

That night they went to the Bull in hope, and came home filled with despair. Although the storm had ceased, the sea was still rough. Great, heavy, sullen waves, sprayless, but crested ominously, from ridges of foam, came rolling into the bay, swelling onward with great speed and resistless force, and bursting over the shallow waste of sand so violently that even any attempt to reach the wreck was out of the question.

As Robert and Tom hurried homeward—they had waited to the latest moment on the Bull, and feared being late—they felt spiritless and dejected. But one more evening remained on which they might possibly visit the wreck, and they feared that even should wind and tide be suitable one hour would not do to explore it.

However, youth is never without hope, and next morning they both had that sanguine feeling which is the outcome of despair—the feeling that the tide of fortune must sometime turn, and that the loser as well as the winner has his time. As they neared the Bull that night their hearts beat so loud that they could almost hear them. They felt that there was ground for hope.

All the way from town they could see the great flats opposite Clontarf lying black in the moonlight, and they thought that over the sands the same calm must surely rest. But, alas, they did not allow for the fact that two great breakwaters protect the harbour, but that the sands of the Bull are open to all the storms that blow—that the great Atlantic billows, broken up on the northern and southern coasts, yet still strong enough to be feared, sweep up and down the Channel, and beat with every tide into the harbours and bays along the coast. Accordingly, on reaching the sand-hills, they saw what dashed their hopes at once.

The moon rose straight before them beyond the Bailey Lighthouse, and the broad belt of light which stretched from it passed over the treasure-ship. The waves, now black, save where the light caught the sloping sides, lay blank, but ever and anon as they passed on far over their usual range, the black hull rose among the gleams of light.

There was not a chance that the wreck could be attempted, and so they went sadly home—remembering the fact that the night of the 24th December was the earliest time at which they could again renew their effort.

# 3

## THE IRON CHEST

The days that intervened were long to both men. To Robert they were endless; even the nepenthe[1] of continued hard work could not quiet his mind. Distracted on one side by his forbidden love for Ellen, and on the other by the expected fortune by which he might win her, he could hardly sleep at night. When he did sleep he always dreamed, and in his dreams Ellen and the wreck were always associated. At one time his dream would be of unqualified good fortune—a vast treasure found and shared with his love; at another, all would be gloom, and in the search for the treasure he would endanger his life, or, what was far greater pain, forfeit her love

However, it is one consolation, that, whatever else may happen in the world, time wears on without ceasing, and the day longest expected comes at last.

On the evening of the 24th December, Tom and Robert took their way to Dollymount in breathless excitement.

As they passed through town, and saw the vast concourse of people all intent on one common object—the preparation for the greatest of all Christian festivals—the greatest festival, which is kept all over the world, wherever the True Light has fallen, they could not but feel a certain regret that they, too, could not join in the throng. Robert's temper was somewhat ruffled by seeing Ellen leaning on the arm of Tomlinson, looking into a brilliantly-lighted shop window, so intently, that she did not notice him passing. When they had left the town, and the crowds, and the overflowing stalls, and brilliant holly-decked shops, they did not so much mind, but hurried on.

So long as they were within city bounds, and even whilst there were brightly-lit shop windows, all seemed light enough. When, however, they were so far from town as to lose the glamour of the lamplight in the sky overhead, they began to fear that the night would indeed be too dark for work.

---

1. nepenthe—a drink or drug to alleviate sorrow.

They were prepared for such an emergency, and when they stood on the slope of sand, below the *dunnes*, they lit a dark lantern and prepared to cross the sands. After a few moments they found that the lantern was a mistake. They saw the ground immediately before them so far as the sharp triangle of light, whose apex was the bulls-eye, extended, but beyond this the darkness rose like a solid black wall. They closed the lantern, but this was even worse, for after leaving the light, small though it was, their eyes were useless in the complete darkness. It took them nearly an hour to reach the wreck.

At last they got to work, and with hammer and chisel and saw commenced to open the treasure ship.

The want of light told sorely against them, and their work progressed slowly despite their exertions. All things have an end, however, and in time they had removed several planks so as to form a hole some four feet wide, by six long—one of the timbers crossed this; but as it was not in the middle, and left a hole large enough to descend by, it did not matter.

It was with beating hearts that the two young men slanted the lantern so as to turn the light in through the aperture. All within was black, and not four feet below them was a calm glassy pool of water that seemed like ink. Even as they looked this began slowly to rise, and they saw that the tide had turned, and that but a few minutes more remained. They reached down as far as they could, plunging their arms up to their shoulders in the water, but could find nothing. Robert stood up and began to undress.

'What are you going to do?' said Tom.

'Going to dive—it is the only chance we have.'

Tom did not hinder him, but got the piece of rope they had brought with them and fastened it under Robert's shoulders and grasped the other end firmly. Robert arranged the lamp so as to throw the light as much downwards as possible, and then, with a silent prayer, let himself down through the aperture and hung on by the beam. The water was deadly cold—so cold, that, despite the fever heat to which he was brought through excitement, he felt chilled. Nevertheless he did not hesitate, but, letting go the beam, dropped into the black water.

'For Ellen,' he said, as he disappeared.

In a quarter of a minute he appeared again, gasping, and with a convulsive effort climbed the short rope, and stood beside his friend.

'Well?' asked Tom, excitedly.

'Oh-h-h-h! good heavens, I am chilled to the heart. I went down about six feet, and then touched a hard substance. I felt round it, and so far as I can tell it is a barrel. Next to it was a square corner of a box, and further still something square made of iron.'

'How do you know it is iron?'

'By the rust. Hold the rope again, there is no time to lose; the tide is rising every minute, and we will soon have to go.'

Again he went into the black water and this time stayed longer. Tom began to be frightened at the delay, and shook the rope for him to ascend. The instant after he appeared with face almost black with suffused blood. Tom hauled at the rope, and once more he stood on the bottom of the vessel. This time he did not complain of the cold. He seemed quivering with a great excitement that overcame the cold. When he had recovered his breath he almost shouted out –

'There's something there. I know it—I feel it.'

'Anything strange?' asked Tom, in fierce excitement.

'Yes, the iron box is heavy—so heavy that I could not stir it. I could easily lift the end of the cask, and two or three other boxes, but I could not stir it.'

Whilst he was speaking, both heard a queer kind of hissing noise, and looking down in alarm saw the water running into the pool around the vessel. A few minutes more and they would be cut off from shore by some of the tidal streams. Tom cried out:

'Quick, quick! or we shall be late. We must put down the beams before the tide rises or it will wash the hold full of sand.'

Without waiting even to dress, Robert assisted him and they

placed the planks on their original position and secured them with a few strong nails. Then they rushed away for shore. When they had reached the sand-hill, Robert, despite his exertions, was so chilled that he was unable to put on his clothes.

To bathe and stay naked for half an hour on a December night is no joke.

Tom drew his clothes on him as well as he could, and after adding his overcoat and giving him a pull from the flask, he was something better. They hurried away, and what with exercise, excitement, and hope were glowing when they reached home.

Before going to bed they held a consultation as to what was best to be done. Both wished to renew their attempt as they could begin at half-past seven o'clock; for although the morrow was Christmas Day, they knew that any attempt to rescue goods from the wreck should be made at once. There were now two dangers to be avoided—rough weather and the drifting of the sand—and so they decided that not a moment was to be lost.

At the daybreak they were up, and the first moment that saw the wreck approachable found them wading out towards it. This time they were prepared for wet and cold. They had left their clothes on the beach and put on old ones, which, even if wet, would still keep off the wind, for a strong, fitful breeze was now blowing in eddies, and the waves were beginning to rise ominously. With beating hearts they examined the closed-up gap; and, as they looked, their hopes fell. One of the timbers had been lifted off by the tide, and from the deposit of sand in the crevices, they feared that much must have found its way in. They had brought several strong pieces of rope with them, for their effort to-day was to be to lift out the iron chest, which both fancied contained a treasure.

Robert prepared himself to descend again. He tied one rope round his waist, as before, and took the other in his hands. Tom waited breathlessly till he returned. He was a long time coming up, and rose with his teeth chattering, but had the rope no longer with him. He told Tom that he had succeeded in putting it under the chest. Then he went down again with the other rope, and when he rose the second time, said that he had put it under also, but crossing the first. He was so chilled that he was unable to go down a third time. Indeed, he was hardly able to stand so cold did he seem; and it was with much shrinking of spirit that his friend prepared to descend to make the ropes fast, for he knew that should anything happen to him Robert could not help him up.

This did not lighten his task or serve to cheer his spirits as he went down for the first time into the black water. He took two pieces of rope; his intention being to tie Robert's ropes round the chest, and then bring the spare ends up. When he rose he told Robert that he had tied one of the ropes round the box, but had not time to tie the others. He was so chilled that he could not venture to go down again, and so both men hurriedly closed the gap as well as they could, and went on shore to change their clothes. When they had dressed, and got tolerably warm, the tide had begun to turn, and so they went home, longing for the evening to come, when they might make the final effort.

## 4

### LOST AND FOUND

Tom was to dine with some relatives where he was living. When he was leaving Robert he said to him, 'Well, Bob, seven o'clock, sharp.'

'Tom, do not forget or be late. Mind, I trust you.'

'Never fear, old boy. Nothing short of death shall keep me away; but if I should happen not to turn up do not wait for me. I will be with you in spirit if I cannot be in the flesh.'

'Tom, don't talk that way. I don't know what I should do if you didn't come. It may be all a phantom we're after, but I do not like to think so. It seems so much to me.'

'All right, old man,' said Tom, cheerily, 'I shan't fail—seven o'clock,' and he was gone.

Robert was in a fever all day. He went to the church where he knew he would see Ellen, and get a smile from her in passing. He did get a smile, and a glance from her lovely dark eyes which said as plainly as if she had spoken the words with her sweet lips, 'How long you have been away; you never come to see me now.' This set Robert's heart bounding, but it increased his fever. 'How would it be,' he thought, 'if the wreck turned out a failure, and the iron box a deception? If I cannot get £100 those dark eyes will have to look sweet things to some other man; that beautiful mouth to whisper in the ears of someone who would not—could not—love her half so well as I do.'

He could not bear to meet her, so when service was over he hurried away. When she came out her eyes were beaming, for she expected to see Robert waiting for her. She looked anxiously, but could only see Mr Tomlinson, who did not rise in her favour for appearing just then.

Robert had to force himself to eat his dinner. Every morsel almost choked him but he knew that strength was necessary for his undertaking, and so compelled himself to eat. As the hour of seven approached he began to get fidgety. He went often to the window, but could see no sign of Tom. Seven o'clock struck, but no Tom came. He began to be alarmed. Tom's words seemed to ring in his ears, 'nothing short of death shall keep me away.' He waited a little while in terrible anxiety, but then bethought him of his companion's other words, 'if I should not happen to turn up do not wait for me,' and knowing that whether he waited or no the tide would still come in all the same, and his chance of getting out the box would pass away, determined to set out alone. His determination was strengthened by the fact that the gusty wind of the morning had much increased, and sometimes swept along laden with heavy clinging mist that bespoke a great fog bank somewhere behind the wind.

Till he had reached the very shore of the 'Bull' he did not give up hopes of Tom, for he thought it just possible that he might have been delayed, and instead of increasing the delay by going home, had come on straight to the scene of operation.

There was, however, no help for it; as Tom had not come he should work alone. With misgivings he prepared himself. He left his clothes on the top of a sand-hill, put on the old ones he had brought with him, took his tools, ropes, and lantern, and set out. There was cause for alarm. The wind was rising, and it whistled in his ears as the gusts swept past. Far away in the darkness the sea was beginning to roar on the edge of the flats, and the mist came driving inland in sheets like the spume from a cataract. The water in the tidal streams as he waded across them beat against his legs and seemed cold as ice. Although now experienced in the road, he had some difficulty in finding the wreck, but at length reached it and commenced operations.

He had taken the precaution of bringing with him a second suit of old clothes and an oilskin coat. His first care was to fix the lamp where the wind could not harm it; his second, to raise the planks, and expose the interior of the wreck. Then he prepared his ropes, and, having undressed once again, went beneath the water to fasten the second rope. This he accomplished safely and let the knot of it be on the opposite side to where the first rope was tied. He then ascended and dressed himself in all his clothes to keep him warm. He then cut off a portion in another plank, so as to expose a second one of the ship's timbers. Round this he tied one of the ropes, keeping it as taut as he could. He took a turn of the other rope round the other beam and commenced to pull. Little by little he raised the great chest from its position, and when he had raised it all he could he made that rope fast and went to the other.

By attacking the ropes alternately he raised the chest, so that he could feel from its situation that it hung suspended in the water. Then he began to shake the ropes till the chest swung like a pendulum. He held firmly both ropes, having a turn of each round its beam, and each time the weight swung he gained a little rope. So he worked on little by little, till at last, to his infinite joy, he saw the top of the box rise above the water. His excitement then changed to frenzy. His strength redoubled, and, as faster and faster the box swung, he gained more and more rope, and raised it higher and higher, till at last it ceased to rise, and he found he had reached the maximum height attainable by this means. As, however, it was now nearly up he detached a long timber, and using it as a lever, slowly, after repeated failures, prized up the chest through the gap till it reached the bottom of the ship, and then, toppling over, fell with a dull thud upon the sand.

With a cry of joy Robert jumped down after it, but in jumping lit on the edge of it and wrenched his ankle so severely that when he rose up and attempted to stand on it it gave way under him, and he fell again. He managed, however, to crawl out of the hulk, and reached his lantern. The wind by this time was blowing louder and louder, and the mist was gathering in white masses, and sweeping by, mingled with sleet. In endeavouring to guard the lantern from the wind he slipped once more on the wet timbers, and fell down, striking his leg against the sharp edge of the chest. So severe was the pain that for a few moments he became almost insensible, and when he recovered his senses found he was quite unable to stir.

The lantern had fallen in a pool of water, and had of course gone out. It was a terrible situation, and Robert's heart sank within him, as well it might, as he thought of what was to come. The wind was rapidly rising to a storm, and swept by him, laden with the deadly mist in fierce gusts. The roaring of the tide grew nearer and nearer, and louder and louder. Overhead was a pall of darkness, save when in the leaden winter sky some white pillar of mist swept onward like an embodied spirit of the storm.

All the past began to crowd Robert's memory, and more especially the recent past. He thought of his friend's words—'Nothing short of death shall keep me away,' and so full of dismal shadows, and forms of horror was all the air, that he could well fancy that Tom was dead, and that his spirit was circling round him, wailing through the night. Then again, arose the memory of his dream, and his very heart stood still, as he thought of how awfully it had been fulfilled. There he now lay; not in a dream, but in reality, beside a ship on a waste of desert sand. Beside him lay a chest such as he had seen in his dreams, and, as before, death seemed flapping his giant wings over his head.

Strange horrors seemed to gather round him, borne on the

wings of the blast. His father, whom he had never seen, he felt to be now beside him. All the dead that he had ever known circled round him in a weird dance. As the stormy gusts swept by, he heard amid their screams the lugubrious tolling of bells; bells seemed to be all around him; whichever way he turned he heard his knell. All forms were gathered there, as in his dreams-all save Ellen. But hark! even as the thought flashed across his brain; his ears seemed to hear her voice as one hears in a dream. He tried to cry out, but was so overcome by cold, that he could barely hear his own voice. He tried to rise, but in vain, and then, overcome by pain and excitement, and disappointed hope, he became insensible.

Was his treasure-hunting to end thus?

As Mr Stedman and Ellen were sitting down to tea that evening, Arthur Tomlinson being the only other guest, a hurried knock came to the cottage door. The little servant came into the room a moment after, looking quite scared, and holding a letter in her hand. She came over to Ellen and faltered out, 'Oh, please, miss, there's a man from the hospital, and he says as how you're to open the letter and to come at once; it's a matter of life and death.'

Ellen grew white as a sheet, and stood up quickly, trembling as she opened the letter. Mr Stedman rose up, too. Arthur Tomlinson sat still, and glared at the young servant till, thinking she had done something wrong, she began to cry. The letter was from the doctor of the hospital, written for Tom, and praying her to come at once, as the latter had something to tell her of the greatest import to one for whom he was sure she would do much. She immediately ran and put on her cloak, and asked her father to come with her.

'Surely you won't go?' said Tomlinson.

'What else should I do?' she asked, scornfully; I must apologise for leaving you, unless you will come with us.'

'No, thank you; I am not a philanthropist.'

In half an hour they had reached the hospital, and had heard Tom's story. Poor fellow, when hurrying home to Robert, he had been knocked down by a car and had his leg broken. As soon as he could he had sent word to Ellen, for he feared for Robert being out alone at the wreck, knowing how chilled he had been on the previous night, and he thought that if anyone would send him aid Ellen would.

No sooner had the story been told, and Ellen had understood the danger Robert was in, than with her father she hurried off to the 'Bull.'

They got a car with some difficulty, and drove as fast as the horse could go, and arriving at the 'Bull,' called to the coast-guard-station. None of the coastguards had seen Robert that evening, but on learning of his possible danger all that were in the station at once turned out. They wrapped Ellen and her father in oilskins, and, taking lanterns and ropes, set out for the wreck. They all knew its position, and went as straight for it as they could, and, as they crossed the sand-hills, found Robert's clothes. At this they grew very grave. They wanted to leave Ellen on the shore, but she refused point blank. By this time the storm was blowing wildly, and the roaring of the sea being borne on the storm was frightful to hear. The tidal streams were running deeper than usual, and there was some difficulty in crossing to the wreck.

In the mist the men lost their way a little, and could not tell exactly how far to go. They shouted as loudly as they could, but there was no reply. Ellen's terror grew into despair. She too, shouted, although fearing that to shout in the teeth of such a wind her woman's voice would be of no avail. However, her clear soprano rang out louder than the hoarse shouts of the sturdy sailors, and cleft the storm like a wedge. Twice or thrice she cried, 'Robert, Robert, Robert,' but still there was no reply. Suddenly she stopped, and, bending her head, cried joyfully, 'He is there, he is there; I hear his voice,' and commenced running as fast as she could through the darkness towards the raging sea. The coastguards called out to her to mind where she was going, and followed her with the lanterns as fast as they could run.

When they came up with her they found her sitting on an

iron chest close to the wreck, with Robert resting on her knees, and his head pillowed on her breast. He had opened his eyes, and was faintly whispering, 'Ellen, my love, my love. It was to win you I risked my life.'

She bent and kissed him, even there among rough sailors, and then, amid the storm, she whispered softly, 'It was not risked in vain.'

# Death in the Wings

*(A.K.A. A Star Trap)*

"When I was apprenticed to theatrical carpentering my master was John Haliday, who was Master Machinist—we called men in his post 'Master Carpenter' in those days—of the old Victoria Theatre, Hulme. It wasn't called Hulme; but that name will do. It would only stir up painful memories if I were to give the real name. I daresay some of you—not the Ladies (this with a gallant bow all round)—will remember the case of a Harlequin as was killed in an accident in the pantomime. We needn't mention names; Mortimer will do for a name to call him by—Henry Mortimer. The cause of it was never found out. But I knew it; and I've kept silence for so long that I may speak now without hurting anyone. They're all dead long ago that was interested in the death of Henry Mortimer or the man who wrought that death."

"Any of you who know of the case will remember what a handsome, dapper, well-built man Mortimer was. To my own mind he was the handsomest man I ever saw."

The Tragedian's low, grumbling whisper, "That's a large order," sounded a warning note. Hempitch, however, did not seem to hear it, but went on:

"Of course, I was only a boy then, and I hadn't seen any of you gentlemen—Yer very good health, Mr Wellesley Dovercourt, sir, and *cettera*. I needn't tell you, Ladies, how well a harlequin's dress sets off a nice slim figure. No wonder that in these days of suffragettes, women wants to be harlequins as well as

356

columbines. Though I hope they won't make the columbine a man's part!"

"Mortimer was the nimblest chap at the traps I ever see. He was so sure of hisself that he would have extra weight put on so that when the counter weights fell he'd shoot up five or six feet higher than anyone else could even try to. Moreover, he had a way of drawing up his legs when in the air—the way a frog does when he is swimming—that made his jump look ever so much higher."

"I think the girls were all in love with him, the way they used to stand in the wings when the time was comin' for his entrance. That wouldn't have mattered much, for girls are always falling in love with some man or other, but it made trouble, as it always does when the married ones take the same start. There were several of these that were always after him, more shame for them, with husbands of their own. That was dangerous enough, and hard to stand for a man who might mean to be decent in any way. But the real trial—and the real trouble, too—was none other than the young wife of my own master, and she was more than flesh and blood could stand.

"She had come into the panto, the season before, as a high-kicker—and she could! She could kick higher than girls that was more than a foot taller than her; for she was a wee bit of a thing and as pretty as pie; a gold-haired, blue-eyed, slim thing with much the figure of a boy, except for. . . and they saved her from any mistaken idea of that kind. Jack Haliday went crazy over her, and when the notice was up, and there was no young spark with plenty of oof coming along to do the proper thing by her, she married him. It was, when they was joined, what you Ladies call a marriage of convenience; but after a bit they two got on very well, and we all thought she was beginning to like the old man—for Jack was old enough to be her father, with a bit to spare.

"In the summer, when the house was closed, he took her to the Isle of Man; and when they came back he made no secret of it that he'd had the happiest time of his life. She looked quite happy, too, and treated him affectionate; and we all began to think that that marriage had not been a failure at any rate."

"Things began to change, however, when the panto, re-hearsals began next year. Old Jack began to look unhappy, and didn't take no interest in his work. Loo—that was Mrs Haliday's name—didn't seem over fond of him now, and was generally impatient when he was by. Nobody said anything about this, however, to us men; but the married women smiled and nodded their heads and whispered that perhaps there were reasons.

"One day on the stage, when the harlequinade rehearsal was beginning, someone mentioned as how perhaps Mrs Haliday wouldn't be dancing that year, and they smiled as if they was all in the secret. Then Mrs Jack ups and gives them Johnny-up-the-orchard for not minding their own business and telling a pack of lies, and such like as you Ladies like to express in your own ways when you get your back hair down. The rest of us tried to soothe her all we could, and she went off home."

"It wasn't long after that that she and Henry Mortimer left together after rehearsal was over, he saying he'd leave her at home. She didn't make no objections—I told you he was a very handsome man."

"Well, from that on she never seemed to take her eyes from him during every rehearsal, right up to the night of the last rehearsal, which, of course, was full dress—'Everybody and Eve-rything.'"

"Jack Haliday never seemed to notice anything that was go-ing on, like the rest of them did.

True, his time was taken up with his own work, for I'm tell-ing you that a Master Machinist hasn't got no loose time on his hands at the first dress rehearsal of a panto. And, of course, none of the company ever said a word or gave a look that would call his attention to it. Men and women are queer beings. They will be blind and deaf whilst danger is being run; and it's only after the scandal is beyond repair that they begin to talk—just the very time when most of all they should be silent."

"I saw all that went on, but I didn't understand it. I liked

Mortimer myself and admired him—like I did Mrs Haliday, too—and I thought he was a very fine fellow. I was only a boy, you know, and Haliday's apprentice, so naturally I wasn't looking for any trouble I could help, even if I'd seen it coming. It was when I looked back afterwards at the whole thing that I began to comprehend; so you will all understand now, I hope, that what I tell you is the result of much knowledge of what I saw and heard and was told of afterwards—all morticed and clamped up by thinking."

"The panto, had been on about three weeks when one Saturday, between the shows, I heard two of our company talking. Both of them was among the extra girls that both sang and danced and had to make theirselves useful. I don't think either of them was better than she should be; they went out to too many champagne suppers with young men that had money to burn. That part doesn't matter in this affair—except that they was naturally enough jealous of women who was married—which was what they was aiming at—and what lived straighter than they did.

"Women of that kind like to see a good woman tumble down; it seems to make them all more even. Now real bad girls what have gone under altogether will try to save a decent one from following their road. That is, so long as they're young; for a bad one what is long in the tooth is the limit. They'll help anyone downhill—so long as they get anything out of it."

"Well—no offence, you Ladies, as has growed up!—these two girls was enjoyin' themselves over Mrs Haliday and the mash she had set up on Mortimer. They didn't see that I was sitting on a stage box behind a built-out piece of the Prologue of the panto., which was set ready for night. They were both in love with Mortimer, who wouldn't look at either of them, so they was miaw'n cruel, like cats on the tiles. Says one:"

"'The Old Man seems worse than blind; he won't see.'"

"'Don't you be too sure of that,' says the other. 'He don't mean to take no chances. I think you must be blind, too, Kissie.' That was her name—on the bills anyhow, Kissie Mountpelier.

'Don't he make a point of taking her home hisself every night after the play. You should know, for you're in the hall yourself waiting for your young man till he comes from his club.'"

"'Wot-ho, you bally geeser,' says the other—which her language was mostly coarse—'don't you know there's two ends to everything? The Old Man looks to one end only!' Then they began to snigger and whisper; and presently the other one says:"

"'Then he thinks harm can be only done when work is over!'"

"'Jest so,' she answers. 'Her and him knows that the old man has to be down long before the risin' of the rag; but she doesn't come in till the Vision of Venus dance after half time; and he not till the harlequinade!'"

"Then I quit. I didn't want to hear any more of that sort."

"All that week things went on as usual. Poor old Haliday wasn't well. He looked worried and had a devil of a temper. I had reason to know that, for what worried him was his work. He was always a hard worker, and the panto season was a terror with him. He didn't ever seem to mind anything else outside his work. I thought at the time that that was how those two chattering girls made up their slanderous story; for, after all, a slander, no matter how false it may be, must have some sort of beginning. Something that seems, if there isn't something that is! But no matter how busy he might be, old Jack always made time to leave the wife at home."

"As the week went on he got more and more pale; and I began to think he was in for some sickness. He generally remained in the theatre between the shows on Saturday; that is, he didn't go home, but took a high tea in the coffee shop close to the theatre, so as to be handy in case there might be a hitch anywhere in the preparation for night. On that Saturday he went out as usual when the first scene was set, and the men were getting ready the packs for the rest of the scenes.

"By and bye there was some trouble—the usual Saturday kind—and I went off to tell him. When I went into the coffee shop I couldn't see him. I thought it best not to ask or to seem to take any notice, so I came back to the theatre, and heard that the trouble had settled itself as usual, by the men who had been quarrelling going off to have another drink. I hustled up those who remained, and we got things smoothed out in time for them all to have their tea.

"Then I had my own. I was just then beginning to feel the responsibility of my business, so I wasn't long over my food, but came back to look things over and see that all was right, especially the trap, for that was a thing Jack Haliday was most particular about. He would overlook a fault for anything else; but if it was along of a trap, the man had to go. He always told the men that that wasn't ordinary work; it was life or death."

"I had just got through my inspection when I saw old Jack coming in from the hall. There was no one about at that hour, and the stage was dark. But dark as it was I could see that the old man was ghastly pale. I didn't speak, for I wasn't near enough, and as he was moving very silently behind the scenes I thought that perhaps he wouldn't like anyone to notice that he had been away. I thought the best thing I could do would be to clear out of the way, so I went back and had another cup of tea."

"I came away a little before the men, who had nothing to think of except to be in their places when Haliday's whistle sounded. I went to report myself to my master, who was in his own little glass-partitioned den at the back of the carpenter's shop. He was there bent over his own bench, and was filing away at something so intently that he did not seem to hear me; so I cleared out. I tell you, Ladies and Gents., that from an apprentice point of view it is not wise to be too obtrusive when your master is attending to some private matter of his own!"

"When the 'get-ready' time came and the lights went up, there was Haliday as usual at his post. He looked very white and ill—so ill that the stage manager, when he came in, said to him that if he liked to go home and rest he would see that all his work would be attended to. He thanked him, and said that he thought he would be able to stay. 'I do feel a little weak and ill, sir,' he said. 'I felt just now for a few moments as if I was going to faint. But that's gone by already, and I'm sure I shall be able to get through the work before us all right.'"

"Then the doors was opened, and the Saturday night audience came rushing and tumbling in. The Victoria was a great Saturday night house. No matter what other nights might be, that was sure to be good. They used to say in the perfesh that the Victoria lived on it, and that the management was on holiday for the rest of the week. The actors knew it, and no matter how slack they might be from Monday to Friday they was all taut and trim then. There was no walking through and no fluffing on Saturday nights—or else they'd have had the bird."

"Mortimer was one of the most particular of the lot in this way. He never was slack at any time—indeed, slackness is not a harlequin's fault, for if there's slackness there's no harlequin, that's all. But Mortimer always put on an extra bit on the Saturday night. When he jumped up through the star trap he always went then a couple of feet higher. To do this we had always to put on a lot more weight. This he always saw to himself; for, mind you, it's no joke being driven up through the trap as if you was shot out of a gun.

"The points of the star had to be kept free, and the hinges at their bases must be well oiled, or else there can be a disaster at any time. Moreover, 'tis the duty of someone appointed for the purpose to see that all is clear upon the stage. I remember hearing that once at New York, many years ago now, a harlequin was killed by a 'grip'—as the Yankees call a carpenter—what outsiders here call a scene-shifter—walking over the trap just as the stroke had been given to let go the counter-weights. It wasn't much satisfaction to the widow to know that the 'grip' was killed too."

"That night Mrs Haliday looked prettier than ever, and kicked even higher than I had ever seen her do. Then, when she got dressed for home, she came as usual and stood in the wings for the beginning of the harlequinade. Old Jack came across the stage and stood beside her; I saw him from the back follow up the sliding ground-row that closed in on the Realms of Delight.

I couldn't help noticing that he still looked ghastly pale. He kept turning his eyes on the star trap. Seeing this, I naturally looked at it too, for I feared lest something might have gone wrong. I had seen that it was in good order, and that the joints were properly oiled when the stage was set for the evening show, and as it wasn't used all night for anything else I was reassured.

"Indeed, I thought I could see it shine a bit as the limelight caught the brass hinges. There was a spot light just above it on the bridge, which was intended to make a good show of harlequin and his big jump. The people used to howl with delight as he came rushing up through the trap and when in the air drew up his legs and spread them wide for an instant and then straightened them again as he came down—only bending his knees just as he touched the stage."

"When the signal was given the counter-weight worked properly. I knew, for the sound of it at that part was all right."

"But something was wrong.

The trap didn't work smooth, and open at once as the harlequin's head touched it. There was a shock and a tearing sound, and the pieces of the star seemed torn about, and some of them were thrown about the stage. And in the middle of them came the coloured and spangled figure that we knew."

"But somehow it didn't come up in the usual way. It was erect enough, but there was not the usual elasticity. The legs never moved; and when it went up a fair height—though nothing like usual—it seemed to topple over and fall on the stage on its side. The audience shrieked, and the people in the wings-actors and staff all the same—closed in, some of them in their stage clothes, others dressed for going home. But the man in the spangles lay quite still."

"The loudest shriek of all was from Mrs Haliday; and she was the first to reach the spot where he—it—lay. Old Jack was close behind her, and caught her as she fell. I had just time to see that, for I made it my business to look after the pieces of the trap; there was plenty of people to look after the corpse. And the pit was by now crossing the orchestra and climbing up on the stage."

"I managed to get the bits together before the rush came. I noticed that there were deep scratches on some of them, but I didn't have time for more than a glance. I put a stage box over the hole lest anyone should put a foot through it. Such would mean a broken leg at least; and if one fell through, it might mean worse. Amongst other things I found a queer-looking piece of flat steel with some bent points on it. I knew it didn't belong to the trap; but it came from somewhere, so I put it in my pocket."

"By this time there was a crowd where Mortimer's body lay. That he was stone dead nobody could doubt. The very attitude was enough. He was all straggled about in queer positions; one of the legs was doubled under him with the toes sticking out in the wrong way. But let that suffice! It doesn't do to go into details of a dead body...I wish someone would give me a drop of punch."

"There was another crowd round Mrs Haliday, who was lying a little on one side nearer the wings where her husband had carried her and laid her down. She, too, looked like a corpse; for she was as white as one and as still, and looked as cold. Old Jack was kneeling beside her, chafing her hands. He was evidently frightened about her, for he, too, was deathly white. However, he kept his head, and called his men round him. He left his wife in care of Mrs Homcroft, the Wardrobe Mistress, who had by this time hurried down. She was a capable woman, and knew how to act promptly. She got one of the men to lift Mrs Haliday and carry her up to the wardrobe. I heard afterwards that when she got her there she turned out all the rest of them that followed up—the women as well as the men—and looked after her herself."

"I put the pieces of the broken trap on the top of the stage box, and told one of our chaps to mind them, and see that no one touched them, as they might be wanted. By this time the police who had been on duty in front had come round, and as they had at once telephoned to headquarters, more police kept coming in all the time. One of them took charge of the place where the broken trap was; and when he heard who put the box and the broken pieces there, sent for me. More of them took the body away to the property room, which was a large room with benches in it, and which could be locked up. Two of them stood at the door, and wouldn't let anyone go in without permission."

"The man who was in charge of the trap asked me if I had seen the accident. When I said I had, he asked me to describe it. I don't think he had much opinion of my powers of description, for he soon dropped that part of his questioning. Then he asked me to point out where I found the bits of the broken trap. I simply said:"

"'Lord bless you, sir, I couldn't tell. They was scattered all over the place. I had to pick them up between people's feet as they were rushing in from all sides.'"

"'All right, my boy,' he said, in quite a kindly way, for a policeman, 'I don't think they'll want to worry you. There are lots of men and women, I am told, who were standing by and saw the whole thing. They will be all subpoenaed.' I was a small-made lad in those days—I ain't a giant now!—and I suppose he thought it was no use having children for witnesses when they had plenty of grown-ups. Then he said something about me and an idiot asylum that was not kind—no, nor wise either, for I dried up and did not say another word."

"Gradually the public was got rid of. Some strolled off by degrees, going off to have a glass before the pubs closed, and talk it all over. The rest us and the police ballooned out. Then, when the police had taken charge of everything and put in men to stay all night, the coroner's officer came and took off the body to the city mortuary, where the police doctor made a post mortem. I was allowed to go home. I did so—and gladly—when I had seen the place settling down.

Mr Haliday took his wife home in a four-wheeler. It was perhaps just as well, for Mrs Homcroft and some other kindly souls had poured so much whisky and brandy and rum and gin and beer and peppermint into her that I don't believe she could have walked if she had tried."

"When I was undressing myself something scratched my leg as I was taking off my trousers. I found it was the piece of flat steel which I had picked up on the stage. It was in the shape of a star fish, but the spikes of it were short. Some of the points were turned down, the rest were pulled out straight again. I stood with it in my hand wondering where it had come from and what it was for, but I couldn't remember anything in the whole theatre that it could have belonged to. I looked at it closely again, and saw that the edges were all filed and quite bright. But that did not help me, so I put it on the table and thought I would take it with me in the morning; perhaps one of the chaps might know. I turned out the gas and went to bed—and to sleep."

"I must have begun to dream at once, and it was, naturally enough, all about the terrible thing that had occurred. But, like all dreams, it was a bit mixed. They were all mixed. Mortimer with his spangles flying up the trap, it breaking, and the pieces scattering round. Old Jack Haliday looking on at one side of the stage with his wife beside him—he as pale as death, and she looking prettier than ever. And then Mortimer coming down all crooked and falling on the stage, Mrs Haliday shrieking, and her and Jack running forward, and me picking up the pieces of the broken trap from between people's legs, and finding the steel star with the bent points."

"I woke in a cold sweat, saying to myself as I sat up in bed in the dark:"

"'That's it!'"

"And then my head began to reel about so that I lay down again and began to think it all over. And it all seemed clear enough then. It was Mr Haliday who made that star and put it over the star trap where the points joined! That was what Jack Haliday was filing at when I saw him at his bench; and he had done it because Mortimer and his wife had been making love to each other. Those girls were right, after all. Of course, the steel points had prevented the trap opening, and when Mortimer was driven up against it his neck was broken."

"But then came the horrible thought that if Jack did it, it was murder, and he would be hung. And, after all, it was his wife that the harlequin had made love to—and old Jack loved her very much indeed himself and had been good to her—and she was his wife. And that bit of steel would hang him if it should be known. But no one but me—and whoever made it, and put it on the trap—even knew of its existence—and Mr Haliday was my master—and the man was dead—and he was a villain!"

"I was living then at Quarry Place; and in the old quarry was a pond so deep that the boys used to say that far down the water was boiling hot, it was so near Hell."

"I softly opened the window, and, there in the dark, threw the bit of steel as far as I could into the quarry."

"No one ever knew, for I have never spoken a word of it till this very minute. I was not called at the inquest. Everyone was in a hurry; the coroner and the jury and the police. Our governor was in a hurry too, because we wanted to go on as usual at night; and too much talk of the tragedy would hurt business. So nothing was known; and all went on as usual. Except that after that Mrs Haliday didn't stand in the wings during the harlequinade, and she was as loving to her old husband as a woman can be. It was him she used to watch now; and always with a sort of respectful adoration. She knew, though no one else did, except her husband—and me."

When he finished there was a big spell of silence. The company had all been listening intently, so that there was no change except the cessation of Hempitch's voice. The eyes of all were now fixed on Mr Wellesley Dovercourt. It was the role of the Tragedian to deal with such an occasion. He was quite alive to the privileges of his status, and spoke at once:

"H'm! Very excellent indeed! You will have to join the ranks of our profession, Mr Master Machinist—the lower ranks, of course. A very thrilling narrative yours, and distinctly true. There may be some errors of detail, such as that Mrs Haliday never flirted again. I . . . I knew John Haliday under, of course, his real

367

name. But I shall preserve the secret you so judiciously suppressed. A very worthy person. He was stage carpenter at the Duke's Theatre, Bolton, where I first dared histrionic triumphs in the year—ah H'm! I saw quite a good deal of Mrs Haliday at that time. And you are wrong about her. Quite wrong! She was a most attractive little woman—very!"

The Wardrobe Mistress here whispered to the Second Old Woman:

"Well, ma'am, they all seem agoin' of it tonight. I think they must have ketched the infection from Mr Bloze.

There isn't a bally word of truth in all Hempitch has said. I was there when the accident occurred—for it was an accident when Jim Bungnose, the clown, was killed. For he was a clown, not a 'arlequin; an' there wasn't no lovemakin' with Mrs 'Aliday. God 'elp the woman as would try to make love to Jim; which she was the Strong Woman in a Circus, and could put up her dooks like a man. Moreover, there wasn't no Mrs 'Aliday. The carpenter at Grimsby, where it is he means, was Tom Elrington, as he was my first 'usband. And as to Mr Dovercourt rememberin'! He's a cure, he is; an' the Limit!"

The effect of the Master Machinist's story was so depressing that the M.C. tried to hurry things on; any change of sentiment would, he thought, be an advantage. So he bustled along:

"Now, Mr Turner Smith, you are the next on the roster. It is a pity we have not an easel and a canvas and paint box here, or even some cartridge pager and charcoal, so that you might give us a touch of your art—what I may call a plastic diversion of the current of narrative genius which has been enlivening the snowy waste around us." The artistic audience applauded this flight of metaphor—all except the young man from Oxford, who contented himself by saying loudly, "Pip-pip!" He had heard something like it before at the Union.

# A Lesson in Pets

'Once before, I spent some time with the Company in a saloon which was not altogether ideal.'

'Oh, do tell us about it,' said the Leading Lady. 'We have hours at least to spend here, and it will help to pass the time.'

'Hear! Hear!' came from the rest of the Company, who at least always seemed to like to hear the Manager speak. The Manager rose and bowed with his hand on his heart as though before the curtain, sat down again, and began:

'It was a good many years ago—about ten, I should think—when I had out the No 1 Company of "Revelations of Society". Some of you will remember the piece. It had a long run both in town and country.'

'I know it well,' said the Heavy Father. 'When I was a Leading Juvenile I played Geoffroi D'Almontiere, the French villain, in the Smalls in old George Bucknill's Company, with Evangeline Destrude as Lady Margaret Skeffington. A ripping good piece it was, too. I often wonder that someone doesn't revive it. It's worth a dozen of these namby-pamby—rot-gut-problem—'

'Hush! Hush!' came the universal interruption, and the growing indignation of the speaker calmed down. The Manager went on:

'That time we had an eruption of dogs.'

'Of what's?'

'How?'

'Of dogs?'

'How that time?'

'Oh, do explain!' from the Company. The Manager resumed:

'Of dogs, and other things. But I had better begin at the beginning. On the previous tour I had out "The Lesson of the Cross", and as we were out to rake in all the goody-goodies, I thought it best to have an ostensibly moral tone about the whole outfit. So I picked them out on purpose for family reasons. There were with us none but married folk, and no matter how old and ugly the women were, I knew they'd pass muster with the outside crowd that we were catering for. But I did not quite expect what would happen. Every one of them brought children. I wouldn't have minded so much if they had brought the bigger ones that could have gone on to swell the crowds. I'd have paid their fares for them, too.

'But they only took babies and little kiddies that needed someone to look after them all the time. The number of young nursemaids and slips of girls from the workhouse and institutions that we had with us you wouldn't credit. When I got down to the station and saw the train that the Inspector pointed out as my special, I could not believe my eyes. There was hardly a window that hadn't a baby being held out of it, and the platform was full of old women and children all crowing, laughing, and crying and snapping their fingers and wiping their eyes and waving pocket-handkerchiefs.

'Somehow the crowd outside had tumbled to it, and it being Sunday afternoon, they kept pouring in and guying the whole outfit. I could do nothing then but get into my own compartment and pull down the blind, and pray that we might get away on time.

'When we got to Manchester, where we opened, there was the usual Sunday crowd to see the actors. When we came sliding round the curve of the Exchange I looked out, and saw with pleasure the public anxiety to catch the first glimpse of the celebrated "Lesson of the Cross" Company, as they had it well displayed on our bills. But I saw run along all the faces in the line, just as you see a breeze sweep over a cornfield, a look of wonder; and then a white flash as the teeth of every man, woman, and child became open with a grin. I looked back, and there again was that infernal row of babies being dandled in front of the windows. The crowd began to cheer; I waited till they closed round the babies, and then I bolted for my hotel.

'It was the same thing over and over again all through that tour. Every place at which we arrived or from which we went away had the same crowd; and we went and came in howls of laughter. I wouldn't have minded so much if it did us any good; but somehow it only disappointed a lot of people who came to the play to see the crowd of babies, and wanted their money back when they found they weren't on.

'I spoke to some of the Company quietly as to whether they couldn't manage to send some of the young 'uns home; but they all told me that domestic arrangements were complete, and that they couldn't change them. The only fun I had was with one young couple who I knew were only just married. They had with them a little girl about three years old, whom they had dressed up as a boy. When I remonstrated with them they frankly told me that as all the others had children with them they thought it would look too conspicuous without, and so they had hired the child from a poor relation, and were responsible for it for the tour. This made me laugh, and I could say no more.

'Then there was another drawback from all the children; there wasn't an infant epidemic within a hundred miles of us that some of them didn't get—measles, whooping-cough, chicken-pock, mumps, ringworm—the whole lot of them, till the train not only looked like a *crèche*, but smelt like a baby-farm and a hospital in one. Why, if you will believe me, during the year that I toured that blessed Company—and we had a mighty prosperous time of it, take it for all in all—the entire railway system of England was strewn with feeding-bottles and rusks.'

'Oh, Mr Benville Nonplusser, how can you?' remonstrated the First Old Woman. The Manager went on:

'Just before the end of the tour I got all the Company together, and told them that never again would I allow a baby to be taken on any tour of mine; at all events, in my special trains. And that resolution I've kept from that day to this.

'Well, the next tour we went on was very different. It was, as I said, with the "Revelations of Society", and, of course, the cast was quite different. We wanted to get a sort of toney, upper-crust effect; so I got a lot of society amateurs to walk on. The big parts were, of course, done by good people, but all the small ones were done by swells. It wasn't altogether a pleasant time, for there was no end to the jealousies. The society amateurs were, as usual, more theatrical than the theatricals; the airs that some of them gave themselves would make you laugh. This put up the backs of our own crowd—and they got their shirts out, I can tell you.

'At first I tried to keep the peace, for these swell supers were mighty good and just what we wanted in the play; but after a bit it got to a regular division of camps, and I found that whatever I did must be wrong. Whatever one got or did they all wanted, and nothing was allowed to pass that gave even a momentary advantage or distinction to any of the crowd. By-and-by I began to have to put my foot down, but every time I did so there was a kick somewhere; so I had to be careful lest I should have no one at all to play the piece.

'I seemed never to be able to get an hour's rest from some of the jealousies that were constantly springing up. If I could have managed to forestall any of them it would have been easy enough, but the worst of it all was that they were perpetually breaking out in a new place; and it was only when it was too late to do anything to prevent a row that I came to know the cause of the one then on.

'Having forbidden babies on the former tour, I did not think it was necessary to forbid anything else; and the consequence was that I suddenly found that we had broken out in an eruption of Pets. My Leading Lady then, Miss Flora Montressor, who had been with me on seven tours and was an established favourite all over the Provinces, had a little toy wheaten terrier that she had taken with her everywhere since ever she had been with me. Often other members had asked my Acting Manager if they too might bring dogs; but he had always put them off, telling them that the railway people didn't allow it, and that it would be better not to press the matter, as Miss Montressor from her position was a privileged person.

'This had always been enough with the regular Company, but the new lot had all of them got pets of some kind, and after the first journey, when their attention had been called to the irregularity, they simply produced dog-tickets, and said they would pay for them themselves. That was enough for the other lot, and before the next journey came there wasn't a soul in the whole crowd but had a pet of some kind. Of course, they were mostly dogs—and a queer lot they were, from the tiniest kind of toy up to the biggest sort of mastiff. The railway people weren't ready for them—it would have taken a new kind of van for them all—and I wasn't ready for them either; so I said nothing then.

'The following Sunday I got them all together, and told them that after that journey I was afraid I could not permit the thing to go on. The station was then like a dog-show, and I could hardly hear myself speak for the barking and yelping and howling. There were mastiffs and St Bernards, and collies and poodles and terriers and bull-dogs and Skyes, and King Charleys and dachshunds and turnspits—every kind of odd illustration of the family of the canine world. One man had got a cat with a silver collar, and led it by a string; another had a tame frog; and several had squirrels, white mice, rabbits, rats, a canary in a cage, and a tame duck. Our Second Low Comedy Merchant had got a young pig, but it got away at the station, and he hadn't time to follow it up. When I spoke to the Company they were silent, and they all held up their dog-tickets—all except Miss Flora Montressor, who said quietly:

'"You gave me leave years ago to bring my little dog."

'Well, I saw that nothing could be done then except with the kind of row that I didn't want. So I went to my own compartment to think the matter over.

'I soon came to the conclusion that an object-lesson of some kind was required; and then a bright idea struck me:

"'I should get a pet myself.'

'We were then bound for Liverpool, and early in the week I slipped down to my old friend Ross, the animal importer, to consult with him. In my early days I had had to do with a circus, and I thought that on this occasion I might turn my knowledge to account. He was out, so I asked one of the men if he could recommend me some sort of pet that wouldn't be pleasant for a nervous person to travel with. He wasn't a humorous man, and at once suggested a tiger. "We have a lovely full-grown one," he said, "just in from Bombay. He's as savage as they make 'em. We have to keep him in a place by himself, for when we put him 'in a room with any of the others, he terrifies them so that they are like to quit in a body."

'I thought this cure might be too drastic, and I didn't want to close my tour in a cemetery or a gaol, so I suggested something milder. He tried me with pumas, leopards, crocodiles, wolves, bears, gorillas, and even with a young elephant; but none of them seemed as if it would suit. Just then Ross himself came in, and took me off to see something new.

"'Just come in," he said; "three ton of boa-constrictor from Surinam. The finest lot I've ever come across." When I looked at them, although my early training had somewhat accustomed me to such matters, I felt a little uneasy. There they lay in cases like melon beds, with nothing over them but a glass frame, with not even a hasp to hold it down. A great slimy, many-coloured mass all folded about and coiled up and down and round and round;—except for a head sticking out here and there one would have thought that it was all one big reptile. Ross saw me move a little, so he said, to reassure me:

"'You needn't be skeered. This weather they're half torpid. It's pretty cold now, and even if the heat were to get at them they wouldn't wake up." I didn't like them, all the same, for whenever one of them would give a gulp, swallowing whatever food he was on at the moment—a rat or a rabbit or what not—the whole mass would stir and heave and writhe a little. I thought how nice a lot of them would look amongst my crowd; so there and then I agreed with Ross to hire a lot of them for the next journey. One of his men was to come down with my workmen to Carlisle, whither we were bound, to take them back again.

'I arranged with the railway company to have for that journey one of their large excursion saloons, so that all the members of the Company would have to travel together instead of going into separate compartments grouped in parties. When they gathered at the station none of them were satisfied. There was, however, no overt grumbling. I had casually mentioned, and the word had gone round, that I was coming with them myself, and had prepared a treat for them.

'That they evidently expected something in the way of a picnic was manifested by the frequent inquiries of some of them from the porters and the Baggage Master as to whether my personal luggage had arrived. I had carefully arranged with Ross's people that my contribution was not to be brought till the last moment, and I had privately tipped the Guard and asked him to be ready for an immediate start after its arrival. The special train had been scheduled for a quick run, and was not to stop between Liverpool and Carlisle.

'As the starting time drew near, the Company took their places as they had secured them in the saloon, the first comers getting to the furthest ends. The carriage became by a sort of natural selection divided into two camps. The dogs belonging to either side were in the centre. When "all aboard" had been called out by my Acting Manager after his usual custom, the last of the Company took their places. Then a heavy truck came quickly along the platform, surrounded by several men. It contained two great boxes with unfastened lids, and as there were many hands available these were quickly lifted into the saloon. One was placed opposite the door on the off-side of the carriage, and the other put just inside the door of entry, which it blocked.

'Then the door was slammed and locked; the Guard's whistle sounded, and we were off.

'I needn't tell you that all this time the dogs were barking and howling for all they were worth, and some of them were only held back by their owners from flying at each other. The cat had taken refuge on a hat-rack, and stood growling, with her tail thickened and lashing about. The frog sat complacently in its box beside its master, and the rats and mice were nowhere to be seen in their cages. When the baskets came in some of the dogs cowered down and shivered, whilst others barked fiercely and could hardly be held back. I got out my Sunday paper and began to read quietly, awaiting developments.

'For a while the angry dogs kept up their clamour, and one of them, the mastiff, became almost unmanageable. His master called out to me:

'"I can't hold him much longer. There must be something in that box that upsets him."

'"Indeed!" I said, and went on reading. Then one or two of the Company began to get alarmed; one of them came over and looked curiously at the box, bent close and sniffed suspiciously, and drew back. This whetted the curiosity of others, and several more came around and bent down and sniffed. Then they began to whisper amongst themselves, and one of them asked me point-blank:

'"Mr Benville Nonplusser, what is in that box?"

'"Only some pets of mine," I answered, without looking up from my paper.

'"Very nasty pets, whatever they are," she answered tartly. "They smell very nasty." To which I replied:

'"We all have our fancies, my dear. You have yours and I have mine; and since all you belonging to this Company have your pets with you, I have determined to establish some of mine. You'll doubtless grow to like them in time. In fact, you'd better begin, for they are likely to be with you every journey henceforth."

'"May we look?" asked one of the young men. I nodded acquiescence, and as he stooped to lift the lid the rest gathered round—all except the man with the mastiff, who had his hands full with that clamorous beast. The young man raised the lid, and as he saw what was within, threw it back as he recoiled, so that it fell over, leaving the whole interior exposed. Then the crowd drew back with a shudder, and some of the women began to scream. I was afraid that they might attract attention, as we were then nearing a station, so I said quietly:

"'You had better be as quiet as you can. Nothing irritates serpents so much as noise. They think it is their opportunity for seeking prey!" This bold statement seemed to be verified by the fact that some of the boa-constrictors sleepily raised their heads with a faint hissing. Whereupon the crowd simply tumbled over each other in their efforts to reach the further corners of the saloon. By this time the man with the mastiff was becoming exhausted by his struggling with the powerful animal. As I wished to push home my lesson, I said:

"'You had better keep those dogs quiet. If you don't, I shall not answer for the consequences. If that mastiff manages to attack the serpents, as he is trying to, they will spring out and fight, and then—" I was silent, for at such a point silence is the true eloquence. The fear of all was manifested by their blanched faces and trembling forms.

"'I'm afraid I can't hold him any longer!" gasped out the man.

"'Then," said I, "some of your companions who have dogs also should try to help you. If not, it will be too late!" So several others came, and by the aid of their rug-straps they managed to tie the brute securely to a leg of the bench. Seeing that they were nearly all half-paralysed with fright, I lifted the lid to the top of the box again; at which they seemed to breathe more freely. When they saw me actually sitting on the box, something like a far-off smile began to glow on the countenances of some of them. I kept urging them to keep the animals quiet; and as this was a never-ceasing work, they had something to occupy them.

'I was a little nervous myself at first, and had any of the boa-constrictors knocked his head against the lid of the box I should have made a jump away. However, as they remained absolutely tranquil, my own courage grew.

'And so some hours passed, with occasional episodes, such as when some one of the many pets would make a disturbance. The singing of the canary, for instance, was resisted with angry curses. But the vials of the wrath of all were emptied forth at its owner when the hitherto silent duck began its homely song, "Quack, quack!"

'"Will you keep that blasted brute quiet?" came an angry whisper from the worn-out owner of the mastiff. Upon which a good many of those on whom time had had a quieting effect smiled.

'When my watch told me that we were within a short distance of Carlisle, I stood upon the box and made a little speech:

'"Ladies and Gentlemen, I trust that the episode of today, unpleasant though it may have been, will not be ultimately without beneficial effect. You have learned that each one of you owes something to the general good, and that the selfish pursuance of your own pleasure in small ways has sooner or later to be accounted for. When I remonstrated with each of you as to this animal business, you chose to take your own way, and even went so far as to reconcile your personal and sectional jealousies in order to unite against me. I therefore thought that I would bring the difficulty home to you in a striking way! Have I done so?"

'For a while there was silence; and then a smile and a faint affirmative answer here and there, so I went on:

'"Now I hope you will all take it in as good part as I have taken all that went before. Anyhow, my mind is made up. Pets shall be included with babies in the Index Expurgatorius of our tour. In the meantime, for the remainder of this tour, if anyone else brings pets, so shall I; and I think you know that I know how to choose my own. Anyone objecting to this can cancel the engagement right here. Has anyone got anything to say?" Some shrugged their shoulders, but all were silent; and I knew that my victory was complete. As I was stepping down, however, I caught Miss Montressor's eye as tearfully she looked at me and then at her little dog, so I added:

'"This does not apply to Miss Montressor, who years ago had

permission to take her dog. I shall certainly not deprive her of that privilege now."

'And not a soul objected.'

# The Spectre of Doom
### *(A.K.A. The Invisible Giant)*

Time goes on in the Country Under the Sunset much as it does here.

Many years have passed away; and they wrought much change. And now we find a time when the people that lived in good King Mago's time would hardly have known their beautiful land if they had seen it again.

It had sadly changed indeed. No longer was there the same love or the same reverence towards the king—no longer was there perfect peace. People had become more selfish and more greedy, and had tried to grasp all they could for themselves. There were some very rich and there were many poor. Most of the beautiful gardens were laid waste. Houses had grown up close round the palace; and in some of these dwelt many persons who could only afford to pay for part of a house.

All the beautiful country was sadly changed, and changed was the life of the dwellers in it. The people had almost forgotten Prince Zaphir, who was dead many, many years ago; and no more roses were spread on the pathways. Those who lived now in the Country Under the Sunset laughed at the idea of more giants, and they did not fear them because they did not see them. Some of them said,

"Tush! what can there be to fear? Even if there ever were giants there are none now."

And so the people sang and danced and feasted as before, and thought only of themselves.

The spirits that guarded the land were very, very sad. Their great white shadowy wings drooped as they stood at their posts at the portals of the land. They hid their faces, and their eyes were dim with continuous weeping, so that they heeded not if any evil thing went by them. They tried to make the people think of their evil-doing; but they could not leave their posts, and the people heard their moaning in the night season and said, "Listen to the sighing of the breeze; how sweet it is!"

So is it ever with us also, that when we hear the wind sighing and moaning and sobbing round our houses in the lonely nights, we do not think our angels may be sorrowing for our misdeeds, but only that there is a storm coming. The angels wept evermore, and they felt the sorrow of dumbness—for though they could speak, those they spoke to would not hear.

Whilst the people laughed at the idea of giants, there was one old man who shook his head, and made answer to them, when he heard them, and said: "Death has many children, and there are giants in the marshes still. You may not see them, perhaps—but they are there, and the only bulwark of safety is in a land of patient, faithful hearts."

The name of this good old man was Knoal, and he lived in a house built of great blocks of stone, in the middle of a wild place far from the city.

In the city there were many great old houses, storey upon storey high; and in these houses lived many poor people. The higher you went up the great steep stairs the poorer were the people that lived there, so that in the garrets were some so poor that when the morning came they did not know whether they should have anything to eat the whole long day. This was very, very sad, and gentle children would have wept if they had seen their pain.

In one of these garrets there lived all alone a little maiden called Zaya. She was an orphan, for her father had died many years before, and her poor mother, who had toiled long and wearily for her dear little daughter—her only child—had died also not long since.

Poor little Zaya had wept so bitterly when she saw her dear mother lying dead, and she had been so sad and sorry for a long time, that she quite forgot that she had no means of living. However, the poor people who lived in the house had given her part of their own food, so that she did not starve.

Then after awhile she had tried to work for herself and earn her own living. Her mother had taught her to make flowers out of paper; so that she made a lot of flowers, and when she had a full basket she took them into the street and sold them. She made flowers of many kinds, roses and lilies, and violets, and snowdrops, and primroses, and mignonette, and many beautiful sweet flowers that only grow in the Country Under the Sunset. Some of them she could make without any pattern, but others she could not, so when she wanted a pattern she took her basket of paper and scissors, and paste, and brushes, and all the things she used, and went into the garden which a kind lady owned, where there grew many beautiful flowers. There she sat down and worked away, looking at the flowers she wanted.

Sometimes she was very sad, and her tears fell thick and fast as she thought of her dear dead mother. Often she seemed to feel that her mother was looking down at her, and to see her tender smile in the sunshine on the water; then her heart was glad, and she sang so sweetly that the birds came around her and stopped their own singing to listen to her.

She and the birds grew great friends, and sometimes when she had sung a song they would all cry out together, as they sat round her in a ring, in a few notes that seemed to say quite plainly:

*Sing to us again.*
*Sing to us again.*

So she would sing again. Then she would ask them to sing, and they would sing till there was quite a concert. After a while the birds knew her so well that they would come into her room, and they even built their nests there, and they followed her wherever she went. The people used to say:

"Look at the girl with the birds; she must be half a bird herself, for see how the birds know and love her." From so many people coming to say things like this, some silly people actually believed that she was partly a bird, and they shook their heads when wise people laughed at them, and said:

"Indeed she must be; listen to her singing; her voice is sweeter even than the birds."

So a nickname was applied to her, and naughty boys called it after her in the street, and the nickname was "Big Bird". But Zaya did not mind the name; and although often naughty boys said it to her, meaning to cause her pain, she did not dislike it, but the contrary, for she so gloried in the love and trust of her little sweet-voiced pets that she wished to be thought like them.

Indeed it would be well for some naughty little boys and girls if they were as good and harmless as the little birds that work all day long for their helpless baby birds, building nests and bringing food, and sitting so patiently hatching their little speckled eggs.

One evening Zaya sat alone in her garret very sad and lonely. It was a lovely summer's evening, and she sat in the window looking out over the city. She could see over the many streets towards the great cathedral whose spire towered aloft into the sky higher by far even than the great tower of the king's palace. There was hardly a breath of wind, and the smoke went up straight from the chimneys, getting further and fainter till it was lost altogether.

Zaya was very sad. For the first time for many days her birds were all away from her at once, and she did not know where they had gone. It seemed to her as if they had deserted her, and she was so lonely, poor little maid, that she wept bitter tears. She was thinking of the story which long ago her dead mother had told her, how Prince Zaphir had slain the giant, and she wondered what the prince was like, and thought how happy the people must have been when Zaphir and Bluebell were king and queen. Then she wondered if there were any hungry children in those good days, and if, indeed, as the people said, there were no more Giants. So she went on with her work before the open window.

Presently she looked up from her work and gazed across the city. There she saw a terrible thing—something so terrible that she gave a low cry of fear and wonder, and leaned out of the window, shading her eyes with her hands to see more clearly.

In the sky beyond the city she saw a vast shadowy form with

its arms raised. It was shrouded in a great misty robe that covered it, fading away into air so that she could only see the face and the grim, spectral hands.

The form was so mighty that the city below it seemed like a child's toy. It was still far off the city.

The little maid's heart seemed to stand still with fear as she thought to herself, "The giants, then, are not dead. This is another of them."

Quickly she ran down the high stairs and out into the street. There she saw some people, and cried to them,

"Look! look! the giant, the giant!" and pointed towards the Form which she still saw moving onwards to the city.

The people looked up, but they could not see anything, and they laughed and said,

"The child is mad."

Then poor little Zaya was more than ever frightened, and ran down the street crying out still,

"Look, look! the giant, the giant!" But no one heeded her, and all said, "The child is mad," and they went on their own ways.

Then the naughty boys came around her and cried out,

"Big Bird has lost her mates. She sees a bigger bird in the sky, and she wants it." And they made rhymes about her, and sang them as they danced round.

Zaya ran away from them; and she hurried right through the city, and out into the country beyond it, for she still saw the great Form before her in the air.

As she went on, and got nearer and nearer to the giant, it grew a little darker. She could see only the clouds; but still there was visible the form of a giant hanging dimly in the air.

A cold mist closed around her as the giant appeared to come onwards towards her. Then she thought of all the poor people in the city, and she hoped that the giant would spare them, and she knelt down before him and lifted up her hands appealingly, and cried aloud:

"Oh, great giant! spare them, spare them!"

But the giant moved onwards still as though he never heard. She cried aloud all the more,

"Oh, great giant! spare them, spare them!" And she bowed her head and wept, and the giant still, though very slowly, moved onward towards the city.

There was an old man not far off standing at the door of a small house built of great stones, but the little maid saw him not.

His face wore a look of fear and wonder, and when he saw the child kneel and raise her hands, he drew nigh and listened to her voice. When he heard her say, "Oh, great giant!" he murmured to himself,

"It is then even as I feared. There are more giants, and truly this is another." He looked upwards, but he saw nothing, and he murmured again,

"I see not, yet this child can see; and yet I feared, for something told me that there was danger. Truly knowledge is blinder than innocence."

The little maid, still not knowing there was any human being near her, cried out again, with a great cry of anguish:

"Oh, do not, do not, great giant, do them harm. If someone must suffer, let it be me. Take me, I am willing to die, but spare them. Spare them, great giant and do with me even as thou wilt." But the giant heeded not.

And Knoal—for he was the old man—felt his eyes fill with tears, and he said to himself,

"Oh, noble child, how brave she is, she would sacrifice herself!" And coming closer to her, he put his hand upon her head.

Zaya, who was again bowing her head, started and looked round when she felt the touch. However, when she saw that it was Knoal, she was comforted, for she knew how wise and good he was, and felt that if any person could help her, he could. So she clung to him, and hid her face in his breast; and he stroked her hair and comforted her. But still he could see nothing.

The cold mist swept by, and when Zaya looked up, she saw that the giant had passed by, and was moving onward to the city.

"Come with me, my child," said the old man; and the two arose, and went into the dwelling built of great stones.

When Zaya entered, she started, for lo! the inside was as a tomb. The old man felt her shudder, for he still held her close to him, and he said,

"Weep not, little one, and fear not. This place reminds me and all who enter it, that to the tomb we must all come at the last. Fear it not, for it has grown to be a cheerful home to me."

Then the little maid was comforted, and began to examine all around her more closely. She saw all sorts of curious instruments, and many strange and many common herbs and simples hung to dry in bunches on the walls. The old man watched her in silence till her fear was gone, and then he said:

"My child, saw you the features of the giant as he passed?"

She answered, "Yes."

"Can you describe his face and form to me?" he asked again.

Whereupon she began to tell him all that she had seen. How the giant was so great that all the sky seemed filled. How the great arms were outspread, veiled in his robe, till far away the shroud was lost in air. How the face was as that of a strong man, pitiless, yet without malice; and that the eyes were blind.

The old man shuddered as he heard, for he knew that the giant was a very terrible one; and his heart wept for the doomed city where so many would perish in the midst of their sin.

They determined to go forth and warn again the doomed people; and making no delay, the old man and the little maid hurried towards the city.

As they left the small house, Zaya saw the giant before them, moving towards the city. They hurried on; and when they had passed through the cold mist, Zaya looked back and saw the giant behind them.

Presently they came to the city.

It was a strange sight to see that old man and that little maid flying to tell people of the terrible plague that was coming upon them. The old man's long white beard and hair and the child's golden locks were swept behind them in the wind, so quick they came. The faces of both were white as death. Behind them, seen only to the eyes of the pure-hearted little maid when she looked back, came ever onward at slow pace the spectral giant that hung a dark shadow in the evening air.

But those in the city never saw the giant; and when the old man and the little maid warned them, still they heeded not, but scoffed and jeered at them, and said,

"Tush! there are no giants now"; and they went on their way, laughing and jeering.

Then the old man came and stood on a raised place amongst them, on the lowest step of the great fountain with the little maid by his side, and he spake thus:

"Oh, people, dwellers in this land, be warned in time. This pure-hearted child, round whose sweet innocence even the little birds that fear men and women gather in peace, has this night seen in the sky the form of a giant that advances ever onward menacingly to our city. Believe, oh, believe; and be warned, whilst ye may. To myself even as to you the sky is a blank; and yet see that I believe. For listen to me: all unknowing that another giant had invaded our land, I sat pensive in my dwelling; and, without cause or motive, there came into my heart a sudden fear for the safety of our city. I arose and looked north and south and east and west, and on high and below, but never a sign of danger could I see. So I said to myself,

'Mine eyes are dim with a hundred years of watching and waiting, and so I cannot see.' And yet, oh people, dwellers in this land, though that century has dimmed mine outer eyes, still it has quickened mine inner eyes—the eyes of my soul.

Again I went forth, and lo! this little maid knelt and implored a giant, unseen by me, to spare the city; but he heard her not, or, if he heard, answered her not, and she fell prone. So hither we come to warn you. Yonder, says the maid, he passes onward to the city. Oh, be warned; be warned in time."

Still the people heeded not; but they scoffed and jeered the more, and said,

"Lo, the maid and the old man both are mad"; and they passed onwards to their homes—to dancing and feasting as before.

Then the naughty boys came and mocked them, and said that Zaya had lost her birds, and gone mad; and they made songs, and sang them as they danced round.

Zaya was so sorely grieved for the poor people that she heeded not the cruel boys. Seeing that she did not heed them, some of them got still more rude and wicked; they went a little way off, and threw things at them, and mocked them all the more.

Then, sad of heart, the old man arose, and took the little maid by the hand, and brought her away into the wilderness; and lodged her with him in the house built with great stones. That night Zaya slept with the sweet smell of the drying herbs all around her; and the old man held her hand that she might have no fear.

In the morning Zaya arose betimes, and awoke the old man, who had fallen asleep in his chair.

She went to the doorway and looked out, and then a thrill of gladness came upon her heart; for outside the door, as though waiting to see her, sat all her little birds, and many, many more. When the birds saw the little maid they sang a few loud joyous notes, and flew about foolishly for very joy—some of them fluttering their wings and looking so funny that she could not help laughing a little.

When Knoal and Zaya had eaten their frugal breakfast and given to their little feathered friends, they set out with sorrowful hearts to visit the city, and to try once more to warn the people. The birds flew around them as they went, and to cheer them sang as joyously as they could, although their little hearts were heavy.

As they walked they saw before them the great shadowy giant; and he had now advanced to the very confines of the city.

Once again they warned the people, and great crowds came around them, but only mocked them more than ever; and naughty boys threw stones and sticks at the little birds and killed some of them. Poor Zaya wept bitterly, and Knoal's heart was very sad. After a time, when they had moved from the fountain, Zaya looked up and started with joyous surprise, for the great shadowy giant was nowhere to be seen. She cried out in joy, and the people laughed and said,

"Cunning child! she sees that we will not believe her, and she pretends that the giant has gone."

They surrounded her, jeering, and some of them said,

"Let us put her under the fountain and duck her, as a lesson to liars who would frighten us." Then they approached her with menaces. She clung close to Knoal, who had looked terribly grave when she had said she did not see the giant any longer, and who was now as if in a dream, thinking. But at her touch he seemed to wake up; and he spoke sternly to the people, and rebuked them. But they cried out on him also, and said that as he had aided Zaya in her lie he should be ducked also, and they advanced to lay hands on them both.

The hand of one who was a ringleader was already outstretched, when he gave a low cry, and pressed his hand to his side; and, whilst the others turned to look at him in wonder, he cried out in great pain, and screamed horribly. Even whilst the people looked, his face grew blacker and blacker, and he fell down before them, and writhed a while in pain, and then died.

All the people screamed out in terror, and ran away, crying aloud:

"The giant! the giant! he is indeed amongst us!" They feared all the more that they could not see him.

But before they could leave the market-place, in the centre of which was the fountain, many fell dead and their corpses lay.

There in the centre knelt the old man and the little maid, praying; and the birds sat perched around the fountain, mute and still, and there was no sound heard save the cries of the people far off. Then their wailing sounded louder and louder, for the giant— plague—was amongst and around them, and there was no escaping, for it was now too late to fly.

Alas! in the Country Under the Sunset there was much weeping that day; and when the night came there was little sleep, for there was fear in some hearts and pain in others. None were still except the dead, who lay stark about the city, so still and lifeless that even the cold light of the moon and the shadows of the drifting clouds moving over them could not make them seem as though they lived.

And for many a long day there was pain and grief and death in the Country Under the Sunset.

Knoal and Zaya did all they could to help the poor people, but it was hard indeed to aid them, for the unseen giant was amongst them, wandering through the city to and fro, so that none could tell where he would lay his ice-cold hand.

Some people fled away out of the city; but it was little use, for go how they would and fly never so fast they were still within the grasp of the unseen giant. Ever and anon he turned their warm hearts to ice with his breath and his touch, and they fell dead.

Some, like those within the city, were spared, and of these some perished of hunger, and the rest crept sadly back to the city and lived or died amongst their friends. And it was all, oh! so sad, for there was nothing but grief and fear and weeping from morn till night.

Now, see how Zaya's little bird friends helped her in her need.

They seemed to see the coming of the giant when no one—not even the little maid herself—could see anything, and they managed to tell her when there was danger just as well as though they could talk.

At first Knoal and she went home every evening to the house built of great stones to sleep, and came again to the city in the morning, and stayed with the poor sick people, comforting them and feeding them, and giving them medicine which Knoal, from his great wisdom, knew would do them good. Thus they saved many precious human lives, and those who were rescued were very thankful, and henceforth ever after lived holier and more unselfish lives.

After a few days, however, they found that the poor sick people needed help even more at night than in the day, and so they came and lived in the city altogether, helping the stricken folk day and night.

At the earliest dawn Zaya would go forth to breathe the morning air; and there, just waked from sleep, would be her feathered friends waiting for her. They sang glad songs of joy, and came and perched on her shoulders and her head, and kissed her. Then, if she went to go towards any place where, during the night, the plague had laid his deadly hand, they would flutter before her, and try to impede her, and scream out in their own tongue,

"Go back! go back!"

They pecked of her bread and drank of her cup before she touched them; and when there was danger—for the cold hand of the giant was placed everywhere—they would cry,

"No, no!" and she would not touch the food, or let anyone else do so. Often it happened that, even whilst it pecked at the bread or drank of the cup, a poor little bird would fall down and flutter its wings and die; but all they that died, did so with a chirp of joy, looking at their little mistress, for whom they had gladly perished. Whenever the little birds found that the bread and the cup were pure and free from danger, they would look up at Zaya jauntily, and flap their wings and try to crow, and seemed so saucy that the poor sad little maiden would smile.

There was one old bird that always took a second, and often a great many pecks at the bread when it was good, so that he got quite a hearty meal; and sometimes he would go on feeding till Zaya would Shake her finger at him and say,

"Greedy!" and he would hop away as if he had done nothing.

There was one other dear little bird—a robin, with a breast as red as the sunset—that loved Zaya more than one can think. When he tried the food and found that it was safe to eat, he would take a tiny piece in his bill, and fly up and put it in her mouth.

Every little bird that drank from Zaya's cup and found it good raised its head to say grace; and ever since then the little birds do the same, and they never forget to say their grace—as some thankless children do.

Thus Knoal and Zaya lived, although many around them died, and the giant still remained in the city. So many people died that one began to wonder that so many were left; for it was only when the town began to get thinned that people thought of the vast numbers that had lived in it.

Poor little Zaya had got so pale and thin that she looked a shadow, and Knoal's form was bent more with the sufferings of a few weeks than it had been by his century of age. But although the two were weary and worn, they still kept on their good work of aiding the sick.

Many of the little birds were dead.

One morning the old man was very weak—so weak that he could hardly stand. Zaya got frightened about him, and said,

"Are you ill, father?" for she always called him father now.

He answered her in a voice alas! hoarse and low, but very, very tender:

"My child, I fear the end is coming: take me home, that there I may die."

At his words Zaya gave a low cry and fell on her knees beside him, and buried her head in his bosom and wept bitterly, whilst she hugged him close. But she had little time for weeping, for the old man struggled up to his feet, and, seeing that he wanted aid, she dried her tears and helped him.

The old man took his staff, and with Zaya helping to support him, got as far as the fountain in the midst of the market-place; and there, on the lowest step, he sank down as though exhausted. Zaya felt him grow cold as ice, and she knew that the chilly hand of the giant had been laid upon him.

Then, without knowing why, she looked up to where she had last seen the giant as Knoal and she had stood beside the fountain.

And lo! as she looked, holding Knoal's hand, she saw the shadowy form of the terrible giant who had been so long invisible growing more and more clearly out of the clouds.

His face was stern as ever, and his eyes were still blind.

Zaya cried to the giant, still holding Knoal tightly by the hand:

"Not him, not him! Oh, mighty giant! not him! not him!" and she bowed her head and wept.

There was such. anguish in her heart that to the blind eyes of the shadowy giant came tears that fell like dew on the forehead of the old man. Knoal spake to Zaya:

"Grieve not, my child. I am glad that you see the giant again, for I have hope that he will leave our city free from woe. I am the last victim, and I gladly die."

Then Zaya knelt to the giant, and said:

"Spare him! oh! spare him and take me! but spare him! spare

him!"

The old man raised himself upon his elbow as he lay, and spake to her:

"Grieve not, my little one, and repine not. Sooth I know that you would gladly give your life for mine. But we must give for the good of others that which is dearer to us than our lives. Bless you, my little one, and be good. Farewell! farewell!"

As he spake the last word he grew cold as death, and his spirit passed away.

Zaya knelt down and prayed; and when she looked up she saw the shadowy giant moving away.

The giant turned as he passed on, and Zaya saw that his blind eyes looked towards her as though he were trying to see. He raised the great shadowy arms, draped still in his shroud of mist, as though blessing her; and she thought that the wind that came by her moaning bore the echo of the words:

"Innocence and devotion save the land."

Presently she saw far off the great shadowy giant plague moving away to the border of the land, and passing between the guardian spirits out through the portal into the deserts beyond—forever.

# The Chain of Destiny

## 1
### A Warning

It was so late in the evening when I arrived at Scarp that I had but little opportunity of observing the external appearance of the house; but, as far as I could judge in the dim twilight, it was a very stately edifice of seemingly great age, built of white stone. When I passed the porch, however, I could observe its internal beauties much more closely, for a large wood fire burned in the hall and all the rooms and passages were lighted. The hall was almost baronial in its size, and opened on to a staircase of dark oak so wide and so generous in its slope that a carriage might almost have been driven up it. The rooms were large and lofty, with their walls, like those of the staircase, panelled with oak black from age.

This sombre material would have made the house intensely gloomy but for the enormous width and height of both rooms and passages. As it was, the effect was a homely combination of size and warmth. The windows were set in deep embrasures, and, on the ground story, reached from quite level with the floor to almost the ceiling. The fireplaces were quite in the old style, large and surrounded with massive oak carvings, representing on each some scene from Biblical history, and at the side of each fireplace rose a pair of massive carved iron fire-dogs. It was altogether just such a house as would have delighted the heart of Washington Irving or Nathaniel Hawthorne.

The house had been lately restored; but in effecting the restoration comfort had not been forgotten, and any modern improvement which tended to increase the homelike appearance of the rooms had been added. The old diamond-paned casements, which had remained probably from the Elizabethan age, had given place to more useful plate glass; and, in like manner, many other changes had taken place. But so judiciously had every change been effected that nothing of the new clashed with the old, but the harmony of all the parts seemed complete.

I thought it no wonder that Mrs. Trevor had fallen in love with Scarp the first time she had seen it. Mrs. Trevor's liking the place was tantamount to her husband's buying it, for he was so wealthy that he could get almost anything money could purchase. He was himself a man of good taste, but still he felt his inferiority to his wife in this respect so much that he never dreamt of differing in opinion from her on any matter of choice or judgment.

Mrs. Trevor had, without exception, the best taste of any one whom I ever knew, and, strange to say, her taste was not confined to any branch of art. She did not write, or paint, or sing; but still her judgment in writing, painting, or music, was unquestioned by her friends. It seemed as if nature had denied to her the power of execution in any separate branch of art, in order to make her perfect in her appreciation of what was beautiful and true in all. She was perfect in *the art of harmonising—the art of every-day life.* Her husband used to say, with a far-fetched joke, that her star must have been in the House of Libra, because everything which she said and did showed such a nicety of balance.

Mr. and Mrs. Trevor were the most model couple I ever knew—they really seemed not twain, but one. They appeared to have adopted something of the French idea of man and wife-that they should not be the less like *friends* because they were linked together by indissoluble bonds—that they should share their pleasures as well as their sorrows. The former outbalanced the latter, for both husband and wife were of that happy temperament which can take pleasure from everything, and find consolation even in the chastening rod of affliction.

Still, through their web of peaceful happiness ran a thread of care. One that cropped up in strange places, and disappeared again, but which left a quiet tone over the whole fabric-they had no child.

> *They had their share of sorrow, for when time was ripe*
> *The still affection of the heart became an outward breathing type,*
> *That into stillness passed again,*
> *But left a want unknown before.*

There was something simple and holy in their patient endurance of their lonely life-for lonely a house must ever be without children to those who love truly. Theirs was not the eager, disappointed longing of those whose union had proved fruitless. It was the simple, patient, hopeless resignation of those who find that a common sorrow draws them more closely together than many common joys. I myself could note the warmth of their hearts and their strong philoprogenitive feeling in their manner towards me.

From the time when I lay sick in college when Mrs. Trevor appeared to my fever-dimmed eyes like an angel of mercy, I felt myself growing in their hearts. Who can imagine my gratitude to the lady who, merely because she heard of my sickness and desolation from a college friend, came and nursed me night and day till the fever left me. When I was sufficiently strong to be moved she had me brought away to the country, where good air, care, and attention soon made me stronger than ever.

From that time I became a constant visitor at the Trevors' house; and as month after month rolled by I felt that I was growing in their affections. For four summers I spent my long vacation in their house, and each year I could feel Mr. Trevor's shake of the hand grow heartier, and his wife's kiss on my forehead-for so she always saluted me-grow more tender and motherly.

Their liking for me had now grown so much that in their heart of hearts—and it was a sanctum common to them both-they secretly loved me as a son. Their love was returned manifold by the lonely boy, whose devotion to the kindest friends of his youth and his trouble had increased with his growth into manhood. Even in my own heart I was ashamed to confess how I loved them both—how I worshipped Mrs. Trevor as I adored the mother whom I had lost so young, and whose eyes shone sometimes even then upon me, like stars, in my sleep.

It is strange how timorous we are when our affections are concerned. Merely because I had never told her how I loved her as a mother, because she had never told me how she loved me as a son, I used sometimes to think of her with a sort of lurking suspicion that I was trusting too much to my imagination. Sometimes even I would try to avoid thinking of her altogether, till my yearning would grow too strong to be repelled, and then I would think of her long and silently, and would love her more and more. My life was so lonely that I clung to her as the only thing I had to love. Of course I loved her husband, too, but I never thought about him in the same way; for men are less demonstrative about their affections to each other, and even acknowledge them to themselves less.

Mrs. Trevor was an excellent hostess. She always let her guests see that they were welcome, and, unless in the case of casual visitors, that they were expected. She was, as may be imagined, very popular with all classes; but what is more rare, she was equally popular with both sexes. To be popular with her own sex is the touchstone of a woman's worth. To the houses of the peasantry she came, they said, like an angel, and brought comfort wherever she came. She knew the proper way to deal with the poor; she always helped them materially, but never offended their feelings in so doing. Young people all adored her.

My curiosity had been aroused as to the sort of place Scarp was; for, in order to give me a surprise, they would not tell me anything about it, but said that I must wait and judge it for myself. I had looked forward to my visit with both expectation and curiosity.

When I entered the hall, Mrs. Trevor came out to welcome me and kissed me on the forehead, after her usual manner. Several of the old servants came near, smiling and bowing, and wishing welcome to "Master Frank." I shook hands with several of them, whilst their mistress looked on with a pleased smile.

As we went into a snug parlour, where a table was laid out with the materials for a comfortable supper, Mrs. Trevor said to me:

"I am glad you came so soon, Frank. We have no one here at present, so you will be quite alone with us for a few days; and you will be quite alone with me this evening, for Charley is gone to a dinner-party at Westholm."

I told her that I was glad that there was no one else at Scarp, for that I would rather be with her and her husband than anyone else in the world. She smiled as she said:

"Frank, if anyone else said that, I would put it down as a mere compliment; but I know you always speak the truth. It is all very well to be alone with an old couple like Charley and me for two or three days; but just you wait till Thursday, and you will look on the intervening days as quite wasted."

"Why?" I inquired.

"Because, Frank, there is a girl coming to stay with me then, with whom I intend you to fall in love."

I answered jocosely:

"Oh, thank you, Mrs. Trevor, very much for your kind intention, but suppose for a moment that they should be impracticable. *One man may lead a horse to the pond's brink. The best laid schemes o' mice an' men.* Eh?"

"Frank, don't be silly. I do not want to make you fall in love against your inclination; but I hope and I believe that you will."

"Well, I'm sure I hope you won't be disappointed; but I never yet heard a person praised that I did not experience a disappointment when I came to know him or her."

"Frank, did I praise any one?"

"Well, I am vain enough to think that your saying that you knew I would fall in love with her was a sort of indirect praise."

"Dear, me, Frank, how modest you have grown. 'A sort of indirect praise!' Your humility is quite touching."

"May I ask who the lady is, as I am supposed to be an interested party?"

"I do not know that I ought to tell you on account of your having expressed any doubt as to her merits. Besides, I might weaken the effect of the introduction. If I stimulate your curiosity it will be a point in my favour."

"Oh, very well; I suppose I must only wait?"

"Ah, well, Frank, I will tell you. It is not fair to keep you waiting. She is a Miss Fothering."

"Fothering? Fothering? I think I know that name. I remember hearing it somewhere, a long time ago, if I do not mistake. Where does she come from?"

"Her father is a clergyman in Norfolk, but he belongs to the Warwickshire family. I met her at Winthrop, Sir Harry Blount's place, a few months ago, and took a great liking for her, which she returned, and so we became fast friends. I made her promise to pay me a visit this summer, so she and her sister are coming here on Thursday to stay for some time."

"And, may I be bold enough to inquire what she is like?"

"You may inquire if you like, Frank; but you won't get an answer. I shall not try to describe her. You must wait and judge for yourself."

"Wait," said I, "three whole days? How can I do that? Do, tell me."

She remained firm to her determination. I tried several times in the course of the evening to find out something more about Miss Fothering, for my curiosity was roused; but all the answer I could get on the subject was—"Wait, Frank; wait, and judge for yourself."

When I was bidding her goodnight, Mrs. Trevor said to me—

"By-the-bye, Frank, you will have to give up the room which you will sleep in tonight, after tomorrow. I will have such a full house that I cannot let you have a doubled-bedded room all to yourself; so I will give that room to the Miss Fotherings, and move you up to the second floor. I just want you to see the room, as it has a romantic look about it, and has all the old furniture that was in it when we came here. There are several pictures in it worth looking at."

My bedroom was a large chamber—immense for a bedroom—with two windows opening level with the floor, like those of the parlours and drawing-rooms. The furniture was old-fashioned, but not old enough to be curious, and on the walls hung many pictures—portraits—the house was full of portraits—and landscapes. I just glanced at these, intending to examine them in the morning, and went to bed. There was a fire in the room, and I lay awake for some time looking dreamily at the shadows of the furniture flitting over the walls and ceiling as the flames of the wood fire leaped and fell, and the red embers dropped whitening on the hearth.

I tried to give the rein to my thoughts, but they kept constantly to the one subject—the mysterious Miss Fothering, with whom I was to fall in love. I was sure that I had heard her name somewhere, and I had at times lazy recollections of a child's face. At such times I would start awake from my growing drowsiness, but before I could collect my scattered thoughts the idea had eluded me. I could remember neither when nor where I had heard the name, nor could I recall even the expression of the child's face. It must have been long, long ago, when I was young. When I was young my mother was alive. My mother—mother—mother. I found myself half awakening, and repeating the word over and over again. At last I fell asleep.

I thought that I awoke suddenly to that peculiar feeling which we sometimes have on starting from sleep, as if someone had been speaking in the room, and the voice is still echoing through it. All was quite silent, and the fire had gone out. I looked out of the window that lay straight opposite the foot of the bed, and observed a light outside, which gradually grew brighter till the room was almost as light as by day. The window looked like a picture in the framework formed by the cornice over the foot of the bed, and the massive pillars shrouded in curtains which supported it.

With the new accession of light I looked round the room, but nothing was changed. All was as before, except that some of the objects of furniture and ornament were shown in stronger relief than hitherto. Amongst these, those most in relief were the other bed, which was placed across the room, and an old picture that hung on the wall at its foot. As the bed was merely the counterpart of the one in which I lay, my attention became fixed on the picture. I observed it closely and with great interest. It seemed old, and was the portrait of a young girl, whose face, though kindly and merry, bore signs of thought and a capacity for deep feeling—almost for passion. At some moments, as I looked at it, it called up before my mind a vision of Shakespeare's Beatrice, and once I thought of Beatrice Cenci. But this was probably caused by the association of ideas suggested by the similarity of names.

The light in the room continued to grow even brighter, so I looked again out of the window to seek its source, and saw there a lovely sight. It seemed as if there were grouped without the window three lovely children, who seemed to float in mid-air. The light seemed to spring from a point far behind them, and by their side was something dark and shadowy, which served to set off their radiance.

The children seemed to be smiling in upon something in the room, and, following their glances, I saw that their eyes rested upon the other bed. There, strange to say, the head which I had lately seen in the picture rested upon the pillow. I looked at the wall, but the frame was empty, the picture was gone. Then I looked at the bed again, and saw the young girl asleep, with the expression of her face constantly changing, as though she were dreaming.

As I was observing her, a sudden look of terror spread over her face, and she sat up like a sleep-walker, with her eyes wide open, staring out of the window.

Again turning to the window, my gaze became fixed, for a great and weird change had taken place. The figures were still there, but their features and expressions had become woefully different. Instead of the happy innocent look of childhood was one of malignity. With the change the children had grown old, and now three hags, decrepit and deformed, like typical witches, were before me.

But a thousand times worse than this transformation was the change in the dark mass that was near them. From a cloud, misty and undefined, it became a sort of shadow with a form. This gradually, as I looked, grew darker and fuller, till at length it made me shudder. There stood before me the phantom of the Fiend.

There was a long period of dead silence, in which I could hear the beating of my heart; but at length the phantom spoke to the others. His words seemed to issue from his lips mechanically, and without expression—"Tomorrow, and tomorrow, and tomorrow. The fairest and the best." He looked so awful that the question arose in my mind—"Would I dare to face him without the window—would any one dare to go amongst those fiends?" A harsh, strident, diabolical laugh from without seemed to answer my unasked question in the negative.

But as well as the laugh I heard another sound—the tones of a sweet sad voice in despair coming across the room.

"Oh, alone, alone! Is there no human thing near me? No hope—no hope. I shall go mad—or die."

The last words were spoken with a gasp.

I tried to jump out of bed, but could not stir, my limbs were bound in sleep. The young girl's head fell suddenly back upon the pillow, and the limp-hanging jaw and wide-open, purposeless mouth spoke but too plainly of what had happened.

Again I heard from without the fierce, diabolical laughter, which swelled louder and louder, till at last it grew so strong that in very horror I shook aside my sleep and sat up in bed. I listened and heard a knocking at the door, but in another moment I became more awake, and knew that the sound came from the hall. It was, no doubt, Mr. Trevor returning from his party.

The hall-door was opened and shut, and then came a subdued sound of tramping and voices, but this soon died away, and there was silence throughout the house.

I lay awake for long thinking, and looking across the room at the picture and at the empty bed; for the moon now shone brightly, and the night was rendered still brighter by occasional flashes of summer lightning. At times the silence was broken by an owl screeching outside.

As I lay awake, pondering, I was very much troubled by what I had seen; but at length, putting several things together, I came to the conclusion that I had had a dream of a kind that might have been expected. The lightning, the knocking at the hall-door, the screeching of the owl, the empty bed, and the face in the picture, when grouped together, supplied materials for the main facts of the vision. The rest was, of course, the offspring of pure fancy, and the natural consequence of the component elements mentioned acting with each other in the mind.

I got up and looked out of the window, but saw nothing but the broad belt of moonlight glittering on the bosom of the lake, which extended miles and miles away, till its farther shore was lost in the night haze, and the green sward, dotted with shrubs and tall grasses, which lay between the lake and the house.

The vision had utterly faded. However, the dream—for so, I suppose, I should call it—was very powerful, and I slept no more till the sunlight was streaming broadly in at the window, and then I fell into a doze.

## 2

### More Links

Late in the morning I was awakened by Parks, Mr. Trevor's man, who always used to attend on me when I visited my friends. He brought me hot water and the local news; and, chatting with him, I forgot for a time my alarm of the night.

Parks was staid and elderly, and a type of a class now rapidly disappearing-the class of old family servants who are as proud of their hereditary loyalty to their masters, as those masters are of name and rank. Like all old servants he had a great loving for all sorts of traditions. He believed them, and feared them, and had the most profound reverence for anything which had a story.

I asked him if he knew anything of the legendary history of Scarp. He answered with an air of doubt and hesitation, as of one carefully delivering an opinion which was still incomplete.

"Well, you see, Master Frank, that Scarp is so old that it must have any number of legends; but it is so long since it was inhabited that no one in the village remembers them. The place seems to have become in a kind of way forgotten, and died out of people's thoughts, and so I am very much afraid, sir, that all the genuine history is lost."

"What do you mean by the genuine history?" I inquired.

"Well, sir, I mean the true tradition, and not the inventions of the village folk. I heard the sexton tell some stories, but I am quite sure that they were not true, for I could see, Master Frank, that he did not believe them himself, but was only trying to frighten us."

"And could you not hear of any story that appeared to you to be true?"

"No, sir, and I tried very hard. You see, Master Frank, that there is a sort of club held every week in the tavern down in the village, composed of very respectable men, sir—very respectable men, indeed—and they asked me to be their chairman. I spoke to the master about it, and he gave me leave to accept their proposal. I accepted it as they made a point of it; and from my position I have of course a fine opportunity of making inquiries. It was at the club, sir, that I was, last night, so that I was not here to attend on you, which I hope that you will excuse."

Parks's air of mingled pride and condescension, as he made the announcement of the club, was very fine, and the effect was heightened by the confiding frankness with which he spoke. I asked him if he could find no clue to any of the legends which must have existed about such an old place. He answered with a very slight reluctance—

"Well, sir, there was one woman in the village who was awfully old and doting, and she evidently knew something about Scarp, for when she heard the name she mumbled out something about 'awful stories,' and 'times of horror,' and such like things, but I couldn't make her understand what it was I wanted to know, or keep her up to the point."

"And have you tried often, Parks? Why do you not try again?"

"She is dead, sir!"

I had felt inclined to laugh at Parks when he was telling me of the old woman. The way in which he gloated over the words "awful stories," and "times of horror," was beyond the power of description; it should have been heard and seen to have been properly appreciated. His voice became deep and mysterious, and he almost smacked his lips at the thought of so much pabulum for nightmares. But when he calmly told me that the woman was dead, a sense of blankness, mingled with awe, came upon me.

Here, the last link between myself and the mysterious past was broken, never to be mended. All the rich stores of legend and tradition that had arisen from strange conjunctures of circumstances, and from the belief and imagination of long lines of villagers, loyal to their suzerain lord, were lost forever. I felt quite sad and disappointed; and no attempt was made either by Parks or myself to continue the conversation. Mr. Trevor came presently into my room, and having greeted each other warmly we went together to breakfast.

At breakfast Mrs. Trevor asked me what I thought of the girl's portrait in my bedroom. We had often had discussions as to characters in faces for we were both physiognomists, and she asked the question as if she were really curious to hear my opinion. I told her that I had only seen it for a short time, and so would rather not attempt to give a final opinion without a more careful study; but from what I had seen of it I had been favourably impressed.

"Well, Frank, after breakfast go and look at it again carefully, and then tell me exactly what you think about it."

After breakfast I did as directed and returned to the breakfast room, where Mrs. Trevor was still sitting.

"Well, Frank, what is your opinion—mind, correctly. I want it for a particular reason?"

I told her what I thought of the girl's character; which, if there be any truth in physiognomy, must have been a very fine one.

"Then you like the face?"

I answered—

"It is a great pity that we have none such now-a-days. They seem to have died out with Sir Joshua and Greuze. If I could meet such a girl as I believe the prototype of that portrait to have been I would never be happy till I had made her my wife."

To my intense astonishment my hostess jumped up and clapped her hands. I asked her why she did it, and she laughed as she replied in a mocking tone imitating my own voice—

"But suppose for a moment that your kind intentions should be frustrated. *One man may lead a horse to the pond's brink. 'The best laid schemes o' mice an' men.* Eh?"

"Well," said I, "there may be some point in the observation. I suppose there must be since you have made it. But for my part I don't see it."

"Oh, I forgot to tell you, Frank, that that portrait might have been painted for Diana Fothering."

I felt a blush stealing over my face. She observed it and took my hand between hers as we sat down on the sofa, and said to me tenderly—

"Frank, my dear boy, I intend to jest with you no more on the subject. I have a conviction that you will like Diana, which has been strengthened by your admiration for her portrait, and from what I know of human nature I am sure that she will like you. Charley and I both wish to see you married, and we would not think of a wife for you who was not in every way eligible. I have never in my life met a girl like Di; and if you and she fancy each other it will be Charley's pleasure and my own to enable you to marry—as far as means are concerned.

"Now, don't speak. You must know perfectly well how much we both love you. We have always regarded you as our son, and

406

we intend to treat you as our only child when it pleases God to separate us. There now, think the matter over, after you have seen Diana. But, mind me, unless you love each other well and truly, we would far rather not see you married. At all events, whatever may happen you have our best wishes and prayers for your happiness. God bless you, Frank, my dear, dear boy."

There were tears in her eyes as she spoke. When she had finished she leaned over, drew down my head and kissed my forehead very, very tenderly, and then got up softly and left the room. I felt inclined to cry myself. Her words to me were tender, and sensible, and womanly, but I cannot attempt to describe the infinite tenderness and gentleness of her voice and manner. I prayed for every blessing on her in my secret heart, and the swelling of my throat did not prevent my prayers finding voice. There may have been women in the world like Mrs. Trevor, but if there had been I had never met any of them, except herself.

As may be imagined, I was most anxious to see Miss Fothering, and or the remainder of the day she was constantly in my thoughts. That evening a letter came from the younger Miss Fothering apologising for her not being able to keep her promise with reference to her visit, on account of the unexpected arrival of her aunt, with whom she was obliged to go to Paris for some months. That night I slept in my new room, and had neither dream nor vision. I awoke in the morning half ashamed of having ever paid any attention to such a silly circumstance as a strange dream in my first night in an old house.

After breakfast next morning, as I was going along the corridor, I saw the door of my old bedroom open, and went in to have another look at the portrait. Whilst I was looking at it I began to wonder how it could be that it was so like Miss Fothering as Mrs. Trevor said it was. The more I thought of this the more it puzzled me, till suddenly the dream came back—the face in the picture, and the figure in the bed, the phantoms out in the night, and the ominous words—"The fairest and the best." As I thought of these things all the possibilities of the lost legends of the old house thronged so quickly into my mind that I began to feel a buzzing in my ears and my head began to swim, so that I was obliged to sit down.

"Could it be possible," I asked myself, "that some old curse hangs over the race that once dwelt within these walls, and can she be of that race? Such things have been before now!"

The idea was a terrible one for me, for it made to me a reality that which I had come to look upon as merely the dream of a distempered imagination. If the thought had come to me in the darkness and stillness of the night it would have been awful. How happy I was that it had come by daylight, when the sun was shining brightly, and the air was cheerful with the trilling of the song birds, and the lively, strident cawing from the old rookery.

I stayed in the room for some little time longer, thinking over the scene, and, as is natural, when I had got over the remnants of my fear, my reason began to question the genuineness—*vraisemblance* of the dream. I began to look for the internal evidence of the untruth to facts; but, after thinking earnestly for some time the only fact that seemed to me of any importance was the confirmatory one of the younger Miss Fothering's apology. In the dream the frightened girl had been alone, and the mere fact of *two* girls coming on a visit had seemed a sort of disproof of its truth. But, just as if things were conspiring to force on the truth of the dream, one of the sisters was not to come, and the other was she who resembled the portrait whose prototype I had seen sleeping in a vision. I could hardly imagine that I had only dreamt.

I determined to ask Mrs. Trevor if she could explain in any way Miss Fothering's resemblance to the portrait, and so went at once to seek her.

I found her in the large drawing-room alone, and, after a few casual remarks, I broached the subject on which I had come to seek for information. She had not said anything further to me about marrying since our conversation on the previous day, but when I mentioned Miss Fothering's name I could see a glad look on her face which gave me great pleasure. She made none of those vulgar commonplace remarks which many women find it necessary to make when talking to a man about a girl for whom he is supposed to have an affection, but by her manner she put me entirely at my ease, as I sat fidgeting on the sofa, pulling purposelessly the woolly tufts of an antimacassar, painfully conscious that my cheeks were red, and my voice slightly forced and unnatural.

She merely said, "Of course, Frank, I am ready if you want to talk about Miss Fothering, or any other subject." She then put a marker in her book and laid it aside, and, folding her arms, looked at me with a grave, kind, expectant smile.

I asked her if she knew anything about the family history of Miss Fothering. She answered—

"Not further than I have already told you. Her father's is a fine old family, although reduced in circumstances."

"Has it ever been connected with any family in this county? With the former owners of Scarp, for instance?"

"Not that I know of. Why do you ask?"

"I want to find out how she comes to be so like that portrait."

"I never thought of that. It may be that there was some remote connection between her family and the Kirks who formerly owned Scarp. I will ask her when she comes. Or stay. Let us go and look if there is any old book or tree in the library that will throw a light upon the subject. We have rather a good library now, Frank, for we have all our own books, and all those which belonged to the Scarp library also. They are in great disorder, for we have been waiting till you came to arrange them, for we knew that you delighted in such work."

"There is nothing I should enjoy more than arranging all these splendid books. What a magnificent library. It is almost a pity to keep it in a private house."

We proceeded to look for some of those old books of family history which are occasionally to be found in old county houses. The library of Scarp, I saw, was very valuable, and as we prosecuted our search I came across many splendid and rare volumes which I determined to examine at my leisure, for I had come to Scarp for a long visit.

We searched first in the old folio shelves, and, after some few disappointments, found at length a large volume, magnificently printed and bound, which contained views and plans of the house, illuminations of the armorial bearings of the family of Kirk, and all the families with whom it was connected, and having the history of all these families carefully set forth. It was called on the title-page *The Book of Kirk*, and was full of anecdotes and legends, and contained a large stock of family tradition. As this was exactly the book which we required, we searched no further, but, having carefully dusted the volume, bore it to Mrs. Trevor's *boudoir* where we could look over it quite undisturbed.

On looking in the index, we found the name of Fothering mentioned, and on turning to the page specified, found the arms of Kirk quartered on those of Fothering. From the text we learned that one of the daughters of Kirk had, in the year 1573, married the brother of Fothering against the united wills of her father and brother, and that after a bitter feud of some ten or twelve years, the latter, then master of Scarp, had met the brother of Fothering in a duel and had killed him.

Upon receiving the news Fothering had sworn a great oath to revenge his brother, invoking the most fearful curses upon himself and his race if he should fail to cut off the hand that had slain his brother, and to nail it over the gate of Fothering. The feud then became so bitter that Kirk seems to have gone quite mad on the subject. When he heard of Fothering's oath he knew that he had but little chance of escape, since his enemy was his master at every weapon; so he determined upon a mode of revenge which, although costing him his own life, he fondly hoped would accomplish the eternal destruction of his brother-in-law through his violated oath.

He sent Fothering a letter cursing him and his race, and praying for the consummation of his own curse invoked in case of failure. He concluded his missive by a prayer for the complete destruction, soul, mind, and body, of the first Fothering who should enter the gate of Scarp, who he hoped would be the fairest and best of the race. Having despatched this letter he cut off his right hand and threw it into the centre of a roaring fire, which he had made for the purpose. When it was entirely consumed he threw himself upon his sword, and so died.

A cold shiver went through me when I read the words "fairest and best." All my dream came back in a moment, and I seemed to hear in my ears again the echo of the fiendish laughter. I looked up at Mrs. Trevor, and saw that she had become very grave. Her face had a half-frightened look, as if some wild thought had struck her. I was more frightened than ever, for nothing increases our alarms so much as the sympathy of others with regard to them; however, I tried to conceal my fear. We sat silent for some minutes, and then Mrs. Trevor rose up saying:

"Come with me, and let us look at the portrait."

I remember her saying *the* and not *that* portrait, as if some concealed thought of it had been occupying her mind. The same dread had assailed her from a coincidence as had grown in me from a vision. Surely—surely I had good grounds for fear!

We went to the bedroom and stood before the picture, which seemed to gaze upon us with an expression which reflected our own fears. My companion said to me in slightly excited tones: "Frank, lift down the picture till we see its back." I did so, and we found written in strange old writing on the grimy canvas a name and a date, which, after a great deal of trouble, we made out to be "Margaret Kirk, 1572." It was the name of the lady in the book.

Mrs. Trevor turned round and faced me slowly, with a look of horror on her face.

"Frank, I don't like this at all. There is something very strange here."

I had it on my tongue to tell her my dream, but was ashamed to do so. Besides, I feared that it might frighten her too much, as she was already alarmed.

I continued to look at the picture as a relief from my embarrassment, and was struck with the excessive griminess of the back in comparison to the freshness of the front. I mentioned my difficulty to my companion, who thought for a moment, and then suddenly said—

"I see how it is. It has been turned with its face to the wall."

I said no word but hung up the picture again; and we went back to the *boudoir*.

On the way I began to think that my fears were too wildly improbable to bear to be spoken about. It was so hard to believe in the horrors of darkness when the sunlight was falling brightly around me. The same idea seemed to have struck Mrs. Trevor, for she said, when we entered the room:

"Frank, it strikes me that we are both rather silly to let our imaginations carry us away so. The story is merely a tradition, and we know how report distorts even the most innocent facts. It is true that the Fothering family was formerly connected with the Kirks, and that the picture is that of the Miss Kirk who married against her father's will; it is likely that he quarrelled with her for so doing, and had her picture turned to the wall—a common trick of angry fathers at all times—but that is all. There can be nothing beyond that. Let us not think any more upon the subject, as it is one likely to lead us into absurdities. However, the picture is a really beautiful one—independent of its being such a likeness of Diana, and I will have it placed in the dining-room."

The change was effected that afternoon, but she did not again allude to the subject. She appeared, when talking to me, to be a little constrained in manner—a very unusual thing with her, and seemed to fear that I would renew the forbidden topic. I think that she did not wish to let her imagination lead her astray, and was distrustful of herself. However, the feeling of constraint wore off before night—but she did not renew the subject.

I slept well that night, without dreams of any kind; and next morning—the third tomorrow promised in the dream—when I came down to breakfast, I was told that I would see Miss Fothering before that evening.

I could not help blushing, and stammered out some commonplace remark, and then glancing up, feeling very sheepish, I saw my hostess looking at me with her kindly smile intensified. She said:

"Do you know, Frank, I felt quite frightened yesterday when we were looking at the picture; but I have been thinking the matter over since, and have come to the conclusion that my folly was perfectly unfounded. I am sure you agree with me. In fact, I look now upon our fright as a good joke, and will tell it to Diana when she arrives."

Once again I was about to tell my dream; but again was restrained by shame. I knew, of course, that Mrs. Trevor would not laugh at me or even think little of me for my fears, for she was too well-bred, and kind-hearted, and sympathetic to do anything of the kind, and, besides, the fear was one which we had shared in common.

But how could I confess my fright at what might appear to others to be a ridiculous dream, when she had conquered the fear that had been common to us both, and which had arisen from a really strange conjuncture of facts. She appeared to look on the matter so lightly that I could not do otherwise. And I did it honestly for the time.

## 3

### THE THIRD TOMORROW

In the afternoon I was out in the garden lying in the shadow of an immense beech, when I saw Mrs. Trevor approaching. I had been reading Shelley's *Stanzas Written in Dejection*, and my heart was full of melancholy and a vague yearning after human sympathy. I had thought of Mrs. Trevor's love for me, but even that did not seem sufficient. I wanted the love of some one more nearly of my own level, some equal spirit, for I looked on her, of course, as I would have regarded my mother.

Somehow my thoughts kept returning to Miss Fothering till I could almost see her before me in my memory of the portrait. I had begun to ask myself the question: "Are you in love?" when

I heard the voice of my hostess as she drew near.

"Ha! Frank, I thought I would find you here. I want you to come to my *boudoir*."

"What for?" I inquired, as I rose from the grass and picked up my volume of Shelley.

"Di has come ever so long ago; and I want to introduce you and have a chat before dinner," said she, as we went towards the house.

"But won't you let me change my dress? I am not in correct costume for the afternoon."

I felt somewhat afraid of the unknown beauty when the introduction was imminent. Perhaps it was because I had come to believe too firmly in Mrs. Trevor's prediction.

"Nonsense, Frank, just as if any woman worth thinking about cares how a man is dressed."

We entered the *boudoir* and found a young lady seated by a window that overlooked the croquet-ground. She turned round as we came in, so Mrs. Trevor introduced us, and we were soon engaged in a lively conversation. I observed her, as may be supposed, with more than curiosity, and shortly found that she was worth looking at. She was very beautiful, and her beauty lay not only in her features but in her expression.

At first her appearance did not seem to me so perfect as it afterwards did, on account of her wonderful resemblance to the portrait with whose beauty I was already acquainted. But it was not long before I came to experience the difference between the portrait and the reality. No matter how well it may be painted a picture falls far short of its prototype. There is something in a real face which cannot exist on canvas—some difference far greater than that contained in the contrast between the one expression, however beautiful of the picture, and the moving features and varying expression of the reality. There is something living and lovable in a real face that no art can represent.

When we had been talking for a while in the usual conventional style, Mrs. Trevor said, "Di, my love, I want to tell you of a discovery Frank and I have made. You must know that I always call Mr. Stanford, Frank—he is more like my own son than my friend, and that I am very fond of him."

She then put her arms round Miss Fothering's waist, as they sat on the sofa together, and kissed her, and then, turning towards me, said, "I don't approve of kissing girls in the presence of gentlemen, but you know that Frank is not supposed to be here. This is my sanctum, and who invades it must take the consequences. But I must tell you about the discovery."

She then proceeded to tell the legend, and about her finding the name of Margaret Kirk on the back of the picture.

Miss Fothering laughed gleefully as she heard the story, and then said, suddenly,

"Oh, I had forgotten to tell you, dear Mrs. Trevor, that I had such a fright the other day. I thought I was going to be prevented coming here. Aunt Deborah came to us last week for a few days, and when she heard that I was about to go on a visit to Scarp she seemed quite frightened, and went straight off to papa and asked him to forbid me to go. Papa asked her why she made the request, so she told a long family legend about any of us coming to Scarp—just the same story that you have been telling me.

"She said she was sure that some misfortune would happen if I came; so you see that the tradition exists in our branch of the family too. Oh, you can't fancy the scene there was between papa and Aunt Deborah. I *must* laugh whenever I think of it, although I did not laugh then, for I was greatly afraid that aunty would prevent me coming. Papa got very grave, and aunty thought she had carried her point when he said, in his dear, old, pompous manner,

"'Deborah, Diana has promised to pay Mrs. Trevor, of Scarp, a visit, and, of course, must keep her engagement. And if it were for no other reason than the one you have just alleged, I would strain a point of convenience to have her go to Scarp. I have always educated my children in such a manner that they ought not to be influenced by such vain superstitions; and with my will their practice shall never be at variance with the precepts which I have instilled into them.'

"Poor aunty was quite overcome. She seemed almost speechless for a time at the thought that her wishes had been neglected, for you know that Aunt Deborah's wishes are commands to all our family."

Mrs. Trevor said—

"I hope Mrs. Howard was not offended?"

"Oh, no. Papa talked to her seriously, and at length—with a great deal of difficulty I must say—succeeded in convincing her that her fears were groundless—at least, he forced her to confess that such things as she was afraid of could not be."

I thought of the couplet—

*A man convinced against his will*
*Is of the same opinion still,*

but said nothing.

Miss Fothering finished her story by saying—

"Aunty ended by hoping that I might enjoy myself, which I am sure, my dear Mrs. Trevor, that I will do."

"I hope you will, my love."

I had been struck during the above conversation by the mention of Mrs. Howard. I was trying to think of where I had heard the name, Deborah Howard, when suddenly it all came back to me. Mrs. Howard had been Miss Fothering, and was an old friend of my mother's. It was thus that I had been accustomed to her name when I was a child. I remembered now that once she had brought a nice little girl, almost a baby, with her to visit. The child was her niece, and it was thus that I now accounted for my half-recollection of the name and the circumstance on the first night of my arrival at Scarp. The thought of my dream here recalled me to Mrs. Trevor's object in bringing Miss Fothering to her *boudoir*, so I said to the latter—

"Do you believe these legends?"

"Indeed I do not, Mr. Stanford; I do not believe in anything half so silly."

"Then you do not believe in ghosts or visions?"

"Most certainly not."

416

How could I tell my dream to a girl who had such profound disbelief? And yet I felt something whispering to me that I ought to tell it to her. It was, no doubt, foolish of me to have this fear of a dream, but I could not help it. I was just going to risk being laughed at, and unburden my mind, when Mrs. Trevor started up, after looking at her watch, saying—

"Dear me, I never thought it was so late. I must go and see if any others have come. It will not do for me to neglect my guests."

We all left the *boudoir*, and as we did so the gong sounded for dressing for dinner, and so we each sought our rooms.

When I came down to the drawing-room I found assembled a number of persons who had arrived during the course of the afternoon. I was introduced to them all, and chatted with them till dinner was announced. I was given Miss Fothering to take into dinner, and when it was over I found that we had improved our acquaintance very much. She was a delightful girl, and as I looked at her I thought with a glow of pleasure of Mrs. Trevor's prediction.

Occasionally I saw our hostess observing us, and as she saw us chatting pleasantly together as though we enjoyed it a more than happy look came into her face. It was one of her most fascinating points that in the midst of gaiety, while she never neglected anyone, she specially remembered her particular friends. No matter what position she might be placed in she would still remember that there were some persons who would treasure up her recognition at such moments.

After dinner, as I did not feel inclined to enter the drawing-room with the other gentlemen, I strolled out into the garden by myself, and thought over things in general, and Miss Fothering in particular. The subject was such a pleasant one that I quite lost myself in it, and strayed off farther than I had intended. Suddenly I remembered myself and looked around. I was far away from the house, and in the midst of a dark, gloomy walk between old yew trees. I could not see through them on either side on account of their thickness, and as the walk was curved

I could see but a short distance either before or behind me. I looked up and saw a yellowish, luminous sky with heavy clouds passing sluggishly across it. The moon had not yet risen, and the general gloom reminded me forcibly of some of the weird pictures which William Blake so loved to paint. There was a sort of vague melancholy and ghostliness in the place that made me shiver, and I hurried on.

At length the walk opened and I came out on a large sloping lawn, dotted here and there with yew trees and tufts of pampas grass of immense height, whose stalks were crowned with large flowers. To the right lay the house, grim and gigantic in the gloom, and to the left the lake which stretched away so far that it was lost in the evening shadow. The lawn sloped from the terrace round the house down to the water's edge, and was only broken by the walk which continued to run on round the house in a wide sweep.

As I came near the house a light appeared in one of the windows which lay before me, and as I looked into the room I saw that it was the chamber of my dream.

Unconsciously I approached nearer and ascended the terrace from the top of which I could see across the deep trench which surrounded the house, and looked earnestly into the room. I shivered as I looked. My spirits had been damped by the gloom and desolation of the yew walk, and now the dream and all the subsequent revelations came before my mind with such vividness that the horror of the thing again seized me, but more forcibly than before. I looked at the sleeping arrangements, and groaned as I saw that the bed where the dying woman had seemed to lie was alone prepared, while the other bed, that in which I had slept, had its curtains drawn all round. This was but another link in the chain of doom.

Whilst I stood looking, the servant who was in the room came and pulled down one of the blinds, but, as she was about to do the same with the other, Miss Fothering entered the room, and, seeing what she was about, evidently gave her contrary directions, for she let go the window string, and then went and pulled up again the blind which she had let down. Having done so she followed her mistress out of the room. So wrapped up was I in all that took place with reference to that chamber, that it never even struck me that I was guilty of any impropriety in watching what took place.

I stayed there for some little time longer purposeless and terrified. The horror grew so great to me as I thought of the events of the last few days, that I determined to tell Miss Fothering of my dream, in order that she might not be frightened in case she should see anything like it, or at least that she might be prepared for anything that might happen. As soon as I had come to this determination the inevitable question "when?" presented itself. The means of making the communication was a subject most disagreeable to contemplate, but as I had made up my mind to do it, I thought that there was no time like the present.

Accordingly I was determined to seek the drawing-room, where I knew I should find Miss Fothering and Mrs. Trevor, for, of course, I had determined to take the latter into our confidence. As I was really afraid to go through the awful yew walk again, I completed the half circle of the house and entered the backdoor, from which I easily found my way to the drawing-room.

When I entered Mrs. Trevor, who was sitting near the door, said to me, "Good gracious, Frank, where have you been to make you look so pale? One would think you had seen a ghost!"

I answered that I had been strolling in the garden, but made no other remark, as I did not wish to say anything about my dream before the persons to whom she was talking, as they were strangers to me. I waited for some time for an opportunity of speaking to her alone, but her duties, as hostess, kept her so constantly occupied that I waited in vain. Accordingly I determined to tell Miss Fothering at all events, at once, and then to tell Mrs. Trevor as soon as an opportunity for doing so presented itself.

With a good deal of difficulty—for I did not wish to do anything marked—I succeeded in getting Miss Fothering away from the persons by whom she was surrounded, and took her to one of the embrasures, under the pretence of looking out at the night view. Here we were quite removed from observation, as the heavy window curtains completely covered the recess, and almost isolated us from the rest of the company as perfectly as if we were in a separate chamber. I proceeded at once to broach the subject for which I had sought the interview; for I feared lest contact with the lively company of the drawing-room would do away with my present fears, and so breakdown the only barrier that stood between her and Fate.

"Miss Fothering, do you ever dream?"

"Oh, yes, often. But I generally find that my dreams are most ridiculous."

"How so?"

"Well, you see, that no matter whether they are good or bad they appear real and coherent whilst I am dreaming them; but when I wake I find them unreal and incoherent, when I remember them at all. They are, in fact, mere disconnected nonsense."

"Are you fond of dreams?"

"Of course I am. I delight in them, for whether they are sense or gibberish when you wake, they are real whilst you are asleep."

"Do you believe in dreams?"

"Indeed, Mr. Stanford, I do not."

"Do you like hearing them told?"

"I do, very much, when they are worth telling. Have you been dreaming anything? If you have, do tell it to me."

"I will be glad to do so. It is about a dream which I had that concerns you, that I came here to tell you."

"About me. Oh, how nice. Do, go on."

I told her all my dream, after calling her attention to our conversation in the *boudoir* as a means of introducing the subject. I did not attempt to heighten the effect in any way or to draw any inferences. I tried to suppress my own emotion and merely to let the facts speak for themselves. She listened with great eagerness, but, as far as I could see, without a particle of either fear or belief in the dream as a warning. When I had finished she laughed a

420

quiet, soft laugh, and said—

"That is delicious. And was I really the girl that you saw afraid of ghosts? If papa heard of such a thing as that even in a dream what a lecture he would give me! I wish I could dream anything like that."

"Take care," said I, "you might find it too awful. It might indeed prove the fulfilling of the ban which we saw in the legend in the old book, and which you heard from your aunt."

She laughed musically again, and shook her head at me wisely and warningly.

"Oh, pray do not talk nonsense and try to frighten me—for I warn you that you will not succeed."

"I assure you on my honour, Miss Fothering, that I was never more in earnest in my whole life."

"Do you not think that we had better go into the room?" said she, after a few moment's pause.

"Stay just a moment, I entreat you," said I. "What I say is true. I am really in earnest."

"Oh, pray forgive me if what I said led you to believe that I doubted your word. It was merely your inference which I disagreed with. I thought you had been jesting to try and frighten me."

"Miss Fothering, I would not presume to take such a liberty. But I am glad that you trust me. May I venture to ask you a favour? Will you promise me one thing?"

Her answer was characteristic—

"No. What is it?"

"That you will not be frightened at anything which may take place tonight?"

She laughed softly again.

"I do not intend to be. But is that all?"

"Yes, Miss Fothering, that is all; but I want to be assured that you will not be alarmed—that you will be prepared for anything which may happen. I have a horrid foreboding of evil—some evil that I dread to think of—and it will be a great comfort to me if you will do one thing."

"Oh, nonsense. Oh, well, if you really wish it I will tell you if I will do it when I hear what it is."

Her levity was all gone when she saw how terribly in earnest I was. She looked at me boldly and fearlessly, but with a tender, half-pitying glance as if conscious of the possession of strength superior to mine. Her fearlessness was in her free, independent attitude, but her pity was in her eyes. I went on—

"Miss Fothering, the worst part of my dream was seeing the look of agony on the face of the girl when she looked round and found herself alone. Will you take some token and keep it with you till morning to remind you, in case anything should happen, that you are not alone—that there is one thinking of you, and one human intelligence awake for you, though all the rest of the world should be asleep or dead?"

In my excitement I spoke with fervour, for the possibility of her enduring the horror which had assailed me seemed to be growing more and more each instant. At times since that awful night I had disbelieved the existence of the warning, but when I thought of it by night I could not but believe, for the very air in the darkness seemed to be peopled by phantoms to my fevered imagination. My belief had been perfected tonight by the horror of the yew walk, and all the sombre, ghostly thoughts that had arisen amid its gloom.

There was a short pause. Miss Fothering leaned on the edge of the window, looking out at the dark, moonless sky. At length she turned and said to me, with some hesitation, "But really, Mr. Stanford, I do not like doing anything from fear of supernatural things, or from a belief in them. What you want me to do is so simple a thing in itself that I would not hesitate a moment to do it, but that papa has always taught me to believe that such occurrences as you seem to dread are quite impossible, and I know that he would be very much displeased if any act of mine showed a belief in them."

"Miss Fothering, I honestly think that there is not a man living who would wish less than I would to see you or anyone else disobeying a father either in word or spirit, and more particularly when that father is a clergyman; but I entreat you to gratify me on this one point. It cannot do you any harm; and I assure you that if you do not I will be inexpressibly miserable. I have endured the greatest tortures of suspense for the last three days, and tonight I feel a nervous horror of which words can give you no conception.

"I know that I have not the smallest right to make the request, and no reason for doing it except that I was fortunate, or unfortunate, enough to get the warning. I apologise most sincerely for the great liberty which I have taken, but believe me that I act with the best intentions."

My excitement was so great that my knees were trembling, and the large drops of perspiration rolling down my face.

There was a long pause, and I had almost made up my mind for a refusal of my request when my companion spoke again.

"Mr. Stanford, on that plea alone I will grant your request. I can see that for some reason which I cannot quite comprehend you are deeply moved; and that I may be the means of saving pain to any one, I will do what you ask. Just please to state what you wish me to do."

I thought from her manner that she was offended with me; however I explained my purpose:

"I want you to keep about you, when you go to bed, some token which will remind you in an instant of what has passed between us, so that you may not feel lonely or frightened—no matter what may happen."

"I will do it. What shall I take?"

She had her handkerchief in her hand as she spoke. So I put my hand upon it and blessed it in the name of the Father, Son, and Holy Ghost. I did this to fix its existence in her memory by awing her slightly about it. "This," said I, "shall be a token that you are not alone." My object in blessing the handkerchief was fully achieved, for she did seem somewhat awed, but still she thanked me with a sweet smile.

"I feel that you act from your heart," said she, "and my heart thanks you." She gave me her hand as she spoke, in an honest, straightforward manner, with more the independence of a man than the timorousness of a woman. As I grasped it I felt the blood rushing to my face, but before I let it go an impulse seized me and I bent down and touched it with my lips. She drew it quickly away, and said more coldly than she had yet spoken: "I did not mean you to do that."

"Believe me I did not mean to take a liberty—it was merely the natural expression of my gratitude. I feel as if you had done me some great personal service. You do not know how much lighter my heart is now than it was an hour ago, or you would forgive me for having so offended."

As I made my apologetic excuse, I looked at her wistfully. She returned my glance fearlessly, but with a bright, forgiving smile. She then shook her head slightly, as if to banish the subject.

There was a short pause, and then she said:

"I am glad to be of any service to you; but if there be any possibility of what you fear happening it is I who will be benefited. But mind, I will depend upon you not to say a word of this to *anybody*. I am afraid that we are both very foolish."

"No, no, Miss Fothering. *I* may be foolish, but you are acting nobly in doing what seems to you to be foolish in order that you may save me from pain. But may I not even tell Mrs. Trevor?"

"No, not even her. I should be ashamed of myself if I thought that anyone except ourselves knew about it."

"You may depend upon me. I will keep it secret if you wish."

"Do so, until morning at all events. Mind, if I laugh at you then I will expect you to join in my laugh."

"I will," said I. "I will be only too glad to be able to laugh at it." And we joined the rest of the company.

When I retired to my bedroom that night I was too much excited to sleep—even had my promise not forbidden me to do so. I paced up and down the room for some time, thinking and doubting. I could not believe completely in what I expected to happen, and yet my heart was filled with a vague dread. I thought over the events of the evening—particularly my stroll after dinner through that awful yew walk and my looking into the bedroom where I had dreamed.

From these my thoughts wandered to the deep embrasure of the window where I had given Miss Fothering the token. I could hardly realise that whole interview as a fact. I knew that it had taken place, but that was all. It was so strange to recall a scene that, now that it was enacted, seemed half comedy and half tragedy, and to remember that it was played in this practical nineteenth century, in secret, within earshot of a room full of people, and only hidden from them by a curtain, I felt myself blushing, half from excitement, half from shame, when I thought of it.

But then my thoughts turned to the way in which Miss Fothering had acceded to my request, strange as it was; and as I thought of her my blundering shame changed to a deeper glow of hope. I remembered Mrs. Trevor's prediction—"from what I know of human nature I think that she will like you"—and as I did so I felt how dear to me Miss Fothering was already becoming. But my joy was turned to anger on thinking what she might be called on to endure; and the thought of her suffering pain or fright caused me greater distress than any suffered myself.

Again my thoughts flew back to the time of my own fright and my dream, with all the subsequent revelations concerning it, rushed across my mind. I felt again the feeling of extreme terror—as if something was about to happen—as if the tragedy was approaching its climax. Naturally I thought of the time of night and so I looked at my watch. It was within a few minutes of one o'clock. I remembered that the clock had struck twelve after Mr. Trevor had come home on the night of my dream. There was a large clock at Scarp which tolled the hours so loudly that for a long way round the estate the country people all regulated their affairs by it. The next few minutes passed so slowly that each moment seemed an age.

I was standing, with my watch in my hand, counting the moments when suddenly a light came into the room that made the candle on the table appear quite dim, and my shadow was reflected on the wall by some brilliant light which streamed in through the window. My heart for an instant ceased to beat, and then the blood rushed so violently to my temples that my eyes grew dim and my brain began to reel. However, I shortly became more composed, and then went to the window expecting to see my dream again repeated.

The light was there as formerly, but there were no figures of children, or witches, or fiends. The moon had just risen, and I could see its reflection upon the far end of the lake. I turned my head in trembling expectation to the ground below where I had seen the children and the hags, but saw merely the dark yew trees and tall crested pampass tufts gently moving in the night wind. The light caught the edges of the flowers of the grass, and made them most conspicuous.

As I looked a sudden thought flashed like a flame of fire through my brain. I saw in one second of time all the folly of my wild fancies. The moonlight and its reflection on the water shining into the room was the light of my dream, or phantasm as I now understood it to be. Those three tufts of pampass grass clumped together were in turn the fair young children and the withered leaves and the dark foliage of the yew beside them gave substance to the semblance of the fiend. For the rest, the empty bed and the face of the picture, my half recollection of the name of Fothering, and the long-forgotten legend of the curse.

Oh, fool! fool that I had been! How I had been the victim of circumstances, and of my own wild imagination! Then came the bitter reflection of the agony of mind which Miss Fothering might be compelled to suffer. Might not the recital of my dream, and my strange request regarding the token, combined with the natural causes of night and scene, produce the very effect which I so dreaded? It was only at that bitter, bitter moment that I realised how foolish I had been. But what was my anguish of mind to hers?

For an instant I conceived the idea of rousing Mrs. Trevor and telling her all the facts of the case so that she might go to Miss Fothering and tell her not to be alarmed. But I had no time to act upon my thought. As I was hastening to the door the clock struck one and a moment later I heard from the room below me a sharp scream—a cry of surprise rather than fear. Miss Fothering had no doubt been awakened by the striking of the clock, and had seen outside the window the very figures which I had described to her.

I rushed madly down the stairs and arrived at the door of her bedroom, which was directly under the one which I now occupied. As I was about to rush in I was instinctively restrained from so doing by the thoughts of propriety; and so for a few moments I stood silent, trembling, with my hand upon the door-handle.

Within I heard a voice—her voice—exclaiming, in tones of stupefied surprise—

"Has it come then? Am I alone?" She then continued joyously, "No, I am not alone. His token! Oh, thank God for that. Thank God for that."

Through my heart at her words came a rush of wild delight. I felt my bosom swell and the tears of gladness spring to my eyes. In that moment I knew that I had strength and courage to face the world, alone, for her sake. But before my hopes had well time to manifest themselves they were destroyed, for again the voice came wailing from the room of blank despair that made me cold from head to foot.

"Ah-h-h! still there? Oh! God, preserve my reason. Oh! for some human thing near me." Then her voice changed slightly to a tone of entreaty: "You will not leave me alone? Your token. Remember your token. Help me. Help me now." Then her voice became more wild, and rose to an inarticulate, wailing scream of horror.

As I heard that agonised cry, I realised the idea that it was madness to delay—that I had hesitated too long already—I must cast aside the shackles of conventionality if I wished to repair my fatal error. Nothing could save her from some serious injury—perhaps madness—perhaps death; save a shock which would break the spell which was over her from fear and her excited imagination. I flung open the door and rushed in, shouting loudly:

"Courage, courage. You are not alone. I am here. Remember the token."

She grasped the handkerchief instinctively, but she hardly comprehended my words, and did not seem to heed my presence. She was sitting up in bed, her face being distorted with terror, and was gazing out upon the scene. I heard from without the hooting of an owl as it flew across the border of the lake. She heard it also, and screamed—

"The laugh, too! Oh, there is no hope. Even he will not dare to go amongst them."

Then she gave vent to a scream, so wild, so appalling that, as I heard it, I trembled, and the hair on the back of my head bristled up. Throughout the house I could hear screams of affright, and the ringing of bells, and the banging of doors, and the rush of hurried feet; but the poor sufferer comprehended not these sounds; she still continued gazing out of the window awaiting the consummation of the dream.

I saw that the time for action and self-sacrifice was come. There was but one way now to repair my fatal error. To burst through the window and try by the shock to wake her from her trance of fear.

I said no word but rushed across the room and hurled myself, back foremost, against the massive plate glass. As I turned I saw Mrs. Trevor rushing into the room, her face wild with excitement. She was calling out—

"Diana, Diana, what is it?"

The glass crashed and shivered into a thousand pieces, and I could feel its sharp edges cutting me like so many knives. But I heeded not the pain, for above the rushing of feet and crashing of glass and the shouting both within and without the room I heard her voice ring forth in a joyous, fervent cry, "Saved. He has dared," as she sank down in the arms of Mrs. Trevor, who had thrown herself upon the bed.

Then I felt a mighty shock, and all the universe seemed filled with sparks of fire that whirled around me with lightning speed, till I seemed to be in the centre of a world of flame, and then came in my ears the rushing of a mighty wind, swelling ever louder, and then came a blackness over all things and a deadness of sound as if all the earth had passed away, and I remembered no more.

## 4

### AFTERWARDS

When I next became conscious I was lying in bed in a dark room. I wondered what this was for, and tried to look around me, but could hardly stir my head. I attempted to speak, but my voice was without power—it was like a whisper from another world. The effort to speak made me feel faint, and again I felt a darkness gathering round me.

I became gradually conscious of something cool on my forehead. I wondered what it was. All sorts of things I conjectured, but could not fix my mind on any of them. I lay thus for some time, and at length opened my eyes and saw my mother bending over me—it was her hand which was so deliciously cool on my brow. I felt amazed somehow. I expected to see her; and yet I was surprised, for I had not seen her for a long time—a long, long time. I knew that she was dead—could I be dead, too? I looked at her again more carefully, and as I looked, the old features died away, but the expression remained the same.

And then the dear, well-known face of Mrs. Trevor grew slowly before me. She smiled as she saw the look of recognition in my eyes, and, bending down, kissed me very tenderly. As she drew back her head something warm fell on my face. I wondered what this could be, and after thinking for a long time, to do which I closed my eyes, I came to the conclusion that it was a tear.

After some more thinking I opened my eyes to see why she was crying; but she was gone, and I could see that although the window-blinds were pulled up the room was almost dark. I felt much more awake and much stronger than I had been before, and tried to call Mrs. Trevor. A woman got up from a chair behind the bed-curtains and went to the door, said something, and came back and settled my pillows.

"Where is Mrs. Trevor?" I asked, feebly. "She was here just now."

The woman smiled at me cheerfully, and answered:

"She will be here in a moment. Dear heart! but she will be glad to see you so strong and sensible."

After a few minutes she came into the room, and, bending over me, asked me how I felt. I said that I was all right—and then a thought struck me, so I asked,

"What was the matter with me?"

I was told that I had been ill, very ill, but that I was now much better. Something, I know not what, suddenly recalled to my memory all the scene of the bedroom, and the fright which my folly had caused, and I grew quite dizzy with the rush of blood to my head. But Mrs. Trevor's arm supported me, and after a time the faintness passed away, and my memory was completely restored. I started violently from the arm that held me up, and called out:

"Is she all right? I heard her say, 'saved.' Is she all right?"

"Hush, dear boy, hush-she is all right. Do not excite yourself."

"Are you deceiving me?" I inquired. "Tell me all—I can bear it. Is she well or no?"

"She has been very ill, but she is now getting strong and well, thank God."

I began to cry, half from weakness and half from joy, and Mrs. Trevor seeing this, and knowing with the sweet instinct of womanhood that I would rather be alone, quickly left the room, after making a sign to the nurse, who sank again to her old place behind the bed-curtain.

I thought for long; and all the time from my first coming to Scarp to the moment of unconsciousness after I sprung through the window came back to me as in a dream. Gradually the room became darker and darker, and my thoughts began to give semblance to the objects around me, till at length the visible world passed away from my wearied eyes, and in my dreams I continued to think of all that had been. I have a hazy recollection of taking some food and then relapsing into sleep; but remember no more distinctly until I woke fully in the morning and found Mrs. Trevor again in the room. She came over to my bedside, and sitting down said gaily—

"Ah, Frank, you look bright and strong this morning, dear boy. You will soon be well now I trust."

Her cool deft fingers settled my pillow and brushed back the hair from my forehead. I took her hand and kissed it, and the doing so made me very happy. By-and-by I asked her how was Miss Fothering.

"Better, much better this morning. She has been asking after you ever since she has been able; and today when I told her how much better you were she brightened up at once."

I felt a flush painfully strong rushing over my face as she spoke, but she went on—

"She has asked me to let her see you as soon as both of you are able. She wants to thank you for your conduct on that awful night. But there, I won't tell any more tales—let her tell you what she likes herself."

"To thank me—me—for what? For having brought her to the verge of madness or perhaps death through my silly fears and imagination. Oh, Mrs. Trevor, I know that you never mock anyone—but to me that sounds like mockery."

She leaned over me as she sat on my bedside and said, oh, so sweetly, yet so firmly that a sense of the truth of her words came at once upon me—

"If I had a son I would wish him to think as you have thought, and to act as you have acted. I would pray for it night and day and if he suffered as you have done, I would lean over him as I lean over you now and feel glad, as I feel now, that he had thought and acted as a true-hearted man should think and act. I would rejoice that God had given me such a son; and if he should die—as I feared at first that you should—I would be a prouder and happier woman kneeling by his dead body than I would in clasping a different son, living, in my arms.

Oh, how my weak fluttering heart did beat as she spoke. With pity for her blighted maternal instincts, with gladness that a true-hearted woman had approved of my conduct toward a woman whom I loved, and with joy for the deep love for myself. There was no mistaking the honesty of her words—her face was perfectly radiant as she spoke them.

I put up my arms—it took all my strength to do it—round her neck, and whispered softly in her ear one word, "mother."

She did not expect it, for it seemed to startle her; but her arms tightened around me convulsively. I could feel a perfect rain of tears falling on my upturned face as I looked into her eyes, full of love and long-sought joy. As I looked I felt stronger and better; my sympathy for her joy did much to restore my strength.

For some little time she was silent, and then she spoke as if to herself—"God *has* given me a son at last. I thank thee, O Father; forgive me if I have at any time repined. The son I prayed for might have been different from what I would wish. Thou doest best in all things."

For some time after this she stayed quite silent, still supporting me in her arms. I felt inexpressibly happy. There was an atmosphere of love around me, for which I had longed all my life. The love of a mother, for which I had pined since my orphan childhood, I had got at last, and the love of a woman to become far dearer to me than a mother I felt was close at hand.

At length I began to feel tired, and Mrs. Trevor laid me back on my pillow. It pleased me inexpressibly to observe her kind motherly manner with me now. The ice between us had at last been broken, we had declared our mutual love, and the white-haired woman was as happy in the declaration as the young man.

The next day I felt a shade stronger, and a similar improvement was manifested on the next. Mrs. Trevor always attended me herself, and her good reports of Miss Fothering's progress helped to cheer me not a little. And so the days wore on, and many passed away before I was allowed to rise from bed.

One day Mrs. Trevor came into the room in a state of suppressed delight. By this time I had been allowed to sit up a little while each day, and was beginning to get strong, or rather less weak, for I was still very helpless.

"Frank, the doctor says that you may be moved into another room tomorrow for a change, and that you may see Di."

As may be supposed I was anxious to see Miss Fothering. Whilst I had been able to think during my illness, I had thought about her all day long, and sometimes all night long. I had been in love with her even before that fatal night. My heart told me that secret whilst I was waiting to hear the clock strike, and saw all my folly about the dream; but now I not only loved the woman but I almost worshipped my own bright ideal which was merged in her. The constant series of kind messages that passed between us tended not a little to increase my attachment, and now I eagerly looked forward to a meeting with her face to face.

I awoke earlier than usual next morning, and grew rather feverish as the time for our interview approached. However, I soon cooled down upon a vague threat being held out, that if I did not become more composed I must defer my visit.

The expected time at length arrived, and I was wheeled in my chair into Mrs. Trevor's *boudoir*. As I entered the door I looked eagerly round and saw, seated in another chair near one of the windows, a girl, who, turning her head round languidly, disclosed the features of Miss Fothering. She was very pale and ethereal looking, and seemed extremely delicate; but in my opinion this only heightened her natural beauty.

As she caught sight of me a beautiful blush rushed over her poor, pale face, and even tinged her alabaster forehead. This passed quickly, and she became calm again, and paler than before. My chair was wheeled over to her, and Mrs. Trevor said, as she bent over and kissed her, after soothing the pillow in her chair—

"Di, my love, I have brought Frank to see you. You may talk

together for a little while; but, mind, the doctor's orders are very strict, and if either of you excite yourselves about anything I must forbid you to meet again until you are both much stronger."

She said the last words as she was leaving the room.

I felt red and pale, hot and cold by turns. I looked at Miss Fothering and faltered. However, in a moment or two I summoned up courage to address her.

"Miss Fothering, I hope you forgive me for the pain and danger I caused you by that foolish fear of mine. I assure you that nothing I ever did"—

Here she interrupted me.

"Mr. Stanford, I beg you will not talk like that. I must thank you for the care you thought me worthy of. I will not say how proud I feel of it, and for the generous courage and wisdom you displayed in rescuing me from the terror of that awful scene."

She grew pale, even paler than she had been before, as she spoke the last words, and trembled all over. I feared for her, and said as cheerfully as I could:

"Don't be alarmed. Do calm yourself. That is all over now and past. Don't let its horror disturb you ever again."

My speaking, although it calmed her somewhat, was not sufficient to banish her fear, and, seeing that she was really excited, I called to Mrs. Trevor, who came in from the next room and talked to us for a little while. She gradually did away with Miss Fothering's fear by her pleasant cheery conversation. She, poor girl, had received a sad shock, and the thought that I had been the cause of it gave me great anguish. After a little quiet chat, however, I grew more cheerful, but presently feeling faintish, was wheeled back to my own room and put to bed.

For many long days I continued very weak, and hardly made any advance. I saw Miss Fothering every day, and each day I loved her more and more. She got stronger as the days advanced, and after a few weeks was comparatively in good health, but still I continued weak. Her illness had been merely the result of the fright she had sustained on that unhappy night; but mine was the nervous prostration consequent on the long period of anxiety between the dream and its seeming fulfilment, united with the physical weakness resulting from my wounds caused by jumping through the window.

During all this time of weakness Mrs. Trevor was, indeed, a mother to me. She watched me day and night, and as far as a woman could, made my life a dream of happiness. But the crowning glory of that time was the thought that sometimes forced itself upon me—that Diana cared for me. She continued to remain at Scarp by Mrs. Trevor's request, as her father had gone to the Continent for the winter, and with my adopted mother she shared the attendance on me.

Day after day her care for my every want grew greater, till I came to fancy her like a guardian angel keeping watch over me. With the peculiar delicate sense that accompanies extreme physical prostration I could see that the growth of her pity kept pace with the growth of her strength. My love kept pace with both. I often wondered if it could be sympathy and not pity that so forestalled my wants and wishes; or if it could be love that answered in her heart when mine beat for her. She only showed pity and tenderness in her acts and words, but still I hoped and longed for something more.

Those days of my long-continued weakness were to me sweet, sweet days. I used to watch her for hours as she sat opposite to me reading or working, and my eyes would fill with tears as I thought how hard it would be to die and leave her behind me. So strong was the flame of my love that I believed, in spite of my religious teaching, that, should I die, I would leave the better part of my being behind me. I used to think in a vague imaginative way, that was no less powerful because it was undefined, of what speeches I would make to her—if I were well. How I would talk to her in nobler language than that in which I would now allow my thoughts to mould themselves.

How, as I talked, my passion, and honesty, and purity would make me so eloquent that she would love to hear me speak. How I would wander with her through the sunny-gladed woods that stretched away before me through the open window, and sit by her feet on a mossy bank beside some purling brook that rippled gaily over the stones, gazing into the depths of her eyes, where my future life was pictured in one long sheen of light. How I would whisper in her ear sweet words that would make me tremble to speak them, and her tremble to hear. How she would bend to me and show me her love by letting me tell her mine without reproof.

And then would come, like the shadow of a sudden rain-cloud over an April landscape, the bitter, bitter thought that all this longing was but a dream, and that when the time had come when such things might have been, I would, most likely, be sleeping under the green turf. And she might, perhaps, be weeping in the silence of her chamber sad, sad tears for her blighted love and for me. Then my thoughts would become less selfish, and I would try to imagine the bitter blow of my death—if she loved me—for I knew that a woman loves not by the value of what she loves, but by the strength of her affection and admiration for her own ideal, which she thinks she sees bodied forth in some man.

But these thoughts had always the proviso that the dreams of happiness were prophetic. Alas! I had altogether lost faith in dreams. Still, I could not but feel that even if I had never frightened Miss Fothering by telling my vision, she might, nevertheless, have been terrified by the effect of the moonlight upon the flowers of the pampas tufts, and that, under Providence, I was the instrument of saving her from a shock even greater than that which she did experience, for help might not have come to her so soon. This thought always gave me hope.

Whenever I thought of her sorrow for my death, I would find my eyes filled with a sudden rush of tears which would shut out from my waking vision the object of my thoughts and fears. Then she would come over to me and place her cool hand on my forehead, and whisper sweet words of comfort and hope in my ears. As I would feel her warm breath upon my cheek and wafting my hair from my brow, I would lose all sense of pain and sorrow and care, and live only in the brightness of the present.

At such times I would cry silently from very happiness, for I was sadly weak, and even trifling things touched me deeply. Many a stray memory of some tender word heard or some gentle deed done, or of some sorrow or distress, would set me thinking for hours and stir all the tender feelings of my nature.

Slowly—very slowly—I began to get stronger, but for many days more I was almost completely helpless. With returning strength came the strengthening of my passion-for passion my love for Diana had become. She had been so woven into my thoughts that my love for her was a part of my being, and I felt that away from her my future life would be but a bare existence and no more. But strange to say, with increasing strength and passion came increasing diffidence.

I felt in her presence so bashful and timorous that I hardly dared to look at her, and could not speak save to answer an occasional question. I had ceased to dream entirely, for such daydreams as I used to have seemed now wild and almost sacrilegious to my sur-excited imagination. But when she was not looking at me I would be happy in merely seeing her or hearing her speak. I could tell the moment she left the house or entered it, and her footfall was the music sweetest to my ears—except her voice.

Sometimes she would catch sight of my bashful looks at her, and then, at my conscious blushing, a bright smile would flit over her face. It was sweet and womanly, but sometimes I would think that it was no more than her pity finding expression. She was always in my thoughts and these doubts and fears constantly assailed me, so that I could feel that the brooding over the subject—a matter which I was powerless to prevent—was doing me an injury; perhaps seriously retarding my recovery.

One day I felt very sad. There had a bitter sense of loneliness come over me which was unusual. It was a good sign of returning health, for it was like the waking from a dream to a world of fact, with all its troubles and cares. There was a sense of coldness and loneliness in the world, and I felt that I had lost something without gaining anything in return—I had, in fact, lost somewhat of my sense of dependence, which is a consequence of prostration, but had not yet regained my strength. I sat opposite a window itself in shade, but looking over a garden that in the summer had been bright with flowers, and sweet with their odours, but which, now, was lit up only in patches by the quiet mellow gleams of the autumn sun, and brightened by a few stray flowers that had survived the first frosts.

As I sat I could not help thinking of what my future would be. I felt that I was getting strong, and the possibilities of my life seemed very real to me. How I longed for courage to ask Diana to be my wife! Any certainty would be better than the suspense I now constantly endured. I had but little hope that she would accept me, for she seemed to care less for me now than in the early days of my illness. As I grew stronger she seemed to hold somewhat aloof from me; and as my fears and doubts grew more and more, I could hardly bear to think of my joy should she accept me, or of my despair should she refuse. Either emotion seemed too great to be borne.

Today when she entered the room my fears were vastly increased. She seemed much stronger than usual, for a glow, as of health, ruddied her cheeks, and she seemed so lovely that I could not conceive that such a woman would ever condescend to be my wife. There was an unusual constraint in her manner as she came and spoke to me, and flitted round me, doing in her own graceful way all the thousand little offices that only a woman's hand can do for an invalid. She turned to me two or three times, as if she was about to speak; but turned away again, each time silent, and with a blush. I could see that her heart was beating violently. At length she spoke.

"Frank."

Oh! what a wild throb went through me as I heard my name from her lips for the first time. The blood rushed to my head, so that for a moment I was quite faint. Her cool hand on my forehead revived me.

"Frank, will you let me speak to you for a few minutes as honestly as I would wish to speak, and as freely?"

"Go on."

"You will promise me not to think me unwomanly or forward, for indeed I act from the best motives—promise me?"

This was said slowly with much hesitation, and a convulsive heaving of the chest.

"I promise."

"We can see that you are not getting as strong as you ought, and the doctor says that there is some idea too much in your mind—that you brood over it, and that it is retarding your recovery. Mrs. Trevor and I have been talking about it. We have been comparing notes, and I think we have found out what your idea is. Now, Frank, you must not pale and red like that, or I will have to leave off."

"I will be calm—indeed, I will. Go on."

"We both thought that it might do you good to talk to you freely, and we want to know if our idea is correct. Mrs. Trevor thought it better that I should speak to you than she should."

"What is the idea?"

Hitherto, although she had manifested considerable emotion, her voice had been full and clear, but she answered this last question very faintly, and with much hesitation.

"You are attached to me, and you are afraid I—I don't love you."

Here her voice was checked by a rush of tears, and she turned her head away.

"Diana," said I, "dear Diana," and I held out my arms with what strength I had.

The colour rushed over her face and neck, and then she turned, and with a convulsive sigh laid her head upon my shoulder. One weak arm fell round her waist, and my other hand rested on her head. I said nothing. I could not speak, but I felt the beating of her heart against mine, and thought that if I died then I must be happy for ever, if there be memory in the other world.

For a long, long, blissful time she kept her place, and gradually our hearts ceased to beat so violently, and we became calm.

Such was the confession of our love. No plighted faith, no passionate vows, but the silence and the thrill of sympathy through our hearts were sweeter than words could be.

Diana raised her head and looked fearlessly but appealingly into my eyes as she asked me—

"Oh, Frank, did I do right to speak? Could it have been better if I had waited?"

She saw my wishes in my eyes, and bent down her head to me. I kissed her on the forehead and fervently prayed, "Thank God that all was as it has been. May He bless my own darling wife forever and ever."

"Amen," said a sweet, tender voice.

We both looked up without shame, for we knew the tones of my second mother. Her face, streaming with tears of joy, was lit up by a sudden ray of sunlight through the casement.

**LEONAUR**

# ALSO FROM LEONAUR
## AVAILABLE IN SOFTCOVER OR HARDCOVER WITH DUST JACKET

**CAPTAIN OF THE 95th (Rifles)** *by Jonathan Leach*—An officer of Wellington's Sharpshooters during the Peninsular, South of France and Waterloo Campaigns of the Napoleonic Wars.

**BUGLER AND OFFICER OF THE RIFLES** *by William Green & Harry Smith* With the 95th (Rifles) during the Peninsular & Waterloo Campaigns of the Napoleonic Wars.

**BAYONETS, BUGLES AND BONNETS** by *James 'Thomas' Todd*—Experiences of hard soldiering with the 71st Foot - the Highland Light Infantry - through many battles of the Napoleonic wars including the Peninsular & Waterloo Campaigns

**THE ADVENTURES OF A LIGHT DRAGOON** *by George Farmer & G.R. Gleig*—A cavalryman during the Peninsular & Waterloo Campaigns, in captivity & at the siege of Bhurtpore, India

**THE COMPLEAT RIFLEMAN HARRIS** *by Benjamin Harris as told to & transcribed by Captain Henry Curling*—The adventures of a soldier of the 95th (Rifles) during the Peninsular Campaign of the Napoleonic Wars

**WITH WELLINGTON'S LIGHT CAVALRY** *by William Tomkinson*—The Experiences of an officer of the 16th Light Dragoons in the Peninsular and Waterloo campaigns of the Napoleonic Wars.

**SURTEES OF THE RIFLES** by *William Surtees*—A Soldier of the 95th (Rifles) in the Peninsular campaign of the Napoleonic Wars.

**ENSIGN BELL IN THE PENINSULAR WAR** *by George Bell*—The Experiences of a young British Soldier of the 34th Regiment 'The Cumberland Gentlemen' in the Napoleonic wars.

**WITH THE LIGHT DIVISION** by *John H. Cooke*—The Experiences of an Officer of the 43rd Light Infantry in the Peninsula and South of France During the Napoleonic Wars

**NAPOLEON'S IMPERIAL GUARD: FROM MARENGO TO WATERLOO** by *J. T. Headley*—This is the story of Napoleon's Imperial Guard from the bearskin caps of the grenadiers to the flamboyance of their mounted chasseurs, their principal characters and the men who commanded them.

**BATTLES & SIEGES OF THE PENINSULAR WAR** by *W. H. Fitchett*—Corunna, Busaco, Albuera, Ciudad Rodrigo, Badajos, Salamanca, San Sebastian & Others

LEONAUR

# ALSO FROM LEONAUR
### AVAILABLE IN SOFTCOVER OR HARDCOVER WITH DUST JACKET

**WELLINGTON AND THE PYRENEES CAMPAIGN VOLUME I: FROM VI-TORIA TO THE BIDASSOA** *by F. C. Beatson*—The final phase of the campaign in the Iberian Peninsula.

**WELLINGTON AND THE INVASION OF FRANCE VOLUME II: THE BIDAS-SOA TO THE BATTLE OF THE NIVELLE** *by F. C. Beatson*—The second of Beatson's series on the fall of Revolutionary France published by Leonaur, the reader is once again taken into the centre of Wellington's strategic and tactical genius.

**WELLINGTON AND THE FALL OF FRANCE VOLUME III: THE GAVES AND THE BATTLE OF ORTHEZ** *by F. C. Beatson*—This final chapter of F. C. Beatson's brilliant trilogy shows the 'captain of the age' at his most inspired and makes all three books essential additions to any Peninsular War library.

**NAVAL BATTLES OF THE NAPOLEONIC WARS** *by W. H. Fitchett*—Cape St. Vincent, the Nile, Cadiz, Copenhagen, Trafalgar & Others

**SERGEANT GUILLEMARD: THE MAN WHO SHOT NELSON?** *by Robert Guillemard*—A Soldier of the Infantry of the French Army of Napoleon on Campaign Throughout Europe

**WITH THE GUARDS ACROSS THE PYRENEES** *by Robert Batty*—The Experiences of a British Officer of Wellington's Army During the Battles for the Fall of Napoleonic France, 1813.

**A STAFF OFFICER IN THE PENINSULA** *by E. W. Buckham*—An Officer of the British Staff Corps Cavalry During the Peninsula Campaign of the Napoleonic Wars

**THE LEIPZIG CAMPAIGN: 1813—NAPOLEON AND THE "BATTLE OF THE NATIONS"** *by F. N. Maude*—Colonel Maude's analysis of Napoleon's campaign of 1813.

**BUGEAUD: A PACK WITH A BATON** *by Thomas Robert Bugeaud*—The Early Campaigns of a Soldier of Napoleon's Army Who Would Become a Marshal of France.

## TWO LEONAUR ORIGINALS

**SERGEANT NICOL** *by Daniel Nicol*—The Experiences of a Gordon Highlander During the Napoleonic Wars in Egypt, the Peninsula and France.

**WATERLOO RECOLLECTIONS** *by Frederick Llewellyn*—Rare First Hand Accounts, Letters, Reports and Retellings from the Campaign of 1815.

LaVergne, TN USA
17 October 2010
201138LV00001B/110/P